"LET ME GO, CLAY."

His body was hard and strong, and he smelled of the mountains and the trees and the wind, and of the night itself.

"Please," she said, and the word clung to the silence around them.

"You're shaking, Kayley. What are you afraid of?"

She wanted to tell him that she was afraid of her father's illness and of being responsible for a ranch that was larger than she'd thought the entire world to be five months ago. She wanted to say that she was afraid of how big the western sky was and how high all the mountains were and how very dark the nights could become. But most of all, she wanted to tell him that she was afraid of how her own life was spinning faster and faster out of control, and that she didn't know what to do to stop it.

"I'm afraid of you," she whispered.

"That, sweetheart, is the first sensible thing I've heard you say."

And then he kissed her. Lightly, gently, his lips brushed across hers, once, twice, hesitating, touching again, lighter, teasing, slower, lingering.

And his hands were touching her as he kept kissing her and caressing her, weaving around her a web of desire too real to be true, too wonderful to ever stop, until she forgot everything except the feel and the smell and the magic of him.

ROMANCE REIGNS
WITH ZEBRA BOOKS!

SILVER ROSE (2275, $3.95)
by Penelope Neri

Fleeing her lecherous boss, Silver Dupres disguised herself as a boy and joined an expedition to chart the wild Colorado River. But with one glance at Jesse Wilder, the explorers' rugged, towering scout, Silver knew she'd have to abandon her protective masquerade or else be consumed by her raging unfulfilled desire!

STARLIT ECSTASY (2134, $3.95)
by Phoebe Conn

Cold-hearted heiress Alicia Caldwell swore that Rafael Ramirez, San Francisco's most successful attorney, would never win her money . . . or her love. But before she could refuse him, she was shamelessly clasped against Rafael's muscular chest and hungrily matching his relentless ardor!

LOVING LIES (2034, $3.95)
by Penelope Neri

When she agreed to wed Joel McCaleb, Seraphina wanted nothing more than to gain her best friend's inheritance. But then she saw the virile stranger . . . and the green-eyed beauty knew she'd never be able to escape the rapture of his kiss and the sweet agony of his caress.

EMERALD FIRE (3193, $4.50)
by Phoebe Conn

When his brother died for loving gorgeous Bianca Antonelli, Evan Sinclair swore to find the killer by seducing the tempress who lured him to his death. But once the blond witch willingly surrendered all he sought, Evan's lust for revenge gave way to the desire for unrestrained rapture.

SEA JEWEL (3013, $4.50)
by Penelope Neri

Hot-tempered Alaric had long planned the humiliation of Freya, the daughter of the most hated foe. He'd make the wench from across the ocean his lowly bedchamber slave—but he never suspected she would become the mistress of his heart, his treasured SEA JEWEL.

Available wherever paperbacks are sold, or order direct from the Publisher. Send cover price plus 50¢ per copy for mailing and handling to Zebra Books, Dept. 3233, 475 Park Avenue South, New York, N.Y. 10016. Residents of New York, New Jersey and Pennsylvania must include sales tax. DO NOT SEND CASH.

SWEET OBSESSION

KATHY JONES

ZEBRA BOOKS
KENSINGTON PUBLISHING CORP.

ZEBRA BOOKS

are published by

Kensington Publishing Corp.
475 Park Avenue South
New York, NY 10016

First printing: December, 1990

Printed in the United States of America

For my parents, because I love them.

I want to thank Wendy McCurdy; Pat Teal; Ernie Kristof; Lester and Kathleen Jones, Cole Jones, Sandy Walker, and all the rest of my family; Jennie Smith; my friends Linda Chase, Diane Hailey, and Mary Pat Koos; the talented members, past and present of my writing group; and Dr. Myles Cohen, who reconstructed my wrist during the writing of this book, and thereby made the writing of it possible.

I want to extend a special thanks to the people of the state of New Mexico for their kindness and assistance, and to the state itself for its beauty, inspiration, and its magic.

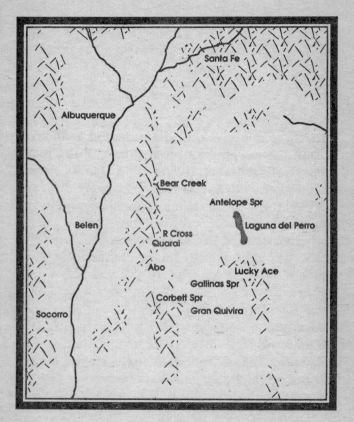

Central Region
Territory of New Mexico
1880

Chapter One

Jack Corbett looked through the bars of the prison gate at the world outside where morning was spreading a golden light across the prairie. A covey of quail lifted on rustling wings from the underbrush and scattered among acres of late-summer wild flowers, their colors so rich and lovely they looked unreal. For a moment, he feared he might awaken and find that the flowers, along with his imminent freedom, were just a dream.

Freedom. The word was a magic elixir, a great shining star that until a week ago had been forever beyond his reach. Now he was inches and minutes away from freedom and a chance to start again the life he'd almost lost the night he followed Sullivan Ryan into a muddy Abilene alley.

Jack was wearing the same clothes now that he'd been wearing that night. The best money could buy, they'd once been symbols of his vanity. The prison storeroom had reduced them to ill-fitting rags smelling of mildew and rot. The tops of his boots had been gnawed by rats, and his hat smelled as though it had housed a nest of the rodents.

His braided gold hatband was missing, as were the bank notes he'd been carrying worth twenty thousand dollars, payment for the biggest herd of steers his Crescent C Ranch had ever driven north. The hatband, those precious notes, and several hundred dollars in cash had also been victims in that alley.

Strangely enough, Jack's pistol had been returned to him. It hung loose against his left leg. Though the pistol was empty of shells, he kept his hand away from the engraved silver handle. He wasn't free yet.

Dogface Sims, a big man with a nose that had been broken so many times he couldn't breathe through it, and Frank Walling, a little man with a tough attitude, were the guards at Lansing's front gate. Walling stepped from the guard house and began to search Jack, even though there was nothing to steal in the prison except the tons of coal inmates were forced to wrest from the unwilling ground.

"We don't get many of these," Sims said. He stabbed a finger at Jack's papers. "Especially for the likes of you, Corbett. Ever since you been here, you ain't been nothin' but trouble."

"Only for people I don't like, Dogface, and I don't like you."

Walling had squatted and was running his hands up Jack's left leg. Although it was the last time he would have to suffer this humiliation, he couldn't endure it in silence.

"Frank doesn't have to worry, though," he said. "The way he's feeling me up, I'm beginning to like him a lot. Maybe he'd like to see how much."

8

Walling glanced up. When he met Jack's hateful stare, he jerked his hands away and got to his feet. "Open the gate, Sims," he said, the words spilling over each other in his haste. "The only thing this bastard's takin' with him is a bad stink."

Hinges creaked and Jack walked forward. The shadows of the bars were cold on his face. When he was in the clear, he stopped to listen to the gate swing shut behind him. Only after silence again claimed the morning, did he take his first free breath.

It smelled sweet and wonderful, and he couldn't get enough of it. Dizzy with freedom and too much air, he noticed a wagon pulled close to the front of the prison. The driver, whose hat was so small it made his head look swollen, held the reins of the sorriest pair of mules Jack had ever seen. They looked incapable of moving themselves, much less the wagon, and stood leaning against each other in a tangle of old harness and sunlight.

"A ride into town'll cost you a dollar," the man said as he tugged at the brim of his hat, as though trying to stretch it down over the thin hair that straggled around his ears.

Jack didn't need to check his pockets to see if he could afford the ride. He had only a few coins, not enough to even make a decent jingle.

"Make it two bits and you have a deal," he said.

"Anybody else gettin' out?"

"I'm all they have to offer today."

"Get in, buddy. Twenty-five cents is better than nothin'."

A slap of the reins across their dusty backs caused the mules to struggle to a standing position. They

9

leaned wearily into their harness, pulling the wagon to a lurching start. Jack settled himself on the uncomfortable seat and put his feet on the rail in front of him. He frowned at the dried mud that covered what had once been beautiful leather. Ryan had taken everything else; surely he couldn't have forgotten the most famous boots in the West.

Jack kicked at the toe of his right boot with the heel of his left. The Abilene mud had turned granite-hard over the years. He had to kick a second time before a chunk broke away. He quickly dropped his feet to the floor of the wagon.

"Is there an assay office in town?"

The driver gave him a sideways glance before nodding.

"Let me off there."

The wagon groaned as it moved onto a road that ran alongside a pair of metal rails, black and empty, stretching out across the Kansas prairie. Before they reached the blur of the horizon, the rails began a slow curve to the southwest.

The mules were relieved when they reached the assay office. Both animals gave heaving groans before, and after, Jack climbed down.

He flipped the driver a quarter. "Thanks for the ride."

"Hope everythin' works out for you, buddy." The driver gave another tug on his tiny hat before shouting at the mules to move.

Jack pulled off his boots and tossed them in a nearby watering trough. An old man, his hands and face scarred by time and work, sat in front of the small office. His beard flashed silver bright in the sun as he tipped his chair back against the wall.

"Just get out?" he asked.

"About an hour ago."

"Lose that eye in there or before?"

Jack involuntarily touched the scrap of cloth that covered his left eye. "Before." He reached into the trough and pulled out the boots. The mud was still hard.

"Nothin' tougher than clay," the old man said.

Jack dropped the boots back into the water before accepting the rolled smoke offered him. He pulled its fumes deep into his lungs and tried to remember the taste of the imported cigars he'd once enjoyed.

The cigarette paper was burning close to his fingers before he checked the mud again. It was soft. He wiped it away with his hand and turned the boots to catch the light.

The old man pointed a shaking finger at them. "There's gold nuggets set in them boots! And the heels are solid gold! Them boots got more color than I seen in forty years of prospecting!"

"Hard to believe a man would wear anything this vulgar," Jack said before taking the sparkling boots into the assay office. When he came out a half hour later, the grizzled old prospector was still there.

He squinted up at Jack. "Sell them boots?"

"Just the shiny parts. Where can I get a new pair? I need clothes, too."

"See Palmer down the street. He asks a fair price."

"Thanks."

"Where you headed for?"

"New Mexico."

"Got family down there?"

11

"Nobody I know of."

"Own land?"

"Not anymore."

"Then, why you going?"

Jack drew his pistol and spun the empty chamber. He sighted along the barrel at the railroad tracks. "Revenge," he said, and for the first time in five years, he smiled.

Chapter Two

Kayley Ryan leaned forward over the pommel of her saddle and drew a deep breath into her lungs. The air smelled of horse sweat and excitement. She stood in the stirrups to let the wind rush unchecked into her face and wondered if this was what it felt like to fly.

She felt more alive than she'd dreamed possible, alive and wild and free. If she could always feel this way, there'd be nothing she couldn't do: run her father's ranch, touch the stars, even catch the devil himself.

This time it was going to happen. This time, before the race was finished, the stallion would feel the touch of her rope around his neck, the weight of her hand upon that rope, and finally, after months of frustration and failure, he would be hers.

"Faster!" she shouted as she lowered herself back into the saddle.

Louisiana, her chestnut gelding, responded immediately to her cry. The world sped past them, a hazy stream of light and color that Kayley knew would make her dizzy unless she kept her attention fixed on the stallion in front of her.

There was no denying that he was magnificent, his tail and mane streaming behind him like the banner of a mighty warrior. The sight of him, head held unnaturally high with nostrils flared wide and eyes bright with hate, brought Kayley to her feet again.

The lash of Louisiana's mane on her face was painful, but she urged the gelding to run faster with her hands and knees and voice, loving the pain and the terror and the thrill of the chase itself almost as much as she'd love catching the wild, white stallion.

From the banks of the Rio Grande, she'd chased him east across a stretch of flat land the color of last year's hay, the whole great expanse of it dry and crackling and quivering with reflected heat. Now they were moving into the foothills of the mountains where junipers, twisted and green, grew thick across the face of the earth. The air was cooler here, and it shimmered with dancing light and sweet-smelling breezes. Through it the two horses ran, their bodies just beginning to lather.

The dark hue of the earth beneath their flying feet gave way to blood-red dirt. Past ancient rock paintings they ran, past a long abandoned pueblo built of sandstone the color of a dying sun, and onto mesas so dry that the air itself tasted of dust and death. It was there, between towering red walls of clay, that Kayley felt the first tremble of exhaustion ripple through her legs and arms.

"Faster, Louie!" she cried. "Please, just a little faster and he'll be mine!"

The sun was hot on her back, burning through the leather of her vest and the flannel of her shirt. Along the crumbling rim of a canyon, the horses ran. Wind, sharp and eager in its rush upward from the depths below, caught hold of her hat, forcing it backward off her head. Her hair tore loose from its heavy braid, spreading out around her like a blazing fire of red and gold.

Kayley pulled on the rawhide ties cutting into her throat. A whiff of moisture softened the air, and she realized she must be near water. And along with its delicious scent, she smelled the smoke of a campfire. Both smells were gone by the time she surrendered the fight with her hat.

A speck of gray, pale as a ghost, appeared in the blur of her vision, moving closer, faster, taking shape and form until she recognized that it was a horse, a gray horse, big and beautiful. Its rider was tall and broad-shouldered, and like Kayley, he rode hunched over his mount's neck.

She wondered who he was and why he was here, chasing her stallion. "He's mine!" she shouted at him. A quick glance in her direction was her competitor's only response.

The land was rising up, up, red sandstone giving way to brittle limestone that caused the hooves of the horses to ring like a blacksmith's hammer on old iron. At the top of the ridge, the ground dropped away into a deep arroyo. The stallion leapt over the edge, and the two horses plunged after him, Louisiana's front hooves striking the bottom with such impact that both he and Kayley shuddered from the shock.

The soft earth that covered the bottom of the arroyo didn't affect the gelding, but the big gray faltered. Kayley felt a rush of satisfaction and, just as quickly, anger when the ground hardened, allowing the gray to regain his speed and pull alongside Louisiana.

The two riders were almost close enough to touch. Kayley leaned across the chasm separating them and screamed, "He's mine! The stallion is mine!"

The man's answering shout was lost in the wind that shrieked around them. It caught his hat in its clutches, whipping it into Kayley's face and blinding her. When it fell away, she saw that ahead of them, the arroyo was blocked by an immense boulder.

The white stallion was running straight for the dark rock. At the last second, he cut to the left. Where the boulder appeared to be touching the dirt wall of the arroyo, a narrow opening was revealed. The stallion entered it without hesitation, although it was scarcely wider than his body.

Kayley reined Louisiana to the left, directly into the gray, hoping to throw the big horse off his stride long enough for her to reach the narrow opening first. The stranger reined his mount into Louisiana at the same moment.

The horses slammed together at the shoulder with such force that Kayley would have been thrown from the saddle if the man's muscular leg hadn't been pressed tightly against hers while the two horses fought for position. The gray's superior weight and size caused Louisiana to stumble, and the gray surged through the opening with a furious Kayley close at his heels.

After they passed the boulder, the gray began moving up on the stallion's left. He made a quick cut to the right, giving Kayley the advantage. She pressed her knees into Louisiana's heaving sides. He responded instantly, pulling a full length ahead of the gray.

Kayley was suddenly closer to the white stallion than she'd ever been before, close enough to taste his sweat and feel the sting of the gravel his sharp hooves threw into the air as he ran up the collapsed sides of the arroyo and onto the grassy plain above.

The extra speed proved too much for the winded gelding. His muscles began to bunch up, his strides shortened and his breathing sounded like a broken bellows.

"No!" Kayley cried in anguish as the gray and his rider shot past her.

The stallion disappeared after cresting a hill crowned with crumbling walls of limestone. Kayley was close enough to the gray to see the sparks caused by his iron shoes striking against brick-shaped rocks that littered the ground. She shouted for Louisiana to follow as the gray also disappeared into the maze of tumbled walls. But the gelding's race was finished. He made it to the top of the hill, and there he stopped, his head falling almost between his legs.

Kayley struggled under the weight of her disappointment for a long moment before dismounting to loosen the cinch to let Louisiana breathe. She dragged the saddle from his sweaty back before climbing to the top of a great mound of black earth to watch the drama unfolding on the plain below her.

Her senses were so attuned to the chase that it was

almost as though she were the one riding the gray with the pounding of his hooves a mighty roaring in her ears. She saw the man shake out his rope, and her own legs tightened on the big gray's sides, and she leaned into the wind as the rope swung free, her fingers opening to let it go, and with it her hope and her heart and her soul.

The rope arched up and over the stallion's head, the loop opening and widening in perfect position. Then it started to fall. She pulled her arm back, eager to close the trap. Too eager.

The rope collapsed on his back instead of around his neck. He reared, screaming his rage and fury, and she screamed with him. Then he was running free again, putting on a burst of such unbelievable speed that the gray appeared to be standing still.

"Like lightning," Kayley whispered, and she spat the bitter taste of defeat from her mouth before collapsing onto a crumbled wall. She was sick and nauseous, and her chest was heaving so that she sounded like Louisiana.

"I was so very close." She dropped her face into her hands. "I almost had him." Then she raised her head. "It wasn't me; it was that man! He missed, he pulled back too soon and he missed!"

The gray was returning to the ruins. Although standing required every ounce of strength in her body, Kayley managed to pull herself erect before the man reined in almost on top of her.

"Damn you," she said, her mouth forming the words but no sound coming out as she glared up at him. "Damn you!" she said again, this time so loud Louisiana shied away. "I would've had him if you hadn't interfered!"

"Like hell," he said and stepped lightly down from the gray's back. Even standing on the ground, he towered over Kayley, and she hated him for that almost as much as for nearly catching her stallion.

Dark hair, long and windblown, fell across his forehead and over his collar. Although he was dressed in the manner of a common cowhand, the handle of the gun hanging low against his left thigh appeared to be made of real silver. Carved into its shining surface was an oddly shaped letter C.

A black leather patch covered the stranger's left eye, lending a menacing air to his appearance that was enhanced by the day's growth of beard that shadowed his face. His other eye was such an incredibly pale shade of gray that it was startling. The effect was made even more unsettling by his incredibly thick, coal-black lashes and by the way he was staring at Kayley, a threatening, angry stare that held her captive in its iron-tight embrace.

Instead of being frightened, it gave her a strange, out-of-control feeling, like being in water over her head.

"That stallion belongs to me," she said and jabbed a finger into his chest. The air felt suddenly charged with energy, the way it did before a lightning storm. She jabbed at him again. "You had no right to go after him."

He grabbed her hand. They were both wearing heavy riding gloves, yet she felt his touch as though it were on her skin. Before she could pull her hand away, he threw it from him.

"A wild horse belongs to no one except the man

smart enough to catch him." The rough texture of his voice was almost as intimidating as his appearance. "You're wearing pants; but that doesn't make you a man, and I don't think you're smart enough to catch that angel of Satan down there."

"It wasn't me who pulled back on the rope too soon."

Instead of being embarrassed by his mistake, he gave her a mocking smile. "At least I tried, kid."

"What does that mean?"

"You were closer to him in the arroyo than I ever got."

Her heart froze within her as her mind flashed back through the churning memory of the chase. Had she missed the opportunity she'd waited for so long? *No, I wasn't close enough,* she told herself firmly. The doubt he'd raised refused to subside, though, and the heat of her anger flared hotter.

"When your horse is ready to ride, mister, get on him and get off this ranch. I won't file charges against you this time, but if I see you chasing my stallion again, I will."

His manner changed from relaxed to rigid. "Charges? For what?"

"For trespassing. And for trying to murder me."

"Are you saying that you weren't partially responsible for that collision?"

"If I'd seen that boulder a second earlier, you'd be picking gravel out of your backside right now. That's not the story I'll tell the sheriff, though."

"And you think he'll believe anything you say while you have those blue eyes turned on him."

"That's right," she said, and couldn't help

20

laughing at his frown of disgust.

Just as quickly as her gratification came, it disappeared, replaced by a growing uneasiness as she realized how very alone they were. All around them lay the open range of the Salinas Valley. It was unlikely there was another person within miles.

He grasped her shoulders. Fear swelled inside her. Her heart skipped a beat, then raced as his hands, strong and powerful, pulled her to him. Images of what he might do to her tumbled through her mind, confusing her, making her breathless and dizzy as he spun her around and pointed past her to the valley below.

"Look," he commanded.

It was the stallion. He was at the bottom of the hill directly below them, the unearthly white of his coat shimmering like a mirage in the brilliant sunlight. When her gaze met his, he rose on his hind legs to paw the air with his front and scream in triumph.

At that moment, Kayley would've traded the entire R Cross Ranch for a Winchester and a single bullet so she could put an end to it.

No! I don't want it to be that easy. First he'll know I'm his master. Then, after I've seen defeat in his eyes instead of arrogance, then I will kill him.

The stallion crashed back onto all fours, tossed his head and raced away. Although his body was lathered with sweat, he appeared as strong as when the chase had started. That was what always defeated her, his strength and stamina. It was an obstacle she had to overcome if she were ever to call herself master of the white killer.

It was only then that she realized the man was still

holding her in what seemed like a very possessive grip, his fingers spreading open across her shoulders and onto the bare skin of her throat where the collar of her shirt had fallen open. She jerked away from him, hooked her thumbs in her belt and turned an accessing eye on his horse.

The big gray was a stallion, and not just a cowpony like Louisiana. This was a blooded animal. An Arabian.

Just like the white stallion.

"I want to buy your horse," she said.

"He's not for sale."

"Everything is for sale, mister. Name your price."

He threw an arm across his saddle and looked at Kayley as though she were the one being considered for sale. His gaze traveled slowly over the curve of her breasts, along the contour of her hips encased in sweat-darkened denim, and down her legs wrapped in stiff leather chaps.

When he met her eyes again, she was irritated to see his expression wasn't only still cold, it was also just a little bored.

"Tell you what I'll do," he said in an exaggerated imitation of a Texas drawl. "The day I throw my saddle across that white devil's back, I'll give Tavira here to you."

"I'd like to have him while I'm still young enough to ride him. Sell him to me now, and if I don't have a rope around the white's neck inside a week, I'll give him back to you."

"You're not giving yourself much of a chance, kid."

Northeast of the ruins, a thin rising of dust stained the crystal air of the valley. It showed the direction of the stallion's flight and the exact place of his disappearance, the cloud of dust ending so abruptly, and so far from cover, it looked as though the stallion had taken to the skies like the mythical beast Pegasus.

His ability to vanish so quickly, and so completely, added to Kayley's frustration. Her fingers began tapping her belt. The best cowpony in New Mexico wouldn't cost more than fifty dollars. But the gray wasn't a cowpony.

"Today's Tuesday," she said. "I'll bet you two hundred dollars against the ownership of . . ."

"Tavira," he supplied.

"Two hundred dollars against the ownership of Tavira that the white stallion will be within a hundred yards of the branding corral on my father's ranch before midnight Saturday."

"What makes you believe that?"

"Because I have his mares."

That morning, while she and her father's ranch hands had been looking for missing cattle, they'd chanced across the white stallion and his herd drinking from the muddy waters of the Rio Grande. The horses had swarmed up the eastern bank of the shallow river and fled.

Although the youngest animals in the herd had at first surged ahead of the other horses, they soon became winded. The mares had ignored their master's commands to continue their flight and allowed themselves to be captured rather than abandon their young. In the resulting confusion, the older foals and non-breeding mares had also been captured, leaving only Kayley and the stallion to continue their race.

"When the stallion comes for them," she said,

"and he will, I know he will, I want to be riding your gray."

The stranger lifted an eyebrow as though considering the offer, then shook his head. "No deal."

"Three hundred dollars." She hated the desperation that edged her voice.

"Sorry, kid." He swung into the saddle. "Your horse is too exhausted to carry you. Climb up behind me and I'll take you part of the way back to your ranch."

Before Kayley had time to even consider the man's offer, he kicked his left foot out of the stirrup and offered his hand. She leaned over and hoisted her saddle onto her back.

"I don't need your help."

"Twenty-five miles is a long way to walk." His hand was still extended. "It'll be dark soon."

The saddle weighed close to fifty pounds. When she wasn't tired, it was almost more than she could lift. Now it felt like she was holding up a horse. She braced her legs apart to keep them from crumbling beneath her.

"I'm not a child to be afraid of the dark," she said, her voice narrow and strained from being forced out between clenched teeth.

He gave her that look again, the one that made her feel she was being auctioned off to the highest bidder. "You're right, Miss Ryan, you're not a child." He turned the big gray west. Before riding off, he glanced back over his shoulder. "About the trespassing charge, it won't stick, since this is government land. You run a good bluff, though, kid."

"The nerve of some people," Kayley said after he'd

gone. She slung the saddle onto Louisiana's back. He tossed his head and snorted in protest. "If I have to walk," she told him, "the least you can do is carry this."

Jack let Tavira choose his own pace as they made their way back to the arroyo. He'd been breaking camp when the white stallion had appeared above the springs. It hadn't occurred to Jack that the beast might still be around, and he'd watched in begrudging admiration as the great Arabian ran with reckless abandon along the very edge of the canyon wall.

Seconds later the girl had appeared, looking like a brilliant spirit born of the sky and sun with her bright blue shirt and fiery hair. There had been something infectious in her manner, something free and wonderful that had drawn Jack to her.

He'd grabbed a rope, mounted Tavira and joined in the chase before he'd even realized what he was doing. After so many years of mind-numbing boredom in Lansing Prison, where shadows had swallowed everything except the absolute darkness of the night, it had been a thrill to ride alongside the girl and let himself be caught up in her excitement. When she'd been forced to give up the chase, he'd been determined to catch Satan's Angel for her. Prison had taken the edge off his skills, though, and he'd missed his throw.

It was when he'd returned to the ruins to speak to her that Jack had recognized, with a sickening disappointment, who she was. She had Sullivan Ryan's eyes, eyes bluer than a New Mexico sky, eyes every bit as bold and arrogant as her father's.

Jack's hat was almost buried in gravel beside the boulder. He leaned over from his saddle to scoop up the dusty hat, slapping it against his leg before putting it on again.

He caressed the leather patch covering his left eye as he remembered the way the girl had trembled at the touch of his hands on her shoulders. That revealing tremble fit perfectly into his plans to take from Sullivan Ryan everything he owned and to destroy everything he valued. What could be more precious to a father than his only child, especially a daughter who was so obviously innocent?

Jack smiled as his sickening disappointment changed into a sudden eagerness for his next encounter with the beautiful Kayley Ryan.

Chapter Three

The day was beginning its death throes when Kayley, to her relief, saw someone riding in her direction. Already her feet were blistered and her legs cramping, and she'd barely walked two miles, a feat not easily accomplished in boots designed for the sole purpose of riding.

She waved her hat to draw the rider's attention, then leaned against Louisiana to watch the waving grasses of the broad valley change from green and gold to lavender and pink as the sky was overtaken by a spectacular sunset. When the last crimson-edged cloud had faded to gray, she couldn't see anything in the darkness that had settled around her.

After what seemed like forever, she heard a horse approaching. She hailed the rider with a shout. It was Sam Butler, foreman of the R Cross. Kayley climbed up behind him and gave him Louisiana's lead.

"I didn't think anyone would ever find me," she said with a sigh.

27

"Where did you lose him?"

"Louie gave out at the ruins." She didn't tell him about the stranger, fearing if she did, he'd again try to dissuade her from riding out alone to search for the stallion. "What happened to his mares?"

"They're in the branding corral. Nineteen mares and eight foals."

"Which we can sell at the Santa Fe stock auction."

"Exactly what I was thinking."

"I must be smarter than I thought."

"You'll do," he said, his voice like an old bear's growl.

Kayley wanted to press her face against his sturdy, buckskin-covered back. "That's the nicest thing anyone's ever said to me, Sam."

She smiled as he put his horse into a teeth-shaking gallop that prevented further confessions, conversations and, as she soon realized, complaints.

The clouds that cloaked the peaks of the Manzano Mountains glinted with silver lightning flashing deep within their stormy depths. Kayley was watching the flashes as Old Joe, Sam's roan mare, topped a rise. Below them, tucked against the eastern slopes of the mountains and glistening like stars at the base of a small canyon, were the lights of the R Cross Ranch headquarters. Laughter and pine smoke drifted on the wind, and the horses in the corral nickered a greeting to the late arrivals who made their exhausted way to the welcoming light.

Standing and sitting and lounging on the porch of the bunkhouse were the familiar faces of the R Cross crew. Mixed among them were four men who didn't belong. Kayley wondered who they were until she saw Vance Moore step off the veranda fronting the house. He owned the Lucky Ace Ranch, the closest neighbor of the R Cross, and never went anywhere without his men accompanying him.

"Welcome, my dear," Vance said. He shoved his way into Kayley so he could help her down. His hazel eyes were almost as black as the sky, and his blond hair looked like a halo in the lamplight. "I've been quite worried about you."

"Not enough to go out looking, though," a faceless voice said from behind them.

"There was no need for you to worry, Vance. Sam, see that Louisiana gets an extra ration of oats tonight." She laid a hand on his forearm. "And thank you."

"Just doing my job," he said, his voice again grumbling and gruff. He led Old Joe and Louisiana to the barn.

Vance pulled Kayley against him. "I don't like it when you're not here to greet me wearing a pretty dress and smelling nice."

She realized how terrible she must look, her face dirtied and her hair blown wild by miles of riding. Vance's expression of distaste added to her discomfort, making her feel like she should crawl under a rock.

Why couldn't he just once look at her the way that rude stranger had? He hadn't seemed to mind her disheveled appearance. She frowned as she remembered not only his final glance, but also his final words.

He knew my name, she realized.

"When are you going to stop wasting your time with that stallion, my dear? This obsession of yours is growing tiresome."

"Is there any reason you're here, other than to reprimand me?" He looked so hurt that she felt instantly ashamed. "I'm sorry," she said, her shoulders slumping and her gaze unable to meet his. "That was uncalled for. It's just that I'm so tired."

"You're forgiven," he said, and she felt even worse. "As for the reason I'm here, other than to see you, I want to know what happened today."

Her eyes stung as she looked up at him. "He outran me again, then disappeared."

"I don't care about that stallion, Kayley. I want to know if you found anything to prove that Sam's right about your cattle being stolen."

"We came across the stallion first."

Vance rolled his eyes and expelled a sigh that sounded forced. "My dear, running a ranch like the R Cross is a job, not something you play at when there's nothing else you'd rather be doing. Let me take over."

"I don't need help."

"Yes, Kayley, you do. Every time I'm here, I'm reminded of just how much you do need help."

She pushed away from him. "Then, stay away."

He threw up his hands and laughed. "You win, as always, my dear. I won't advise, I won't help, and I won't offer again." He drew her into his arms. "Will you at least let me kiss you?"

"No!" she cried, looking quickly across at the cowboys on the bunkhouse porch. She could feel

30

them staring at her.

"Then, how about inviting me to dinner on Saturday night?"

"I didn't think you needed an invitation. You eat here more often than you do at the Lucky Ace."

"That's your father's fault for having the best cook in the territory. Did you know that after I founded the Lucky Ace, I tried to coax Elda away?" he asked, referring to the R Cross cook and housekeeper.

"You mean after you won it in a poker game."

He frowned down at her. "Have you been listening to range gossip, my dear? It's not a becoming habit."

"You did win the Lucky Ace, didn't you?"

"I won the land; the ranch I built myself. And in case you've heard otherwise, I didn't cheat anyone, which is more than your father can say about this place; so don't be looking down that little freckled nose at me."

"My nose isn't freckled! And my father didn't cheat anyone!"

"Your trust in him is most charming, my dear."

Kayley didn't like to be patronized. "I'm glad Elda refused to work for you."

"I'm glad, too. Now, whenever I want an excuse to visit you, I can plead the desire for a good meal. Which brings us back to my requested invitation to dine with you, my dear. I'm tired of eating in the kitchen instead of the dining room. Your habit of eating with your hired hands is most tiresome and unattractive. Didn't that fancy school teach you that employees shouldn't be treated as friends?"

There were a lot of ways to describe the boarding school where Kayley had grown up—fancy wasn't one of them.

"All right," she said, too tired to argue. "We'll eat in the dining room. Don't think just because you forced me into this that you can push your way into managing this ranch, though."

She signalled Bede, Elda Moraillon's fifteen-year-old son, to join them. Snow, a grizzled oldster and the ranch's trail cook ambled over, too.

"Mr. Moore and his men are leaving, Bede," Kayley said. "Bring their horses around. Good night, Vance."

His fingers closed around her arm, pulling her to him as he leaned down to whisper in her ear. "I still want that kiss."

Snow pushed between them. "Miss Ryan done told you so long, so you'd best whistle up them poisoned pups kickin' their boots up on our bunkhouse wall and ride."

"If I don't, are you planning to make me regret it, old man?" Vance asked in an amused tone.

Snow laid a hand on the pistol shoved into the front of his belt. "I ain't no dime novel cowboy, son, so you'd best think a spell before startin' somethin' this Peacemaker will finish."

Vance's smile looked forced as he released Kayley's arm and lifted his hands into the air to signal defeat. "Remind me never to play poker with this man, my dear. He bluffs too well." He touched the brim of his hat to her, then to Snow, before swinging onto his horse and riding away with his men surrounding him.

"Would you really have shot him, Snow?" Kayley asked.

"That gambler ain't worth wastin' a bullet. Now, them boys he's got ridin' with him's a whole different story. They's mean enough to have a reserved seat in hell, no offense intended, Miss Ryan."

"None taken. Good night, Snow."

"Don't let the bedbugs get you."

She shuddered at the memory of all the nighttime creatures she'd encountered on her way to the R Cross five months ago. Not a single bed between Boston and New Mexico had been free from the biting horrors. She'd arrived at the ranch practically bitten blue.

"If they do, I'll send for you and your Peacemaker."

Snow patted the handle of the big Colt. "We'll be ready with a new box of shells."

The fire in the living room had died away to embers. Kayley stirred the glowing coals into flames and added more wood. While waiting for it to ignite, she crossed her arms on top of the mantle and laid her forehead on them, too tired to even move to one of the chairs behind her.

The sound of approaching footsteps caused her to stand quickly upright before Gunning entered the living room from the hall leading to the bedrooms. He was the Ryan butler, for lack of a better term to describe his varied duties in the house. And though he rarely acknowledged it, he was also Elda's brother. He was in his late fifties and had a way about him that made him appear to be starched and unfriendly.

In truth, he was the kindest, gentlest man Kayley had ever known. Although exhausted to the point of near collapse, just seeing him renewed her strength so that she found herself smiling.

"He's awake, Miss Ryan."

Her shoulders slumped, and the smile failed her. "I thought he might be."

"What would you like prepared for your supper?"

"I'm too tired to eat." She pushed her hair back from her face. "Do you have a string I could tie this up with before I go in?"

He pulled a blue ribbon from his pocket. "A lady shouldn't wear string." He tied the ribbon around her hair with a quick twist of his knobby wrists. "Did you have luck today, miss?"

"I need a miracle, Gunning, not luck."

The distance from the living room to her father's bedroom seemed longer than the miles she'd walked earlier, and Kayley traveled it slowly. She'd rather face a pit of angry scorpions than face him after failing again.

A candle was burning on the table beside his bed. When she entered the room, its tiny circle of light quivered in the draft from an open window, alternately revealing and concealing the scene before her.

Sullivan Ryan's hands lay on top of the quilt like last year's leaves, so frail and trembling they appeared to be crumbling beneath their own weight.

"Good evening, Poppa." She crossed the room to smile down at the cavernous cheeks, motionless lips, and the almost translucent skin of the specter he'd become. Only the ridged scar that curved across his forehead and into the wisps of his hair had any color to it, an ugly purple color that time hadn't faded.

His eyes were open, his pupils huge and dark. The sparkle of laughter that had been Kayley's only memory of him for so many years was gone now, lost in that terrible darkness.

She sat on the chair beside his bed and carefully lifted one of his cold hands in hers. "I had a wonderful ride today, Poppa."

In the softly flickering light, she told him how the Rio Grande had been more mud than water and what the red earth of the arroyo had looked like with the afternoon sun shining on it and how the limestone of the Gran Quivira ruins had been stained dark by time on the outside, yet were chalky white inside.

Not once did she mention the stallion, his herd or the stranger who'd appeared from nowhere. It wasn't that she didn't want to tell her father these things. She wanted to so much that the unspoken words were almost choking her. It might worry him, though, and she wanted him to save all his strength for getting well, not worrying about her.

"Vance was here tonight, Poppa, and he's coming to supper this Saturday. I hope you'll be better by then so you can join us."

The limp muscles of her father's face tightened. Sounds that were more like groans than an attempt to speak spilled from his paralyzed lips, causing Kayley's heart to fill with desperate hope.

"Marr . . . moor . . ."

"Say it again, Poppa."

His skeletonlike fingers moved slightly within her gentle grasp. For one wonderful moment, she thought he was going to grip her hand. Then they went limp again. His eyes closed and his breathing slowed until it was barely perceptible beneath the weight of the heavy quilt.

After her disappointment drained away, leaving her feeling weak and alone, Kayley leaned over to kiss the cold flesh of her father's cheek while swearing anew her oath of revenge against the white stallion.

Chapter Four

Two mornings later, just as Kayley was leaving her room, a harsh clanging intruded on the peaceful quiet of the ranch, announcing that breakfast was ready. She ran down the hall, stopping outside the carved double doors of her father's room to wait for Gunning to answer her knock before entering.

This room was beautiful, especially when filled with sunlight, as it was now. The high ceiling was supported by beams called *vigas*, which were made of hewn ponderosa pine. The ceiling itself was covered in *latillas*, which were made of peeled aspen logs the color of fresh butter. The dark maplewood floor was so highly polished it reflected like a mirror.

The most outstanding feature in the room, though, was an entire wall of windows. Such a great expanse of glass was unusual in an adobe house, but the house had been angled so very little heat entered the room while allowing the windows to let in lots of light and fresh air and an uninterrupted view of the endless New Mexico sky.

Gunning was standing in front of the windows, his arms filled with clean linen that smelled of warm winds and lye soap. He stood stiff and straight, his clothes and his manner so starched, he looked incapable of bending.

"I haven't changed his sheets yet this morning, Miss Ryan," he said.

"I just wanted to see him before I go out."

The odors from the bed turned her stomach as she bent down to kiss her father's cheek. The pucker of his scar pulled grotesquely at his face, the purple color startling in the bright sunlight.

"Good morning, Poppa. Did you sleep well?"

There was no movement of his hand within hers, no attempt to speak, no tightening of the muscles in his face to prove he'd even heard her. She swallowed her disappointment before kissing him again, then left him and Gunning to their morning routine.

Kayley was thinking about her father as she entered the living room and almost walked directly into Elda Moraillon. "Elda!" she cried in surprise. "You startled me. I didn't expect anyone to be in here. I thought you'd be serving breakfast."

Elda was tall and stately like her brother, yet completely unlike him in personality. Where he was quiet and reserved, she was outspoken and opinionated and possessed a maternal instinct that overwhelmed Kayley, even though Bede was its victim instead of her.

Right now, she felt like a different type of victim as Elda stood in front of the rolltop desk, an incredibly thin knife held in front of her as though ready to defend herself against attack.

38

"Those are men working for you, not little boys to have their plates filled for them." She slid the knife into a pocket of her apron.

"Not even Bede?"

Elda's attitude softened instantly. "Bede's my baby." She smiled down at an imaginary infant in her arms.

"A very big baby!" Kayley laughed at the remembered image of Bede running across the yard last night, his too big hat flopping around him.

Elda drew herself up in indignant anger. "Now you laugh at me, but someday you'll have a child and you'll know what it is to want to give him everything you never had. It's this work you do. I think you should let a man do this work before you become the kind of woman no man wants."

"I think you should be serving breakfast, not thinking about what I should be doing."

Elda shrugged away the reproach. She rubbed the top of the already spotless desk with the corner of her apron. "There's too much dirt to clean in this house for me to be serving grown men."

Lizard and snake skins, beaten silver conchas, turquoise beads, turkey feathers, and braided horse-hair decorated the sweat-stained hats of the R Cross cowboys who filled the kitchen with their chaps and spurs and flowing moustaches. Their hatbands were like badges of identity, each as different as the man who wore it.

Wood scraped against wood as they pushed their chairs back, standing to greet Kayley and make room for her. She sat at the head of the table between Sam and Snow, who handed her a plate piled high with flapjacks and sausage. She smothered everything in so much honey it dripped like golden nectar onto the well-scrubbed table.

"You're lookin' prettier'n a newborn heifer today," Snow said to her.

Joe Duke, the only black cowboy on the R Cross, rolled his eyes. "What a thing to say to a lady, old man."

Slowhand Smith, who claimed to be the best bronco buster west of anything east, lowered his chin into his bandanna and said, "You're just mad 'cause you didn't say it first."

"Miss Ryan ain't no heifer," Joe said.

"She ain't no bull," Snow said, "and that ain't bull!"

Kayley laughed with the men, enjoying the camaraderie of their boisterous, and sometimes embarrassing, banter.

Sam Butler spread a worn map on the table. She recognized it as the map of the R Cross her father had shown her the day she arrived at the ranch. It was covered in scribbled handwriting and crude drawings that marked every important location in the Salinas Valley. Streams, wet and dry, canyons and arroyos, springs and waterholes and dry lake beds, all had been carefully recorded on the yellowing paper.

"This," Sam said as he planted a calloused forefinger on a wavy line labeled Bear Creek, "can't wait any longer, Miss Ryan."

Bear Creek was owned by Peters McDonnell, a Scotsman who'd been living in the Manzano Mountains for the better part of thirty years. Last month, Peters had sent word that he was planning to return to Scotland and was offering Sullivan Ryan first refusal on the rights to Bear Creek.

Sam had been pressing Kayley to visit the old Scotsman ever since then. She'd kept putting it off, not only because she preferred to search for the stallion, but because she didn't know anything about buying land.

"Tell me how to get there," she said.

Snow punched a finger onto the map. "Ride north until you see the old church right here, then turn around and go back south until you see an abandoned adobe hut beside a creek. That's Bear Creek."

"Why don't I just look for the adobe hut on the way north?" Kayley asked.

Snow grunted. "If you wanna do it the hard way, go ahead."

"I think we should shoot him," Joe Duke said.

Sam pulled the map away from Snow. "When you reach Bear Creek, Miss Ryan, just turn west and follow the creek up the mountain. It'll take you right to McDonnell's." He nodded at the map. "That piece of land will give the R Cross undisputed ownership of the three best natural sources of water in the entire valley."

He punched a finger at the other two: Antelope Springs, which lay west of the ranch house, and Gallinas Spring to the south. Elda pushed between Kayley and Sam with the coffeepot. A cloud of steam billowed across the table and rushed to the ceiling as Elda slowly filled Sam's half-empty cup.

"We'll also be saving five steers a year," he said,

41

referring to the price they paid for the agreement the ranch had with Peters that guaranteed the only obstruction of the creek would be a beaver dam at the eastern boundary of his property. The water that crossed over that dam fell on R Cross property, and it was vital to the ranch's survival.

"At the rate our beef is bein' rustled," Slowhand said, "we might not have that many cows left by spring."

"Vance thinks I'm the problem, not rustlers," Kayley said.

Willie Pete, who at just under seven feet was the tallest person Kayley had ever seen, pushed his empty cup at Elda, who ignored him. "There's bound to be something besides dust in the draws and washes we passed while we was chasing those mustangs the other day," he said with a scowl. "I'd like to ride back that way today and take a good look around for them missing steers."

"Good idea," Sam said. He tipped his turquoise-banded hat onto the back of his head. "Take Bede here with you and teach him how to track something besides his ma's apron strings."

Bede's face lit up like a freshly struck match. He jumped to his feet, knocking his chair backward and causing it to crash to the floor.

"I'll get our gear," Willie said. He thrust an empty provision sack at Bede. "You fill this."

Elda took the sack from him. "I know what a boy must eat to work so hard."

Whenever any attention was paid to Bede, he blushed scarlet and looked like he wanted to disappear. Now, with the men laughing at Sam's comment and under the pressure of his mother's loving smile, he looked more miserable than Kayley had ever seen him. His hazel eyes were fixed on the floor in front of him as he lifted a thin hand to push at the scraggly blond hair that fell from beneath his hat.

"It ain't his ma's apron strings that's got him followin' her around," Snow said. "It's them goodies she keeps bakin' him. He eats more cakes and cookies and pies in a week than I had in my whole life."

"These men," Elda said to Bede, "are jealous their mamma isn't here to do for them what I do for you."

"The only thing my ma done for me was kick me out on my own," Snow said.

"She probably couldn't stand the way you smelled," Kayley said and laughed at Snow's offended expression. "Not that I mind it, but I did hear your mules complaining."

The room exploded with guffaws of laughter. Even Sam let out a gasping choke that was the closest Kayley had ever heard him come to laughing. Suddenly she didn't care what Vance thought about her eating in the kitchen with her father's men. She liked it here.

"You'll do just fine with McDonnell," Sam said. He folded the map and handed it to her. "Day's wasting, boys."

Chairs scraped and spurs jingled as the men began filing out of the kitchen, ready to face another long day of dust, cattle, and sunshine.

Bede came out of his stupor of embarrassment when Elda put enough salt pork in the sack to feed the entire crew for a week. "There's only two of us, Ma."

43

He took out most of the meat and replaced it with peppermint sticks. Sacks of beans, coffee, and cornmeal were matched with licorice whips and jawbreakers and horehound candy.

Elda slapped his hand away when he tried to put in a tin of cookies. "You're looking for cows, not little children!"

Willie came back in the kitchen and took the sack from Elda. He frowned and dropped it on the table. "Too heavy. I'll shoot jackrabbits."

"I'll carry it," Bede said. "Maybe we should ride into town, Willie, and see if Miss Charity's ma has some of that fudge of hers for sell at Señor Chaves' store. Remember that fudge she made for the picnic at the Stormer ranch?"

"Picnic?" Kayley asked, looking up at him from her breakfast.

Elda tweaked his arm. "You stay away from that Calhoun girl!"

"The Flying S gave a barbecue after spring roundup this year," Willie said to Kayley. "They invited the men from every ranch in the county to join them."

Bede nodded. "They roasted dozens of hogs and steers, and the women from Mrs. Stormer's church made enough cakes and pies to feed the whole country. Charity Calhoun's mother made chocolate fudge just like she sells at Chaves' store in Belen. The men working their spread said they had picnics, I mean barbecues, a lot, only not so big."

It was the most she'd ever heard Bede say. It seemed to surprise him as much as it did his mother, who pinched him on the arm again.

"I've never been on a picnic or a barbecue," Kayley said.

"I sure am sorry, Miss Ryan," Bede said before imitating Willie by ducking his head as he left the kitchen. Kayley was unsure if he'd meant he was sorry for talking so much, or for her having missed out on what he obviously considered the most fun anyone could ever have.

Snow stood up with a grunt and a groan, his joints creaking like rusty hinges. "I'd best be headin' for town to get them supplies you want, Elda."

"Not what I want, what you want if you want to eat for the next month." Her mood was as black as the crud she was scraping off the bottom of a skillet.

"Snow, would it be much trouble for us to have a barbecue?" Kayley asked. "Just a little one, for the men?"

"No more trouble than tryin' to get a smile out of this woman," he said, sidling up behind Elda and acting like he was going to grab her. She stopped him with a threatening glare. He cowered back from her in mock fear and threw Kayley a wink. "Come to think of it, givin' a barbecue would be a sight easier. You want me to fix things up?"

"For Saturday night," she said. "And tell Willie and Bede so they can be back in time." She ran a finger along a crease in her father's map while looking at Elda out of the corner of her eye. "Maybe we should invite the Calhouns. I'd like to taste that fudge, and Bede might enjoy Charity's company."

"That girl isn't fit to keep my son company!" Elda cried, her face turning redder with every word.

Both Sam and Snow made for the door, leaving

Kayley alone to face what she'd caused.

"My son must not marry the daughter of a woman like Amanda Calhoun. She will do anything to make money."

"It was a joke," Kayley said. "Besides, you know I don't want anyone visiting the ranch until Poppa gets well."

Elda lifted a questioning eyebrow. "Not even Vance Moore?"

"Vance is Poppa's friend; he wouldn't betray our secret, especially since it was his idea we keep it a secret."

"He's a handsome man, this Vance Moore, and it's not your father he comes here so often to see."

Kayley busied herself with stuffing the last of the peppermint sticks into her vest pocket. "I'll be late for supper tonight." She went to the living room to lock her father's map in his desk before starting for Peters McDonnell's mountain.

The flat landscape of the southern valley folded into rolling hills north of the ranch house. Ancient apple orchards gave way to junipers on their gentle slopes. When Kayley turned west into the Manzano Mountains, the junipers gave way to white oaks that lent a dappled shade to the warm day. The temperature was noticeably cooler by the time Louisiana entered the forest of the stately ponderosa pines that capped the towering mountains.

The winding banks of Bear Creek were lined with yellow coneflowers, mile after mile of them that reached up to Kayley on slender stems that swayed gently in the wind.

The air here smelled rich and moist. It was a familiar scent that reminded her unexpectedly of boarding school. Every night, after the other girls had fallen asleep, Kayley had slipped from her narrow bed and crept on bare feet to the end of the dormitory. There she'd opened the window that faced out onto the wooded glen behind the school-yard fence.

Shivering with excitement, she'd stood wrapped in a blanket woven of the sounds and smells of the night while looking at the stars sparkling like bright tears. For hours, she'd watched them move slowly across her little corner of the sky, leaving her to wonder where they were going and if she would ever go there, too.

The dense forest on the eastern slopes of the Manzanos opened quite suddenly onto a sun-drenched meadow where the scent of flowering locoweed chased away the shadows of the past. She turned Louisiana in the direction of the beaver pond that lay behind a rambling expanse of berry bushes.

The gelding moved through the bushes with caution, even though his hair, already starting to grow thick and shaggy for the coming winter, protected him from the thorns. Kayley wasn't so fortunate. Because she wasn't wearing her chaps, she was kept busy pulling off the branches that snagged on her pantlegs. Her gloves were useless, the fringe around the cuffs becoming entrapped by the thorns more easily than the denim. She removed the doeskin gloves and suffered in silence the painful punctures.

When she reached blindly for one clinging branch,

her fingers closed on a clump of wet cloth. She jerked her hand back and looked in confusion at the bush. Stretched across it was a pair of men's underwear dripping water in a steady stream onto the ripe berries below. Other bushes were adorned with an equally wet shirt and pants, and a single red sock.

A hat was balanced on the end of a spiky branch. There was no hatband encircling the crown. A man without an identity, Kayley thought. A nicker of greeting drew her attention to where a gray stallion was tethered away from poisonous purple blossoms that grew in great profusion in the meadow. The Arabian's sleek coat glistened in the light as he tossed his head, causing his silken mane to fall in wild disarray across his eyes.

"Tavira," Kayley whispered, remembering with distaste the blooded stallion's owner. She glanced back down at the clothes on the bushes. This was an opportunity too good to ignore.

Bending close to Louisiana's twitching ear, she whispered, "Quiet now, Louie," and urged him forward until they broke out of the grasp of the bushes at the very edge of the pond.

The stranger was standing knee-deep in the water with his back to Kayley. A mirror was in his right hand, a razor in his left. Although she'd known he'd be nude, she'd assumed he'd be immersed in the pond and suffered a blush of embarrassment at the unexpected sight of his tall, naked body.

His shoulders were wide, and they, along with his arms and upper back, were corded with sinewy muscles. His waist and hips were narrow, almost slender, like a cowboy's. Men who worked cattle carried their strength in wiry, thin muscles, though. This man was muscled by years of hard, physical labor that had shaped his body like a magnificent sculpture.

The rawhide strings securing his eyepatch in place were knotted on the back of his head, the ends tangling with his dark hair and falling onto his upper back where they seemed to be pointing directly at a scar, long and white, that sliced across the sun-bronzed skin just above his waist.

Knife, she thought, and tried not to imagine the retribution a man like this would extract from whoever had dared to cut him. *Or from someone who sneaks up on him while he bathes.* She bit her lower lip to silence the fear pulsing within her. *I'll leave before he sees me.*

At that moment, he began walking deeper into the pond, his movement through the water slow and confident, his legs and buttocks alternately tensing and relaxing in a seductive rhythm that made Kayley slightly breathless.

When the water reached his upper thighs, he lowered the razor into the pool to rinse the froth of soap from its shining length. He lifted the blade again, touched it beneath his chin and tilted his head back, raising the mirror simultaneously.

A bright flash of golden-red hair appeared in the silver glass, letting Kayley know even before the stranger froze that he'd seen her. Her heart slammed to a stop, and her hands gripped Louisiana's reins so tightly that he gave a violent shake of his head that filled the clearing with a jangling of bit and bridle.

The man spun around, his face beneath the eye

patch contorted by surprise. Before he turned completely, though, he froze in an awkward stance that was almost comic, and Kayley realized that he'd just remembered he was naked.

He held that pose for a long moment before dropping into the water to his neck. The surface of the pond convulsed with his sudden immersion, and a wave slapped him in the face, washing away most of the soapy lather and revealing the angry set of his jaw.

His obvious discomfort, and the fact that she had him at such a complete disadvantage, restored Kayley's confidence. She rode into the pond, stopping a few feet away from her crouching victim to kick her feet clear of the stirrups and fold her right leg across the saddle in front of her. It was an awkward position that made her feel she was about to tumble over backward, but she'd often seen the R Cross ranch hands sit that way while relaxing and was determined not to look any less comfortable than they had.

Once settled, she dumped the stale contents of her canteen in the pond. She dropped the canteen on the surface of the water and pushed it under with her left foot so it could fill.

"I take it you haven't caught my stallion yet," she said.

"Not yet."

She lifted the canteen by its strap and took a long drink. Then, as though the thought had just occurred to her, she looked down at him in mock concern. "It's not cold in there, is it?"

The muscles in his left cheek twitched, then

hardened again. "No."

"Good, I wouldn't want you to catch a chill on my account." She released her hold on Louisiana's reins to allow him to drink. "Have you changed your mind about selling Tavira?"

"No."

His abrupt answers irritated her. "You're on private land," she said, nodding her head in the direction of the boundary marker below the beaver dam.

"I know," he said. To her surprise, the scowl on his face turned into an amused smile as he rose far enough out of the water for the hair on his chest to glisten in the sunlight. "And I know that this isn't your land, either, kid."

Kayley gave a predatory glance around her. *Not yet*, she thought, and decided to come back after her visit with Peters McDonnell and throw this man off what would then be her land. "I'll be going now," she said and dropped her feet back into the stirrups.

"I look forward to our next meeting, Miss Ryan, when I hope to be at less of a disadvantage."

"I preferred it this way," she said with a laugh, and lifted a hand in farewell.

Kayley curled her fingers into fists and tried to keep her voice calm. "What do you mean you've already sold out? You offered my father first refusal on this land."

Peters McDonnell was sitting in a chair made of braided willow branches. He was nearly seventy, his hair and beard completely gray. "That I did, lass. I

51

couldn't be waitin' forever for him to be takin' me up on me offer.''

"I'll double whatever you've been offered and pay your way to Scotland.''

He shook his head to stop her. "Save your breath, girl, 'tis done and I'll not be backin' out of a handshake." He gave a noisy suck on the peppermint stick she'd given him. "Tell your pa not to be worryin' that his beasts will want for water. The lad will honor the treaty for me stream.''

Although furious that her negligence had cost her the land, Kayley felt a rush of relief that she'd not lost the rights to the water.

"My father will be grateful for your concern, Mr. McDonnell. I hope the new owner will be as good a neighbor as you've been.'' She gave Louisiana what remained of her own peppermint stick to eat while she swung into the saddle.

"If you're eager to be meetin' him, lass, come inside and have a bowl of mush. He'll be back soon.''

She looked past McDonnell to the windowless shack that was almost buried in the debris that thirty years of accumulation had heaped around its exterior. "Elda's waiting supper for me," she said.

Peters pushed himself out of the willow chair. He appeared to be too frail for the long journey to Scotland, but Kayley had no doubt he'd make it. The story Snow had told her about the grizzly skin tacked to the wall behind McDonnell proved that.

The animal had charged into the Scotsman's cabin during a snowstorm one night last fall. Alone, in the dark, and with no weapon except a knife, Peters had managed to kill the bear while receiving what he'd called "a few wee scratches," the worst of which had almost sliced his left arm off.

He'd then tied himself to his old mule and let the animal carry him off the mountain and into town where he'd argued that he didn't want a doctor, just a bottle of "good Scotch whiskey."

"Maybe you'll be seein' your new neighbor goin' off the mountain," Peters said. "The boy went to take himself a bath." He shook his head in disbelief and chuckled while scratching at his own reasons for needing to bathe.

It can't be, Kayley thought. *Fate wouldn't be that cruel.*

"A tall man with a patch over one eye?" she asked.

"That be him! Said to call him somethin' to do wi' dirt." Peters frowned up at his bushy eyebrows. "Clay, I think he said. Used to be a rancher and has a hankerin' to run a few head again."

It was all Kayley could do to keep from screaming with frustration. "I'm sorry we couldn't do business, Mr. McDonnell," she said. "Have a good trip home."

To avoid another encounter with the man named Clay, Kayley turned off the trail and rode south, hoping she'd find a canyon to follow to the valley below. With each step Louisiana took, his hooves making soft crunching sounds as they broke through the debris carpeting the moist ground, Kayley felt a fresh burst of anger at how she'd been made to look a fool.

"The nerve of him," she punctuated each word by slamming her fist against her right leg, "telling me that he knew this wasn't my land and not saying it was his! He just stood there in that terribly cold water . . ."

Her voice trailed off as she remembered how the crystal drops of water had streamed down his skin, tanned and firm, stretched tight over the hard muscles of his shoulders, arms, chest . . .

Brought back to the present by the realization that Louisiana had stopped, Kayley glanced down to see what was wrong and found herself looking into the chilling winter gray of Clay's unblinking stare.

"What are you doing riding a horse so lame he can barely walk?"

She was so surprised to see him that she offered no resistance when he pulled the reins from her limp fingers. His hair was damp, the ends curling beneath his hat, lending a boyish charm to his otherwise piratical appearance.

"Get down and let me look at his foot."

He reached up to help her dismount, his fingers closing around her right arm just below the elbow. Slivers of pain shot outward from his fingertips, bringing her back to reality with a jolting suddenness.

"Have you been following me?"

He half lifted and half dragged her from the saddle. Like a rag doll, she was pulled and dropped and forgotten as his attention was turned to Louisiana, who was holding his front left hoof off the ground.

Concern immediately overcame Kayley's anger. "It's probably a rock," she said as she knelt beside the injured gelding.

"He's too lame for that. He must've picked up

something at McDonnell's. That place is a hazard."

Tavira was tied beneath the autumn-bright leaves of an oak tree. Clay laid a gentling hand on the stallion's neck before taking a knife from his saddlebag.

"I can do it," Kayley said.

The sharp blade flashed in the sunlight that filtered through the forest canopy as Clay laid the knife in her outstretched hand. The handle was made of polished antler. It felt pleasantly smooth beneath her fingers as she bent to lift Louisiana's hoof.

Before she could even begin to look for the rock she was certain would be there, the gelding leaned his head against her and gave a hard push that sent her sprawling on the ground.

She had to look a long way up to see if Clay was laughing. The brim of his hat cast a dark shadow across his face. All she could see was the rigid set of his jaw as he extended his hand to her.

"I don't need your help," she said, then stumbled so clumsily to her feet that he had to grab her around the waist to keep her from falling into him.

He held her possessively against him, sparking within Kayley feelings and emotions that were more powerful than anything she'd ever experienced before.

"You said that the first time we met, too, kid. How far did you walk that night?"

She jerked away from him. "Louisiana doesn't like having his feet lifted, but I can handle him." She bent again to lift the gelding's foot. Still staggered with surprise by her reaction to Clay's embrace, she forgot to brace herself, and the gelding promptly knocked

55

her back to the ground.

"So I see," Clay said with a short laugh. "Does your father know how well you handle your horse?"

She ignored him, concentrating instead on tying Louisiana's reins to the trunk of a fir tree, snubbing his head so close to the knobby bark that he couldn't move more than an inch. "Show's over," she said to Clay with a caustic smile.

"Too bad." He leaned a shoulder against the tree. "I was just beginning to enjoy myself."

"Don't you have something better to do?"

"Not until I'm paid the cattle your father owes me for Bear Creek."

"Mr. McDonnell has already received his five steers this year."

"Peters sold out cheap. I won't."

"The agreement—"

"Was made with Peters nine years ago, kid. Now I own this land. If your father wants Bear Creek water, he'll have to pay my price. That's one of the reasons I was waiting here for you, so you could take a message to him for me."

How could he have been waiting for her when she wasn't even on a trail?

"My father's away on business."

His smile seemed to suddenly surround her. "Leaving his daughter at the mercy of unscrupulous strangers? How long do I have to take advantage of his fortuitous absence?"

She tried to pretend that his smile was having absolutely no affect on her. *And it isn't*, she told herself, even though she was having a great deal of trouble keeping her knees from sinking beneath her.

"How many cattle do you want?" she asked.

"Twenty-five head per year."

It was an extravagant price, one that she couldn't possibly afford to pay. Neither could she afford to stand here any longer with him looking at her like that.

"Agreed," she said. "I'll have our foreman bring ten steers to your cabin after roundup next month."

"Twenty-five, not ten, and I want to chose my own animals, and I want them now, not next month."

"We've already paid five head this year for that creek. Since the year is almost over, an offer of ten cattle for the remaining months is more than fair."

He crossed his arms over his chest. "Twenty-five is what I want, and what I expect to get."

Kayley wasn't about to be pushed another inch. "Then, you'll have to talk to my father."

"When will he be back?"

She shrugged. "Certainly not before roundup, and maybe not before spring."

The muscles in Clay's neck were rigid against his tightly knotted black bandanna. "I'll take the ten," he said, almost spitting the words at her.

She turned her attention quickly to Louisiana so Clay wouldn't see the laughter in her eyes. She scraped away the mud, dead pine needles and smashed mushrooms that covered the gelding's hoof. Clay had been right. Instead of the rock she'd expected, she found the head of a nail embedded in the gelding's hoof. She wedged the tip of the knife under it, held it tight with her thumb and pulled with every ounce of strength she could muster. The nail refused to budge.

She stopped to catch her breath and noticed that Clay appeared to be calmer now. "When will you be bringing the cattle to the house for me to see?" she asked him.

He glowered at her. "What are you talking about?"

"I have to see which steers you select, otherwise how will I know which animals to describe on the transfer of ownership papers?" She looked at him across Louisiana's saddle. "Or that you took only ten?"

He moved around beside her. Before she could stop him, he took the gelding's leg from her and pulled the nail free. It was long and rusted, and a gush of bright blood poured out of the wound and across his hand. He gently lowered the injured hoof to the ground.

"I'm many things, Miss Ryan, but I'm not a rustler."

His closeness was more unsettling to Kayley than his interference. She looked around for a way to escape, but found herself trapped between him, Louisiana and the tree. Clay made her position even more unbearable by reaching out to brush a strand of hair from her cheek. Even after he moved his hand away, she could still feel the lingering tenderness of that gentle caress.

"What was the second reason you were waiting here for me?" she asked, her voice breaking after the first few words so that she had to finish in almost a whisper.

"To give you this." He produced from behind him a braided chain of the yellow flowers that had blanketed the banks of Bear Creek.

Kayley couldn't believe it when he placed them around her shoulders like a living necklace. "You made this?"

"While I was waiting for you."

No one had ever given her flowers before. "How did you know I'd come this way?"

He was watching her lips. It made her unbelievably nervous. She lifted her left hand to fumble with the delicate petals of the flowers. He put his hands on the tree behind her, one on each side of her head so that she was imprisoned by his arms.

"I knew you wouldn't want to ride past the pond again, so I chose the next most obvious route off the mountain to give you this." His hand covered hers where it was still fumbling with the flowers. "And because I wanted to tell you . . ."

He gave her a slow smile, his head lowering until it was very close to hers. Only moments before, the forest had been filled with sounds born of wind and birds and insects. Now it was so silent that Kayley could hear the flutter of her breath catching in her throat.

"I want you," he said, and the silver fire of his gaze caused her to feel suddenly faint, "to get off my land, Miss Ryan. You're trespassing."

Her fingers cramped from the spasmed grip she took on the handle of the knife. She thrust it at him, forcing him to move back or be stabbed, then turned and drove the sharp blade into the tree behind her.

She untied Louisiana and began leading him down the mountain. It was hard to believe that twice in one week she'd been reduced to walking, both times in front of this overgrown, overbearing, overwhelming man.

"I could give you a ride back to your ranch," he called after her.

"I like walking," she snapped, feeling already the rub of her boots against her unhealed blisters.

Chapter Five

Saturday morning, Jack saddled Tavira and started for R Cross Ranch headquarters. There was no reason for him to avoid the house with Sullivan out of town, so he rode confidently across the familiar rolling hills of grass and juniper. When the corrals first appeared out of a shimmering wave of valley heat, he tensed. Seconds later he saw the house. His heart started to race, and he felt as though he were choking.

He'd built this place. He'd molded the adobe bricks, erected the corral posts and dug the well that provided the house with sweet, cool water. Not until it had all been stolen from him had he realized how much he loved this ranch, and not until this moment had he realized the full extent of his hatred for the man who had been his partner.

The horses in the branding corral were in a frenzy that bordered on panic. The white's herd, Jack realized, and was surprised by how agitated they were this long after their capture. There were also fewer animals than he expected, less than a dozen.

They were forgotten at the first sight of his rose garden. Not a single bush was in bloom. There weren't even any buds. The plants were withered and dry. A few even appeared dead. His anger flared fresh and hot, filling his mouth with the bitter taste of his hate.

He tied Tavira in the shade near the first enclosure he'd built on the ranch, a corral made of juniper wood. Imprisoned behind the weathered gray rails was the biggest longhorn bull he'd ever seen. The animal was the color of old adobe and absolutely huge, at least seventeen hundred pounds. The twisted horns rose to a height of eight feet above its head and had a seven-foot spread from tip to tip.

On the bull's right shoulder was a tremendous gash, which had been sewn with what looked like thin strips of rawhide. A smear of foul-smelling ointment discouraged a buzzing hoard of flies hovering around the wound.

When Jack first arrived, the bull had been pawing at the ground. Now it stopped and charged directly at Jack. The animal's massive head slammed against a corral post with a resounding thud. Jack jumped back from the horns, even though they'd missed him by several feet.

The shade from the lattice-roofed veranda along the front of the house was a welcome relief from the hot sun. He paused to wipe the sweat from his forehead. The front door opened, and he started in surprise at the face that greeted him.

"Gunning! I didn't think you'd still be here, old man. It's good to see you."

The perpetually solemn eyes widened. "Mr. Corbett! I was told that you were dead."

"Ryan tried; but I managed to survive, so he bought me a lifetime sentence in a Kansas penitentiary."

"How terrible for you, sir. Did you escape?"

"Don't start counting your reward money yet. An old friend lucked into a position of influence and managed to wrangle me a release."

A smile flickered among the stern features. "I would've helped if I'd known."

"Next time, try reading your mail before Ryan burns it. Incidentally, old man, I'm going by Clay now, and I'm a stranger to these parts." He hesitated a moment before asking, "Will that be a problem for you?"

Gunning looked offended. "Did you really think you needed to ask, sir?"

Jack put a hand on his shoulder. "I learned the hard way not to take anything for granted, friend. Is there anyone else around who might know me?"

"Mr. Ryan brought in his own men after he took over the ranch."

"Except for you."

"If he'd ordered me to go, I wouldn't have gone far. If you're here to see him," Gunning seemed to hesitate, "he's not available."

"His daughter told me he's out of town." Jack looked past Gunning at the interior of the house. "Is she here?"

"Yes, please come in, sir." Gunning stepped aside for Jack to enter. "I shouldn't have kept you standing outside, only I was so surprised to see you. If you'll excuse my asking, sir, is that patch over your eye a diguise?"

"It's real."

"I'm sorry, sir. I'll summon Miss Ryan for you."

"I'm sorry, too, old friend," Jack muttered to himself as he glanced around what had once been his home.

It was like stepping back in time. The massive rolltop desk he'd transported from his grandparents' farm in West Virginia still dominated the room, its surface as crowded with papers as it had been the day he left for Abilene five years ago. The sofa and the chairs, the bookcases and tables, everything was just as it had been the last time he'd been in this room.

The only change was the rug in front of his grandmother's easy chairs which were still pulled close to the fireplace hearth. The rug was woven from several beautiful shades of blue wool. It complemented to perfection the dark gleam of the hardwood floor he'd put in his last winter on the ranch.

Another change, he realized, was that his personal mementos were gone. What had happened to his father's rifle from the Civil War? Although the pegs on which it had been mounted were still in the wall above the desk, the rifle was gone. Its absence left an ugly blemish of emptiness on the plaster wall. And where were his grandmother's crocheted doilies and the daguerreotype of his mother and him as a baby?

Ryan probably burned that along with everything else that proved he didn't own this place.

It was strange how empty the room looked. Almost lonely. It wasn't just his own missing remembrances that gave it such an abandoned appearance, though.

It was that the Ryans hadn't replaced his things with any of their own. There were no pictures of their family, no pieces of feminine handiwork, no open books or discarded newspapers, not a single thing to show that this room was ever used.

Except for the desk. Jack's attention moved back to it, and his heart came to a sudden, jolting stop. Beneath the tumbled papers, was a thin book bound in white leather.

It can't be, not after all these years.

But what else could it be? The white cashbooks he'd used to keep the ranch accounts had been custom made. It was unlikely Sullivan would've continued ordering the expensive books. "A waste of money" had been his comment when auditing Jack's accounts prior to their partnership.

Jack crossed to the desk, drawn by an impossible hope.

"Miss Ryan will be right in," Gunning said from behind Jack, startling him. He'd forgotten his long-time friend's unsettling ability to move about in such complete silence.

"How about offering me a drink, old man?" he asked, his attention fixed on the book.

"What would you like, sir?"

"Whiskey. Wait, better cancel that. The last time I tried dealing with a member of the Ryan clan while I was drinking, I regained consciousness two weeks later, half dead and locked in prison."

"We've lemonade."

"Perfect."

He waited impatiently for Gunning to leave. Before he could do anything more than take a step closer to the desk, he heard the unmistakable sound of rustling skirts approaching from the hallway.

At first, he didn't recognize the vision who entered the room as Kayley Ryan. Her transformation from a foul-tempered tomboy to this spun-sugar confection of a girl was so unexpected that he found himself not only speechless, but also a little breathless.

She was wearing a white dress that clung to her like a gentle embrace. Delicate ruffles trailed from the edges of her elbow-length sleeves. More ruffles swirled around her slippered feet. A yellow ribbon was tied around her waist, another threaded through the bright fire of her hair. The satin glowed like nuggets of gold between the shining curls.

She slipped a piece of violet stationery into a pocket in the skirt of her dress and crossed to the desk, which she closed and locked with a determined twist of a key. "Welcome to the R Cross, Mr. Clay."

Her voice was sweeter and gentler than he remembered, matching her innocent, almost child-like, appearance. He couldn't believe his good fortune at Sullivan's having fathered such a creature.

"Have you chosen your ten steers so soon?"

"Tavira isn't trained to work cattle. I was hoping to persuade you to sell me an R Cross bronc."

"Our foreman can show you our stock. I'll send someone to locate him for you."

Jack caught her arm to prevent her from leaving. Her skin was softer than anything he'd ever touched, softer even than the skin he'd imagined caressing on sleepless nights when the sounds and smells and reality of Lansing Prison had been more than he could bear, and inventing fantasies had been his only means of escape.

"Can't you show me?"

"Sam knows the horses better than I do. He'll help you pick out a good mount."

"I prefer your company to a foreman's," he said, hoping that she wouldn't recognize the need that had deepened his voice and twisted his insides into painful knots.

"Your drink, sir," Gunning said, and Jack silently cursed both the man's timing and his soft tread.

"The horses are on the other side of the barn," Kayley said. The hem of her skirt swirled across the toes of Jack's boots as she slipped away from him, leaving the room.

He took the lemonade and drank the cool deliciousness of it in one long swallow. "Thanks," he said, thrusting the empty glass back at Gunning, who moved to block him from leaving.

"Don't do this, sir."

"He took everything I had, Gunning."

"Miss Ryan isn't responsible for that. It's not right for you to vent your hate on her."

"This isn't hate," Jack said. He touched the rough leather of his eyepatch. "It's justice."

Kayley's arm refused to stop tingling where Clay had held it, even though, as they walked to the barn, she tried repeatedly to rub away the lingering effect of his touch.

"That must be the stallion's herd," he said, pointing at the nervous horses in the branding corral. "I recognize his bloodline in those youngsters. Since the corral gate is still in one piece, I assume he hadn't tried to free them.''

"Not yet.''

"Maybe I should've taken your bet for Tavira.''

"It's not too late,'' she said, glancing up at him. ''There are still ten hours until midnight.''

"You're a very determined woman.'' He wrapped her in a smile. ''I like that.''

Her face flushed hot, and she looked quickly away. She could still see him out of the corner of her eye, though, and as they crossed the yard, she let herself enjoy the sight of him walking beside her, his spurless boots almost silent on the hard-packed dirt.

He wore a day's growth of beard, just as he had the first time they met. It made his hard, handsome face appear even more rugged and uncompromising. The silver handle of his gun had been polished until it reflected light like a mirror. She remembered with a warm shiver how it had pressed against her when he'd caught her to him on the mountain.

Tavira was tied near the corral where Toro the bull was tearing at the ground with its front feet and snorting its hatred at the world. The Arabian's elegant ears flattened back as he stared at the gigantic bull in wide-eyed terror.

"How did this ugly beast get hurt?'' Clay asked. He leaned on the fence, apparently undisturbed by Toro's intimidating display.

Ever since the bull had been brought in from the range to have its terrible wound treated, it had taken every bit of nerve that Kayley possessed just to walk past the corral. Now, as she forced herself to stand beside Clay, instead of turning and running like she wanted to do, her knees began to shake so violently she feared he would hear them knocking together.

"Another bull was eating Toro's favorite stand of prickly pear cactus. My father's men said he ripped the poor animal into so many pieces they couldn't find a piece of hide bigger than the palm of my hand." To show how small those pieces had been, she held out her hand.

Clay captured it in his. Holding both it and her gaze captive, he traced a finger around the edges of her open palm. "Tell me more about Toro, Kayley."

The gentle way he said her name was as unnerving as his caress. "He's the best bull we own," she said, repeating what Sam had told her. "My father's as proud of Toro as he is of this ranch."

Clay's fingers constricted painfully around hers. She jerked her hand away. The pressure that had been building inside her faded immediately.

"There's Sam." She hurried in the direction of the leanto where he was making new shoes for Old Joe. The surly mare was tied, along with Louisiana, to a post which Old Joe was chewing on with her big, yellow teeth. "Sam, this is the man who bought Peters McDonnell's land out from under us. Clay, meet Sam Butler, the R Cross foreman."

"Kayley speaks highly of you," Clay said.

Sam thrust a piece of iron deep into the glimmering coals of his fire with a pair of tongs. "I can't say the same for you."

Kayley tensed, expecting Clay to take offense. Instead, a slow smile spread across his face. "I can see her praise was justified." He extended his hand.

Sam pulled out the hot iron and laid it aside. Then

he took off his gloves and reached out his own hand. "Welcome to the valley."

Kayley gave a silent sigh of relief. "Clay needs a horse trained to work cattle. I was about to show him our stock."

Sam fell into step with them. "Have you worked cattle before?"

"It's been a few years."

"Most of our herd is running north of Bear Creek until we need them for roundup. I'll ride back that way with you if there's nothing here you like." One of the horses in the adobe corral trotted toward them and nickered a greeting. "That friendly pinto is the only horse not for sale in here."

"No wonder, she wouldn't make good—"

"She belongs to Miss Ryan," Sam said, interrupting Clay.

Kayley nuzzled her face against the little mare's neck. "Father gave Sophia to me the day I arrived at the ranch. What were you saying about her, Clay?"

He ran a hand down Sophia's concave backbone. "Just that she's too small for me."

He picked up a bridle from outside the corral, then opened the gate and pushed his way into the center of the milling horses. He watched them for a minute before slipping the bridle onto a big gelding the color of dirty ice.

Sam crossed his arms over his chest and nodded. "That's Boxer. He's a good cutting horse. I've seen him hold a troublesome steer at bay even without a rider."

Kayley pushed her face into Sophia's broom-straw mane to keep from laughing. The incident to which

Sam referred had occurred last month, and he'd been the rider Boxer wasn't carrying. The animal had thrown Sam when he'd set off after a different steer than the big gelding wanted to cut from the herd.

Clay ran his hands over Boxer's back and legs, checked his teeth, then stared the big gelding straight in the eye. "I'll take him. How much, Kayley?"

She read the answer that Sam mouthed to her. "Forty-five without an outfit," she said, "sixty-five dollars complete."

Clay frowned. "That's a lot of money."

"That's a good horse," Sam said.

Clay looked again at Boxer, then shrugged his surrender. "It's too hot to argue. It's a deal."

Without knowing why, Kayley tensed. The air around her had become strangely still. Her heart skipped a beat as she slowly turned, knowing even before she moved what she'd see.

Less than a hundred yards away, standing under the cottonwoods at the edge of the arroyo with dappled sunlight strewn around him like fallen stars, was the white stallion.

In the fathomless depths of his eyes, she saw the outline of a person. *A reflection*, she realized, *my reflection*. The memory of her second day at the ranch came rushing back. The sun had been hot that day, hot and blinding and murderous. Just like today. Just like now.

Kayley had never been on a horse, had never even touched one until that morning when she'd insisted that she be allowed to join the search party. Sam had put her on Louisiana, and she'd spent the next six hours riding across the vast expanse of the Salinas

Valley with the R Cross hands, searching for her father.

It was the circling crows that finally lead them to the terrible scene where blood was seeping slowly from her father's torn flesh and falling on the dry earth beneath him, turning it red, turning it dark. His eyes had been open, staring at the sky, staring at the terrible sun. Then they, too, had turned dark.

That terrible darkness had reflected, along with Kayley's tear-stained face, the shattered pieces of her dreams. Truth had always been her enemy. On that day, it became a nightmare that she'd lived with, both asleep and awake, every moment of the last five months.

The white stallion exploded into action, charging directly at Kayley. His nostrils flared wide and wild. His long mane and tail floated around him so that he looked like a ghostly apparition. His sharp hooves tore at the earth as he ran, faster and faster, straight at her, his hoofbeats like rifle fire in the eerie silence that had descended on the ranch.

"Miss Ryan!" Sam shouted. "Watch out!"

Unable to move, Kayley saw her foreman running toward her to pull her out of the stallion's path.

The beast reached her first. He didn't touch her, though. He just ran past her, rocking her with his gusting wake and slapping her with his tail, but leaving her otherwise unmarked.

Staggered, uncertain of what was happening, she watched the great animal slam into the heavy gate of the adobe corral. Already unfastened, the gate swung open. The stallion rushed in, neck arched, teeth bared. Then he froze.

His coal black eyes were fixed on Clay. The white beast dipped his head and shook it as though confused, his silky mane whipping from side to side. His front hooves clattered on the ground in a rapid flurry of motion. A guttural cry ripped from his throat as he reared and slashed with his razor-sharp front hooves at Clay, not touching him, yet coming so close that Kayley shrank back in involuntary reaction.

"Easy, Angel," Clay soothed, "I'm not here to hurt you."

The stallion, still poised high above him, seemed both angered and bewildered by his victim's lack of fear and calming voice. He slashed at the air again, this time missing Clay by several feet, then dropping onto all fours, spun around and bolted from the corral.

The R Cross horses ran with him, taking with them Kayley's best chance to catch the white demon that Clay had twice called Angel. *Tavira,* she thought, and ran to where the gray Arabian was tied. She tore his reins loose from the hitching post and grasped his mane to hold him steady while she vaulted into the saddle.

Her skirt and petticoats shackled her legs. She hiked them higher than a saloon girl's dress. Because her feet didn't reach the stirrups, she had to use the pressure of her knees to keep herself in the saddle. She dug her heels into Tavira's sides. They leapt out of the shadows and into the sunlight with Clay and Boxer right behind them.

Men were pouring out of the bunkhouse, a jumble of checkered shirts and blue denims. Someone tossed Kayley a rope. She grabbed it just as the white stallion crashed through the sturdy gate of the branding corral. The sound of wood splintering underlined the shouts of the men and the excited whinnies of the caged horses.

Once he'd opened the way to his mares' freedom, the stallion leapt the shattered gate and headed for open ground. Kayley and Clay tried to follow him. Both were caught in a seething tide of escaping horseflesh.

She saw that Clay, hampered by his lack of a saddle, couldn't fight his way clear. Her seating, although almost as precarious, was enough to keep her astride Tavira as she guided him across the flow of the herd and into the clear.

Given the room he needed to run, Tavira's strides became immediately long and powerful. He was the perfect match for the white stallion. His big gray body surged beneath Kayley with such confident speed that she wanted to shout in exhilaration.

Although caught up in the thrill of the chase, she was aware when Clay broke away from the stamp-ing herd. He appeared to be motioning for her to do something. She turned in the saddle to see him better, causing her hair to whip into her eyes and blind her. She faced forward again without understanding Clay's frantic signalling.

To avoid the stones being flung upward by the stallion's pounding hooves, she reined Tavira close to the edge of the arroyo, positioning herself between it and the white stallion.

Wind whistled in her ears, a single-noted song beneath which she could hear the thundering hooves of the two stallions as they pounded against the hard, dry earth. She heard the snorts and sounds of the horses behind her fading in loudness and intensity and, almost smothered by noise and distance, heard Clay shouting to her.

"Get on the other side, Kayley! He won't let you app—"

He stopped mid-word. She looked around for him, seeing only a riderless horse that looked like Boxer near the fleeing herd. She didn't have time to look further for Clay or to try to understand what he'd been trying to tell her because at that second, she reached the place she'd dreamed of being every minute during the past five months.

She was close enough to catch the white stallion.

Too nervous even to whisper a prayer, she shook out the horsehair rope, hesitated a brief moment while her heart leapt into her throat, then made her throw, hearing through the roar of excitement that filled her head Clay's cry of "Now!"

The loop opened, wider, wider, growing bigger and longer, stretching out and up, and then, like an unbelievable wish come true, dropping around the stallion's proud head.

A quick snap of her wrist closed the loop around his neck. Moving as though she were in a dream, Kayley double looped the rope around the saddle horn between her legs and pulled back on Tavira's reins to bring him to a stop.

He wasn't trained to take the weight of a roped quarry and began taking plunging leaps forward. Kayley had to struggle to regain control of him while trying to keep the rope secure. Because she wasn't wearing gloves, her skin became quickly blistered by her efforts.

Soon exhausted by both his fear and the stallion's struggle for freedom, the big gray steadied. Kayley maneuvered him to keep sufficient tension on the rope to slow, then stop, the white stallion's panicked flight. His hooves flashed in the sun as he reared and screamed and reared again in raging fury.

"He's mine, he's really mine!"

The white's ears pricked forward at the sound of her voice, even though his attention was fixed on his fleeing herd. They were running east across the flat valley floor like huge antelope racing through acres of waving grasses.

The stallion looked from them to Kayley. Hate danced like fire in his eyes. Without warning, without reason, without even a moment's hesitation to let her prepare for what might happen next, he began moving toward her.

The rope went immediately slack. She tried to make Tavira back up, but he refused to obey. She coiled the rope around her arm in a desperate attempt to keep it taut. Her blisters tore open, and the braided horsehair was stained red by her blood.

No matter how fast she worked to pull the rope in, she couldn't compensate for the white stallion's steady advance. She spun Tavira around and forced him into a run. Once moving, she made a quick cut to the left, then right, then left again.

The white stallion anticipated her every move so accurately that the rope remained consistently slack. Kayley could almost picture the noose slipping open. If she didn't do something soon, he'd be free.

Before she could even think of what to do, the

stallion was beside her, magnificent in size and beautiful in form, his white hair dark with the lather of his sweat that smelled raw and wild and exciting. She realized that it wasn't just sweat that darkened his incredible coat. An ugly black mark high on his left side scarred his perfection.

She caught only a glimpse of it, not enough to be certain if it was natural or man made, before the stallion charged in front of Tavira. The rope snapped tight against the gray's neck. He was almost dragged off his feet before Kayley could lift it up and over his head.

The stallion's change in direction caused the rough horsehair to twist around her arms and tangle with her skirts. She tried to free herself, but was still entangled in its deadly embrace when the white stallion made a breathtaking leap into the arroyo.

Then he began to run.

"No!" Kayley screamed, the word ripping from her throat as the rope tightened around her.

She dug her knees into Tavira, forcing him down into the arroyo. The soft ground on the bottom caused him to founder. Even after he regained his footing, he was still dragged like a reluctant dog by the white stallion's power and speed through dead brush and over rocks and across patches of siltlike sand.

Each time they encountered one of those puddles of soft earth, Tavira's speed was cut so drastically that the rope imprisoned Kayley even tighter in its terrible grasp. Her arms were being pulled from her shoulders, the flesh of her hands and wrists ripped open by the braided horsehair.

She began to fear that she'd be pulled from the saddle and dragged to death. Visions of that horror made her clutch Tavira's sides so tightly that the muscles in her legs knotted with cramps.

On and on the white stallion ran, towing Kayley and Tavira behind him. The farther they went, the more her fear surged out of control until it was like a great weight pressing in around her, leaving nothing within her except the knowledge of what she must do.

When next they came to a stretch of firm ground, she desperately urged Tavira forward. The valiant Arabian responded to her urgent plea with a heroic burst of speed.

The rope slackened.

Every second was a lifetime now. At any moment, the white stallion could snap the rope taut again, and she'd be lost.

With bleeding fingers, Kayley fought to unwind the rope from her hands and her arms, to disentangle it from her skirts, to unwrap it from the saddle horn.

Then, with a sob of defeat and pain, she let it go.

Chapter Six

It was quiet in the arroyo after the white stallion was gone. Kayley slumped in the saddle, blinded by the throbbing misery of her hands and arms, and by disappointment.

The sound of a horseshoe striking against stone caused her to sit upright just as Clay, who was riding Boxer bareback, reached the edge of the flats above her. The gelding slid on his haunches down the steep incline.

"Are you hurt?" Clay asked as he brought Boxer to a rearing stop beside her.

"I had him, my rope was around his neck. Then I had to let him go." Her voice failed her.

"Don't think about it, sweetheart." He slid off Boxer's back and lifted her down beside him.

She was so unsteady on her feet that he had to lean her back against Tavira before inspecting her hands and arms, his fingers gently probing through the torn flesh and blood.

"You shouldn't have tried to hold him without

gloves, Kayley. Nothing's broken, but your hands are ripped to shreds."

"I don't care about my hands; I care about losing the stallion. Sell me Tavira, Clay. Without him, I'll never catch that white devil. How much do you want? Five hundred? A thousand? I'll pay it, somehow, just please sell him to me!"

"Your problem isn't which horse you're riding, Kayley." He took the bandanna from around his neck and tied it over the worst of her cuts. "The white stallion's just too much for you."

A blaze of anger filled her and was as quickly forgotten when she realized he was covered with dirt. "Did Boxer throw you?"

He made a swipe at the front of his shirt and grinned at her through the resulting cloud of dust. "Twice."

She laughed. "Good for him!"

"I thought you might consider cutting his price in sympathy."

"Not a chance, though it's about ten dollars more than he's worth."

"Twenty, but I'll take him anyway."

"I thought you would. You look like a man who likes trouble."

He seemed to hesitate for a moment, then lifted his hands to her face, cupping it gently and turning it up to him. "You're trouble," he said.

She could feel herself falling, tumbling deeper and deeper into the magic of his caress as his fingers moved slowly, softly, across her face and into her hair.

"Please, Clay, this isn't right. Let me go."

He pulled free the satin ribbon and let the weight of her curls fall through his hands. "Is that what you want, Kayley? Do you want me to let you go?"

He was holding her now. Pulling her closer. Leaning over her, his embrace warm and strong, his nearness making her dizzy and afraid.

"Tell me, Kayley," he whispered, and his breath touched her lips. "Tell me what you want."

A sound that was in rhythm with the beating of her heart filled her head. She recognized it as the hoofbeats of an approaching horse, yet even after Clay's arms fell from around her, she didn't fully realize what the sound meant until he touched a finger to her cheek and trailed it down the side of her face.

"Dry your tears," he said.

She stumbled away from him, embarrassed and confused, wiping her face almost violently with a torn sleeve in an attempt to erase both the stain of her tears and the memory of his caress.

A black horse appeared on the flats above them. Vance Moore peered with a scowl of distaste into the arroyo. He was wearing a dove-gray suit, a white shirt with a starched collar, and a gray vest and black tie.

He looked like he belonged at a piano recital in Boston instead of astride a sweating horse in New Mexico. Not even his hat fit the surroundings. It was white and so incredibly clean that Kayley wondered if he'd been carrying it in a sack and had put it on only moments ago.

Vance pointedly looked from Clay to Kayley, as though commenting on how close they were standing. "You look terrible, my dear," he said.

"No, I'm not hurt, Vance. Thank you for asking," she said beneath her breath, causing Clay to laugh, which caused Vance to frown.

His disapproval had again caused her to become uncomfortably aware of her disheveled appearance, though. She picked up handfuls of her dress to shake out the dirt.

The crackle of paper stopped her. "My letter!" The dress fell out of her suddenly cold hands, and her heart stopped as she took from her pocket a ripped sheet of violet paper.

"What's going on down there?" Vance asked.

Kayley tried to match the pieces together, but her fingers wouldn't stop shaking.

"Was it important?" Clay asked.

"My mother wrote it to me. It's the only thing I have that was hers."

"You're getting blood on it, sweetheart. Let me."

"It's only one sheet."

He easily reassembled the letter. "It's all here."

She glanced down at her torn pocket. "How am I going to carry it?"

"Kayley?" The sunlight made Vance's suit look like a shimmering mirage above them.

Clay put the letter in his vest pocket. "I'll carry it for you."

"Don't let Boxer throw you again."

"I'd like to think that comment was as much out of concern for me as your mother's letter, kid."

"Since you owe me sixty-five dollars, I'm very concerned."

"Kayley?" Vance called again. "Is there a problem?

Should I come down?"

"And chance looking as terrible as I do, Vance? I wouldn't hear of it."

She winced in pain when she tried to mount Tavira. Clay didn't bother to ask if she needed help. He simply lifted her and placed her in the saddle. She put her hand on his shoulder, intending to stop him from moving away before she could thank him. The touch brought back the flood of emotions his embrace had created, and it was with trembling lips that she smiled down at him.

He turned his head just enough to press a kiss to the back of her fingers. Shivers of pleasure raced up her arm. She pulled her hand back and held it close against her while he swung onto Boxer's back. The gelding lead the way out of the arroyo, Tavira following close behind.

When they reached the flats, Vance was there waiting, along with Sam, who'd just arrived astride Old Joe.

"Did we lose them all, Sam?" Kayley asked.

"We couldn't even stop our own horses." He shifted his weight in the saddle and stared at the ground between Old Joe and Tavira. "Sophia's gone, Miss Ryan."

"Sophia," she said, the word a whisper that sounded like shattered glass. A spasm of pain twisted around her heart, and she wished it was night so that she could wish away the hurt on a star.

"Twelve dollars will buy you a dozen just like that nag at the glueworks," Vance said.

The thought of Sophia being made into glue was more upsetting to Kayley than knowing the little mare was running with the white stallion.

"How did he get so close to the house without anyone seeing him?" she asked.

"He probably came up this arroyo," Clay said. "You should've posted a lookout on that rise south of the house. From there, you can see inside the arroyo as well as all the other directions of approach from the valley."

"Put someone there now, Sam, in case he comes back for the rest of his herd."

"The rest?" Vance asked. He scowled at Old Joe, who'd taken a snapping bite at him.

Bede came galloping up on his bay mare. "Me and Willie just got back. What happened?"

"The white stallion's wearing my rope as a necklace; that's what happened," Kayley announced.

His eyes grew wide, his mouth split open in a tremendous grin and he threw his hat into the air with a whoop of excitement.

"Looks like he was almost wearing you as an ornament," Sam said.

"Or an anchor," Clay added, and Kayley purposely caused Tavira to bump into Boxer, who greeted the collision by trying to pitch Clay off. His failure brought a grin to Clay's dusty face.

"I asked what you meant about the rest of his herd, my dear." Vance's voice was almost as stiff as his collar.

"We put only the oldest and youngest horses from the white's herd in the branding corral," she explained. "The best animals are locked up in the barn."

"I'll bring them out now for bait, Miss Ryan," Sam

said. "Bede can stand first watch on the rise."

"Me? Really? Right now? Stand guard? Really? Where?"

"There." Sam pointed.

"Yippee!" Bede shouted and galloped away.

"Hold it, boy," Sam called after him. "You don't have a gun to signal with."

Bede didn't stop his dead-out run, though, and Sam set after him while Kayley, Vance, and Clay started for the ranch house.

"The white won't take that bait, Kayley," Clay said. "Not after feeling your rope."

"You seem to know a lot for a stranger," Vance said.

He tried to move up between Kayley and Clay. The intrusion caused Boxer to start pitching again. Vance pulled his mare away. After Clay brought the gelding under control, Kayley introduced him. He frowned when she mentioned that Vance was the owner of the Lucky Ace Ranch.

"I've never heard of it. Where is it?"

"My headquarters are on Jumanos Mesa," Vance said.

"That's east of here," Kayley added.

"Southeast," Clay said. "I thought the R Cross was the only ranch in the eastern Salinas Valley."

"It was," Vance said, "until Sullivan Ryan dealt me an ace of diamonds."

Kayley stared at him. "You won the Lucky Ace from my father? When?"

"Not long before he sent for you, my dear."

"I was in a boarding school in Boston," she explained to Clay. "Why didn't you tell me this before, Vance?"

"Why didn't your father tell you?" Clay asked.

Kayley fumbled with Tavira's reins. "I guess because it isn't really important since we own two of the three best sources of good water in the valley." She gave Clay a disdainful glance. "You own the third."

"Leaving me with the exclusive rights to all the salt water," Vance said.

Kayley laughed. "I hope the steer Snow's cooking for the barbecue wasn't one of yours. I'm too hungry for salted beef."

"Barbecue?" Vance scowled at her. "When we discussed this the other night, my dear, I made my position on this issue clear."

"Yes, you did. What wasn't made clear was my position." She turned away from him. "Why don't you join us, Clay?"

"I don't like crowds."

"There isn't one, just the R Cross hands, Vance and you, if you'll stay."

"I'd love to," he said with a smile that turned her heart upside down. Then he looked pointedly at Vance and added, "My dear."

Chapter Seven

Sam Butler unfolded the map of the ranch and laid it on the kitchen table. Kayley set a tin of baking powder on it to make it lie flat. Willie Pete frowned at the map for a minute, then leaned over to take a closer look at the scribbles and scrawls. He placed a finger on the eastern slopes of the Los Piños Mountains.

"Here," he said. "There's a draw leading down to the flats. An old branding fire, tracks for one horse, one man, a few cattle." He moved his finger to the southern edge of the Manzano Mountains, stopping beside the pueblo ruins at Abo. "And here. Same horse, same man, same number of cattle, all of them with calves."

"Maybe he was just camping," Kayley said, "and the cattle wandered by."

The wild turkey feathers on Willie's hat fluttered as he shook his head. "Both fires were too small for cooking or to keep a man warm."

"It doesn't take much of a fire to heat an iron," Sam explained. "Which way did he head after he put his mark on our calves?"

"Couldn't tell you. He didn't leave enough of a trail to trip an ant."

"How did you find his fires?" Kayley asked.

"I'd like to credit my grandfather's Indian blood," Willie said, "but it was a coyote who found the first fire. He'd dug it up looking for food, and we chanced across it. Bede found the second fire by stumbling over it when he was looking for the horses, which he forgot to stake."

"I didn't know you were part Indian," Kayley said. "I thought you were just tall."

"Maybe that's why you couldn't see any tracks," Sam said. "You're too high off the ground. You'd better get yourself some supper before Mrs. Moraillon's boy eats it all."

Willie rubbed his jaw and laughed. "That Bede's about as useless on the trail as setting a milk bucket under a bull, but I've never seen nobody try harder in my life. No matter what task I set him, he did it with a grin."

The sounds of the barbecue spilled into the kitchen when Willie opened the door. The men were laughing, telling jokes and swapping lies as big and long as the Salinas Valley. He went out to join them, leaving the door open in his hurry to add his own laughter, jokes and lies to the chaos of noise.

Above the other voices, Snow could be heard talking in his drum of a voice about what was in the sauce he'd generously smeared over the steaks and beef ribs he'd roasted. "A possum that's been dead the better part of a week tastes best. Yesterday I found somethin' almost as good, though. Bet none of you boys can guess what."

"Scorpions," Joe Duke said. His suggestion for the secret ingredient met with a cheer from the men whose mouths had been blistered by the sauce.

Kayley had eaten a little of the gooey hot sauce before Willie Pete and Bede returned. Now she ran across the kitchen to close the door before Snow could deny, or confirm, Joe Duke's guess. She preferred to think of the old trail cook's sauce, along with everything else he concocted, as something to be tolerated, not understood.

Instead of closing the door, though, she used it as a blind while she looked at the men sitting around the makeshift table outside. Clay wasn't among them. Vance was, though, sitting at the head of the table. Bede was beside him, having been relieved of his lookout duties at Elda's angry insistence. His hair looked like ripe wheat where it spilled wildly from beneath his hat. Kayley noticed it was decorated with a fresh snakeskin hatband. According to Snow, Bede changed snakeskins more often than he changed socks.

Elda was standing between Vance and Bede, patting Vance on the arm as she served him a great piece of bread, its cornmeal goodness enhanced by the cheese, chiles, and bacon Snow had put in the batter. She gave Bede an equally huge slice, patting him repeatedly on the arm just as she had Vance, a habit that made her appear both maternal and possessive.

Bede shrugged off her attention, as he always did, and turned away from whatever she was saying. His attitude toward his mother caused the cowhands at the table to give him their usual looks of disapproval. In response to their frowns, Elda, who refused to believe it was her son's rejection of her that caused the men's censure, turned a cold shoulder on the crew and left after another maternal caress on Bede's flinching arm.

The angry frown that had creased Vance's thin, handsome face ever since learning of the barbecue was still quite evident. Kayley felt a pang of regret for turning what he'd wanted to be an intimate dinner into a party for the R Cross cowboys. Sitting there in his starched collar, Vance looked so out of place and uncomfortable that she felt sorry for him.

I should ask him to come in the kitchen with me, she thought. *I don't have to listen to anything he suggests for solving Sam's problem with Poppa's missing cattle.*

"Skunk!" Snow announced proudly, and she slammed the door closed, leaving Vance outside. After all, it hadn't been her idea to invite him to supper.

If only her father were well. He'd convince Clay to sell Tavira and tell Vance that his daughter could eat with whomever she wanted. If her father were well, he'd known how to find those missing cows, even if he had to move the mountains themselves . . . if only he were well.

"Are any other ranchers complaining about trouble with rustlers?" she asked.

"None of the men were talking about losing beef in town last Saturday."

Kayley met and held Sam's gaze. "Were ours?"

"R Cross hands don't talk about the ranch or its

business," he said, repeating the first order she'd ever given on the ranch.

The sky the morning she had taken over the ranch had been like a great bowl of immaculate blue turned upside down over the land, which was still wet from the storm that had filled the long night with thunder and lightning and rain. When both the night and the storm passed, the morning air had been so clean that it had hurt to breath it.

Charles Easterday, a physician from Albuquerque, had just driven away, his buggy leaving deep scars in the muddy ground of the yard. "Hopeless" had been his diagnosis the night before after examining Sullivan Ryan.

"Your father has suffered a major stroke," Dr. Easterday had said. "He's paralyzed completely on the right side, partially on the left. There's nothing that can be done."

Kayley had stared at him, trying to look past the spectacles and beard to see how many years he'd been telling people such outrageous lies. It had been Vance who told Dr. Easterday that his diagnosis was unacceptable and that he was to leave the R Cross at first light.

The next morning, under that incredible sky, Kayley had given Sam the order that would keep her father's condition a secret.

"It's for your own good, my dear," Vance had told her the previous night. "Because of your age, the courts will appoint a guardian for you. Not only will you have no say in your father's care, you'll probably be sent back to school."

That had been five months ago, and she and Sam

were still fighting to protect their secret. *How much longer,* she wondered, and regretted questioning the loyalty of his men.

A strange feeling, like the chill of anticipation she'd felt before seeing the white stallion beside the arroyo, came over Kayley. She moved her gaze from Sam to the uncurtained window that looked out on the courtyard separating the kitchen from the main house.

There, alone and moving quickly across the flagstones toward the door that opened onto the living room, was Clay. Before she could even wonder what he was doing, he stopped, turned and saw her watching him.

For a moment, terror gripped her as something dark and ugly flickered in the pale silver of his eye. Then his gaze turned soft, caressing, just as it had been in the arroyo when he'd held her.

Kayley was shaken anew by a storm of emotions as she remembered how his body, hard and hot and strong, had felt pressed against hers. She saw again his lips bending so near to hers that she could almost taste them, felt his arms pulling her to him, closer, tighter . . .

"Miss Ryan," Sam said, bringing her abruptly back to the kitchen, where the unsolved problem with the missing cattle was as distasteful as the smell of old grease that permeated the room.

"One man putting his brand on a few calves won't make the kind of difference we've been seeing in the herd," Sam said.

"How much of a difference?" Kayley asked.

"I'd guess two hundred animals in the last three

months alone."

"They could just be lost and we'll find them at roundup."

"It's not a good idea to wait another six weeks to find out. If we're being rustled, we could lose another hundred animals by then. If we're not, then we'll be the first herd to make the fall market." He pointed at the twisted lines on the map that marked the rugged canyons and mesas south of Abo. "This is the easiest place for cattle to avoid our counts. We'll start here and work north."

Kayley watched Sam's finger slide across the marking for Corbett Springs. "Is that the only water in those canyons?"

"All we've found. Wouldn't even know about it if it hadn't been for this map. Still took us nearly a whole day to find it the first time."

And yet Clay, a stranger, had been camped there the day she met him. She remembered smelling the sweet juniper wood smoke of his fire moments before he joined in the chase of the white stallion.

"I'll take the boys north tomorrow to gather the horses on the northern range," Sam said.

"Take Louisiana if you need him."

Sam nodded. "We will if our ponies don't come back tonight. I'm riding out now to see if any broke away from the stallion's herd and are on their way back."

"Why go after them if they're already headed this way?"

"I'd like to put some distance between me and Snow's skunk sauce."

"You're not the only one," Kayley said and looked

out the kitchen window. The courtyard was empty now except for the first shadows of evening that lay blue and silent on the flagstones outside the open door of the living room.

Jack gave a sigh of relief when Kayley's attention was drawn away from him. He pushed the garden door open and stepped inside. The living room was cool, a haven from the muggy heat outside, and so dark that he couldn't see anything except ribbons of sunlight filtering in through the shuttered windows.

With the image of the room clear in his mind, he started for the desk. The floor groaned a protest beneath his boots. He froze, hearing from somewhere in the room the sound of something being slammed shut, then muffled footsteps retreating from the room.

By the time his eyes had adjusted enough to the dim light for him to be certain he was now alone, the only sound in the house was the ticking of the clock on the mantle.

He crossed quickly to the desk, touching the rose-colored wood with gentle hands as he ran his fingertips down to the lock. He'd have to force it open and regretted the damage it would cause to his grandfather's desk.

To his delight, the desk was unlocked. He rolled the top open with a smile of relief. He shoved aside the letters piled on top of the white cashbook and saw, burned into the leather, a crescent moon. It had been stamped there by him with the same iron he'd used to brand Crescent C cattle.

Inside the front cover of the ledger, where he'd inscribed the name of the ranch, black ink had been used to smudge his scribbled handwriting that had given the name of the ranch and the year. None of the pages contained accounting entries, though.

Jack remembered that before he left for the Abilene drive, he'd filled the last line in a cashbook and had started a new one. This must be it. The first few pages in the book had been torn out, leaving ragged edges along the binding. The rest of the pages were filled with notes and lists written in Sullivan's flowing script, the sight of which sent a spasm of anger through Jack.

As he dropped the useless book on the desktop, a sheet of stationery protruding from one of the cubbyholes at the back of the desk caught his eye. The letterhead on the stationery revealed it was from an Albuquerque physician. What caused Jack to frown in surprise was that the letter was addressed not to Sullivan, but to Kayley.

Jack froze. Someone was behind him. He wasn't sure how he knew. There'd been no sound. Yet still he knew someone was there, just as he'd known in that dark, muddy alley in Abilene a split second before he'd felt a white-hot stab of pain in his lower back.

Then he heard the distinctive sound of rustling silk. His fear drained away, and he turned to face the daughter of his enemy.

"What are you doing?" she asked, the question cracking like a whip in the quiet room.

"Waiting for you."

There was no schoolgirl blush of pleasure as he'd

expected. Instead, he recognized in Kayley's flashing eyes the same fierce determination he'd once seen in a mountain lion protecting its young.

He'd tracked the big cat, which had been killing Crescent C calves, to a sandstone cliff deep in the Manzano Mountains. Instead of escaping up the rocky incline where Jack couldn't follow, the tawny-coat she-cat had turned to face him, teeth bared, yellow eyes ablaze with the resolve to protect, even at the sacrifice of her own life, the cubs crying in helpless fear in the cave behind her.

What was Kayley Ryan trying to protect?

"While I waited to pay you for Boxer," he said, "I was admiring this desk. It's quite a work of art, don't you agree?"

"What did you do, break into it so you could admire it?"

"I came in here to pay you the money I owe you, not to steal whatever might be buried under all this." He flicked a hand through the piled letters, toppling them onto the white ledger to hide the brand that was an exact replica of the engraving on his pistol.

"The desk was locked," she said, "and I have the only key." She produced it from the breast pocket of her dress.

"Look for yourself, kid. The lock hasn't been forced."

He stepped aside while she inspected the brass plate around the lock. Not a single scratch marred its shining surface. She frowned at it in confusion.

"I don't understand. I'm certain I locked it again after I took this out for Sam."

Jack recognized what she was holding as the map

he'd drawn of the ranch when he and Sullivan were negotiating a partnership.

"Maybe with those bandages Gunning put on your hands, you just thought it was locked, kid." He took his wallet from his back pocket and counted out sixty-five dollars.

She sat at the desk and dipped a pen in a bottle of ink. "What name do you want on this?"

"Describe the buyer as the Bar C Bar brand."

He folded the bill of sale she gave him into his wallet while she put his money in the top drawer. Then she closed the desk, turned the key, and checked to be certain it was locked by trying to roll open the top and pull out the drawer. They refused to yield to her persistent tugs.

"This time it's really locked," she said and stood. "Now that our business is finished, Mr. Bar-C-Bar, why don't we join the others outside?"

Jack ran his fingertips lightly down the tucked sleeve of her dress which was made of soft cotton. "I heard silk when you came up behind me." The blush he'd expected earlier surfaced now, turning the ivory skin of her throat the same beautiful peach color as her dress. "Petticoats?" he asked, and the delicate skin of her cheeks flushed deeper.

"A gentleman doesn't talk about such things," she said, unable to meet his gaze.

He touched a finger to the curls spilling across her shoulder. "I'm not a gentleman, Kayley."

"I know," she whispered while staring at the key clutched tightly in her fingers.

Gunning entered the living room from the hallway that led to the bedrooms. "Miss Ryan, if you've a moment, I could use your assistance."

All the color drained from her face. Jack heard the sound of metal striking wood as she quickened into motion, almost running across the room to the arched doorway. There she stopped, turning back to look at him, her eyes wide and a shadow of fear clouding their crystal depths.

"Gunning will see you out," she said and turned to flee into the hallway beyond.

"I won't make it rough on you, old man," Jack said. "I'll leave without even asking what's going on."

"Thank you, sir."

He closed the front door behind him, stepped down off the veranda and went around the corner of the house to the western wall. Peering through the cracks in the shutters, he saw Gunning disappearing down the hallway.

Jack retraced his steps back into the quiet house. He searched around and under the desk, shoved aside the sofa and chairs and tables, lifted the blue rug and gave it a violent shake. All he found was dust. The little brass key was gone.

Chapter Eight

Breathless and afraid, Kayley rushed into her father's bedroom. The windows were thrown open, letting in a beautiful view of the valley which seemed to extend forever. The sky was growing dark with clouds, and the grass was bending beneath the wind that heralded the gathering storm.

Sullivan Ryan lay in the center of the great four-poster bed, oblivious to the spectacle unfolding outside. His right hand was frantically clenching and unclenching, and air erupted from his lungs, carrying with it a gasping cry.

"Kay . . ."

"I'm here!"

She ran to the bed and sat beside him, capturing his grasping hand in hers. It was the first time he'd asked for her, the first time since the accident that any of his attempts to speak had made any sense. Best of all, though, his eyes were blue again. As she bent close to him, they followed her, trying to focus, trying to see.

"Hear . . ."

"Yes, I'm here!"

His fingers crushed hers. She winced as the pain from her encounter with the stallion came flooding back beneath her father's bruising grasp.

"Know . . . voi . . ."

"No what, Poppa?"

He drew a rasping breath. "Loo . . . sec . . . dra . . ."

He seemed to be trying so desperately to make her understand, but the words just didn't make sense. Some weren't even words, just parts of them, scattered syllables and nonsensical sounds.

Except for when he'd said Kay.

A despairing moan filled the room as his hand and face went limp. He seemed to be shrinking away from Kayley, sinking deeper into the mattress and pillow until she feared he might disappear completely.

"What did he say?"

Startled, she dropped her father's hand and jumped to her feet. Vance was standing in the doorway, looking past her to the bed.

"You heard him?" she asked.

"I heard sounds. Did they mean anything to you?"

She smiled. "He said my name."

"I'd like to talk to you about this Clay person, my dear."

She pulled Vance out into the hall. "What about Clay?" she asked in a hushed voice.

"I understand your association with him regarding the water rights to that stream of his, but a drifter like that has no business being invited to supper."

"He isn't a drifter."

"You're very quick to defend him, aren't you, my dear?"

"That's because you're so quick to accuse him."

"Enough." He pulled her to him. "I didn't come looking for you to start an argument."

His arms felt strange around her, as though they were made of wood. Why hadn't she ever noticed before that his embraces felt like he performed them out of a duty, not pleasure.

"I want to go back in with Poppa in case he tries to talk again."

"What was Clay doing in the house?" Vance asked, surprising her with his venomous tone.

"Looking for me."

"Did you do anything to encourage his interest in finding you?"

"Yes," she said, "I did. I sold him a horse, and he wanted to pay me for it."

Vance considered her answer for a moment, then nodded. "I believe you."

She shoved free from his embrace. "If you're trying to impress me by pretending to be jealous, it's not working."

"I'm not pretending, Kayley."

"And you're not impressing me. My father said my name a few minutes ago, Vance. Have you any idea how important that moment was to me? No, you couldn't, because if you did, then you wouldn't be trying to ruin it with these petty accusations and untimely declarations."

She went into her father's room, closing the door behind her and running to his side. But it was too late. Sullivan Ryan's eyes were as dark as the storm-black sky behind him.

Kayley slipped quietly from the house. It was late,

almost midnight, and she welcomed the cool embrace of the night wind. She'd been sitting by her father's side for hours, hoping he'd try to talk again, and being disappointed. Finally she'd been unable to stand it another moment and had sought escape.

She stayed concealed beneath the veranda until a jingling of spurs told her that the lookout Sam posted on top of the house every night had moved to the far side of the roof. Then she ran down the two steps and crossed the barren yard, not daring to even breathe until she passed both the bunkhouse and the barn.

The grass grew tall along the narrow path that led west into the canyon behind the ranch. Because of it, Kayley no longer feared detection, yet still she hurried past the old rose garden where the air smelled of freshly turned earth, running under the cottonwoods and across the arroyo where a trickle of water made its slow way through pebbly, red sand. Once across the arroyo, she crossed the dew-moistened meadow and entered the silent ruins called Quarai.

Once this ancient settlement had been home to hundreds of people—families, friends, priests and soldiers—and its mission church had been a place of faith and beauty. But fear and fire destroyed the grandeur of La Purisima Concepción de Cuarac, and it, along with the pueblo it served, was abandoned. Now only a few crumbling walls of red sandstone remained, and they looked black and forbidding in the darkness.

Kayley shivered as she walked through the baptistry and entered the holy ground of the sanctuary. This was where she came when she needed to be alone with her dreams and the night. Except tonight there was no sky filled with promises to greet her. Just the heavy, uncomfortable threat of rain.

The clouds which had gathered above the Manzanos during the evening were beginning to flow down the forested slopes of the mountains. Long, pale fingers of fog moved like phantoms across the flagstone floor of the church, drifting over the blanket of moss where the altar had been and floating up into the choir loft, where flowers grew wild on the old support beams.

Feeling lost and alone in the fog, Kayley was unable to bring her imaginings and fantasies to life. Tonight, not even Quarai could help her forget the darkness in her father's eyes.

A sound startled her: a footstep, without an accompanying jingle. She whirled around, thinking it came from behind her, then heard it from yet another direction. Muffled and misdirected by the drifting fog, the footsteps seemed to surround her.

She slipped into the cross-shaped transept, and there, with her back against the smooth stones of the centuries-old wall, waited in breathless silence for the footsteps to find her.

Before they sounded again, the wind freshened, blowing away the clinging white mist of fog.

Terror tightened around Kayley's chest and throat as she saw that the corner where she'd chosen to cower was less than a foot away from where a man was standing in the doorway to the sacristy. His face beneath his hat was hidden in the shadows of the starless night. He stepped into the ruined church, and Kayley felt so suddenly overwhelmed that she knew instantly who he was.

"Clay!" she cried, her voice choked with the lingering effects of her fear.

He came quickly to her side. "Kayley? What's wrong?"

"You frightened me," she said and moved away from him to the center of the church. High above her, the storm clouds appeared to be resting on the beautiful carved corbels that once supported the roof of the church.

Her hair where it fell loose across her shoulders felt as though it were being stirred by an unseen hand, and so she knew when Clay came to stand beside her.

"I thought you'd gone back up the mountain," she said and tried unsuccessfully to picture him in Peters McDonnell's dirty shack of a cabin.

"Sam offered me the hospitality of a bed for the night."

Clay brushed away a curl that had blown across her face. His hand lingered on her shoulder, warm and comforting and very disturbing.

"I'm going back to the house," Kayley said. "It'll be raining soon."

As though on cue, a flash of lightning spiked across the sky, creating a ceiling of brilliant white light above the ruined church. She turned away from it, hiding her face behind Clay's arm just as the thunder erupted, the great sound of it billowing and curling in the shifting air currents around them.

When the last rumble had faded into silence and her eyes no longer burned with the remembered image of the lightning, she lifted her head and tried to move away from her protector. Her attempt failed because his powerful arms were holding her captive. He pushed her back into the corner and up against the wall, shielding her from the whipping anger of wind with his body.

"I have to go, Clay."

"Stay just a little longer," he said, his lips almost touching her hair.

"It's going to rain."

"Not yet. That was just the first warning."

She was becoming confused by the softness of his voice and the way his legs were pressing close against hers.

"Why did you come up here tonight? No one ever comes here."

"Except you," he said, then stiffened. "And maybe that overdressed gambler, Moore. Is that why you're here, Kayley? To meet him?"

"No!" She pushed against Clay's chest, trying to force him back. "Please, I can't breathe!"

He moved closer to her. His body was hard and strong, and he smelled of the mountains and the trees and the wind, and of the night itself.

"Please," she said again, and the word clung to the silence around them.

"You're shaking, Kayley. What are you afraid of?"

She wanted to tell him that she was afraid of her father's illness and of being responsible for a ranch that was larger than she'd thought the entire world to be five months ago. She wanted to say that she was afraid of how big the western sky was and how high all the mountains were and how very dark the nights could become. But most of all, she wanted to tell him that she was afraid of how her own life was spinning faster and faster out of control, and that she didn't know what to do to stop it.

"I'm afraid of you," she whispered.

"That, sweetheart, is the first sensible thing I've heard you say."

And then he kissed her. Lightly, gently, his lips brushed across hers, once, twice, hesitating, touching again, lighter, teasing, slower, lingering.

And his hands, they were touching her, moving across the curve of her breasts, onto her waist, down to her hips and legs. He kept kissing her and caressing her, weaving around her a web of desire too real to be true, too wonderful to ever stop, until she forgot everything except the feel and the smell and the magic of him.

He moved his kisses from her lips, across her face, into her unbound hair. "Why did you run away from me in the house today?"

She pressed her face against the warm strength of his shoulder and slid her arms up and around him. At the first brush of her fingertips on his back, his arms crushed her so tightly against him that she thought she'd die with pleasure.

"Gunning came for me," she whispered against his neck.

Clay's teeth were gentle on her ear, biting, nipping, sending chills and fevers racing over her, through her, sweeping her away with the storm-tossed wind.

"Why?"

He whispered the word against her lips, and she knew that she couldn't stop herself from telling him.

A bolt of lightning exploded in the air around

them. It struck the ground just outside the church, causing the wall behind her to shudder. Clay pushed her down to the ground and fell across her just as the thunder began to scream. Kayley thought the wall was going to collapse on top of them, burying them in the sound and the fear and the terrible darkness of the night.

The moment the thunder died, Clay got to his feet, dragging her up with him. She stared at the wall, surprised to find it still standing.

"We'll have to run for it!" he shouted and, taking her by the hand, pulled her with him, out the church through the door where she'd first seen him, over the walls of the tumbled *convento*, and across the meadow where the grasses were bent and broken by the wind.

One of the old cottonwoods caught the next bolt of lightning in its branches as they ran beneath it. Fire and timber showered down upon them. Kayley's skirt caught on a shattered limb. Clay jerked it free, half dragging and half carrying her across the arroyo, which was already beginning to fill with a torrent of rushing waters the storm had unleashed at the top of the mountain. A few seconds later, and they would've been swept away to a muddy death.

And then the rain began to fall, big, heavy drops of water that struck with the impact of hailstones. The faster the rain fell, the faster Clay ran, dragging Kayley with him. Past the barn and bunkhouse, across the yard, now a sea of black mud, up the steps and across the veranda they ran until they reached the haven of the doorway set deep into the thick adobe walls of the house.

Exhausted, her breathing labored and painful, Kayley leaned against Clay for support. His heart was beating as unevenly and rapidly as her own. She wanted to push aside the wet shirt and lay her face against his bare chest, to know what it felt like to touch his skin.

Embarrassed by her thoughts, she glanced up at him just as he tilted his head down to look at her. The brim of his hat spilled a river of trapped rain onto her upturned face. She gasped at the cold shock of it, then began to laugh as she reached to wipe away the droplets of water clinging to the rough beard of his face.

He trapped her bandaged hands beneath his own and brought them to his lips, where he gently kissed her fingertips. "Do you have any idea how lovely you look right now?"

"No one's ever told me that I was even pretty before."

"I find it very hard to believe that Vance Moore doesn't ride over here at least once a week just to tell you how lovely you are with your lips moist with sweet, unspoken promises and your lashes heavy with raindrops begging to be kissed away."

"It's been a dry summer," she said, and was so horrified that she buried her face against Clay's shoulder to hide from his laughter.

He touched a finger beneath her chin and gently forced her to look up at him. With a smile that caught at the corners of her heart, he took off his hat and leaned toward her, enveloping her in the warm promise of another kiss.

This time she wanted more than the teasing touch

of his lips on hers, and she leaned into him, opening her lips and entrusting herself to his will. He tensed and pulled away. Horrified by his response to her daring boldness, she tried to escape from him. He stopped her, though, turning her back to face him and pulling her close against him.

"Please," he said, "don't go," and his voice was as soft as the rain that was now falling in a gentle shower from the silent sky.

His fingers were cold, and they touched the rain-wet cotton clinging like a second skin to her breasts, causing her to shiver, then melt as he traced the outline of her right nipple with light, circling carresses, around and around. Lighter, lighter, they circled slower, then faster until he was touching her there, there at the tip that was hard and rigid with the ache of desire.

Her knees gave way beneath her. He pulled her to him, holding her close against his warmth and his need while his hand kept melting her, molding her, making her breathless and helpless and afraid. And when she was his, completely, absolutely, leaning away from him and arching into him and wanting him more than she'd ever dreamed possible, he kissed her.

Not teasing this time, not gentle. Hot, hard kisses, searing, fiery kisses that drew her up and into him, claiming her, branding her, his tongue violating her softness, her innocence, her very soul.

When she knew she couldn't bear it another moment, when she thought her heart would shatter if his kiss lasted even another second, he released her.

Kayley collapsed against the wall behind her, her

hands grasping at the rough adobe bricks for support. Clay braced his hands on either side of her head and leaned his face against his left arm. His breathing was as labored as it had been after running the long mile down the mountain from Quarai. When he lifted his head to look at her, his expression was as unreadable as the emotions raging within her.

"I should've let you go, sweetheart." He touched his lips to hers for a moment as brief as a single beat of her heart. Then he was gone, moving off into the night and the rain, leaving her shivering and alone.

She pushed away from the wall and ran to the edge of the veranda, where raindrops fell like tears onto her face. She couldn't see him. She couldn't see anything except the darkness.

"Miss Ryan." Gunning was standing in the open doorway, the room beyond him warm with firelight. "You should come in, miss, before you get hurt."

"The storm's over, Gunning."

"I know," he said. "It wasn't the storm I was concerned about."

Chapter Nine

Morning spread slowly across the wet land. A misty haze clung to the foot of the mountains where night's shadows crouched low to avoid the light. Above the arroyo, fog drifted aimlessly until touched by the warm breath of the sun, then drifted into nothingless.

Kayley watched the day begin from the veranda. Water dripping from the lattice roof above her brought back the emotions and memories of last night with such disturbing clarity she felt disoriented, and just a little lost.

The ranch felt empty this morning, the men having left early to bring in the mustangs grazing on the northern range.

Clay was gone, too. He'd left in the middle of the night while rain spilled from the sky and Kayley stood alone, shivering, just as she was doing now.

In the distance, behind a tangled fence of wire, was the stooped figure of a man. It was Gunning. She hugged the warmth of her shawl close about her before going to join him, taking care to avoid the shiny paths of snails and the tiny pools of rainwater that paved the trail leading to the little cemetery.

Gunning's hands hung motionless beside him. Though he stared at the grave before him, he seemed to be seeing not it, but the past that lay buried beneath the carefully piled stones covering the narrow grave.

Kayley made her way to his side through the crosses built of weathered juniper and the markers of unetched stone that were gathered into the fenced ground where the ranch buried its dead.

"I've never seen you here before," she said.

"I come here every day."

"Did you know one of the cowboys well?"

"Not a cowboy, Miss Ryan. My wife."

"Gunning, I'm sorry. I didn't know. When, how?" She stopped, uncertain of what to say, or if she'd already said too much.

He looked east across the rolling vista of the Salinas Valley. "I came here when this ranch was so new the adobe wasn't yet dry. Melissa came with me. This valley was different then. It was a wild, savage place."

"Indians?"

"Not all savages are red, Miss Ryan," He paused. "But the ones that took Melissa were. Everyone said it was useless to look for her. We didn't stop searching, though, and eventually we learned where they were holding her."

"We?" she asked.

"Me, not that I was much help, and the man who built this ranch from nothing more than sweat and a

dream. Jack took from this land what he wanted."
Gunning pointed in the direction of the garden
beside the path. "And he gave back to it."

Kayley couldn't believe that a man capable of
building a ranch like the R Cross would plant roses.
She'd never thought much about the garden, only
that it was there and she should do something to stop
the plants from dying. What that was, she didn't
know.

"When Jack asked me to come here and work for
him, he assured me that he could keep Melissa
safe. He couldn't be everywhere at once, though,
and he wasn't here when they took her. So he promised me that he'd bring her back."

Gunning bent to pick a flower growing wild
among the graves. He laid it at the foot of Melissa's
cross. The raindrops on the lavender petals glistened
like tears in the morning light.

"And he did," Kayley said.

"Yes, he brought her back," Gunning said, his
voice breaking, then steadying again. "Jack was a
good man, Miss Ryan. Stubborn and arrogant and
vain, but a good man."

"The stubborn and arrogant part sounds like
Clay."

"Jack was younger than Clay." Gunning offered
Kayley his arm. "Shall we go, miss?"

"I'm sorry about Melissa," she said after they'd left
the cemetery and closed the gate behind them.

"It was a long time ago."

"Whatever happened to Jack?"

Gunning slowed his pace. "I don't know yet," he
said quietly.

Kayley was about to question his strange reply when she suddenly noticed the rose garden. When she'd passed it earlier, she'd been concentrating on the path itself and hadn't even glanced at the three rows of overgrown and dying plants. Now she stared in disbelief at them.

The scraggly bushes had been trimmed and shaped. The dirt around them was freshly turned and mounded around the base of each plant, most probably to prepare them for the coming winter. The irrigation ditch had been cleared, and the water that trickled between the neat rows sparkled in the morning light.

"Clay asked me for a shovel last evening," Gunning said. "Now I know why."

First, the braided necklace of wild flowers. Now this. Kayley lifted a hand to her chest where a strange ache had lodged beside her heart.

"It must've been to repay me for inviting him to supper."

"Perhaps," Gunning said.

They walked on in silence for a time.

"What do you think of him?" Kayley asked.

"This isn't something you should ask me, Miss Ryan."

"But, you're my friend. In fact, you're the first friend I ever had."

He looked uncomfortable. "What about at school?"

She shook her head. "Mrs. Potter's Boarding School for Young Ladies wasn't a good place to make friends. The other girls were rarely there for more than a year."

"How long were you there?"

"Twelve years," she said with a sigh. "Before that, I lived with my Aunt Lo. She died when I was eight, and I was sent to Mrs. Potter's the day after the funeral."

Gunning opened the front door and stood aside for her to enter. "Your father sent you there?" he asked.

"No, the judge who handled Aunt Lo's estate. She'd left all her money in a trust for my tuition." Kayley smiled as she warmed her hands over the fire. "Poppa did come to visit me, though, a few weeks later. I'd never seen anyone with eyes like his. They looked like they were dancing. I couldn't stop staring at them while Mrs. Potter explained to him about Aunt Lo's trust." Kayley ran a finger along the top of the clock on the mantle. "Then he left."

"But he came back."

She shook her head. "His work kept him too busy traveling. Finally he settled here and sent for me."

"Why didn't you leave school then?"

"I did!" she cried and spun around in a circle as she remembered that wonderful day. "I was on the next train out of Boston!"

"Miss Ryan," Gunning said, speaking slower and with more caution than was normal even for him. "Your father took over this ranch five years ago."

She stared at him. "Five years? I don't understand."

"He must've wanted you to finish your education."

"I graduated two years ago. I was still at the school because I had to work for Mrs. Potter to pay for the tuition she was owed because Aunt Lo's money had run out."

"Mr. Ryan couldn't have known, miss."

"No," Kayley said. Her temples were pounding so hard she couldn't think. "No, he couldn't have known. And he did send for me. I had to wait a long time, but he did send for me. That's what's important." She covered her face with her hands and tried to push the pain away. "That's all that's important."

Chapter Ten

Jack slapped his coiled rope against his thigh to frighten the longhorn hiding in the brush. The animal ignored him. He rode Boxer into the tangle of limbs and slapped the rope against the brindled steer's bony rump while shouting, "Hiyaa!"

The steer bawled a loud protest before bolting into the narrow stretch of open land bordering the southern edge of Laguna del Perro, twenty convoluted miles of salt lakes, dry beds, and towering dunes in the heart of the Salinas Valley.

Light shimmered over the acres of white salt like a threat from hell. The steer stopped its blind rush and turned to face its pursuer, giving Jack a good view of twisted horns stained green with moss. The steer feinted to its left, and Boxer cut off the attempted escape with agile speed.

The ten cattle that Sullivan Ryan owed Jack had to be the best ten on the R Cross, not a tough, stringy animal like this.

"Let him go, boy," Jack said. "He's too old to

make good shoe leather.''

For three days, he'd been flushing cattle out of draws and gullies and arroyos, working day and night. Now he was so tired he could hardly stay in the saddle.

The mossy-horned steer lunged back into the brush, leaving behind broken limbs and silence. Jack dismounted and loosened the cinch of his saddle to let Boxer breath while he dampened his thirst with the stale water in his canteen.

He longed for a drink of fresh water and thought of Antelope Springs. It had the sweetest water in New Mexico, but was a two-hour ride north of him. If he closed his eyes, he could almost see the glittering surface of the pond that held the overrun of the free-flowing spring.

The only thing that prevented him from heading for it immediately was the other need possessing him, this one greater than any thirst he could ever suffer. This need had been the reason he left the R Cross in the middle of the night, riding through rain and darkness to reach the crowded, noisy saloons of Socorro.

The ride had been in vain, though, because when he took that first drink of whiskey, it wasn't escape he found in its burning taste; it was memories. So he'd taken a second drink, then a third and the fourth. Yet still his mind had refused to forget Kayley Ryan's face and hair, her lips and sighs, her cries of passion, and her laughter.

There'd been only one goal in his mind when he chanced across her at the ruins, and that was find out what happened to the key she'd dropped. With kisses to distract her and caresses to cover his search of her pockets, it hadn't taken him long to discover she wasn't carrying it.

Holding her, hearing her sigh against his neck and feeling her heart beating faster with each caress had affected him more than he'd anticipated. It had been a struggle to keep control of his emotions while working to make her so dizzy with passion she'd tell him anything he asked. He'd managed, though, and had been ready to start interrogating her when the storm struck.

Once they reached the safety of the veranda, he'd planned to continue his assault on her senses. But in the shelter of the doorway, it was Jack who fell victim to desire.

The water spilling from his hat onto her face had ignited the trouble. He'd expected her temper to flare. Instead, she'd looked up at him, her sparkling eyes framed by rain-wet lashes, and she'd laughed. It had been the sweetest music he'd ever heard, and he'd found himself suddenly desperate to lose himself, and his hate, in the beautiful innocence of her.

Jack took off his hat to let the burning sun cool him, and he wiped his forehead with his sleeve, staining it with sweat and dust.

He'd left Socorro the next day and gone back to Peters' cabin, where he'd exchanged Tavira for Boxer. Then he'd headed for the valley, intending to work the lingering desire for Kayley Ryan out of his system.

Three days of riding beneath a sky colored the same pure, innocent, beautiful blue as her eyes had only served to heighten, not lessen, his memories of that night, and of the last kiss they'd shared on the veranda.

Boxer pawed the ground, eager to start working again. Jack narrowed his eyes as he looked out across Laguna del Perro. Longhorns were smart animals, too smart to go into that wasteland. It would be a smarter move to head for Antelope Springs and wait for the cattle to come to him. Except during that wait, there'd be nothing for him to do but stare at the sky and remember how close he'd come to letting a Ryan get the best of him again.

He tightened the cinch on his saddle, mounted, and with a whoop of determination, headed straight into Laguna del Perro's blinding white hell.

Chapter Eleven

It was a week before the R Cross cowhands returned to the ranch with the captured herd of ranch horses. They were accompanied by a cold wind that had chapped their faces and stiffened their muscles until they looked like tired statues.

By the time the last lathered pony had been driven into the corral and Kayley had pushed the gate closed, it was dark. The wind had died, and a pale moon was suspended in the star-filled sky. After supper, she updated the ranch accounts while Sam made out a list of winter gear the crew needed. He wet the point of his pencil and added an extra line ordering a new pair of boots for himself.

The next morning, the men began readying the horses for the early roundup. Kayley listened to the frightened screams of the horses for a moment, then went inside.

I should relieve Elda, she thought, and went down the hall to her father's room. He'd been restless ever since the day of the barbecue, unable to sleep and occasionally thrashing about so violently at night that he had to be dosed with laudanum. During the day, he wasn't left unattended for even a moment.

Outside the double oak doors of his room, Kayley stopped. In her mind, she heard again Gunning telling her that her father had lived on the ranch for five years before he sent for her. She moved away from the doors, avoiding looking at them or touching them, afraid that if she did, she'd be trapped into facing him again with her doubt.

She went instead to her own room, seeking its quiet and solitude. She sat by the window facing east across the valley. From the old cigar box on the dresser beside her, she took out the torn pieces of her mother's letter and pieced them together on her lap, the violet paper looking pretty against the bright blue of Kayley's gingham dress.

She didn't remember her mother. Alicia Ann Ryan had died of tuberculosis when Kayley was two years old, leaving her in the care of her only sister, Lona. When Kayley arrived at Mrs. Potter's school that lonely day so many years ago, clutched tight in her hands had been the cigar box, which she used to pretend smelled just like her father. In the box had been the two most precious things in her life—a pink seashell her Aunt Lo had loved, and the violet letter.

"My darling baby girl," the letter started, the words flowing across the page in a fragile script that told more about Alicia Ann than the words themselves.

Kayley closed her eyes and tried to imagine her mother writing the letter. She placed her at an open window with a breeze stirring her golden-red hair and the lacy collar of her gown. The pen she held was made from a white gull's feather, and the ink well on the desk beside her was cut from beautiful crystal that caught the light from the window and scattered it across the empty paper in a thousand rainbows.

Alicia Ann would have glanced across the room at the bassinet where her new baby lay sleeping before dipping her pen in the dark ink and beginning to write.

This letter is the only thing I have to leave you, dearest Kayley Ann, except for my love. Be kind to your Aunt Lona, she is too frail for the task that I must leave her. And yet there's no one else I would entrust you to, my most precious child, except my most precious sister. Be happy, daughter.

Alicia had never signed the letter. "She couldn't bring herself to say good-bye," Aunt Lo had explained the day she gave Kayley the letter. That was on her eighth birthday. A few days later, Aunt Lo had succumbed to her lifelong frailty and died. She hadn't said good-bye, either.

Kayley folded the pieces of the letter and slipped them back into the worn cigar box. Aunt Lo's pink seashell was in it, too, along with the dried circlet of yellow flowers Clay had given her, the key to her father's desk, and the letter from him that had changed her life.

"I want you to come live on my new ranch," he'd written, and with one sweeping stroke of his pen, her dreams had come true and her life had changed forever. At least the truth couldn't take that away from her.

She lifted her face into the cold breeze that stirred the lace curtains on her window. It was a beautiful day, the sky clear and blue, the land golden and green. A group of cattle surged into sight at the top of a small rise. Behind them was a horse the color of dirty ice.

"Boxer," Kayley whispered, and she trembled at the sight of the tall man riding the big gelding.

The oval mirror hanging on the wall above the dressing table gave her a polished picture of herself; flushed cheeks and sparkling eyes; hair arranged in a braided knot at the nap of her neck, the way Aunt Lo had worn her hair, only instead of auburn brown, Kayley's pinned masses sparkled like fire in the sunlight that spilled into the tiny bedroom.

She fussed with her collar. It was made of white lace, and it looked fresh and pretty spread out across the crisp gingham checks. She straightened her full skirts, checked the wide ribbon tied snugly around her waist, and then, with her heart beating so fast that she was breathless, went to meet Clay.

The cattle were making their hurried way across the hard-packed dirt of the yard to the watering trough beside the barn. Clay turned away from them. He reined Boxer in so close to where Kayley was standing on the veranda that she could feel the gelding's steaming breath on her face.

Clay looked as though he hadn't slept in days. His face was lined by cold and exhaustion and his shoulders weren't as solidly squared as they'd been before. Although he was obviously close to physical collapse, his silver gaze glowed like a freshly fired branding iron as he caught, and forcibly held, Kayley's hesitant gaze.

The last time she'd seen him, he'd been bending close to kiss her. Now he stared down at her from a great height, his lips set in a brutal line that sent chills racing down her arms and along the edges of her fingers.

The silence between them was so brittle that each time she inhaled, it was like breathing broken glass. Unable to remember even a single word of the welcome she'd rehearsed for his return, she blurted out the first thing that came to her mind.

"Those cattle you were driving. They're not steers."

"That's because they're cows," he said in a disgusted tone that made her feel stupid and dull. "The nine best cows I could find with the R Cross brand."

She pressed her fingernails deep into her palms and tried to match her tone to his. "Have the rustlers left us so few animals that you couldn't find a tenth?"

"The tenth is already here."

"The only cattle within a mile of this house are the ones you just brought here."

He swung down from the saddle. "There's a longhorn now two hundred yards from where we're standing."

Kayley followed the direction of his gaze to where Toro was pawing the ground in furious discontent. The big bull had wedged its massive horns between the slats of the fence and was trying to wrench the post out of the ground.

"No," she said with a determined shake of her head. "Absolutely not. You can have any other bull on the ranch, but you're not taking Toro."

Clay leaned a shoulder against the post beside her, and victory flashed like winter starlight in his eye. "If I don't get him, your father doesn't get my water."

"We'll manage without it," she said, knowing they couldn't.

"That's fine," Clay said in a distracted tone that drew Kayley's immediate attention. He was looking at Elda, who was standing outside the kitchen and staring out across the valley.

"What's she looking at?" Kayley asked.

"I'm not sure," he said, then lifted his arm to stab a finger in a northeasterly direction. "There!"

Kayley couldn't see anything until she stretched up onto her toes. Surging suddenly upward into the clear skies was a soot-colored cloud. It looked like a thunderhead rising higher and higher until finally Kayley didn't need to stretch to see it.

"What is it?" she asked.

"Smoke." Clay's fingers closed around hers for a brief moment. Then he was moving, running to the branding corral and shouting. "Sam, there's a fire at Antelope Springs!"

Sam had been sitting on the corral fence beside Slowhand Smith, who was adding hairs from the horses he'd just finished breaking to his braided hatband. Sam swung down at Clay's shout, and together they studied the blackening eastern sky while Kayley ran to join them.

"Snow," Sam said, "load every barrel and cask you can find on the chuckwagon and follow us. You can

126

fill them at the spring. Clay, you'll need a fresh horse. Bede, you can stop looking excited right now. You're staying here with Miss Ryan."

"I'm not staying here!" she cried. "Bede, saddle Louisiana while I change."

Clay grabbed her arms. "You're not going."

"That's my grass out there, grass I need to get my cattle through the winter. I can't just sit here while it's burning."

"Your grass and your cattle? I thought this was your father's ranch."

"I'm not staying," she repeated.

"I don't want to have to worry about you out there, Kayley."

She met his fierce gaze. "Then don't. Bede, don't just stand there with your mouth hanging open. Saddle my horse."

Chapter Twelve

The fire burned itself out before they arrived. The wind, which had pushed it south across the richest grazing acres in the valley, began to blow from the west, ending the fire's destruction by pushing it directly into the unburnable waste of Laguna del Perro.

Starting at the edge of the salt flats, in approximately the same spot Jack had been four days ago, he and Kayley began walking north through the center of the devastated acres while her father's men patrolled the edges, searching for and stamping out any smoldering threats that could start the fire raging again.

The air was still. Terribly, horribly still. No wind, no rustling grasses. No insects or rabbits or snakes or birds. Nothing. Just the sound of his and Kayley's boots on the blackened earth, and the sound of their breathing, each gasping intake of air bringing with it the stench of burned trees and grass, of scorched dirt and rocks and sand, and of charred flesh.

With each breath he took, Jack regretted having given Kayley his bandanna. The gesture had been intended to put him back in her goodwill after their confrontation over Toro. At first she'd refused the bandanna. But after an hour of coughing on the ash and being sickened by the smells, she'd not protested when he tied it around her neck and lifted its protecting veil over her face. She hadn't thanked him, though, nor had his sacrifice softened her attitude toward him.

When he'd ridden into the yard of the ranch house that morning, he'd been certain that his feelings for her had been brought under tight rein. The moment he'd seen her waiting for him on the veranda with a smile in her eyes and a tremble of anticipation on her soft lips, Jack's hard-won control had shattered, and he'd turned his self-anger on her.

Last night, while he slept, one of the cattle he'd selected had wandered away. It had been a stupid decision to replace that cow with Toro, one he regretted more with each glance of Kayley's ice-blue eyes in his direction and with every breath he took of this stinking air.

He ground a lump of scorched grass beneath the heel of his boot until it turned to ash. How long would it take for this land to recover, if it ever would? And how many acres of government scrubland would he have to lease to replace this rich grassland?

"I had no idea so many animals died in a fire," Kayley said, speaking for the first time since they left the salt flats. She was standing beside the burned body of a rabbit, gently nudging its lifeless body with her toe. "I hope the stallion wasn't one of them."

Since starting their gruesome walk, they'd seen dozens of animals who'd met a sad fate in the flames. The closer they came to Antelope Springs, the higher the toll became. Deer, antelope, and cattle had fallen victim to the fire in greater numbers than even Jack had imagined possible.

"I didn't realize the ground would be this hot, either." She pulled his scarf off her face and removed her gloves. "I feel like my feet are being baked inside my boots."

She was wearing a heavy wool coat several sizes too large for her. It made her look like a child bundled up to play in the snow. Jack ran his fingers along the coat's collar.

"Why don't you take this off?"

She looked down at her wiggling fingers, which barely extended from the ends of the bulky sleeves. "Gunning told me it would protect me from the fire."

Jack made a show of intently scanning the horizons. "I think it's safe to take it off now, kid. I don't see a flame anywhere in sight." He tensed. "There's five riders approaching us from the south. Sam and his men are north of us."

Kayley slid a foot into one of her gelding's stirrups and stood up in it so she could see. "I recognize Vance Moore's black mare in that group."

"I don't like that man."

She jumped down. "How can you say that? You hardly know him."

"I know him well enough. He's a gambler who won his ranch, such as it is, from your father in a poker game. He considers himself better than everyone else, including you, kid. He's condescending, reproachful, afraid to travel without an armed escort—"

"Enough!" she cried with a laugh. "Can't you think of one good thing to say about him?"

Jack smiled into her sparkling eyes which were so much like her father's, and yet so different. "He hasn't put a wedding ring on your finger yet."

Her laugh shied away. He cupped her chin with his hand to prevent her from dropping her head. His touch brought a blush to her cheeks, which had been protected by his scarf from the dust and ash that had left smudging stains around her eyes and across her nose.

In prison, Jack had learned to put a wall between himself and emotions that had no outlet. Now he found himself having to do that again, only this time the wall was to defend him from golden lashes and hair the color of fire, against musical laughter and schoolgirl innocence.

"You look like a raccoon," he said.

His insides tied themselves into knots as she touched his cheek with a gentle caress. "And you, sir, look like a chimney sweep."

He captured her hand and turned it over to press a kiss against her palm. Her fingers closed around his. "That won't make me change my mind about Toro," she said before releasing his hand and stepping away from him just as Moore reined in alongside them.

Jack didn't like the looks of the men riding with Moore any better than he liked Moore himself. While the gambler was merely a dandy in riding boots, his men looked as though they either belonged in prison

131

or had just gotten out. Their hands were held close to the Colt insignia on the handles of their pistols, and their eyes were dark with insult when they looked at Kayley.

Jack noticed there were no triggers on their guns. It was a trait of professional gunmen, who gained an edge by using only the hammer of their pistols when firing. Jack dropped his left hand onto the handle of his own triggerless gun.

"What are you doing here?" Moore asked Kayley in a disapproving tone of voice that reminded Jack of the warden at Lansing Prison. He added another debit to Moore's mounting tally of unlikable traits.

"Where should I be?" Kayley asked. "Sipping lemonade on the veranda while I wait for news of how many acres of grass and how many head of cattle I lost?"

"Exactly," Moore said and motioned to one of his men. "Take Miss Ryan to her house and see that she stays there." He pointed at Jack. "You aren't needed here, either. Clear out."

Jack had his gun halfway out of the holster before Kayley stopped him by putting her hand over his.

"This isn't your land, Vance, so stop giving orders as though it were."

"Clive, put her on her horse."

The surliest looking of the foursome moved his lathered mount in Kayley's direction.

Jack shook off her restraining hand and took an aggressive step forward. "If you touch her, I'll kill you."

"Stop being dramatic, Clay. Vance, I'm not going anywhere until I know what started this fire."

"Heat lightning. Now get on your horse."

"It wasn't hot enough this morning for heat lightning," Jack said.

"Are you calling me a liar?" Moore's voice was edged as sharp as a skinning knife.

"If you're saying that you saw heat lightning in this valley today, I'm calling you a liar."

The four Lucky Ace men cleared their guns from their holsters at a speed that lent strength to Jack's opinion of them. He pulled his own and pressed his thumb onto the hammer, holding it open and ready for action.

"Kayley, get behind me."

"Both of you, stop this right now! Vance, make those men put their guns away. And you," she said to Jack, "stop trying to start trouble. If Vance said he saw lightning, I believe him."

"Miss Ryan!"

Jack turned sideways so he could see who had shouted and still keep an eye on Moore and his men. Sam Butler was riding toward them. He reined in beside Kayley, flicked his cool gaze over the situation and then pulled his own gun, which he pointed directly at Moore.

"What's going on here?"

"We're discussing the weather," Kayley said. "Is something wrong?"

"The spring's been poisoned."

"Antelope Springs?" Jack asked in surprise. "What makes you think that?"

"The dead animals."

Moore gave a snort of disgust. "Of course there are dead animals, Butler. There's been a fire."

"That doesn't explain the carcasses north of the springs. There's at least fifty head of dead cattle up there and not one burned blade of grass. Then there's Snow's mules. After they drank from the pond, they went into convulsions."

"Arsenic," Jack said, and Sam nodded without taking his gaze, or his gun, off Moore.

"Why would anyone poison our water?" Kayley asked. Her face was pale beneath its smudging black stains.

"Maybe it was an accident," Moore said.

"That's as believable as heat lightning on a cold day," Jack said. "Has your father made any recent enemies, Kayley?"

"Poppa doesn't have any enemies at all."

"At least, no recent ones," Moore said, and Kayley gave him a withering glance.

"Sam," she said, turning her back on Moore. "Were there really a lot of animals killed?"

"Enough. But no horses, at least none we've found. The boys are still looking."

"I'll look, too," she said and swung into her saddle.

Moore grabbed her gelding's bridle. "There's no need for that, my dear. Clive, you and the boys put your guns away and check out those dead animals. You know which stallion Miss Ryan's concerned about."

The four men were reluctant to follow his order. They kept staring at Jack while impatiently thumbing the hammers of their guns.

"Now," Moore said. They holstered their pistols and gave Jack another contemptuous scowl before

134

galloping away.

"If you don't release my bridle, Vance, I'll tell Sam to shoot you," Kayley said. Her hands were steady on her gelding's reins, but her lower lip kept trying to tremble.

"There's no need for theatrics, my dear," Moore said. "I won't stop you if you really want to go." He released her reins, and she galloped after his men.

"The next time your hired guns want to practice their manhood, Moore," Sam said, "make sure it isn't around Miss Ryan." He backed his horse away, dropped his gun into his holster, and went in pursuit of Kayley.

"Now that the lady isn't here to witness my bid to be a hero," Jack said, "shall we call this one quits, Moore?"

"I saw lightning," Moore said, not sounding quite so sure of himself without his men.

Jack eased the pressure he'd been maintaining on his Colt's hammer and slipped the gun back into his holster. "Maybe it was off that vulgar diamond you're sporting."

"Maybe it was," Moore said, looking down at the ring on his right hand. "This thing's been bad luck ever since I won it."

"From Kayley's father?"

"The only thing Sullivan owns worth more than a plug nickle is this ranch."

"Which you want. You'd have a better chance convincing him to give it to you than you'll have by trying to marry his daughter for it. She's too smart for that."

"She's a foolish child."

"Obviously you don't know her as well as I do," Jack said, and Moore's eyes went black with indignation.

"Somebody needs to teach you some manners, cowboy!" He clutched at his gun, which was strapped too high and too tight to be of any real use.

"Maybe," Jack said as his pistol cleared leather.

His first bullet sliced through Moore's trigger guard. The second one clipped the Colt's pearl handle, dragging the gun out of its tooled-leather holster and sending it spinning through the air to drop beside the body of the burned rabbit.

Jack slipped his pistol into its snug holster and swung into the saddle. He gave Moore a cold smile.

"But it won't be you, city boy."

Kayley sat beside Snow on one of the rocks that crowded the shore of Antelope Springs. Sam had put Willie Pete and Joe Duke to work digging ditches to drain the poisoned water from the pond. They were wielding their shovels so inexpertly it would probably be morning before they finished.

It was the type of scene Snow loved. He didn't seem to even notice their clumsy efforts, though, because a hundred feet away lay Silly and Sip, his beloved mules. They'd been shot through the head, but not before their agony at drinking the poisoned water had caused them to twist their harness into a tangled mess of knots.

"I shot them," Snow said. His grizzled face was buried in his hands, and his grumbling voice sounded thicker and rougher than normal. "They was hurtin' bad and I shot them."

Kayley laid a hand on his arm. "They were good animals, Snow."

Clay and Vance came riding up, Clay gifting Kayley with a satisfied smile and Vance wearing the same grimace of displeasure he'd worn at the barbecue.

"Arsenic isn't a pretty way to die," Clay said as he looked down at the mules. He dismounted and tied the reins of the white-faced sorrel he was riding to the back wheel of the chuckwagon beside Louisiana. "Did you find the stallion, kid?"

Kayley shook her head. "A lot of my father's cattle were killed, though." Her shoulders felt as though they were being punched down by a great weight. "And so many wild animals."

Snow got up and went over to his mules. He began to gently untangle the reins twisted around their heads while Slowhand cut away the tangled harness.

"If it wasn't for the mules," Kayley said, "and for the wind pushing the fire south, we might be dead, too."

Vance propped a shiny boot on the rock beside her. "That same wind would've destroyed the Lucky Ace if my boys hadn't set a backfire on Coyote Run to stop it."

Kayley stared up at him. "They did what?"

"It had to be done, my dear. Otherwise, the fire would've burned straight up the mesa and destroyed the Lucky Ace."

"The wind turned it east at least ten miles north of your mesa, Vance."

"And even if it hadn't," Clay said, "the junipers on the slopes of Los Jumanos would've stopped it."

137

"I couldn't take a chance on that," Vance said, his eyes narrowing in anger.

Kayley dug the heel of her boot into the black dirt around the rock. "I guess not," she mumbled.

"And next spring, my dear, your cattle will have even better grazing. Burning lets the land breathe and stimulates stronger growth."

"That's bullcrap," Clay said.

"It's a well-known fact," Vance replied.

"That only idiots believe. There'll be grass here next spring, all right, a good crop of it, if the roots survive the winter. And if they do, then you'll have to worry that the summer heat will dry them out or whether the storms will wash them away. Then you'll have to start worrying about winter killing them again. If everything goes perfectly, it could take ten years before this land recovers."

"That's a long time to worry," Kayley said and tugged on the bulky sleeves of her coat with her fingertips.

"Don't listen to him," Vance said. "Getting rid of the matted, dead grass in this valley is the best thing that could happen to the R Cross cattle. Eating the new growth might keep them from looking so scrawny."

"Sam told me that longhorns are supposed to look like that," she said.

"Scrawny, bony and ugly as homemade sin," Clay said. He'd taken off his hat and filled it with water from his canteen. The white-faced sorrel drank his offering with noisy slurps. "But they don't need a rancher to coddle them like eastern breeds, and they can turn that grass Moore thinks is dead into money on the hoof."

"That matted stuff isn't dead?" Kayley asked. She looked past the springs to the great stretch of land that extended north as far as the eye could see. It was covered in grass so yellow and dead looking that it was hard to imagine it had ever been alive.

"Dig down through that mat and you'll find new growth," Clay said, "even in the middle of winter." He filled his hat again and offered Louisiana a drink.

"I still say that a fire is good for the land," Vance said. Kayley had to struggle not to smile at his petulant tone.

When she first arrived at the R Cross, the valley had been full of new spring growth. She remembered Vance describing this area to her, saying it had the richest grazing in the whole valley.

"If the R Cross had more fresh water, this section alone," he'd said and pointed at her father's map, "would make this ranch worth a fortune."

"To whom?" Kayley had asked.

"Cattle companies, my dear. Big, beautiful, rich cattle companies. They're buying up ranches throughout the southwest. If the Lucky Ace had fresh water instead of salt, I'd sell out to them myself."

Vance took his boot off the rock beside Kayley. "The few acres of grass I own aren't worth wasting a match," he said, "but if I owned the R Cross, I'd set fire to all of it."

"Like you did here?" Clay asked.

Kayley gave an audible gasp while every man in camp stopped whatever he was doing to stare first at Clay, and then Vance, whose face had gone as white as the handle of his gun.

"You—you good for nothing trail bum!" he sputtered. He made a grab for his pistol. His fingers clutched into a fist before he reached it, and his hand froze at his side.

"Clay, that was uncalled for," Kayley said.

He knelt beside her and scraped up a handful of the dirt she'd displaced with her boots. "Smell this."

She looked into his pale silver gaze while sniffing the dirt on his glove. Her nose wrinkled as she recognized the unpleasant odor.

"Kerosene," she said. "What does it mean?"

"See how the ground around these rocks is blacker than the rest of the burned area? The fire was hotter here because it was soaked in kerosene."

He searched among the rocks, stopping beside two boulders propped against each other. He motioned for Kayley to join him. Both of the big rocks were covered with soot. Between them was a narrow space resembling a miniature cave. From it, Clay pulled out a piece of red cloth onto which had been melted a lump of wax.

He pressed a thumb into the wax, sniffed it and then handed it to Kayley, who followed his example. It was more malleable than the wax she was used to seeing from the candles made of tallow that they used on the R Cross. This didn't smell as rancid as tallow, either.

"What is it?" she asked.

"Beeswax," Clay said. He reached between the rocks again.

Flakes of white ash filled the air around him as he pulled out a scorched can. Only part of the label was still readable, enough to confirm that it had contained kerosene.

"Someone soaked the ground with kerosene, stuck the empty can in here along with a lighted candle and that wool rag. The candle burned down, caught the rag on fire. There was probably grass piled up around these rocks, which accounts for all this soot and ash. The rag caught the grass on fire, which started the inferno blazing."

Vance gingerly picked up the burned can, using only two fingers and holding it from him with a grimace of distaste. "That's quite a story." He set the can on the ground beside Kayley. "We have an old kerosene can and what looks like a piece of a sock with wax on the toe. Hardly what I'd call conclusive evidence of arson. These were probably tossed out of the chuckwagon last spring after roundup, or left by a cowboy who camped here overnight."

"I don't know many ranch hands who can afford beeswax candles," Clay said.

"And we don't carry kerosene on the chuckwagon," Sam said.

"Where these things came from," Vance said, "isn't half as interesting as the fact that Clay knew just where to look for them."

The air sparked with tension as Clay slowly stood. "I didn't."

"And yet it looked to me like you went directly to them. Isn't that how it looked to you, my dear?"

"Why would he show us the proof if he set the fire?"

"To impress you." Vance pulled out a handkerchief and wiped his fingers. "Is there something he wants from you? A job, a loan? Or, my dear, is it

141

something more personal?'' He turned and strode away.

"Toro," Kayley whispered as she looked at Clay. "You want Toro."

"The fire was already burning before I told you I wanted him, Kayley."

"The candle," she said.

Sam shook his head. "They don't make candles that big, Miss Ryan. It took us almost four hours to reach here, and we were riding full out. He was driving cattle."

"That's right!" Kayley cried and jumped to her feet to hug both Sam and Clay. Realizing how much that would embarrass them, and her, she ran instead after Vance, who was untying his mare's reins from the front of the chuckwagon. "It couldn't have been Clay," she told him. "We were talking on the veranda, and he saw Elda looking this way; and then we saw the smoke, and they don't make candles that long."

"Your obsession with defending this man is becoming tiresome, my dear."

"You're just angry because he accused you of setting the fire."

Vance sighed. "I'm not angry; I'm frustrated and I'm jealous. I love you, Kayley, and lately, whenever I'm with you, all you talk about is this gunslinger. What is it about him that you find so fascinating?"

He swung into the saddle and pulled the mare into such a sharp turn Kayley was almost knocked down. She grasped Vance's leg to prevent him from riding away.

"Did you say that you loved me?"

"Yes, my dear, I did. I've loved you ever since your first night on the ranch when you kept waiting, hour after hour, for Sullivan to join us for supper. I almost starved to death, but I also fell in love."

Kayley glanced at Clay, who'd taken over digging the nearest ditch. Had he heard what Vance said, she wondered, and wondered why she should wonder that at one of the happiest moments of her life. Not since Aunt Lo died had anyone said they loved her. Now someone had, and all she could think about was whether someone else had overheard.

No, not someone. Clay.

Her hand fell away from Vance's leg. "Why didn't you tell me?"

"Because I've been waiting for you to grow up, only I'm beginning to think that may never happen." His men rode out of the gathering dusk and reined their mounts in beside him. "Where have you been?" he snapped.

"Looking for that horse," Clive said. "It ain't there."

Kayley's relief disappeared beneath the surprising touch of Vance's hand on the side of her face.

"I hope it won't take long for you to realize your future is with me, Kayley, and not running after a gunslinging trail bum who will never care about anyone except himself." He spurred his mare and rode away surrounded by his men.

"Bad news, kid?"

Clay was leaning on the handle of his shovel. The ditch he'd been digging was finished. Water was just beginning to flow out of the pond, reaching out across the burned land and leaking its poison into the blackened earth.

Kayley was as unsure of her feelings for Vance as she was about what she should do about the attacks against the R Cross. What she was sure of, was that when her grass was being burned, Clay hadn't hesitated in offering his assistance. And now, while a man who claimed to love her was riding away, Clay was here digging ditches. If he was doing this just to impress her, it was working.

"Good news," she said, "at least, for you." She waved a hand at the poisoned water rushing through the ditch between them. "This means that Toro belongs to you."

Chapter Thirteen

Sam lifted the branding iron from the fire. The sculpted R and Spanish cross had turned a glowing red that looked unreal in the fading orange light of sunset.

Kayley stiffened, but refused to let herself look away from that bright iron as Sam moved from the fire to where a calf lay on its side a short distance away. Bede was sitting on the calf's head, and Joe Duke held its feet.

"Last one," Sam said and applied the hot iron to the animal's dusty brown hide. Its hair burst into flame, the calf bellowed in pain, and Joe Duke spat out an unintelligible curse as he was kicked by a flailing hoof.

Smoke and the stench of burning skin turned Kayley's stomach. She curled her hands into fists and fought down a wave of nausea. After what seemed like hours, Sam lifted the iron away from the flinching hide of the poor calf, and Kayley sighed in relief.

"Castrate him," Sam said and threw the iron in the direction of the fire.

Willie Pete knelt behind the calf, reached between its legs and, with a quick flick of his knife, turned Bede's captive from a bullock into a steer.

"Yum yum," Willie said as tossed the severed testicles into the bucket Snow held out to him.

"These are gonna make fine eats for supper," Snow said.

"You eat those?" Kayley asked in horror. She covered her cramping stomach with her hands and wished that her father had bought a hotel instead of a ranch.

"Best vittles this side of heaven," Joe Duke said, "even if it is Snow that's cookin' them. You can let that critter up now, Bede."

The boy jumped off the little steer's head. It clambered to its feet and charged back to the milling herd, where its mother licked its wounded rear.

Bede glanced in the bucket. His face paled, and he swallowed hard. "Ma would skin me if I ate those things. I'd better not have any."

"We're about an hour away from the house," Sam said to Kayley. "Are you going to head back or camp here with us?"

"I want to compare these figures"—she indicated the little book in which she'd listed the numbers of cows, steers, bulls, yearlings and calves they'd counted during the roundup—"with the spring count."

"You just want an excuse not to eat these," Snow said as he sloshed the contents of his bucket.

She pretended to look surprised. "I thought you said he wasn't very smart, Joe."

"Don't get me into this or he'll be feedin' me that bucket instead of what's in it."

"You two the one's gettin' too smart," Snow said with an indignant sniff. He went off in the direction of his chuckwagon.

Sam put a hand on Bede's shoulder. "Get Miss Ryan's horse, and yours, too. You're riding back to the ranch with her."

"I thought I was going with you tomorrow."

"There's not enough men working this ranch to protect me from your mother if I said yes."

"But, Sam—"

"No arguments, boy, or I'll tell Snow you're staying for supper."

"I'm going," Bede said. He untied the saddle horses from the tether line Slowhand had put up and handed Louisiana's reins to Kayley.

Sam gave the boy a leg up onto his mare. "You stick close to Miss Ryan on the ride back."

Bede squared his shoulders. "Don't worry, Sam, I'll watch out for her."

Sam brought his smile under quick control. "Yeah, you do that, boy." He lifted the stirrup on Louisiana's saddle and tightened the cinch. "Don't be surprised, Miss Ryan, if you find those figures show a big drop in the tally." He moved aside for her to mount.

"Nothing personal, Sam, but I hope you're wrong."

"Me, too," he said and slapped the flat of his hand on Louisiana's rump. "Keep the north star on your right!" he called after them.

Bede brought his mare up even with Louisiana. "I

ride at night a lot, Miss Ryan, so you don't need to worry about getting lost."

"I'll depend on you, then."

"I won't let you down." He glanced across at her, his face looking even younger than usual in the moonlight. "Thank you for having that barbecue. I liked it a lot."

"Maybe the next time we can invite Charity Calhoun."

He rolled his eyes. "Ma'd have a fit."

"She'd probably shoot me," Kayley said.

"Nope. She'd definitely shoot you."

"You'll have to help me hide all the guns first."

He grinned. "It's a deal."

It didn't take long for Kayley to discover that Sam was right. The herd count was lower. A lot lower.

In March, the R Cross had 1,719 cattle on its books. Now there were only 1,072. Clay had been paid ten animals, Felipe Chaves in Belen had received twenty-five in payment for supplies, Pedro Baca had been paid eight steers for a year's supply of grain for the horses, and 127 had been lost in the Antelope Springs tragedy.

That left 477 animals unaccounted for, and not even Kayley could believe than many cattle simply got lost, no matter how stupid Slowhand said long-horns were.

"Is something wrong, Miss Ryan?" Gunning asked.

He took a candle from his pocket, lit it from the one about to die on the desk and set the new candle in the melted tallow wax pooled in the bottom of the brass candlestick. Then he took a small box out of his pocket, put the old candle stub in it and slipped the box back into the pocket that Kayley was beginning to believe was bigger than the ranch storeroom.

"You don't have any miracles in there, do you?"

He almost smiled, but subdued the urge before it became too obvious. "No, miss. Just a pencil," he said, then proved himself wrong by producing not only a pencil, but also a knife he used to sharpen it with. He exchanged the bit of a pencil Kayley was using for the new one. The pencil shavings went into a different box, which came out of, and went back into, the same pocket.

"How about cattle?"

"Sorry."

"A donut?" she asked, and laughed when he pulled a lint-covered pastry from the incredible pocket. "You're the answer to my dreams, Gunning."

"I hardly think you're that desperate, miss."

"You don't know how hungry I am," she said and reached for the pastry.

The smile came back. "You'll find a way to stop the rustling."

"What about the arsonist?" she asked between bites. "And let's not forget the poisoner. Will I find a way to stop him or them, too?"

"You'll do what you have to."

She finished off the pastry and rubbed her tired eyes with sticky fingers. "That's what I've been doing my whole life, Gunning. I'm sick of doing what I have to."

"What would you like to do?"

She leaned her head against the back of the leather chair and sighed at the ceiling. "I'd like to make my father well and I'd like to stop being intimidated by Vance and I'd like to know why he never sweats and why Clay always needs a shave."

An image of a very angry Clay submerged to his chin in the beaver pond caused her to laugh.

"Well, almost always," she said and laughed again. "I'd like to order one of those chairs with wheels on it so we can take Poppa out in the sun every afternoon, and I'd like to look out the window and see 477 cows stampeding into the yard complaining because they missed roundup."

She looked at the desktop. It was covered with letters she'd received from doctors regarding the possibility of recovery for stroke patients. Their answers to her pleas for hope had been as disappointing as the results of the herd count.

"But more than anything else, Gunning, I'd like to make the white stallion pay for what he did to Poppa."

"It won't bring him back, miss."

She lifted her suddenly angry gaze to his kind and caring face. "He isn't gone."

"Isn't he?"

A log in the fire popped, startling Kayley. She jumped to her feet and went over to stab at the embered logs. "We need more wood," she said and, after throwing the poker onto the overflowing box of firewood, escaped out the front door.

Clouds had gathered overhead. They hid the stars and moon, turning the night into a dark chasm lit only by an occasional flash of lightning along the southern horizon.

Kayley took deep, gasping breaths of the cool air, using it to ease the ache inside her chest and the burning in her eyes.

"Miss Ryan." The voice came out of the darkness beyond the veranda.

Kayley turned, wanting the voice to belong to Clay. *Poppa isn't gone,* she wanted to tell him. *He hasn't left me again; please say he hasn't.*

But it wasn't Clay. It was Sam. His spurs were loud in the silence between the thunder, and his hat was pulled low across his face.

"You were right," she said and told him what the roundup had revealed.

His hat dropped still lower. "We need help, Miss Ryan."

She curled her fingers into fists. "Vance said I couldn't run the ranch alone. It looks like he's right."

"The spring counts were low by a hundred fifty head," Sam said. "You can't take the blame for that."

"But Vance said I—"

"In Texas, the big ranches are hiring professional trackers to find rustlers and dispose of them."

"But Vance said—"

"We should be able to get a line on where we can hire one in Santa Fe."

"But Vance—"

"I'm starting the herd out at first light. Don't be late."

"But—"

"Good night, Miss Ryan."

He jingled his way toward the corral. Kayley heard the creak of saddle leather, then the drumming of

151

hoofbeats fading into the distance.

It was a long time before she stopped trying to understand what had happened. By then, the wind smelled of faraway rain, and the southern sky was dark, the storm's lightning spent, its thunder silent.

"I won't have to ask Vance for help," she realized.

If Sam had still been there, she would have hugged him, no matter how embarrassed it would have made him.

Chapter Fourteen

Sante Fe was the wildest, most completely alive place Kayley had ever seen. The city's heart was its plaza, and the heart of the plaza was the Palace of the Governors. Government officials had been gathering in the Palace, and the plaza, since the early 1600's. Bull fights had once been held here, it had been the end of the long trail for wagon caravans, and the flags of four nations had waved in the breeze above it.

Between encounters with history, the plaza was a marketplace. Dominating the square from the porch fronting the Palace, Indians dressed in calico and buckskin sold turquoise and silver jewelry. They sat behind brightly woven blankets spread with their skillful creations, watching the spectators, bargaining with the shoppers, and occasionally rearranging their glittering wares to catch the eye of a passerby.

Elsewhere in the plaza, Mexicans wearing serapes sold vegetables and fruits, livestock and spicy enchiladas. String of dark red chiles dangled from rooftops along with onions and garlic. Beneath the dried vegetables, burros, goats and children added their harmony to the cacophony of plaza noise.

Horses were stamping and snorting their way around the square. Wagons creaked and flung themselves after the horses while their drivers shouted and spat and whistled at raven-haired señoritas wearing silk dresses and lace mantillas.

Cottonwood trees cast dappled shadows over the chaotic scene, and the wind smelled of boiled beans and fried cornbread. The wind tugged at Kayley's hat, and she held firmly to the straw brim with one hand, using her other hand to lift the hem of her skirt above the smelly dropping of a horse being led by an even smellier man.

A huge black dog was tied to a post of the Palace porch. Snow walked past the looming beast without even noticing its slathering fangs, then stopped at the next seller's blanket to look over the displayed wares. Kayley edged past the drooling monster, almost falling into the center of a display of bracelets.

"Snow!" she shouted, trying to be heard over the dog's roaring barks. "I want to take this money to the bank!"

The dog stopped barking suddenly, allowing her last remark to be heard by everyone within three miles of the plaza. Kayley gave the dog a deadly glance as she closed her hand protectively around her purse, which was stuffed with thirty-two hundred-dollar bank notes.

That morning, Sam Butler had bickered and bargained and threatened and argued with Juan Delgado, a Sante Fe livestock agent, until poor Señor

Delgado, who'd insisted he couldn't afford to pay $12.50 a head for their cattle, offered $12.80.

Sam had jumped on the slip, much to Señor Delgado's frustration, and Kayley had walked away from the livestock office with what she considered a fortune and what Sam considered "almost a fair price."

Because he had to take the cattle to the pens near the rail line, he'd handed Kayley and the money into Snow's care. The old trail cook was more interested in a beautiful Spanish comb that a Navajo woman was showing him, however, than in Sam's orders or Kayley's panic.

"Snow, we need to go to the bank," she said and darted her eyes across the crowd to see how many of them planned to rob her.

Snow nodded in her general direction before offering five dollars for the comb.

"One hundred U.S. gold dollars," the woman said, and Snow protested the price by spitting a stream of tobacco juice over the dog's head and into the street.

"Six," he said when the splatter stopped.

"One hundred U.S. gold dollars."

"What do you want a comb for anyway?" Kayley asked.

"It's a present for Elda. I'm gonna win that she-male's affections even if I gotta spend," he leaned close to Kayley's ear and rasped in a loud whisper, "fifty dollars."

"Sold," the Navajo woman cried, and Snow almost swallowed his chaw.

Kayley left the two combatants arguing and went in search of the Second National Bank of Santa Fe.

Outside the bank, she paused to press a reassuring hand to the back of her head where her hair was confined in a knot. Its pinned neatness made her feel mature and capable.

The bank's front door was extremely heavy. She had to pull with all her strength to swing it open. Once she was inside, she just stood there, catching her breath and letting the wonderful silence envelope her.

There was only one clerk. He was standing behind a cage built of carved wooden bars and was counting a huge stack of paper money for a big man dressed in a silk suit every bit as shiny and black as his skin. His most distinguishing feature was his stomach. It was positively the biggest stomach Kayley had ever seen in her life.

Although she tried not to stare, she couldn't help sneaking glances at him as he took his receipt from the clerk and walked past the two women in line behind him who were acting like he'd just committed a heinous murder instead of making a deposit.

"Pardon me," he said to Kayley.

Surprised by the deep music of his voice, she lifted her gaze from his ponderous girth to his dark-brown eyes, so completely overwhelmed by him that she didn't remember what he'd just said. It wasn't as though she'd never spoken to a black person before. Joe Duke was black; but he wasn't very big, and his voice was nothing like the bass violin voice of this large man.

"You're blocking the door, miss."

She stumbled out of the way. "I'm sorry, sir. I was just so stunned at how quiet it is in here that I forgot where I was standing."

"Think nothing of it, miss. I did the same thing when I came in." The floor shook as he passed her.

"Do you need assistance?" the clerk asked. He was peering at Kayley through his thick spectacles and between the oak bars.

"I'm looking for Mr. Claude Asken."

"He's with someone right now. Have a seat on the bench against the far wall and I'll let you know when he's finished." The clerk turned his attention to the handful of silver coins one of the whispering women had given him. "Let me guess, Mrs. Mottram, a deposit from your egg business. Here it is Friday, and this is only your third deposit this week. Your chickens must be slowing down. What a surprise," he said after counting the coins and sounding not the least bit surprised. "Two dollars in nickels."

Kayley had trouble settling herself on the uncomfortable bench. The legs were all different lengths, causing it to pitch beneath her like a bronc on a cold morning. She scrunched herself into the most stable corner of the bench and braced her feet firmly on the floor to avoid being thrown.

"I wonder if this is where Slowhand learned to ride," she mumbled to herself.

The wall behind her separated the main room of the bank from the private offices. The wall groaned above her head, as though someone were leaning against it on the other side. "You can't find a copy because the court didn't issue an order," the suspected leaner said, his voice booming through the thin wall.

Kayley heard another man's voice coming from

deeper within the room. "Defend our action" was the only thing she could understand.

"You will if Lew Wallace calls for an audit of your books."

The second man mumbled something; then the first man laughed, and the wall groaned in relief as he moved away.

"That's right, Governor Lew Wallace," he said, his voice slightly muted, but still audible. "At breakfast this morning, we were talking about what the grand jury would do with the results of that audit. Can you imagine handing a roomful of ranchers and miners a case of land title fraud? It would be like tossing a lit match into a keg of gunpowder."

The second man's voice sounded wobbly. He said something about evidence, and the first man cut him off by shouting, "Ten thousand dollars in the hands of a convicted conman isn't overwhelming evidence; it's a bribe!"

There was something familiar about the first man's voice. When the door beside Kayley slammed open a second later, she looked to see who came out.

It was Clay. His beard was several days longer than usual, his hat was low across his forehead and his hands were clenched into fists. He looked tall and handsome and incredibly intimidating, and Kayley's heart lurched into her throat at the sight of him.

Before she could gather herself enough to call out to him, he'd already crossed the polished floor of the bank with great, angry strides. He threw open the front door so violently that the glass in the front window continued to shudder long after he'd bullied his way into the crowd outside and disappeared.

The two whispering women were cowering behind the door, having retreated there during Clay's advance. Mrs. Mottram was holding her deposit receipt in front of her like a shield of protection. The other lady was clutching in gloved hands the ribbon of her bonnet, which was so large and so decorated it looked like a display case for cabbage roses and feathers.

"This is just too much," Mrs. Mottram said. "First, a negro man, then a madman with an eyepatch. I'm changing banks." Together, arms clasped around each other for support, they fled back to the clerk's cage. "I want all my money," she demanded, "every nickel of it, and make certain you return the exact same coinage I deposited, starting with the two dollars I opened my account with three years ago."

The clerk looked at her over the rim of his spectacles. Then he unbuckled the leather cuffs that protected his shirt sleeves. "I'm going to lunch," he said and released himself from his barred confinement. He was about to leave the bank entirely when he paused in front of Kayley and whispered, "Mr. Asken's free now. If you don't go in now, Mrs. Mottram will, and you'll be still sitting there when we close tonight. His office is right behind you."

"I'm here about the letter you sent my father, Mr. Asken, and to make a deposit to his account."

Kayley was seated in a stiff leather chair across a gigantic desk from Claude Asken. He was short and overweight and had hair the color of soap scum and a

159

moustache that had been dyed black. It was also terribly askew, a condition Kayley assumed had occurred during his confrontation with Clay.

"What letter was that?"

There was an open file on his desk. He shuffled through it while he spoke, his attention riveted on whatever secrets it contained. Mrs. Potter had frequently used the same technique when confronted with a situation she was unprepared for, and Kayley hoped that she fared better with Mr. Asken than she ever had in boarding school.

"The letter you wrote Sullivan Ryan four weeks ago," she said.

"He's your father?" Asken stopped shuffling and looked up at her. "This is quite a coincidence."

"I hardly think so, Mr. Asken. You wrote my father requesting he come to see you regarding an 'urgent matter' that affected the R Cross. Because he's away on business, I came on his behalf."

"Where is Sullivan?"

"Away on business," she repeated.

"That, too, is quite a coincidence." He dropped his gaze from Kayley to his reflection in the highly polished surface of his desk. His bottom lip dropped open as his top lip tried to twitch his moustache back into alignment with his nose.

"What is the urgent matter, Mr. Asken?"

"If your father were here instead of you, Miss Ryan, I wouldn't need to tell him what the problem was." Asken glanced at the door of his office and seemed to shudder at something only he could see there. "Sullivan would already know." He looked at Kayley. "You obviously don't know anything."

160

I know you're the most irritating man I've ever met, Kayley thought and twisted the handle of her purse around the arm of the chair so she wouldn't be tempted to hit him with its beaded bulk.

Asken gave his moustache a final pat and his reflection a satisfied smile. "When did you say your father would be joining us?"

No wonder Clay had been shouting. Kayley wanted to shout, too, and would have except she didn't want the cashier and anyone else who might be in the bank to hear her.

"I'm handling my father's business until he returns."

"When will that be?"

"I don't know," she said through teeth that hurt from being clenched.

"And you've no way of communicating with him?"

"If I could, I would, but I can't, so why don't you tell me what the urgent matter is or was or will be so I can begin taking care of it or handling it or whatever it takes to eliminate it from your life and this conversation!"

"There's no need for anger, Miss Ryan," he said with a lift of his eyebrows, which hadn't been dyed black and so looked like two smears of soap at the bottom of his forehead. "Did you say you were here to make a deposit?"

It took Kayley a moment to remember she was here for some other purpose than to learn to hate Claude Asken. "Yes, I did want to do that, didn't I? I have sixteen hundred dollars to deposit from our fall cattle drive."

Asken frowned. "That's not very much money, even for a fall herd."

"That's not all we received; it's just all I'm depositing. The rest I'll need to exchange for cash to pay the ranch employees for the next six months."

"And the sixteen hundred? What's that for?"

She didn't know there had to be a reason for a deposit. "Taxes," she said. "And supplies and mules and a chair. And a gift for a friend."

"What about your father's loan? Are you planning to make a payment on that, or were you going to ignore it, like Sullivan did in April."

What loan, Kayley wondered. "Of course I wasn't going to ignore it. How much is a payment?"

"Two payments, Miss Ryan. And there's his regular mortgage. That's overdue, too."

Panic swelled inside her. "Just tell me how much, Mr. Asken, and I'll take care of both of them."

"Because I personally handle Sullivan Ryan's dealings with this bank, I can tell you that if there's an audit, these unpaid loans would be just the beginning of the end. The key to Pandora's box. The tip of the iceberg. We don't want that, do we, Miss Ryan? We don't want to face the Sword of Damocles."

Kayley had no idea what he was talking about. "How much are the payments, Mr. Asken?"

He dove back into the already shuffled file and madly shuffled through it again. He extracted a document, looked it over, took a blank sheet of paper from his desk drawer and began madly scribbling, looking from the document to the paper and back, all the while madly mumbling.

"Two thousand dollars received by the borrower

162

September twenty-ninth of last year, loaned for a period not to exceed three years and payable semi-annually with an interest rate of fifteen percent—"

"Fifteen?" Kayley sounded like she'd been stuffed inside a barrel.

"That's standard for high risk loans, Miss Ryan." He began to drool as the lid of her barrel was nailed shut. "You can ask any banker west of the Mississippi, and he'll tell you that fifteen percent is standard, especially considering there was already a loan outstanding." He smiled fondly at his scribblings. "This isn't good," he said and lifted his foot to give her barrel a kick.

"How much is it, Mr. Asken?"

"It's the interest," he said, and Kayley's barrel began plummeting down a steep hill. "Interest is a borrower's worst enemy, especially when the payments are late."

"How much is it?"

"I hope your taxes aren't very high," he said, and her barrel picked up speed in its rush to reach the bottom.

"How much?" she asked, her voice rising uncontrollably as the end loomed near.

He looked at her the way the clerk had, except Claude Asken wasn't wearing glasses. "Don't you even want to know how much you owe, Miss Ryan?"

The barrel exploded on impact.

"Yes," she said calmly, "I want to know that. I want very much to know that. I want very much for you to tell me that, Mr. Asken."

"Then, you should've asked. I can't read minds, you know, especially not female minds. Women have such scattered, unorganized minds."

"How much, Mr. Asken?" Kayley shouted, jumping to her feet and slamming her chair back against the wall, hoping that she'd frightened the life out of whoever was listening on the other side of the wall. "Just tell me how much!"

Chapter Fifteen

Kayley stood on tiptoe as she tried to look through the window into the smoky darkness of the City Beer Hall. Both the sidewalk and the street outside the saloon were crowded with huge pasteboard placards that advertised the saloon as "The Only Place Of Amusement In The City." It didn't look very amusing to Kayley. After her meeting with Claude Asken, she doubted she'd ever be amused by anything again.

The City Beer Hall was humming with activity. Men were coming and going through the front doors, each of which were only half as tall as the opening and half as wide. They swung to and fro with such speed and frequency, Kayley feared she might be killed if she ventured too close. But the window was too high to see much of anything except hats, so she was forced to confront the doors.

The smell of the "Fine Wine, Liquors, And Cigars" that a nearby placard promised awaited customers inside the Beer Hall caused Kayley to wrinkle her nose in displeasure as she looked over the top of one of the doors.

"Excuse me," a cowboy, who didn't look much older than Bede, said to her. He was trying to get around her and into the saloon.

"Would you please tell the manager I'd like to speak with him."

"Sure thing, miss. You just wait right here."

Kayley huddled against the wall, out of reach of the doors, and waited. A few minutes passed, then a big-faced man, wearing a starched collar and a black vest so shiny it looked waxed, stepped out of the saloon. He looked around, and when his gaze fell on Kayley, he shook his head.

"Ain't got no job you'd fit."

"Are you the manager?"

"Conway's the name. I own the Hall, and I don't hire youngsters."

"My name's Kayley Ryan, Mr. Conway, and I'm not looking for work; I'm looking for Sam Butler, my father's ranch foreman. He told me this morning that if I need him, to check here first."

"Hire her, Conway," said a man who was looking at Kayley through the narrow opening between the swinging doors. "I like that hair."

"Shut up, Fetch, and get back to work. What's this Butler look like, Miss Ryan?"

"He's as tall as you, slender, wears a black-handled pistol and a buckskin shirt."

"You just described half the men in here. Anything else?"

She tried to think of what it was that made Sam different from everyone else. It came to her suddenly, and she smiled. "He has the kindest eyes in the whole world."

Conway snorted. "That narrows it down. Wait a minute, has he been asking around for a tracker?"

"That's him."

"Wait here." Conway started to leave, then added, "If Fetch comes out, scream and I'll come running." He broke through the double doors with a swat of his hand.

Another few minutes passed, then Sam came out of the saloon. He looked left, then right, his eyes narrowing as he saw Kayley. "You shouldn't be here, Miss Ryan. I meant for you to send Snow if you needed me." He took her arm and lead her to the corner.

"Have you found anybody yet?" she asked.

"I've been to half the saloons in town, and all I've found in most of them are Slowhand and Joe Duke."

"Sam, did Poppa ever say anything about having trouble paying the mortgage?"

"Most ranches have that problem occasionally, Miss Ryan."

"What about taking out a second loan last fall?"

"I don't know anything about it."

Kayley related what had happened at the bank.

"How much was it?" Sam asked when she finished.

"We have the tax money left and wages for the next six months."

Sam pushed his hat onto the back of his head and gave a low, incredulous whistle. "That was some loan payment."

"We still have the stallion's foals to sell," she said

and her hands reached out, as though grasping at straws. Her fingers closed on empty air.

"Those wages, do they include the job I'm hiring for?"

Kayley shook her head. "We'll have to make another cattle drive."

"By the time we round the herd up again and cut out the best steers and drive them north, the market will be flooded with herds from the other ranches, and the price will've dropped."

Kayley refused to blame her father for the situation she was facing. There had to be a reason he didn't make payments on the mortgage and the personal loan. It was Claude Asken's fault for demanding all the payments be made now. He'd whittled her money down so efficiently, carving away dollar after dollar with words like interest and penalties and processing fees, it was almost as though he'd planned it that way.

She stopped pacing, stood motionless for a second, then almost ran back to Sam. "We'll pay with cattle," she said, "a percentage of the herd. The quicker the tracker finds and stops whoever's causing our trouble, the more cattle we'll have to pay him with."

Sam frowned. "There's a lot of men who don't like getting paid in stock."

"But some who do."

"It'll be hard—"

"You'll find a man."

"I can't even—"

"You have to find a man."

"There might not be—"

"Sam, Poppa and I are depending on you."

He started to say something, closed his mouth and turned to look at the parade of placards crowding the sidewalk.

"Your job is depending on you," Kayley said.

He gave a rueful shake of his head and looked at her with laughter in his eyes. "Snow's right, you're getting too smart."

She grinned. "I learned from the best."

Jack slipped behind a placard that promised "At The City Beer Hall Not Only Can A Man Find Five Cent Beer, But He Can Try His Hand At The Sport Of Billiards—Or Prove His Skill In Our Shooting Gallery." Because it had so much to say, the placard was bigger than the others. But it wasn't as big as Jack, so he had to scrunch and hunch and bunch himself up like a wadded piece of paper to conceal himself from Kayley and Sam.

Although he was close enough to see the intensity on Kayley's face and the doubt on Sam's, Jack wasn't close enough to hear what they were saying. Kayley gave Sam a sudden smile. Then she lifted her pretty chin and began sashaying her way down the sidewalk, directly toward Jack.

He pulled his head behind the placard and tried to make himself even smaller. A man wearing so much fringed buckskin that he looked like a deer in fancy dress, stopped square in the middle of the sidewalk to stare at Jack's contortions.

So much for being inconspicuous, he thought and was about to give up the game when he saw Kayley edging around the buckskinned man. The mountain man's fringe was Jack's salvation. It acted as a protective veil, concealing him from her questioning glance. After she'd passed, he straightened up and offered his hand to his protector.

"My wife," Jack said with a grimace as he glanced after Kayley. "I owe you a beer, friend." They went through the swinging doors into the City Beer Hall a step behind Sam Butler.

Smoke choked the room, and the smell of stale beer choked Jack. He and his fringed friend made their way to the bar, which filled one entire wall of the saloon. In the rest of the room, cards were being slapped down on green felt tables, and pegged wheels were spinning.

"Set up a glass for my friend here," Jack said to the bartender.

He stayed on the lee side of the big man, using his size and fringe as cover while Jack watched Sam talk to Conway, the proprietor. Sam nodded, pulled his hat lower across his eyes and crossed the room to a table where two men were letting their tongues trip over a string of compliments to a tired-looking blonde wearing a red dress and a painted face.

While the men listened to Sam, the woman struck up a conversation with a fat man. He was seated at the next table and was wearing a diamond stickpin that sparkled like trouble in the dim lamplight. After Sam left the two men, they realized their girl had deserted them for brighter pastures. They abandoned their table, heading for the bar to drown their disappointment, and it wasn't coincidence that Jack was there to meet them.

"Let me buy you a drink," he said.

"Ain't saying no, just why?" one of the two asked while the other lifted two fingers to signal their order.

"Need an answer," Jack said.

He dropped two nickels on the bar and pushed them at the bartender through a puddle of spilled beer. The two men inhaled most of the contents of their glasses in one swallow. One wiped his moustache dry with his sleeve; the other let his moustache drip. Then they set their glasses down and looked at Jack.

"What did that hombre want?" He nodded in the direction of their abandoned table.

"What's it to you?"

"Just curious."

"That's a dangerous disease in these parts," said the man with the wet sleeve.

Jack pulled a twenty-dollar gold piece out of his vest pocket. "This is a remedy for that disease, and it'll put you back in that blonde's favor."

"It might do just that," the dripping man said. "It weren't nothin' secret nohow. He's lookin' to hire somebody good at trackin' down and stoppin' trouble. Conway sent him to us 'cause we're just up from Lincoln."

"You're trackers?"

"That's what they called us when we were riding east of the Pecos. In Lincoln, we're called Regulators." The wet-armed man grinned at his buddy and gave him a sharp jab with an elbow. "Let's go regulate that little lady, Chinspot."

Jack handed the gold piece to them, but didn't release it. "Did you take that man up on his offer?"

"We got work waitin' on us," the dripping man said, and the money fell into his outstretched hand. They drained the last of their beer and left in search of the red-skirted blonde.

Jack leaned his elbow on the bar and spun one of the empty glasses with the tips of his fingers. He'd watched the R Cross roundup through binoculars and knew the count was low. Kayley must've contacted Sullivan about that, and the problems on the ranch, although when or how Jack didn't know. He'd been watching her every move for weeks, and not once had she or any of her men gone near a telegraph or post office.

"Things must be a lot worse than I realized," Jack muttered to himself. "Otherwise, the old skinflint would never part with his precious pennies to hire professional help."

Fire, poison, rustling.

A government audit would take months to order and complete. Add a few more months for the grand jury to hand down an indictment against Sullivan, Asken, and the bank. Then it would go to the courts, where more time would be wasted.

Jack's only hope of getting the ranch back while it was still worth owning was to get the proof he needed against Sullivan from the bastard himself. The only way to do that was to beard the lion in his own den, and the easiest way to enter a den was by invitation.

Chapter Sixteen

Kayley sat on the very edge of the splintery seat of the very top row of the crowded grandstands at the Sante Fe Stock Auction. She didn't want Snow, who was sitting beside her, to know how nervous she was, so she tried not to figit. It was almost impossible for her to sit still, though, when Sam led the first of the eight foals sired by the white stallion into the bidding paddock.

"My word," Snow said with a sharp clap of his hands that sent Kayley's frazzled nerves into a quivering frenzy. "That colt looks so purty I feel like takin' my hat off to him."

"Nothing's that pretty," Kayley said, knowing that the old trail cook didn't even take off his hat with its decoration of lizard skins when he went to get his annual haircut. He just told the barber to cut anything sticking out.

The leggy, two-year-old colt was causing quite a stir among the bidders. He'd been curried until his white coat glistened like summer frost in early-morning light. His smoky eyes smoldered with intelligence and pride. As he paraded around the paddock, his muscles rippled with a promise of fluid speed that was so strongly reminiscent of his father, Kayley stiffened in a unexpected spasm of hate.

And yet it was on the white stallion's value as a sire that she was depending. If his offspring sold for even half of what she'd been unable to stop herself from hoping they'd bring, the unknown money troubles of the fast approaching winter wouldn't be nearly as frightening as they'd been yesterday when she left Claude Asken's office.

The white stallion's beauty and breeding, along with his ability to avoid capture by even the most skilled and determined mustangers, had made him famous throughout the Southwest. The R Cross hands had purposely leaked word several weeks ago in Socorro and Belen that several of the legendary stallion's foals were being offered for sale at the Santa Fe auction. Since then every trail, road and train into town had been crowded with interested buyers.

Now the fateful morning had arrived. The fairgrounds were overflowing with curious spectators, serious collectors of fine horseflesh, and several well-known renegades. While Sam Butler walked around the paddock with the high-spirited colt, the other R Cross men were keeping a close eye on the more famous members of the audience, among them the Apache Kid, Marino Leyba, and a man known to some as Sallie Parker, to others as Jim Lowe, and to still others as Butch Cassidy. There was even a rumor that Billy the Kid had been sighted in the crowd.

"He ain't here," Snow had said when they first

arrived at the fairgrounds. "If he was, the governor wouldn't be showin' himself around like he's doin' down there, not after the threats the Kid made to gun him down."

Even with one less thief to worry about, it was still a tense situation, and it reassured Kayley to see the familiar faces of the R Cross men among the crowd. She ached with pride that they cared so much about her father they were willing to sacrifice their own interests, which included not only a day of having fun, but also their own lives, to protect the foals.

The bidding for the colt was so fast and furious that it was difficult for Kayley to keep track of the offers. When the auctioneer banged his gavel down on the unbelievable final bid of two hundred dollars, she couldn't stop her hope from soaring as high as the lone white cloud that was drifting across the porcelain blue sky.

The next six foals went for prices that ranged from sixty to ninety dollars. Although the amounts weren't nearly as spectacular as that of the first sale, each crash of the gavel added to Kayley's growing excitement until she couldn't possibly sit still, and she began to twist and figit as the last foal was led into the ring.

This was Kayley's favorite of the stallion's offspring, a dainty-footed filly Sam had guessed to be barely weaned. The filly practically danced at the end of her lead as she was led around the ring.

"Looks like she's skippin' through dew," Snow said.

Like the first colt, the filly had inherited her father's spectacular white coat and dark eyes. Because she was still young, though, it was impossible to tell if she'd develop the long-legged potential of her older brother. As a result, Kayley expected the bids to be low, but wasn't prepared for the first offer made.

She directed a quick scowl of disapproval at the originator of the insulting one-dollar bid and felt the blood draining from her face. "Claude Asken," she whispered in disbelief, wincing at the bitter taste the name brought to her mouth.

"Twenty-five!" a man seated a few rows down from her shouted. She gave him a smile of thanks while the skinny auctioneer changed his staccato cries to accommodate the new bid.

"Twenty-six," Asken said. He sounded bored, and Kayley glared at him while he flicked something offensive from the sleeve of his black coat.

"Thirty!" was the next bid.

Asken immediately topped it, again by a single dollar, then bestowed on Kayley a mewling smile that caused his pencil-thin moustache to wriggle like a worm perched above his lip. She grasped the edge of the seat with sweating hands as she was gripped by a sudden nausea.

He lied about the loan being overdue.

The lie was there, easy for her to see in his twitchy eyes and disgusting smile, along with the fact that he was buying the filly only to irritate her and that he was using his position in the bank to intimidate the other bidders.

"ThirtyonethirtyoneIgotthirtyone!" the auctioneer cried. He stopped calling, mopped his florid face with a green bandanna and fixed the crowd with a questioning stare. "This here filly ain't no range

176

mustang, folks. She was sired by the same wild stallion as that colt bought by Señon Montoya of the High Chaparral. In my opinion, that makes her worth more than thirty-one dollars. So how about it, folks? Why don't you start taking this here auction seriously and let me hear them bids." He took a deep breath and began to call:

"DoIhearfiftyfiftyfifty?Nofifty?Howabout
fortyfivefortyfivefortyfive?Nofortyfive?
LetmehearfortyfortyfortydoIhearforty?
Thirtyfivethirtyfiveanybodythirtyfive?
ComeonsomeoneanyoneIwantthirtyfive!"

No one responded to his pleading efforts. He stopped, wiped his face again and raised the gavel, ready to signal the end of the bidding.

Kayley jumped to her feet and shouted, "One hundred dollars!"

Snow almost swallowed his chaw. "You're crazy as a sheepherder, girl!" he sputtered.

Sam's jaw fell open in surprise. Asken's smirking smile dripped off his face and the auctioneer knocked the podium over in his attempt to stop the gavel from descending.

He shaded his eyes and squinted up at Kayley. Then he frowned and motioned for her to sit back down. "You can't bid on your own animal, Miss Ryan."

A roar of laughter filled the stands. She could feel her body actually swaying under the impact of that wall of disapproving sound.

"Hey, girlie, why don't you go buy yourself a new

bonnet and let your menfolk handle this?'' a man shouted. "It's gonna be a long enough day without no females messin' things up!''

Her shoulders straightened. "I'm not trying to mess up the auction. I simply don't want to sell that filly to anyone who thinks he can buy a quality animal for a dollar.''

"Thirty-one dollars,'' Asken said. He was standing close to the paddock gate, ready to claim his prize.

"I wouldn't sell her to you even if you offered me a thousand and one dollars. Sam, get her out of there. I'm pulling her from the auction.''

The auctioneer held up his hand to quiet the crowd. "Once an animal is put under the gavel, Miss Ryan, it can't be withdrawn.''

She dropped the handfuls of skirt she'd gathered in anticipation of climbing down out of the grandstand. "I wasn't informed of that rule when I paid my entry fee.''

"Men don't need to be told!'' the heckler shouted.

"You need to be told something, mister, but I'm too much of a lady to do it,'' she responded, and the crowd roared again, only this time their laughter didn't attack her.

Snow gave a hoot and slapped his leg. "You made that old son shut his face so fast I'm bettin' he busted his gums!''

"Let's all settle down now,'' the auctioneer said. "Mr. Asken's bid is legal, Miss Ryan, so unless somebody out there wants to bid more'n thirty-one dollars before I can bang this gavel, I'm gonna be collecting his money.''

"I bids five hundred dollars for the little lady's

filly," said a man whose voice was so deep it was like a bass violin.

"Somebody's off their mental reservation," Snow said.

Kayley sat down so abruptly that the wind was knocked out of her. Claude Asken's moustache stopped wiggling at the same crooked angle it had been stuck in after his confrontation with Clay yesterday.

Kayley followed Asken's line of vision to where the source of that incredible bid was standing beside the cattle pens. It was the big-stomached man from the bank.

"He's big enough to hunt bears with a switch," Snow said, "and blacker'n my best skillet."

"What's your name?" the auctioneer asked.

"I don't recollects you askin' for no other names of peoples here today, Mr. Fast-Talking Man, buts my mama taught me to never argue with a white man holdin' a hammer, so I'll tells you."

Kayley was surprised by the way he spoke. The educated accent and stately poise she'd witnessed in the bank had vanished beneath a slur and a shuffle.

"On the night the Yankees tooks Atlanta, bless their blue-bellied souls, my gran'pap named me Jefferson Davis Abraham Lincoln Robert E. Lee Pollet, buts don't you worrys none about rememberin' all that. You can just call me 'boy' likes you was plannin' to anyway."

The auctioneer waved his gavel to quiet the hostile murmuring of the crowd. "I'll need to see your money before I can accept your bid, boy."

Because Kayley remembered the stack of bills Mr.

179

Pollet had deposited yesterday, she was the only one who wasn't surprised when he opened his wallet to reveal an equally huge pile of paper money.

He rifled it with his thumb like a deck of cards, then pointed a slender finger at Claude Asken. "Ifn you, Mr. Bank Man, is thinkin' of uppin' my bid by a dollar likes you done them other folks, I'll be warnin' you that come first thing Monday, I'll be at your bank to empty that account I just finished stuffin' full."

Asken huffed himself up like an indignant chicken. "My bank doesn't have any black depositors."

The bespectacled bank clerk stumbled out of the grandstand and hurried over to Asken to whisper in his ear. When he finished, Asken looked like an unstarched petticoat.

"I withdraw from the bidding," he said in a strangled voice. "And you," he said to the clerk, "can consider yourself fired effective whatever time yesterday you let him open an account! Get out of my way!" He shoved the clerk aside, spun around on the spiky heel of his boots and left the fairgrounds.

Kayley would have cheered if the mood of the crowd, which had been behind her only moments before, hadn't shifted. Cheering for the humiliation of the banker who controlled half the mortgages in the territory wasn't the way to get them back on her side.

Even though Snow was beside her and the other R Cross men were close by, she felt terribly alone. She huddled down, thinking if she could make herself small enough, she'd be invisible and unimportant and, maybe, less miserable.

"Five hundred's the top bid," the auctioneer said. He raised his gavel in the air.

"No!" Kayley shouted and jumped to her feet again. "Mr. Pollet, I can't let you do this, sir. That's a good filly, but she's not worth five hundred dollars."

"I knows that. Buts having a lady likes you callin' me sir yesterday, then again just now in fronts of all these peoples, that's worth more than all the money I gots, and that's a powerful lot."

"You can't buy respect, Mr. Pollet."

"I knows that, too."

"Then why?"

He looked at the money in his open wallet, then back up at her. "Maybe 'cause I can affords it. Maybe 'cause them Yankees that died the night I was borned showed my gran'pap how important it was to them that he was free." He closed the wallet and sighed. "Maybe just 'cause I don't knows why; I just knows I wants to do this. Let me, Miz Ryan. Let me do this."

A smile of gratitude was the only answer she could give him. Tears clouded her eyes, and her throat ached so deep inside that it hurt to even breath as the dancing white filly was lead away by the kindest gentleman in New Mexico, and maybe the whole world.

"That's a good man," Snow said, his drumming voice raspy with respect.

Kayley felt strong fingers closing about hers and looked up into Clay's familiar gray gaze. Her feelings of loneliness melted beneath his warm smile.

"What would you've done if your black knight hadn't salvaged the day with that spectacular last-round joust?" he asked while leaning so close to her

181

that she could feel the brim of his hat brushing hers.

"I would've had Sam shoot that filly right between the eyes."

Clay laughed. "I believe you would've, too. Snow, we'd better get her out of here before the fine upstanding citizens of Santa Fe start looking for a lynching tree."

"What for?" Kayley asked.

"Negroes might be free, kid; but they're not very well liked by some folks, and right now, neither are you. Besides, you're in imminent danger of making a complete fool of yourself."

"It's too late to prevent it. I can't believe I bid on my own animal."

"The friend I was sitting with when this started isn't impressed with fools, Kayley, and he was quite impressed with you today. If you can resist the temptation to break down and start crying right now, which is what I was referring to, he might even put you in his next book. Let's go," he said and began leading her down the grandstand through the uncooperative crowds.

"This here's almost as fun as bein' burned at the stake," Snow said from behind them, and Clay shot him a threatening look.

"What kind of book?" Kayley asked to distract Clay from Snow's antics and herself from the guilt that assailed her as she saw the worried faces of Sam and the rest of the R Cross men waiting for her at the bottom of the grandstand.

"The last one was about heroes," Clay said. "People who do what's right no matter what it might cost them." He lifted her down the final two steps, setting her before him and touching her trembling chin with a steadying finger. "Just like you, kid."

Leaving the fairgrounds was a frightening experience for Kayley. Although she felt safe with Clay and the R Cross ranch hands surrounding her like a protective barrier, she still saw and heard things she couldn't believe.

People stared and pointed at her, spoke sharp words and threatened to toss even sharper stones. And all because she'd called a black man sir.

She didn't take an easy breath until she, Sam and Clay were standing in the hallway outside her room in the Hotel Capitol. The rest of her men stayed in the lobby and on the street in front of the hotel, making certain no one tried to follow her.

"The boys and me will stand guard outside her room until we leave tomorrow," Sam said.

Clay was working Kayley's key in the lock. His hat was pulled low across his face, and the angled slices of light in the hall made only the left side of his unshaven jaw visible to her.

"You should change that departure to tonight," he said as he swung the door open and motioned for Kayley to enter.

"That's a good idea," Sam said. "It's best we cut our losses and run for home while we can still run. Most of the men are out of money anyway."

"Not anymore," Kayley said. "I want you to give each of them a twenty-dollar bonus out of the money you collect for me at the auction, and double that for yourself. As for running away, Sam, that's not your

183

style, and I don't want it to be mine. Besides, this furor will die down by this afternoon, and no one will even remember what happened, much less care that I was involved."

"I still think we should leave."

"The men were promised two nights in Santa Fe. On the way here all they talked about was spending the last night at that nice little club they thought was so special. I'm not going to deprive them of it."

"What nice little club?" Clay asked.

"The Cowhand's Social Club," Sam said in an undertone.

Clay suppressed what sounded suspiciously like a guffaw, and Sam's face, which had been aged beyond his thirty-odd years by a lifetime of looking at sunbright horizons, crinkled unexpectedly into a schoolboy grin that made Kayley wonder how many hearts he'd broken in his youth.

"The boys will be glad to know they have the approval of the boss on going there, Miss Ryan, and they'll appreciate having some cash to spend on the entertainment. I'll go tell Snow to bring your lunch up here to your room, then I'll be back to watch your door."

"I have to get McDonnell to the station by noon," Clay said, "but I'll stay with Kayley until you get back."

"I won't be long," Sam said and closed the door behind him.

Clay leaned against it and crossed his arms over his chest while he let his gaze travel from Kayley's face to her toes, then back up again.

He seemed to fill the room with his presence. She

was so very aware of him, and so very aware of him looking at her, that when she tried to take off her hat in front of the dressing table mirror, she almost impaled her thumb with her hatpin.

"How could such a small girl inspire so much animosity in such a peaceful town?" he asked in a teasing voice. "Did you take lessons in starting riots at school?"

She lifted her chin in anger and liked how that made her mirror-wavy reflection look more sure of itself. "I'm not a small girl, nor am I a kid, which you take such delight in calling me." She lifted her chin a little higher. "I'm a woman."

"That's impossible to tell from the dresses you wear."

She spread her hands open protectively across the full skirt of her dress. It was made of a red and gold plaid wool so soft it felt like thick silk. The high collar and neatly tucked bodice, along with the bright colors of the plaid, made her feel very stylish and continental.

"This is a wonderful dress," she said, disappointed beyond reason that he didn't like it, especially since she loved it so much. "It's exactly like the one that Marsha Watkins was wearing last year when she left Mrs. Potter's to join her parents on a trip to England. All the girls at school thought it was the most elegant dress they'd ever seen."

"The key word in that speech, Kayley, is girls."

A heavy knock at the door caused him to straighten up. He opened it enough to see who was there before swinging it wider. Kayley could see Sam in the hallway, but couldn't hear what he was saying. Then he turned and left, and Clay closed the door again.

"Sam has to take care of a little business on the outskirts of town. Since I can't leave you here alone, you'll have to suffer coming to the train with me to see Peters off."

"What business, and where are my father's other men? Can't one of them stay with me?"

She was casting about desperately for alternatives to being with him. Not because she didn't want to, but because she did, and that frightened her.

"Sam's taking the men with him," Clay said. "It might be cool on the ride to the station, so take a shawl. And, sweetheart, do me a favor and leave that ridiculous hat here."

First, her dress. Now her hat. She was becoming overwhelmed by her inability to overwhelm him.

"What's wrong with my hat?" she asked, and frowned indignantly at him because the petulant question made her sound exactly like the child he'd accused her of being.

"Everything," he said. "If you demand specifics, I'll say only that it hides your hair. Red hair is too rare in this part of the country to be kept hidden, especially when it's as lovely as yours."

He took the hat from her suddenly limp fingers and tossed it dramatically away from them. It sailed across the room like a straw bird and fell from sight behind the bed.

"Shall we go?" He tucked her hand into the crook of his arm. "We'll need all the time we can get to wrest Peters away from his mule."

They went into the hall, and while Clay closed and locked the door, Kayley asked, "Why did Mr.

186

McDonnell bring his mule to Santa Fe?"

"He rode it," Clay said.

He took her hand again, and her entire arm tingled with pleasant excitement.

"Peters wanted to see a friend of his in Golden, so we camped there overnight. That stupid animal ate every mouthful of the grain in his friend's barn. Peters cussed and fumed and threatened to shoot it, then gave it his supper." Clay shook his head in disbelief. "I didn't know mules ate beans."

The street outside the hotel was empty. There were no Spanish guitars playing, no children running, no wagons creaking and squeaking their way through town.

"How strange," Kayley said as she looked around.

"At least we won't have to fight our way to John Allen's."

Kayley didn't question Clay again, but his casual disregard for a reason to the unusually quiet street would have been more convincing if it hadn't been for how obviously he was keeping his gaze diverted from hers.

Chapter Seventeen

John Allen was the enterprising owner of a livery stable in Santa Fe. When the Atchison, Topeka and Santa Fe Railroad located its station for the New Mexico territorial capital in Lamy, a town eighteen miles southeast of Santa Fe, Allen took advantage of the railroad's delay in building a siderail to diversify his business.

Anytime of the day or night, he hired out his biggest and best livery wagon, with himself as driver, to transport passengers and baggage to and from the station. As a sideline to his service, Allen graciously rented blankets to his customers in cold weather and unbrellas in wet.

Kayley sat enthroned on the front row of passenger seats in Mr. Allen's wagon, wrapped by Clay in one of the blankets, because she'd forgotten her shawl, and holding one of the umbrellas, which he'd also insisted on renting, even though there wasn't a cloud in sight.

It was also much too warm for the blanket, a fact

Clay had overlooked. Kayley didn't mind his oversight, though, because after renting the unnecessary items, he'd spent several minutes tucking the blanket around her knees and adjusting the umbrella over her head so that it would protect her from the sun.

"You don't want freckles," he'd said with a smile that made her forget her continued curiosity over Santa Fe appearing to be deserted.

That had been ten minutes ago. Now Kayley, along with the angle of the umbrella, was beginning to wilt. Instead of protecting her from the sun, the canvas covering stretched across the thin wire spokes seemed to be magnifying it. The increased heat, coupled with the suffocating effects of the wool blanket, was giving her an excellent idea of what it must feel like inside an Indian sweathouse.

While she sweltered, Clay paced up and down the street beside the wagon, muttering curses at Peters, who was missing, and his mule, who wasn't. The ugly animal was following close behind Clay, making a great deal of noise by alternating bouts of braying with bouts of breaking wind.

There were two other passengers in the wagon waiting for the ride to the Lamy station. Both were nicely dressed gentlemen with bowler hats perched high on their balding heads and sample cases, which they were holding on to with fierce intent, tucked between their feet.

"Ready to give a quick display of their goods should a stray merchant wander by," Clay said to Kayley when he came over for the third time to adjust the angle of her umbrella. "Why are you sweating, kid?"

John Allen snapped shut the gold cover of his watch. "We gotta get movin' or we'll miss the train."

John Allen reminded Kayley of the scarecrow in Elda's vegetable garden at the ranch. Its stick legs and arms, and oversized head, had been a great source of amusement to the ranch hands, especially after a crow built a nest in its baggy pants. The crow had spent the entire summer with its greasy black head sticking out between the gaping buttons on the front of the sun-bleached denims.

"Please, can't we wait just another minute?" Kayley asked, her gaze fixed firmly on John Allen's face. "I'm certain Mr. McDonnell is on his way here now. He probably just wanted a last look at Santa Fe."

"Peters hates Santa Fe," Clay said. "He hates everything except this mule."

"We really must make this train," said the younger of the two gentleman. "My father and I have important business in St. Louis."

"We sell corsets," the older gentleman said. "Perhaps you're wearing one of ours right now, miss."

"I'm not even wearing my own corset," Kayley said, and was even more embarrassed by what she'd said than what he'd said. Her gaze flew to Clay's face. The way he was looking at her made her feel faint, and she flapped the edge of the blanket like a fan to cool her face.

"We also sell buttonhooks," his son said.

"She's not wearing one of those, either," Clay said, and Kayley bit back a laugh.

"They're hand carved," the younger gentleman

continued, oblivious to everything except his sales speech, "from the finest whale ivory in the world."

"Sperm whale teeth," Clay said. He shoved the mule away from him and fixed both gentlemen with a frowning stare. "Ivory is from walruses and elephants."

The older gentleman's face flushed, and his forehead began to sweat, causing his bowler hat to begin a slow slide forward. When it reached the pronounced arch of his eyebrows, it stopped.

"Perhaps," he said and peered at Kayley from beneath the lip of his hat, "I can interest you in purchasing one of our corsets. They're made of a whale's finest bones and are guaranteed for life."

"Whalebone," Clay said, "which is actually baleen, not a whale's bone. Your corsets would be the size of California if you used an actual bone from a whale."

The younger gentleman was sweating now, which was causing the slow descent of his bowler hat. Because his eyebrows were much less arched than his father's, Kayley wondered where the hat would stop.

"You certainly know a lot," John Allen said to Clay.

"Except where his friend is," the younger gentleman said. Kayley couldn't see his eyes at all now, and the hat was still descending.

"Yes, you don't seem to know that," his father added with a nod of his head that sent his hat crashing down over his brows and onto his nose.

"There he is!" Kayley cried.

And indeed, it was Peters. With his coattails flying out behind him and elbows flapping beside him, he looked like a chicken being threatened with beheading as he sprinted down the center of the street, holding a brown paper sack aloft and shouting, "Don't ye be leavin' without me, John Allen! Don't ye be leavin' without me! It's home to Scotland I'm goin' today, and I canna be late for me boat!"

"Your ship doesn't sail for a month," Clay grumbled. "It's the train you almost missed, you old fool." He gently lifted the skinny old man and deposited him beside Kayley.

"Where were you, Mr. McDonnell?" she asked.

Peters proffered his sack in explanation. "Peppermint," he gasped. "For me pet, Cleo."

Clay climbed into the wagon on Kayley's other side. He sat so close to her that his leg pressed against hers. She flapped the blanket faster.

"That mule's name is Cleo?" he asked in the most disgusted tone she'd ever heard. "Why would anyone name such an ugly animal Cleo?"

"Cleopatra," Peters wheezed. "She was a beautiful thing when I bought her, an' I named her after the queen of Egypt."

"That's ridiculous," Clay said.

"That's sweet," Kayley said.

"That's weird," the younger gentleman said.

"We're late," John Allen said. "And since we're havin' to take a different road than normal, we'll be goin' at a gallop. Hang on," he warned and, with a slap of the reins across the backs of his matched bays, sent the wagon hurdling forward.

"Why are we taking a different road?" Kayley shouted over the din of noise caused by the hooves of the horses, the rattling of the wagon, and the gasping brays of a galloping Cleopatra.

"The regular is the same road the lynch crowd took!" John Allen yelled over his shoulder as the wagon plunged into a ravine, rolling so quickly forward that it almost clipped the heels of the team.

Kayley found herself suddenly in midair with nothing to grasp hold of except the rented blanket. It was ripped from her hand by the screaming wind, and she was just beginning to panic when she felt Clay's hands encircle her waist, grabbing her back into the wagon and forcing her down onto the seat.

"I thought we'd lost ye, lass!" Peters pointed behind the wagon at his mule. "Cleo hasn't run this fast in two decades!"

"What lynch crowd?" Kayley asked Clay, who was still holding on to her.

"I can't hear you, kid! Too much noise!"

"I heard her!" the younger gentleman shouted. "A few citizens have taken it upon themselves to teach that uppity—" Clay's elbow slammed backward into the younger gentleman's face. "Ouch!" he cried, and the bowler hat flew up in the air. Cleo caught it on the fly.

"She didn't even break stride!"

"You hit my son!"

"It was an accident!"

"That mule's eating my hat!"

"Mr. Pollet," Kayley said in a horrified whisper. She turned on Clay. "That's where Sam went! They're trying to hang Mr. Pollet and Sam went to help him and you didn't want me to know!"

The wagon shot out of the forest and into the open.

In the distance was Lamy. Beyond its clutch of buildings was the train, looking like a giant black caterpillar curled between dark green mountains. Its presence at the station inspired John Allen to bring his team under control so that the wagon no longer felt like part of a stampede. The father and son salesmen showed their appreciation by giving a synchronized sigh of relief.

Kayley pounded on John Allen's back with the umbrella. "Take me to where they're hanging Mr. Pollet!"

Clay took the weapon away from her. "There's nothing you can do there except get in the way, kid."

"But, it's my fault this is happening."

"The problems of the world aren't your fault, Kayley."

His voice was so caring that the fight drained away from her. She felt limp and weak and sick, and she turned her face into the soft leather of his jacket. "This one is," she whispered, and his arms tightened around her.

"Don't worry, kid. Sam will save him."

She closed her eyes. In her mind, she saw a rope dangling from a tree and Mr. Pollet dangling from the rope. The kindness in his eyes and the gentleness of his hands were gone. Wasted. Because of her. Because she'd been too proud to let Claude Asken buy the white stallion's filly.

The white stallion. All her problems stemmed from that devil horse. His image appeared in her mind, too, an image so sharp and clear and so incredibly real that she sat abruptly upright and stared around her, fully expecting to see him standing nearby, breathing fire through flared nostrils and screaming hatred at her and at the world.

What she saw were towering mountains and the platform in front of the Lamy train station and Peters McDonnell trying not to look scared.

Clay's embrace had loosened the pins in her hair. He brushed several golden-red strands from her face and smiled. "Are you all right, kid?"

She thought of the moment when the white stallion's spirit would be broken and the dancing light in his eyes gone forever.

"Yes," she said and curled her hands into fists of anticipation. "I'm fine now."

Chapter Eighteen

Jack had to go almost to the end of the train to load Peters McDonnell's baggage. As he walked back to the platform, the intensity in the Scotsman's voice as he stood talking to Kayley caused Jack to quicken his step.

"I was scarcely more than thirty and three, lass, just a youngster. 'Tis harder on the young ones." Peters smacked his lips against his gums. "The lad here will tell ye that when ye be young and they turn that key in yer lock, 'tis no picnic."

"Here," Jack said. "You left this in the wagon." He thrust the sack of peppermints at Peters and took Kayley's hand to lead her away before Peters could impart more of his wisdom on her.

"Were you really in prison, Clay?"

Jack didn't answer. Instead, he slowly traced the delicate lines of her upturned face with his gaze until she blushed and lowered her eyes.

"I'm sorry. I had no right to ask that."

"The answer is yes, Kayley. I spent five years in

Lansing Prison."

"What did you do?"

He walked a short distance away from her. The mountains north of Lamy were the blue-green color of spruce and pine. They looked close enough to touch, if only he reached out his hand.

"I needed money and no one was lending, so I offered a man who didn't know the difference between a steer and a bull the opportunity to invest in my ranch. What he didn't know about ranching turned out to be less important than what I didn't know about him."

Jack turned and looked at her. He was sorry that he'd insulted her dress. Although the style was intended for a young girl, the red and gold colors were a perfect foil for her hair and her sun-bright complexion. She looked like a maple tree dressed in the colors of an early autumn.

My favorite season.

"What I didn't know, kid, was that my partner wanted more than a return on his investment. The day I collected enough from the sale of a herd to stop using red ink in our cashbook, he decided to collect on his investment by taking the ranch, my freedom, and almost my life."

"The scar on your back," Kayley said, and her face turned immediately red. "I saw you, I mean it, the scar, at the pond, on the mountain. You were shaving."

He gave her a slow smile. "I was also naked."

"Yes," she said, sounding like she was about to faint. "You were."

Jack slipped a hand around her waist. "Let's see

how Peters is holding up, kid."

The old Scotsman was squatting at the edge of the platform. Cleopatra was on the ground below him, eating the stick of candy he was holding out to her. She took the proffered peppermint in yellow teeth that were so chipped and broken it looked as though she was more used to eating rocks than candy.

Behind Peters, framing his silver hair with its black bulk, was an engine of the AT&SF railroad. It billowed and hissed and rattled and fumed in its impatience to be about the business of hauling its load through the winding mountains of northern New Mexico.

The wheels sparked on the tracks, flat cars groaned beneath their loaded weight of timber, and at the very rear of the train, the cattle cars, smelling of dung and dusty hides, crept closer to the Lamy station as the train lurched forward and stopped again, looking like a horse straining at the bit to begin a race.

"All aboard!" the conductor shouted above the screech of escaping steam. He gave a brief wave of his hand to the Lamy station manager before climbing into the railcar behind the mountainous stack of wood that fueled the engine.

Peters' fingers tightened on the stick of peppermint. He kept his eyes fixed on Cleo, who was taking tender bites of the candy.

"Are you ready?" Jack asked Peters. The Scotsman's knuckles turned white, but the peppermint didn't move out of the mule's reach.

"Last call!" the conductor cried. He'd walked back between two of the passenger cars and was standing on the steps, opening and closing the cover of his watch with anxious clicks. "If you're taking that mule, old timer, you should've had him loaded already."

Cleo finished the stick of candy with a popping crack of her teeth. Jack helped Peters to his feet. Cleo bolted up the ramp to the platform and butted her head against the Scotsman's shaking shoulders. He put an arm around her neck and pressed his face against her ratty mane.

"I have to go," Peters said. "I wrote me baby brother to get me room ready in the castle. I have to go. I can't be changin' my mind now; me brother would not understand."

"Do you own a castle, Mr. McDonnell?" Kayley asked. She took the bag of candy from him and fished a stick out for Cleo while Jack pulled Peters away from the mule and led him to the train.

"Not a very big one, but I'd not be wantin' to change the rushes every day. And 'tis not mine, 'tis me brother Raine's. It was to him I gave it when I went chasin' adventure." He grabbed Jack's arm. "You'll feed me mule, boy?"

"I'll treat her like a queen."

"She don't like boats."

"I won't put her on one."

"And she don't like bears."

"I won't put her on one of those, either. You have to get aboard, Peters." He peeled the old man's fingers off his sleeve.

"Where's the griz skin I want to be givin' me brother's wife?"

Jack pointed at the rear of the train. "In the baggage car. The conductor thought it was a live

199

grizzly and almost died of fright, so I wrapped it in a tarp. Your name's pinned on both the tarp and the skin, so don't worry about it getting lost."

"I must go. I promised Raine."

"It's all right, Peters. I'll take care of Cleo."

"And I'll see to it she gets all the candy she wants," Kayley said.

"Not too much! 'Tis a terrible racket she'll be makin' if she gets the colic."

"She must have it all the time," Jack said. "Stop yammering, old man, and get aboard before the train leaves without you." The train seconded his suggestion by expelling a great breath of steam that drowned out Cleo's suddenly frantic brays.

Peters started to step onto the bottom step of the last passenger car. He stopped and turned instead to lay a hand on the side of Kayley's face. "There's no need for you to be thinkin' that ye must pay for what yer father's done, lass. Do like I've been tellin' the lad here, and leave the past be."

Jack shoved Peters into the car. "Good-bye," he said firmly. "And good riddance," he muttered before taking a firm grasp of Kayley's arm to drag her away.

She pulled free and ran down the platform after the fast-retreating Scotsman. "What did you mean? What did Poppa do?"

"I'm glad the boy has ye to be pinin' for, lassie! Mayhaps now he'll act like a man instead of that sour-tempered bull he took from ye!" Peters' head was bombed by cinders as he thrust it as far out the window of the car as his bony shoulders would allow. "Take care of me mule, Jack, me boy! Good-bye,

Cleopatra, me darlin' girl, I'm missin' ye already! Scotland, here I come!"

Cleo stopped braying and began to howl like a demented dog. Jack grabbed her bridle just before she could leap between two freight cars. The rapid-fire sound of pistols was added to the symphony of noise the train, Kayley, Peters and Cleo were causing.

"Hold up! Hold the train!"

Two horses were stampeding in the direction of the station down Lamy's main, and only, street. Their riders kept firing their pistols in the air as the horses galloped up onto the platform, almost knocking down the station manager, who was removing cinders and mule manure from a bench.

"I got another passenger for you!" one of the dusty, sweat-soaked riders shouted to the shoveling manager.

As the rider dropped his pistol into his holster, Jack recognized him as Sam Butler. The other man was easier to recognize, not just because of his black face, but because of his ponderous girth.

"Mr. Pollet!" Kayley cried and threw herself into Jefferson Pollet's arms the moment he dismounted.

The white filly's lead was tied to Sam's saddle horn. "Give me a hand here, Clay. This rope got tangled in the fray."

"Pollet, hold on to this mule for me."

The big man set Kayley from him and reached for Cleo's harness, revealing a bloody welt on the back of his hand.

Kayley's face went completely white. "They whipped you."

"He's also got a nasty rope burn around his neck,"

Sam said. "We got to him just in time to keep it from becoming fatal."

Jack untangled the rope and led the filly away from the sweating saddle horses. She looked as fresh as she had in the paddock that morning.

"It doesn't hurt too much, Miss Ryan," Pollet said. "Even if it did, being whipped is better than being hung."

"If you're going on this train, boy, you'll have to jump onto one of the cattle cars when they come by," the station manager said. "You can move up and pay for your ticket at the next station."

"I'm sorry," Kayley said. "I'm so sorry all this happened, Mr. Pollet. I should've let Mr. Asken have the filly."

Pollet released Cleo and grabbed Kayley by the shoulders. "Don't ever be sorry for doing what you know is right, Miss Ryan."

"But you were hurt and the men—"

"The boys are fine," Sam said. "They've been snarling for a fight ever since they hit town, and this suited them just fine. Pollet's alive, and he has a first-rate filly for his daughter; so everything worked out fine."

"That's who I bought her for," Pollet said. "Shani, that's my baby girl. She's in Atlanta with her mama and my mama. Whenever I travel on business, I bring back something special for my girl. This little pony is the best present yet."

"What business?" Kayley asked. "I've wondered about that ever since I saw you at the bank with all that money."

"Ask your foreman after I'm gone." Pollet handed

Kayley over to Jack. "You'd better take good care of this little girl, mister, or I'll be coming back to take care of you." Pollet lifted the filly like she was a sack of grain and, with surprising speed, ran down the platform and jumped into the last cattle car before it moved out of reach. "By the by, son, that mule of yours sure is ugly!"

The train pulled itself out of sight around a forested bend, leaving only a trail of soot hanging in the air. The station manager heaved the last pile of mule droppings off into the street and went inside to answer the tapping of the telegraph machine.

"What business is Pollet in, Sam?" Jack asked.

"You're not going to believe it." He picked up the trailing reins of the two exhausted horses and walked with Kayley and Jack down the platform ramp. "He's a bank robber."

Kayley's eyes grew wide. "A what?"

"A bank robber, Miss Ryan. He robs a bank, then goes to a town where he's never been before and opens an account into which he deposits exactly half of what he stole; then he heads home to Georgia. He said the accounts are for his retirement, and he's lost count of how many he's got scattered around the country."

"What about his stomach?" Kayley asked. "It would be easy to find a bank robber described as having the biggest stomach in the world."

"It's false," Sam said, "just like the act he put on in front of the crowd this morning. He says acting like white people expect a black man to act makes him invisible to them. When he's not robbing banks, he stuffs a half dozen or so pillows in his underwear. He

203

claims that there's not a sheriff in the whole world stupid enough to arrest a man with a stomach that big for a robbery committed a week earlier by a man without a paunch. He also drops his accent and dresses in expensive clothes. Bank robbers aren't known for making themselves conspicuous, and so again he becomes invisible, this time to the law."

Jack laughed. "That's the slickest thing I ever heard."

"No wonder Miss Ryan got along so well with him," Sam observed.

"What do you mean?" she asked.

"Pollet reminds me of your father, crooked as the day is long but a lovable rascal."

"Why is everyone picking on my father today? First Mr. McDonnell, now you, Sam. Poppa isn't a bank robber. He's a rancher."

"What did he do before that?" Jack asked. "And just what is he doing now?"

"I don't know, except that it wasn't, I mean isn't, robbing banks."

"Maybe he's charming lonely women into letting him steal their husband's money." Jack watched her closely for any reaction that would reveal how much she knew about her father's past. Her only reaction, though, was a crinkling of her pretty nose.

"If you don't stop teasing me, Clay, I'm going to give Cleopatra this entire bag of candy, and then you'll be up all night with a colicky mule."

"That mule's name is Cleopatra?" Sam gave a hoot of laughter. "That's funnier than Pollet being a bank robber."

"I think he was just pulling your leg, Sam,"

Kayley said. "And as for this mule, I'm not really sure her name is Cleo. Mr. McDonnell called her that, but he also called Clay by the wrong name."

Jack stopped so suddenly that Cleo bumped into him. "Peters was upset. He just used the wrong name."

"That's what I said," she replied with a lift of her chin. "Besides, you look less like someone named Jack than that mule looks like Cleopatra."

Jack almost kissed her in relief. Instead he gave Cleo a pat on the head. The mule responded by lifting her tail in a perfumed echo of the train's distant whistle.

Chapter Nineteen

Jack held on to Kayley to keep her from being bounced out of the wagon as John Allen brought it to a skidding stop in front of his livery stable. The R Cross hands were waiting by the corral. They hurried to the wagon and lifted Kayley down among them.

Their faces were bruised, their noses, lips and knuckles stained with dried blood. They were wearing ripped shirts and dirty pants, scuffed boots and crushed hats. And all of them, to a man, sported a grin wider than the Rockies.

Kayley looked small and defenseless in their unruly midst, and she greeted the outrageous lies being told her with just the right mixture of fear, astonishment, and laughter.

One story, which involved the cutting of the rope around Jefferson Pollet's neck by Joe Duke, who'd risked his own dusky neck by joining in the fight, affected Kayley so much she laid her hand on Duke's arm in genuine concern as he told his tale.

The other men immediately began to elaborate on

their own stories until soon not even the prose of the most imaginative dime novelist in New York could've matched the amazing acts of death defying heroism these cowhands had performed. When they ran out of both breath and lies, Sam came to the rescue.

"The marshal locked up the troublemakers that we didn't knock senseless, Miss Ryan, which means that you won't need a guard anymore, so I'm going to take the boys over to the Social Club for a drink."

Kayley waited until the last cowboy had touched the brim of his hat to her and strutted away before coming to stand beside Jack, who was helping John Allen unhitch his team.

"After talking to my father's men, I'm glad you kept me away from Mr. Pollet's hanging," she said.

"They were lying, Kayley."

"I know." She leaned her head back against the side of the wagon and smiled at the sky. "And I know that whatever they really did to save Mr. Pollet was brave and wonderful. If I'd been there, they'd have spent the rest of the day trying to convince me it was nothing. Because I wasn't there they can brag about being heroes, like your friend writes about, instead of being just plain cowhands who did someone a good turn. It'll be more fun for them to spend their last night here as heroes."

Jack stopped unbuckling straps to stare at her. It was hard to believe anyone who would wear a ridiculous straw hat like she'd had on that morning could be so smart. *And beautiful*, he thought, noticing for the first time that when she smiled, a tiny dimple appeared in her left cheek.

He turned his attention back to the harness straps but couldn't remember if he'd been closing the buckles or opening them.

"Do you really know Governor Wallace, Clay, or were you just trying to impress Mr. Asken yesterday?"

All thoughts of her dimple disappeared as Jack's head snapped around and he fixed her with an unblinking stare.

"What did you say?"

"I was in the bank when you were yelling at Claude Asken, and I overheard you say that you had breakfast with the governor. Did you really?"

Jack wondered what it would feel like to put his hands around her slender throat and squeeze. He balled his hands into fists.

"What else did you hear, Kayley?"

Clay looked so very frightening and threatening as he stood there, hands clenched into fists as he leaned over her with lightning flashing in the pale silver of his eye that Kayley almost swallowed her tongue.

"Ju-just that," she stuttered. "Then you left but you didn't see me because I was on the bench behind the office door so when you came out you couldn't see me." She tried to stop, but the words just kept pouring out of her, all stuck together like dolls cut from a piece of folded paper. "I was there because Mr. Asken sent my father a letter last month saying it was urgent that Poppa come see him but Poppa was away on business so I came instead and that's why I was there and how I heard you yelling at him."

She stopped because she was completely out of breath, and because she'd bitten the inside of her lip and her mouth was filling with the unpleasant taste of blood.

"I yelled at him, too," she added as an after-thought.

Clay looked confused. "Your father?"

"Mr. Asken."

"He's a jackass."

She looked down at her empty purse. "I know."

"So here you are!"

Kayley looked up to see Snow limping across the street. She ran to help him. When they reached the livery wagon, Snow almost collapsed against it, wheezing and blowing and pulling on his hat.

"What happened to your foot?" Clay asked.

"It was them vittels Sam sent me to fetch for Miss Ryan. The cook at the hotel ladled up some soup that looked like it was made from dirty socks."

"And you couldn't resist telling him," Kayley said.

"I mighta said somethin', but nothin' that would embarrass a Sunday go-to-meetin' crowd. When you wasn't in your room, I took that runny soup back to the kitchen, and that worthless cook asked what was wrong, did I get lost; and I said the problem was his cookin' wasn't fit for no lady and I wasn't gonna offer it to you."

"Just to put him in his place," Kayley said.

"That's right. He didn't take kindly to it, though, and flung a meathook at me." Snow pointed at his right boot. A wicked tear marred the worn leather. "Dang near took off my big toe!"

"What did you do?" Clay asked.

"Only thing I could do. I shot him."

"Snow!" Kayley cried and grabbed his arm. "Tell me you didn't!"

"I did, but I didn't kill him. Just let a little wind out of his saddle. But the hotel people took it bad, and they sent for the sheriff. I waited around for him, and when he didn't show up, I left." He stomped his right foot in the dirt. "Don't hurt so much anymore. Guess I ain't crippled after all."

Kayley didn't know whether to laugh or reproach him for taking such chances. Instead of doing either, she told him about the lynching and how the R Cross men had saved Jefferson Pollet.

"I missed all the fun! Where are they now?"

"Sam took them to that nice little club on the other side of the stockyard," Clay said.

Snow frowned in confusion, then snorted out a laugh. "I got you, son. Now, don't you worry none, Miss Ryan, I won't get so drunk that I can't hit the ground in three tries." His injured foot raised a cloud of dust in the street as he limped away at great speed while singing, "Mississippi Sue, I'm a comin' to see you, so don't be blue, Mississippi Suuuuuuue!"

She winced as Snow belted out the next verse of his song, which had to do with someone called French City Lannie and what he was going to do her—

"I wonder why they like it?" Kayley asked, almost shouting the question to drown out Snow.

"The social club?" Clay asked.

"I know why they like that," she said, casting a look after Snow, "even though they think I don't. It's drinking I don't understand."

"I take it your father doesn't let you drink his whiskey."

"I've never even tasted sarsaparilla," she said and felt trapped by the sudden intensity of Clay's gaze.

210

"Have supper with me tonight," he said.

She couldn't think with him looking at her like that. He moved closer to her, his legs pushing into the folds of her skirts so that she could feel the press of them against her own legs. She looked up at him, at the unshaven chin, the cruel fullness of his lips, the rugged, almost harsh, shape of his cheekbones, the black patch over his left eye and the long lashes that framed his right eye like sooty silk.

He wasn't at all like Vance. He wasn't like anyone she'd ever met, or anyone she'd ever dreamed about.

"Please," he said; and though he didn't kiss her, or even try to, her eyes drifted closed, and she felt the hot memory of his kisses pressing down upon her.

"Yes," she whispered, and felt his smile.

Chapter Twenty

The night was crisp and clear, and it smelled of pine needles and moist earth. Jack stopped the rented buggy at the edge of a small meadow near the Santa Fe River. The wind, which held a chilling promise of the coming winter, pushed at the edges of his shirt collar, tussled with the manes of the horses and painted Kayley's face the color of excitement.

The mountain grasses were moist with dew that sparkled almost as brightly as the lights of Santa Fe nestled in the valley below, and it dampened Jack's pantlegs as he crossed to the other side of the buggy.

Kayley laid a hand on his shoulder as he lifted her down beside him. Her head was tilted back, and her eyes were wide as she stared at the sky spangled with silver stardust.

"I used to dream about standing under a sky like this," she said. "The window in the dormitory at my boarding school opened onto such a small piece of it. I watched the stars crossing it every night, and I wanted to go with them and see what wonderful place they were rushing away to."

Jack spread a blanket near the center of the meadow, set the picnic basket down and dropped down beside it, stretching his legs out and crossing his feet at the ankles. With his head propped up on his hand, he watched Kayley turn in a circle with her arms spread open as though she were trying to embrace the sky.

"Are you hungry?" he asked.

"Starved."

"A lady should never admit to being starved."

Her laughter shimmered like the starlight. "Nor should she go unchaperoned into the wilds of northern New Mexico in the middle of the night to share supper on the top of a mountain with a man who stole her father's best bull."

"It's not the middle of the night, and I didn't steal Toro; I acquired him in payment of a debt."

Her dress was ivory wool. Soft and clinging, it flowed like sweet cream, swirling gently around her as she came to him through the wet grass.

Jack lit the candle he'd taken from the basket while Kayley sat beside him, curling her legs beneath her so that her skirts spread out between them like a saucer of milk. The candlelight tamed her crimson hair into a red as rich and fine as expensive burgundy wine, and her eyelashes cast entrancing shadows across her delicate cheekbones.

She caught a droplet of wax sliding down the side of the candle. "Beeswax?" she asked.

"Spermaceti, kid. You'll have to look elsewhere for

your arsonist.''

She blushed. "I just wondered." She smiled. "This is nice, Clay. I'm glad you didn't listen to me at the hotel.''

When she'd first learned of his plans for their evening, she'd refused to go. "You're crazy; it's dark and there might be bears out there!"

"Of course there'll be bears out there. Where else would they be? There will also be mountain lions and wolves and coyotes and Indians plotting to add our scalps to their collections.''

"Then, why do you want to go?"

"Because it'll be fun.''

Laughter had been her only answer, that and the trusting touch of her hand on his arm as they left the hotel. The light pressure of her fingers had sent his head reeling, and he'd almost hit a man who'd smiled and tipped his hat to her outside the hotel.

"What's that delicious smell wafting from your basket?"

"Let's see," he said and began sorting through the basket. "The Bon Ton Restaurant has provided us with enough fried chicken to feed an entire army. The bread's from the City Bakery. I can't remember where I got the cheese, just that there were two children playing hide and seek behind the pickle and cracker barrels.''

As he named each item, Jack set it out on the blanket. The place he'd chosen to display his wares was so far away from Kayley that she had to almost lean across him when she reached to break off a tiny piece of the cheese.

214

He took quick advantage of her disadvantage by kissing the top of her head. Her hair smelled like wild clover. He closed his eyes and allowed his lips to linger for a moment before pulling away.

"The pears are courtesy of Pentland's Fruit Confectionery Shop," he continued in a voice that had been more than a little affected by her closeness, "along with an assortment of sweets for dessert, although it's not cake or candy that I crave."

He winked at her. She didn't react to his flirting, though, and he realized that because of his eyepatch, a wink looked just like a blink.

Another reason to hate Sullivan.

"That's all we have," he said, "except for two bottles of wine, an assortment of crystal, linen, china, and silver. Wait, I almost forgot. There is something else."

He lifted from the basket a huge white flower with a pale yellow center that looked dark gold in the candlelight. The edges of the petals fluttered like butterflies as he laid the flower in Kayley's lap.

"Clay," she whispered, the word catching in her throat. "I've never seen anything so beautiful."

"It's an orchid. Quite rare, I understand, and a favorite of Mr. Elster, who grew it."

She brushed the flower against her cheek. "It's so soft."

Jack opened the wine, tasted it, then poured a glass and handed it to her. She crinkled her nose at its heady aroma and looked at him with a suspicious frown.

"Is it supposed to smell like this?"

215

"That smell is called a bouquet."

She took a sip and grimaced. "It must be an acquired taste, like Snow's barbecue sauce."

"By the time we finish the first bottle, you'll love it," Jack said.

In fact, he added silently, *I'm counting on you loving it quite a lot.*

He's right, Kayley decided as the last drop of wine from her third glass slid onto her tongue. "I do love it," she announced before handing her glass to Clay. She pushed a finger into the bread crumbs on her plate. "And I'm not a lady," she confessed. Her lips felt strange. Words stuck to them, tripping and falling and stumbling around like a bee drunk on nectar. "Because I ate so much," she added, rushing to finish the thought before she forgot what she'd been saying.

Clay filled her glass from the newly opened second bottle of wine. "There's more chicken."

"If I ate anything else, my corset laces would pop, except I'm not wearing any."

"Laces?" he asked with a lift of an eyebrow.

"Corset," she replied and fanned her face with her hands. "Vance wouldn't approve of me telling you that. He's a gentleman, you know."

"Is he?" Clay was lying beside her on the blanket, one hand propping his head up, the other exploring the folds of her skirt.

"Yes," she said with an affirmative shake of her head that sent hairpins scattering into the night. "I

216

don't know if I like gentlemen." She tried to push her hair back into shape. It insisted on falling through her clumsy fingers, and she let it go so she could concentrate on holding on to her wine, which was trying to slide out of the glass and onto her fingers.

"Kayley," Clay said, and she forgot about the wine to look at him instead.

The candle was almost out, its tiny flame flickering in a wild panic as it consumed the last of the wick and tried to survive on melted wax. The dying light softened the lines of his face, making him less intimidating and more handsome. The last flicker of the candlelight was bright and sudden, then it was gone, plunging them into the midnight-blue night where the only light was from the stars and a crescent moon.

She reached to touch his eyepatch. Her fingers were hungry to know what secrets it concealed. He captured her hand in his, turned it over and pressed a kiss to her palm. Wine splashed over her other hand, and she laughed as it dripped onto the blanket between them.

"I spilled some," she said, and then spilled more as he slid one of her fingers into his mouth.

"Tell me what you heard at the bank, Kayley."

His tongue began to do strange and delightful things to her fingertip.

"I—I heard you."

"What was I saying?"

"You said, I heard you say, you had breakfast, with the governor."

He was kissing her wrist now, turning his face and

hair into the embrace of her open palm while he moved his lips around the cuffed edge of her sleeve.

"Is that all you heard?"

"Something about a bribe," she managed to whisper. "Did you bribe the governor, Clay?"

He wrapped her cascading hair around his hand and pulled her down to him. "No, Kayley, I didn't bribe the governor."

"Did you bribe Mr. Asken?"

"I didn't bribe him, either."

The mother-of-pearl buttons on her dress opened easily beneath his exploring touch, and he pushed the soft wool aside, exposing her breasts to the night wind and the glittering brilliance of his piercing gaze.

"Who did you bribe, Clay?"

"Joseph Elster," he said, and kissed the hollow at the base of her throat.

"Who's that?"

"He grew the orchid. Give me your wine, Kayley."

He released her hair and took the glass from her. He dipped a finger in the ruby-red liquid and wet her lips with it. He dipped again and trailed a finger down the sensitive skin of her throat. He dipped his finger into the glass a third time and traced a path across the curve of her breasts where they pushed against the lacy edge of her camisole.

"Silk," he said and slid his finger onto the ivory lace. "Are you cold?"

Kayley was shivering so hard that she couldn't speak. She nodded her head.

He sat up and put his arms around her. "Is that better?"

His silver-gray eye was like a star shining above her. She realized that she was lying on the blanket beside him, nestled close to the long line of his body.

"I think I had too much to drink, Clay. I don't remember lying down."

He licked the wine from her lips. Chills raced through her. She pressed against him for warmth.

"Why is the desk at the ranch kept locked, Kayley?"

"My father kept it locked."

He ran a finger along the moon-bright tracing of wine on her breasts.

"Where's the key?"

"Clay!" she cried as his lips followed the path of his finger. His breath was hot and moist as he touched a kiss to the rigid peak of first one nipple, then the other. "This isn't right," she said, and he moved his kiss to her mouth.

His lips were barely touching hers. "Don't you want me to kiss you?"

"No," she said and raised her head to press the word against his mouth. His hand moved onto her waist, down across her hips. His fingers caught in the folds of her skirt, raising it slowly, pulling it up and up, higher and higher while he kept teasing her with his tongue and his lips and his mouth, not giving to her, not taking, just tasting and teasing and touching.

"Where's the key, Kayley?"

His hand was on her leg now, at the top of her stocking. Warm flesh against bare thigh. Not moving, just resting there, just touching. His hand moved, just a bit, just a little, slipping up higher, making her quiver beneath him, making her gasp for breath.

He kissed her, making her mind spin faster than the world beneath her and the sky above her. She closed her eyes and fell into that spinning void, opening herself to the searching thrust of his tongue and the hot taste of his mouth.

When he stopped kissing her, she realized that his hand had moved still higher. It was so close now, so very terribly close to the pulsing center of her that she couldn't breath.

And he was kissing her nipples again, pulling a silk-covered peak into his mouth and stroking it with his tongue and warming it with his breath, ragged and fast, the way his heart was beating, the way hers was beating.

His fingers played with the tender skin of her inner thigh while his kiss moved slowly across her wine-sweetened breasts, onto her throat, hesitating above her mouth, his tongue touching the tips of her teeth.

His hand moved suddenly higher. "The key, Kayley, where is it?"

She couldn't think, couldn't breathe. His fingers were brushing across her private curls, tormenting her, tantalizing her.

"In my room."

"At the hotel?"

"The ranch," she said, and her body arched suddenly upward, shaking and quivering as he touched the moist heat of her need.

It had been a light touch, barely anything at all, and yet enough to cause her to gasp and moan and clutch at him, holding him, pulling him closer, feeling beneath the leather vest he wore that his shirt was wet with sweat and his muscles tight with tension.

She buried her face against his neck and breathed in the hot smell of him. "Why are you asking me these strange questions?"

He moved his hand from her leg to the forgotten glass of burgundy. "You need another drink," he said and poured the ruby-red liquid into his mouth. Then he lowered his lips to hers, and she drank the wine from his kiss.

"Kayley, are there any white cashbooks in your father's desk?" Jack asked, but the last drink of wine had been too much for her. She'd fallen asleep in his arms.

He lowered her onto the blanket and ran a hand through his damp hair. Her lips glistened with the lingering wetness of his kiss. A desperate need to taste again their wonderful sweetness grew within him. He jumped to his feet with a muttered curse and began pacing around the quiet meadow.

"It doesn't mean anything that she affects me like this. It's just all those years in prison."

All those nights of dreaming, his mind whispered.

"About revenge!"

Every night?

"I'm a man."

And she's a woman.

He paced faster, his heart and body at war with his hate, his mind full of images of prison and Sullivan and the perfect softness of Kayley's skin.

"I'll break into the desk."

Nonsense, his mind said. *Get her to give you the key. She'll do anything you want. Just ask her.*

Jack stopped pacing and turned to look at Kayley. She was curled on the blanket, her eyes closed, and her lower lip pouting in sleep. She looked too peaceful to be drunk. Was she just pretending, the way her father had pretended the night he lured Jack into the alley in Abilene?

Sullivan had become staggering drunk during their celebration of the successful cattle drive. He'd been slurring his words and had bumped so violently into the corner of the saloon they'd just left that he'd practically fallen into the alley. Jack had followed his partner into the shadowed darkness, expecting to find the old drunk sprawled in the mud.

Instead, he'd found the sharp end of a knife. It had plunged quickly and deeply into his back, slicing and stabbing and digging for his kidney. Then it had slashed at his face, and the last thing Jack remembered seeing that night were Sullivan's blue eyes aflame with greed.

Kayley was holding the orchid in her hands. The wind was pushing at the delicate flower, trying to tug it out of her grasp. Jack saw her fingers tighten around its slender stem, and he knew the truth.

He threw aside the empty glass he'd been clutching in his own stiff fingers and crossed the meadow in long strides that brought him quickly to her side. He knelt, smashed the flower in his fist and jerked Kayley off the blanket and into his arms.

"Let's see if you can pretend to sleep through this," he said and crushed his lips against hers. He thrust his tongue deep into her mouth, plunging fast and hard, hurting, angry thrusts intended to punish her for everything that her bastard father had done to him.

But it wasn't hate Jack felt as he plundered her lips. It was something else, something frightening that grew stronger within him as she began to respond to his brutal kiss with a hesitant gentleness that gave way to a burning eagerness that made Jack forget everything except how much he wanted her and needed her and how he was going to have her, right here on top of this mountain, so close to the stars and the moon that they were almost a part of the sky itself.

Her tongue pressed against his, sparring and circling, teasing and exciting. Her lips nibbled at his, her teeth tasting and biting, her hands caressing his back, his shoulders and neck. Her breasts pushed against his chest, softness against steel, silk against leather. Her fingers slipped into his hair, into the tangle of rawhide laces that held his eyepatch in place.

And her legs, those long, delicious legs that he'd first seen encased in sweaty denim and dirty chaps, they wrapped slowly, sensuously, around his, holding him captive in a possessive embrace that made him shudder with desire.

She wrenched her mouth from his and let her head fall back onto the blanket to draw a gasping breath between her bruised and swollen lips.

Jack wanted her more than he'd ever wanted

anything in his life, and he pushed his hips tight against hers, letting her feel the swollen, hard surge of his need.

"Clay!" she cried, and he lifted his face into the breath of the wind, letting her cry surround him.

She raised her head and laid her cheek against his. "Clay," she said again, this time whispering the word so softly that if his ear hadn't been pressed close to her lips, he wouldn't have heard the gentle sound.

"What is it, my love?" he said, turning his head to feel her answer against his lips.

"I'm going to be sick."

Chapter Twenty-One

The sky grew dark with clouds on the drive back to Santa Fe. Kayley didn't look at Jack once during the nine-mile ride, nor did she speak. When they reached her hotel, she didn't put her hands on his shoulders as he lifted her down from the wagon or take his arm when he offered it.

She looked pale in the bright hotel lights and didn't seem to even notice the boisterous crowd that had spilled out of the bar and into the lobby where the low ceiling turned their laughter into noise and conversation into chaos.

Jack stayed in the shadows near the front door of the hotel, searching the room for familiar faces and seeing appreciative glances follow Kayley to the registry desk, where she collected her room key. Jack moved quickly to join her, letting everyone know she was under his protection by putting his hand on her waist.

In the hall outside her room, she tried repeatedly to fit her key into the lock. Finally she stopped and pressed her forehead against the door.

"I'm so ashamed that I got sick."

So that's what's upsetting her.

"Don't worry about it, kid. It happens to the best of us. Half your crew will be throwing up tomorrow morning, and the other half will be too sick to try."

He took the key from her, opened the door and leaned a shoulder against the doorframe to prevent her from entering.

"It did happen to you at a most inopportune moment, however," he said and touched a finger to her lips. "I was just starting to have fun."

"How could that be?" she asked and slipped past him into the room. "There weren't any bears or mountain lions, and not a single scalp-collecting Indian showed his face all night." Mischief danced in her eyes.

"There was a rather lonely coyote, though," he said and threw a piercing howl at the ceiling, which needed painting.

Someone in a nearby room banged on the wall. "There's no dogs allowed in here!"

"Snow told me that coyotes were lying, deceitful, treacherous animals. I can't imagine you behaving like that, Clay."

The dark horror of Lansing Prison had turned Jack into just such an animal. "Why not?" he asked, almost snarling the words.

"Because you didn't ravage me."

His anger disappeared in his sudden laughter. "Ravish, sweetheart, not ravage. And who knows what might've happened up on that mountain if you hadn't decided to throw up everything you'd eaten

226

for the last week."

"It was your wine that made me sick!"

"That's a relief. I thought it might've been my kisses."

She blushed, and her gaze shied away from his. He put a finger beneath her chin and forced her to look at him.

"Thank you for tonight," she said.

He slid his thumb along the curve of her lower lip. "You're welcome, kid."

She pushed the door partly closed, then stopped and met his gaze again. "Why was my father's loan file on Claude Asken's desk when you were in his office?"

Jack managed a casual shrug in spite of the caution that gripped his shoulders. "Was it?"

"He wasn't expecting me; yet there it was. And it was open."

"He wasn't expecting me, either."

Jack remembered with pleasure the expression on Asken's face when he recognized his surprise visitor. It hadn't been an expression of surprise, though, and Jack realized that the news of his release must have preceded him.

"He did say it was a coincidence that I was there," Kayley said. "Maybe he had the file out so he could write to my father and warn him."

Jack's nerves vibrated like a guitar string about to break.

"He should've just told Poppa in his first letter, but I guess he didn't want to take a chance that the bank president or the auditors might see it. But everything's fine now." She covered a yawn with her

227

hand and gave Jack a guilty smile. "It must be the wine that's making me talk so much and feel so sleepy. I'd better get to bed."

"What do you mean, everything's fine?"

"I paid Mr. Asken off. Good night, Clay," she said and shut the door in his disbelieving face.

Kayley was throwing the latch when the door suddenly exploded inward, knocking her to her knees at the foot of the bed.

"I've had enough of this!" Clay thundered. He slammed into the room, and the door crashed closed behind him.

She stared up at him in jealous awe. If at the bank today she could have managed to look even half as frightening as he did now, Asken wouldn't have dared threaten her with foreclosure to wring that last hundred dollars out of her.

Clay grasped her arms and dragged her to her feet. "Where's your father?"

"Why are you so determined to know where Poppa is?"

"If you know enough to pay Asken off, you know the answer to that question."

"Not you, too." She wrenched away from him. "What I know is that my father almost lost the ranch because he missed a few payments on our loans, which Claude Asken insisted that I pay, along with enough interest to break Cleo's back."

The answer didn't satisfy him. He still looked capable of throttling her without suffering even a moment's regret. She moved around to the other side of the bed to put the wide expanse of it between them. It was covered in a quilt sewn in a double wedding band pattern that was a replica of the one she'd often imagined her mother making for her.

He began stalking toward her. "Where is Sullivan?"

She didn't understand why he was angry or why he cared where her father was or why it was becoming more difficult with each passing day to lie to him. Instead, she wanted to run to him, to feel his arms encircle her in that strong embrace that chased away the shadows and the fear and the loneliness, a whole lifetime of loneliness and shattered dreams.

What stopped her was that with each threatening step Clay took toward her, he came closer to becoming one of those broken dreams.

She couldn't meet his gaze, so she stared instead at his chin and hoped he wouldn't hear the lie in her voice.

"Poppa's away on business."

His hands never touched her—just his body, tall and unyielding as he forced her back into a corner that smelled of wallpaper glue and cobwebs.

"Where is he?"

She felt crushed by his presence, suffocated by his confusing anger. "I don't know," she said, the words hurting her throat.

"How long has he been away?"

His voice cut into her like a rawhide rope. She flinched from it, unable to remember anything except what had almost happened between them on the mountain. He'd been asking her questions then, too. Why? What questions?

She tried to remember exactly how long it had been since she met him. "Three weeks ago," she said. "No, four, I mean five. He left seven weeks ago."

"You're lying." His fingers clamped onto her face, and he forced her head back until she thought her neck would break. "Is Sullivan dead?"

"No!" she cried and broke away from him, clambering across the bed and moving as far away from him as the confining room would allow. "Poppa's not dead, he's not! He's just away!" she repeated, holding on to the words and not letting herself fall.

Clay was standing close to her again. She could sense him testing her strength with his will, trying to find the biggest weakness in the crumbling front she was presenting to him.

"You're not lying, are you, kid?" he asked, not trying to break her or hurt her, just understand her, and she knew that he'd found her weakness.

She dropped her head and looked at the floor, bare and bleached around the edges of the rug. "He's not dead."

"And it was a loan that you paid off."

"Two of them, and I didn't pay them off; I paid the overdue payments and interest." She looked up at him. "Why did you kick in my door? And why do you want to know so much about my father?"

"Because I care about you."

His answer made no sense, but it was like a salve on a burn, soothing and easing the pain inside her, a pain she'd lived with for so long, she'd stopped believing it would ever heal.

"And I wanted to be certain you'd be all right while

230

I'm gone."

His words fell like heavy silence into her suddenly empty heart.

"Gone?" she asked and tasted the tears she couldn't let him see. "To where?"

"Texas. I'm leaving tonight."

He cupped her face in tender hands. She tried to memorize everything about him; the gray that softened the harsh darkness of his unshaven beard, the curve of his lips, so gentle and passionate as they lowered onto hers, branding her, claiming her as his. Not just for one kiss or one night. Forever.

"Don't go," she whispered.

He straightened up, taking her strength with him.

"I have to. My land will support a lot more than the ten cattle I currently own, and buying them is going to cost me more than a winter's logging in the Manzanos will bring."

"But Texas." It was hard to believe a word could sound so far away. "Why there?"

"They have bigger ranches there, and more of them. I can find work punching cattle for a dollar a day or if I'm lucky, get a job doing the type of work I do best and which pays a lot more."

"What's that?"

He moved away from her to the door. "I'm a tracker. Take care of yourself, kid."

Chapter Twenty-Two

Kayley stood motionless, staring at the place where Clay had been standing. "I'm in shock," she said and jumped at the sound of her own voice. "Or I'm still drunk. Or I'm asleep and I dreamed it. Or I'm crazy and I imagined it."

Or it was real and she was letting it slip away.

She ran out of her room, down the hall and into the lobby which smelled of too many people in too small a space. She fought her way through them, looking at the faces, searching for but not finding Clay.

Out of the hotel she ran and into the street. The ground was soft beneath her feet with the rain that was falling and pouring and pelting its way out of the dark sky. It wet her hair, her face and dress, seeping through the wool and onto her skin. A cold rain, a drenching rain. And nowhere within it could she see Clay.

"How could such a tall person disappear so fast?"

She slogged her way back to the hotel, where a clerk was sorting mail behind the registry desk. Kayley dripped across the room to him.

"I need a message delivered."

"It's after midnight, Miss Ryan. What are you sending messages for at this hour?"

"Because I need to, that's why." She wrote a few lines on a piece of hotel stationery, folded it and handed it to him. "Take that to Sam Butler. He's staying in the rooms behind the Burro Alley Saloon. If he's not there, check the Cowhand's Social Club. And hurry."

It was an hour before a knock sounded on Kayley's door. She opened it to Sam. "Did you find him?" she asked before he'd even entered the room.

Water sheeted off his rain slicker. He took off his hat and slapped it dry. "Already gone. He must've headed out of town right after leaving you."

Kayley curled her fingers into fists. "He's probably halfway to Texas by now."

Sam rubbed his chin to stop a grin. "Hardly that far, but at least a few miles along."

A knock on the door caused Kayley's heart to stop. She flung the flimsy wood open, ready to throw herself into Clay's arms in appreciation for his return. It wasn't him. She scowled her disappointment at the hotel manager, a man named Parker, who was looking at her with a very disapproving expression.

"I've been informed by my clerk that you have men visiting you in your room and that you're using hotel employees to send messages to other men, inviting them to visit you here." He looked past Kayley to

Sam. "The Hotel Capitol won't tolerate this behavior from our female guests."

Kayley pulled herself to her full height, which brought the top of her head to just under Parker's chin. "Mr. Butler is here on business," she said.

"Exactly, Miss Ryan, and we don't want that kind of business in our hotel. Please gather your belongings and vacate these premises immediately."

"And tell her to take her dog with her!" came a shout from a nearby room.

Parker's eyes widened in horror. "You have a dog in here?"

Kayley lifted her chin. "It was a coyote. Sam, shoot this man."

Sam pulled his gun and leveled it at Parker. "Say your prayers, mister."

"You can't shoot me!"

"I have a gun; I have bullets; I have orders."

"I'm just doing my job!"

"And that's what I'm doing," Kayley said. "Mr. Butler is foreman of my father's ranch. And the gentleman who was here earlier is a tracker we're interested in hiring."

"No, he isn't," Parker said. "He's a criminal. Claude Asken told me he escaped from Lansing Prison in Kansas where he was serving a life sentence for murder."

Kayley's teeth chattered from a sudden chill. "That's a lie," she said with more conviction than she could force herself to feel. She'd recognized Clay all along as a man capable of murder and realized with an unpleasant sinking feeling that he'd never told her what happened to the partner who'd tried to kill him.

"I'm sorry for any trouble I've caused you, Mr. Parker, but I'm not leaving until morning. Now, if you'll excuse us, Mr. Butler and I have business to discuss."

She closed the door in Parker's face, and Sam slid his gun into his holster. "Yes, she said before he could ask. "I knew he'd been in jail."

"That describes half the men in this territory. Most of them weren't in there for murder, though."

"He didn't kill anyone," Kayley said, forcing herself to believe the words as she said them. "I want you to go after him. Offer him whatever it takes to bring him back."

"You sure you want to do this, Miss Ryan?"

"The R Cross is all I have, Sam. If I lose it, I lose Poppa and Gunning and you." She drew a shaky breath. "And I'll lose Clay."

"I thought it was Moore who had the best odds of getting put on that list."

"He did, until I met Clay." She sat on the edge of the bed. "From the first moment, he took up so much room in my life. The valley didn't seem quite so wide or the mountains so tall or the sky so intimidating. I needed that, Sam; I needed someone to put my life in perspective, someone who was bigger than the things I fear."

"Moore won't like this."

Kayley sighed. "I'm not sure I like it, either."

It was still dark the next morning when Kayley

finished packing her valise. She picked up her straw hat and stroked her fingers along the edge of the brim. It was exactly like the hat Marsha Watkins had worn with the plaid dress Kayley had duplicated with her needle on the trip to New Mexico.

In the oily light from the Hotel Capitol's lanterns, she saw it for what it was—the hat of a little girl, the hat of a spoiled and pampered child.

With a flick of her hand, she sent the hat sailing across the room. Before it fell, she was gone, closing and locking the door behind her.

Dawn looked as cold as the wind felt as it whipped through Santa Fe. Kayley faced the bitter chill bravely as she splashed through mud up to her ankles on her way to John Allen's stable.

"That's it," Snow said as he snapped the last line of the harness of his new mules. Both animals had grizzled faces that resembled his own.

"What are their names?" Kayley asked.

"Gypsy One and Gypsy Two."

Joe Duke tossed a rope to Willie Pete across the top of the tarp protecting the crates of supplies in the back of the wagon.

"I suggested Beer and Whiskey," Joe said. The silver conchas circling his hat flashed in the morning light. "Snow didn't think Elda would cook anything hauled to the ranch by mules named after liquor, though."

Snow pulled a faded red bandanna from his pocket. "See this," he said and turned back the folds to reveal the shining beauty of the Spanish comb. "This should warm the cockles of that old girl's heart."

"How much did you finally pay for it?" Kayley asked.

"I got a fair deal."

"How much?" she insisted.

"A month's pay," he mumbled into the ear of one of the Gypsies.

"Thirty dollars?" Willie Pete asked. "You're a fool, old man."

Slowhand rubbed a finger across the designs carved into the Spanish comb. "It's sure enough fancy, but Mrs. Moraillon won't take it." He threw a saddle onto his horse. "That woman don't want nothin' from you, Snow, but a permanent good-bye."

"If she don't like this, it'll be her that'll be sayin' *adiós*," Snow grumbled as he folded the comb back into its cotton protection.

"Good idea," Joe said. "I'm tired of that boy of hers comin' and goin' in the middle of the night. I can't sleep with all the noise he makes."

Kayley remembered Bede telling her that he rode a lot at night. "Where does he go?" she asked.

"He's deliverin' something for his ma," Slowhand said.

Joe shook his head. "Couldn't be. She don't like nobody enough to send them nothin' but complaints."

"All I know is what Bede told me when I threatened to take my razor strap to him for wearin' out a horse. That bay was covered in so much lather it looked like a barber was set to shave him. He must've ridden that pony flat out the whole night to get it so lathered."

237

"If he's gonna ride like that," Snow said, "he needs a horse like that gray stallion Clay rode up here."

Kayley stopped scraping mud off her boots. "Clay rode Tavira to Sante Fe?"

"Sure did. I seen him in the stable here when I was buyin' the Gypsies from John Allen. Seen that mule of Peters', too. Can you believe that boy paid money to have that stupid animal stabled and fed good grain?"

"Did you see Boxer?"

"Nope, just the stallion and that stupid mule. I can't tolerate a mule dumber than wood."

"He left Boxer up on the mountain," Slowhand said.

"Did he tell you that?"

Slowhand nodded as he swung into the saddle. His dun mare began to pitch, and he spurred her to get more action. Together they kicked up dust and filled the air with snorts and shouts. After a few minutes, the dun calmed down, and Slowhand reined her in.

"Told me last night at the Social Club. Walked in dripping wet, came up to me and started talking about leaving Boxer on the mountain."

Kayley pulled Louisiana's reins off the hitching post and swung into the saddle. "Slowhand, I want you to go after Sam and tell him to come back."

"Where you headed, girl?" Snow asked.

"To hire us a tracker."

Chapter Twenty-Three

The Manzanos were cloaked in silence. It was an eerie silence, a waiting, watchful silence in which the only sound was an infrequent click of Louisiana's shoes on the rocks as he climbed steadily higher along the winding banks of Bear Creek.

Occasionally pieces of sky showed through the clouds that crowned the mountains, scattering sunshine at random through the forest. Kayley rode into several of those pockets of winter warmth. She was riding out of one when it began to snow.

Tiny flakes, bits of white wonder swirling and falling through the forest canopy, tumbled and tossed their way to earth beneath Louisiana's feet. The higher Kayley rode, the bigger the flakes became.

There was no wind and no sound. Just snow. Falling and falling and falling until it seemed impossible there could be any left to fall, yet there was. It clumped on the ground below and on the branches above, causing the trees to snap beneath its weight and making the quiet between the echoing snaps seem suffocating and complete.

Kayley's shoulders began to bend beneath the cold and weight of the snow. Her fingers were freezing. She couldn't feel her face or her ears. She couldn't see or smell or taste anything except snow.

She wound her hands into Louisiana's mane and pressed her face against his neck. He was warm and wet with melted snow. As they climbed higher and the temperature dropped lower, the wetness became ice that scraped Kayley's skin.

"We should've reached the cabin by now." The words cut through the frozen flesh of her throat and lips. "We're lost, Louie. We have to go back down to the valley."

She was too cold to hold the reins, too cold to make the gelding turn. And even if she did, which way was down? Which way was back? They might be going down now. Or they might already be dead.

"Trust your horse," she heard Sam say, and suddenly it wasn't cold anymore. It was a sun-washed day in summer, and she was ready to set out on her first solo search for the white stallion.

"If you get lost, trust your horse, Miss Ryan. He'll take you to safety."

The sun faded, Sam's voice and his kind eyes blurred, the world became cold again and Kayley's teeth were frozen to her lips where she'd tried to smile.

"I trust you," she whispered to Louisiana. "I trust you."

The gelding kept walking . . . on and on, through the snow and the storm and the forest of muffled death.

"So white," Kayley heard herself say. "So very white."

The first time she saw the stallion, she hadn't believed it was possible for anything to be so white. It had been at dawn, the first light of day pouring across the valley, climbing to the top of the ridge where Kayley had been lying flat on her stomach to look into the draw below. It had taken her a month to find the wild herd, a month of trying to learn everything a lifetime in a Boston boarding school hadn't taught her.

She'd learned to ride and care for her horse, to start a fire in the open and cook over it. She'd learned to sleep under an open sky with her saddle blanket for warmth and her saddle for a pillow. She'd learned to rope and to ignore the pain of blisters and tired muscles and sunburn and range-tired eyes. She'd learned everything necessary to bring her to that ridge, and to that moment when she first saw her enemy.

Kayley had inched closer, just a little, just a bit, peering over the edge of the ridge, looking, searching among the lingering shadows. And there, among a tumble of limestone boulders, beside a scraggly bush of silver sage, standing with one foot in a pool of water shimmering with the chilling beauty of the reflected white sky, had been the stallion. Devil creature. Spawn of hell. Satan himself, standing there, looking up. Looking at her.

She hadn't believed how white he was, so pure, so perfect, turning the bright world around him to gray, dimming it to shadows, exiling it to darkness.

And his eyes. Black as hell itself, black as fear and

241

loneliness, black as death.

They were looking at her. Watching her. Daring her to come closer and face his anger and his strength and his hatred. To face everything she feared.

She stood. The stallion tensed, his ears pricking forward, his nostrils flaring, his eyes opening wider.

"I'm going to kill you," she said, her voice pouring out of her and into the draw where he waited, unmoving and unafraid.

He raised his head higher and flung his tail into the gathering wind before snorting a response to her promise.

He's laughing, Kayley thought. *Laughter like storms raging above the valley, like mountains crumbling, like the world coming to an end.*

Laughter like snow, falling and falling and falling.

Laughter like death, like suffocating, slow, cold death. Pressing upon her, around her. Pressing inside of her where she was growing weaker, colder. Growing quiet and still.

Louisiana was moving slower now, forcing his way through piles and drifts and mountains of snow. It rose to his knees, then his chest so that Kayley's feet dragged through it as he walked. She could see it close to her face which was still pressed against the gelding's neck because she couldn't move it away.

Kayley thought of Clay, of how he smiled and the way he laughed, so bold and unafraid. And she thought of how he'd kissed her and said that he cared for her and how she wished that he were here now, holding her, making her warm again.

She thought of Vance, his hazel eyes so dark, his

242

hair sleek and perfect, his manners always so right, always so remote. Where was he now? What was he doing while she froze?

And she thought of her father, but all she could remember of him was when she was eight years old and he'd come to see her at Mrs. Potter's. His eyes had been so blue, and Kayley had wanted so much for him to tell her that he loved her and he was sorry about her mother and Aunt Lo. She'd wanted him to smile at her and say her name. All he said, though, was that Lona had no right to dictate his daughter's future and the money should have been his.

Kayley remembered how Mrs. Potter had explained and explained, how she'd given him tea and smiled at him and laughed a silly laugh.

And then her father had left. He'd just left. Without a word, without a hug or a kiss. Without saying her name, without looking at her. Without saying good-bye.

"Clay," she whispered.

The word cut through the silence and through her fear. And the world, the world that had been white, terrible, blinding and white, turned black. A quiet, peaceful black.

Jack stabbed at the fire with a poker, punching it, beating it into higher and higher flames, shoving blocks of wood back and forth, chipping at them, releasing explosions of heat from deep inside their smoldering hearts, then stabbing at them again to hide the heat away.

It was a familiar game, and fast becoming a

243

tiresome one. Ever since the first snowflake had floated down from the velvet white sky, he'd been stabbing and punching at the fire he'd built to warm the cabin.

"Maybe she didn't come after me."

The look on her face as he closed her hotel door was enough to convince him otherwise, though. It had been a look of astonishment, disbelief and hope. So much hope that Jack had almost regretted setting her up that way.

He'd been waiting for this moment for five years, plotting and planning and waiting. Now that it was here, instead of anticipation, he felt regret. And all because of one quick moment's flash of joy in the perfect blue of her eyes when Jack had said he cared for her. It had flared quick and bright and desperate, and it had touched him.

A young girl's happiness, a young girl's hope, had touched him. His enemy's daughter. The weapon of his revenge.

Even now, just the memory of it caused him to stab harder and faster at the flames and to hate himself because he knew she was out there in that storm, fighting her way through a blizzard just so he could have the pleasure of knowing she'd chased after him before he listened to her beg for his help.

He shoved the poker from him, walked to the window and pressed his hands on the icy glass, spreading his fingers wide and staring out at the snow.

Out there, in that world of white, there was a movement that didn't belong. He stared harder, trying to see through the flurry of snow. There it was again, a form taking shape out of a formless world.

Jack didn't hesitate. He tied a rope around his waist, knotted it once, then again, opened the door and plunged out into the storm.

He didn't feel the cold, not at first. It hit him suddenly, knifing into his lungs, freezing his face and fingers, pouring into his shirt and up inside his pant legs, filling his boots with cold and wet and a quickening numbness that made him stumble and fall.

But not into snow. Into something big and solid, something as cold as ice and yet somehow alive. Then there was a snort of welcome and the feel of living flesh beneath a mantle of snow.

Jack grabbed the horse's bridle and began to fight his way back along the rope to the welcoming brightness of the open door. Once he was under the eaves of the cabin roof, he felt down the animal's neck until he found her, stiff and unmoving and quiet as death. He pulled her to him, holding her, cradling her.

"You're safe, Kayley. You're with me now; you're safe."

And his tears turned to ice as they fell onto her frozen face.

Chapter Twenty-Four

It wasn't the feeling of being warm that caused her to awaken. It was the feeling of being on fire. Her body, her very skin, was being burned and blistered. Hearing the roar of a fire and smelling its heat confirmed her long-time fear that hating Mrs. Potter had, indeed, been a sin.

"I'm in hell," Kayley said and opened her eyes. -

What she saw, was Clay—eye darker than she'd ever seen it, hair falling in unruly shagginess across his face and onto the open collar of his shirt of gray and black flannel that was tucked into black pants that were being worn over black boots that were standing very close to the tin bathtub in which she was sitting and which was almost as shiny as the silver buckle of his belt.

"I thought the devil would be much uglier and carry a pitchfork."

His eye lightened a little. "I left it in the shed."

"I also thought Mr. McDonnell's cabin would

smell like one of those rooms where sunlight never reaches."

"It did until I put in a window. Close your eyes."

"Why?" she asked, and was almost blinded by the bucket of water he dumped over her head.

"It hurts!"

"That means you're going to live," he said, managing to sound incredibly impersonal considering the circumstances, which were, Kayley realized, that she was naked and there was barely enough water in the tub to cover her toes, much less the rest of her. She curled herself into a very nervous knot, knees against her chest and arms around her knees with wet clumps of hair covering everything else.

"Where's Louisiana?" she asked, hoping to distract Clay from whatever he planned to do to her next by sending him out into the storm to find her horse.

"I rubbed him down, buried him in blankets and wedged him into the shed with Boxer, Tavira, and Cleo."

"Louie saved me."

"I saved you, he almost killed you."

"Sam told me to trust my horse, that he'd take me to safety. He was right—Louie brought me here."

Clay went to the fireplace, which was only a few feet away, and began refilling his bucket from a kettle hanging over the flames. Kayley considered escaping from his torture tub, until she realized there was nowhere to go and nothing to put on when she got there.

Diversionary tactics are my only hope, if only I could think of one.

"Close your eyes," he said.

247

This time she obeyed before the flood struck.

"It's too hot."

"It's warm. You feel hot because you're thawing out. When the blood comes back into the frozen skin, it feels like it's burning."

She stared at her hands hugging her legs. "I thought I was going to die."

He knelt beside her. His hands were warm and dry, and he touched her face with them, turning it up until she looked at him.

"There were tears frozen on your face," he said, and the impersonal tone was gone.

"I don't remember crying."

He released her and stood. "Are you ready to get out?"

"My skin doesn't hurt anymore; it just feels wet."

Clay unfolded a blanket and held it up before the fire. His face was turned away from her, so she could see only his profile, etched in light and scarred by the black leather of his eyepatch.

"Stand up," he said and turned to spread the blanket open between them.

Her legs were more than a little shaky, and her body glowed in the firelight. It seemed to take forever for him to wrap the blanket around her. Her skin tingled with awareness of his hands touching her through the scratchy wool as he lifted her, carried her, and laid her on a bed in the corner of the cabin.

It was a wide bed. And long. And comfortable.

She felt it give slightly beneath her weight. Felt the blanket, now wet and cold with that wetness, being taken off her and the warmth of a dry one replacing it. Felt Clay's arms around her. Felt his lips on hers. Soft. Tender. Then she slept.

When she awoke the second time, she was warm. She turned her head, burying one cheek in the softness of a pillow while she looked at the cabin. It was small, the bed filling almost half the space. There was a shelf with folded clothes in one corner. In another, shelves were filled with cans and sacks and boxes of supplies, pots and a skillet and a cigar box with a picture on the side of a tropical island surrounded by turquoise water.

Across the room was the window. It was so large it occupied almost the whole wall and opened the cabin up to the outside world where snow still fell, its brilliance shaded gray by the dimming twilight.

Beneath the window sat a table on which a can spouted a lacy green plant that looked out of place in this rough-hewn cabin.

The bathtub was gone, revealing beside the table a mountain of firewood, pieces and chunks and logs and kindling, sprawled and sprawling against the cabin wall and a flagstone hearth. The fireplace itself was as impressive as the stack of wood. It was massive, built of stone and mortar that had been grayed and blackened by time and smoke.

There were no lanterns in the room. The only light came from a single candle on the mantle, and from the fire itself. It was like the fires of hell Kayley had pictured earlier, huge, leaping, dancing flames that demanded attention.

Pulled close to the hearth, and to those snapping flames, was a chair whose dimensions matched the oversized scale of the other furnishings. And in the chair, long legs stretched out in front of him and feet crossed at the ankles, sat Clay.

He was watching the fire, his eye pale again, the silver-gray sparking with reflected flames, the smoke of the cigar he held drifting up past his face, filling the room with its earth-rich aroma.

Never had Kayley felt as safe as she did in this snow-buried cabin with a man who was dangerous, frightening and intimidating; and intriguing, entrancing, and wonderful.

"I'm awake," she said, and her heart grew still as that wonderful man turned to look at her, embracing her with his gaze.

He stood, took the candle from the mantle and crossed the room to her. He was dressed as before, the gray and black plaid of his shirt making his shoulders look broader, his hair darker, his face kinder.

"How do you feel?"

"Warm."

He set the candle in a niche cut into the wall. Bathed in the burning wick's light, he sat beside her and put the back of his hand to her forehead, her cheek and neck.

"No fever. That's a good sign."

"I'm hungry."

"Another good sign. I'll get you a plate of venison stew."

It was hot and as rich tasting as the scent of his

cigar. She ate every bite and handed the empty plate back to him.

"I like the way that smells," she said.

He rolled the cigar between his fingers. "I have them imported from Mistral, an island in the Caribbean."

"I thought you were broke."

"A man should never be too broke to buy a good cigar."

"Then, you're still looking for work?"

He walked to the table and stood with his back to her. "After the storm breaks, and after I take you home."

Home. The word sounded strange. She didn't know if it was the empty way he'd said it or because she'd never thought of the ranch house as home. This cabin felt more like a home than anywhere she'd lived since Aunt Lo died.

Why is that, she wondered.

When Clay turned back to her and she met his intense gaze again, she knew why.

She pulled a quilt close around her and got onto her knees to face him. "I want to hire you. That's why I came here, to hire you to stop the trouble the R Cross is having. And I'll pay you in cattle, a percentage of our herd."

"What about Sullivan?" There it was again, the ever present question about her father. "Did he approve this, Kayley?"

"Yes," she said, then dropped her chin. "I mean, he would if I could tell him. He'd never question anything I did to save the ranch, though."

251

For a moment, she thought she saw victory flash like starlight in Clay's eye. It made her feel like a trapped animal. He laid his cigar on the edge of the table and began stalking toward her. He stopped when his knees were touching hers as she knelt on the edge of the bed.

"Anything, Kayley?"

Her heart grew still within her, and she knew that if she said no, it would never beat again.

"Anything," she said, breathing the word, letting the whispered sound of it be her commitment.

He pulled her hands away from the quilt, holding them out beside her like wings. The quilt loosened its protection of her, and the folds began to slip, sliding down across her breasts, exposing them; her waist and hips, exposing them; falling about her knees, the crests and mounds of material surrounding her, presenting her to him.

"Then, let me teach you to fly," he said, and kissed her, folding her arms behind her and drawing her up into his kiss, pulling her so close that the buckle on his belt pushed cold against her flesh.

His tongue was touching hers, swirling and thrusting, gentle and bold. Exciting her, burning her, his passion ignited her, lifting her up with him into the storm, above it and beyond. She melted against his strength, feeling his heart beat, feeling his hands still holding hers as he caught at the ends of her hair with his fingers.

She became aware of something pressing against her—something big and hard, something that made her feel small, weak, and incredibly alive.

"Your belt," she said, turning her lips away from his. "It's pushing into me."

"That's not my belt, Kayley."

She flushed beneath his laughing gaze. "I know," she said in a whisper, "that's why I want you to take your belt off," and the laughter turned to silver fire.

Slowly, like time standing still, he released her hands, ran his open palms up along her arms, across her shoulders, down her chest. Onto her breasts.

Slowly. Slower. His fingers pulled away just before they touched her nipples.

He unfastened the silver buckle, dragged the tooled leather from the cold metal, and the belt hung free. He moved his hands to the waist of his pants. Unbuttoned one button. Another. A third, a fourth.

He reached for her again, slipping his arms around her waist, his hands warming her as they moved lower to press her hips against the front of his need, his desire. His manhood.

"Take off my shirt," he ordered, and she began to tremble. Deep within her, where secrets and fantasies and unknown desires were hidden, she trembled.

With more nerve than she knew she possessed, Kayley lifted her hands to his face. "You shaved," she said, and for the first time since he'd unbuckled his belt, she met his gaze. Sinking back onto her heels, she drew her touch down across his jaw and onto the collar of his shirt.

By the time she'd freed the last button above the waist of his pants, his breathing had quickened and her secret tremble had spread to her lips and hands.

He pulled the shirt from her grasp and shrugged

253

out of it. His pants were next. Kayley refused to take her eyes off his face as the tight denim was pushed down off his hips and legs.

Naked, his flesh golden in the flickering firelight and tiny candle flame, he stood before her. "Look at me," he ordered.

She couldn't breathe. He was even more perfect, more magnificent than she remembered. His chest, matted with hair as dark as midnight, tapered into a narrow line across his flat stomach, flaring out to surround his erect penis, its swollen size exciting and frightening her.

Before she could react to that fear, his arms were around her again, and he was lifting her and laying her among the quilts and blankets.

Suddenly his hands were in her hair, on her face, her breasts and waist, her legs and thighs, awakening her, seducing her, inflaming her.

Kisses rained on her throat, across her chest, kisses on her breasts, soft and light and sucking while still his hands, always his hands, were everywhere, stroking, patting, touching, teasing.

His kisses became more demanding; his caresses, more possessive; his demands, more exciting.

Breaths arose in quick, aching gasps as his knees wedged between her knees, pushing up, higher, pressing against her at the same moment as his teeth embraced her nipple.

A cry sounded, filling the cabin, filling her. Then his hands cupped her breasts, kneading them, making her twist beneath him, making her seek his mouth with hers, making her clutch and grab at him.

Making her want him so much that she couldn't think or be, only want, and fear that wanting.

Jack raised himself above her. The innocence in those beautiful blue eyes seared him as she looked upon him and his hate, and what he was doing to her because of that hate.

"Are you sure you want to do this, Kayley? It's not too late to say no."

She lifted her hands to his face, her mere touch arousing him so much that his heart trembled with need.

"I trust you," she said.

He pulled away from her. "Don't say that; don't say you trust me."

"I don't want to, Clay. I don't want to trust anyone, because whenever I do, I get hurt." She closed her eyes. "But, I trust you," she said and hid her face in the pillow beside his hand.

Jack saw her again as she'd looked when he'd told he was a tracker, and how she'd looked when he'd lifted her, frozen and dying, from the back of her horse.

He slid his fingers beneath her cheek and forced her to look up at him. "If you ask me now, I'll swear an oath to never hurt you."

For a long moment, the only sound in the room was the crackling of the fire.

"Ask me, Kayley," he whispered.

"I can't."

He felt cold. "Isn't that what you want?"

"Only if you freely give it. If I have to ask for a promise, it means nothing."

"I can't give it," he said. "And I can't do this."

Kayley hadn't known there could be such fear as this, fear born out of the sanity and reason that his talk of oaths and promises and forever had allowed into the room. She'd had a lifetime of reality. Tonight she wanted dreams. She wanted hopes and wishes. Tonight, she wanted magic.

She raised herself off the pillow, sitting up beside him. His feet were on the floor, and his hands were balled into fists.

"I don't want promises, Clay. And I don't want sworn oaths that have to last beyond this room, beyond this moment. All I want is now. All I want, is you."

She could almost feel the shudder that went through him. He stood and moved away from her, the scar on his back so white it seemed to glow in the light from the fire. He was fighting something terrible that lay between them, a barrier she couldn't see, only feel, something alive and tangible that filled the cabin, flowing like heavy water between them, making the short distance between them uncrossable and deadly.

Kayley wanted to reach out to him. But it was his chasm to cross, his vow to break, or to make. All she could do was wait.

*　　　*　　　*

With hands knotted into fists, Jack leaned against the stone mantle. The muscles in his arms and back, his shoulders and neck, were as knotted as his hands, and he drew them still tighter as he heard in his mind, and his heart, Kayley's soft voice repeat over and over, *I trust you.*

He straightened up and turned to face her. She sat where he'd left her, crimson hair tumbled like melting gold around her face and shoulders, her eyes lovely with unshed tears.

All I want is now. All I want, is you.

It was all Jack wanted, too. There would be time tomorrow for hate, time tomorrow to rebuild his defenses and reach again for victory and vindication.

He crossed the cabin to her, and when he reached her, he took her face in his hands and felt her surrender.

"Why did you have to be everything I've ever wanted?" he asked, his voice a whisper in the stillness.

"Clay," she said, and he stopped her by putting a finger on her lips to stop the music of her voice and erase the word she'd whispered.

"No names. No yesterdays, no tomorrows. Just now. Just us."

He touched his lips to hers, then moved his hands from her face to her back, dropping them lower, cupping the rounded perfection of her buttocks in his hands and lifting her, pressing her to him and drinking deeply of her kisses.

Soft, softer than roses in springtime, softer than a drop of rain on a warm summer night, softer than a single flake of snow.

And sweet. He tasted her lips, her kisses and her sighs. Sweet, and perfect in that sweetness.

Her neck, graceful and long. Down, onto her shoulders, her flesh warm beneath his kisses. Her heart beat fast, faster, causing her breast to flutter as he touched it with his lips.

His hands slipping between her legs caused her to shiver. She pulled his face to hers and kissed him, her lips tender, her kisses like dreams as they moved across his face, onto his neck and down to his chest.

Her hands caressed his shoulders, slipping into his hair, catching at and holding the rawhide strings of his eyepatch. Her fingers lightly touched his arms, his waist, moving onto his back, caressing his scar and making him ache anew with the remembered pain of that betrayal, then erasing the memory with the quickening of her heart where it pressed against his.

He held her tighter, kissed her deeper.

Her hands moved lower, stroking his hips, his buttocks, the scratch of her nails exciting on his fevered flesh. Her tongue moved quickly against him, her body pressing and clinging, caressing him, molding his need, pushing a leg between his legs, lifting a knee between his thighs.

"Slowly," he said. "I want this to last all night."

"Tell me what to do," she whispered.

"Enjoy," he said, laying her on the bed and covering her with his need.

*   *   *

Hands roamed across her bottom, her back, her sides. In her hair, on her arms, touching her breasts, grasping and holding and making her ache and gasp and moan beneath his kiss.

And her hands, her own hands, touched him in places that caused his fingers to grip her tighter, that made him pinch and squeeze her, that made him groan his pleasure against her lips.

Dropping her head, she tasted the flesh of his neck, kissing his chest, touching his nipples, causing his head to raise up and his breathing to become rapid and ragged.

Lower, her lips on his stomach.

Lower, hesitating, her trembling lips touched him there; then her hands grasped his penis, rubbing it between her fingers as she brought her lips back to his chest, his neck, beneath his chin.

His hands, caressing her breasts now, holding them, stroking them with his fingers, tracing patterns of fire on her flesh as he reached for, and touched, her nipples. Thumb and forefinger, rolling, twisting. The muscles in her stomach tightened, the tension moving down, down into her legs, turning to darkness, drawing tighter, making her forget to touch him as the heat of her fire, the burn of her passion, began to grow.

He slipped his arms around her, lifting her, arching her into him. Lowering his lips onto a nipple, he sucked it to him, making her moan, making her die.

Bites, tender, hard and fast.

Kissing, licking, wet, faster.

Her face. Her nipples. Her stomach, her thighs. Caressing, tasting.

Stroking and patting and feeling and exciting.

Her skin on fire. Her muscles tense, her lips gasping, her body writhing.

Her need—her burning, longing, stinging need, hot and wet and painful in its desire—consumed her, controlled her, crying out for more, for completion, crying out for love.

His lips kissed her hair, her neck and ears, her eyes and tongue and her whimpers of need.

"Now," he said, and he touched her, there, on the moist heat of her passion. Spreading her legs, he ran his fingers through her cries, dipping them into her, making her tremble and moan and clutch at his arms and shoulders, his face and his heart.

He was over her, arms braced beside her face, hands tangled in the fire of her hair, his lips close to hers and the hair of his chest torturing and teasing her nipples and breasts.

"Now," he said again, and he was inside her. One quick, sudden, powerful thrust of his hips, and his penis, hard and hot and big, was buried deep inside her.

She cried her pain into his kiss while he held motionless. When the spasmed ache of his entry had passed, he made a slight movement, a shifting of his hips. More pain. Another move took him deeper, taking her with him, and then, pleasure.

Her hands trembled on his chest. He buried his face in her hair, and she touched her lips to the pulse of his throat.

"Again," she whispered.

He pulled out, away from her, taking almost everything that she'd become because of him. Then, before he was gone entirely, before he destroyed her completely, he pushed into her. Slow, purposeful, achingly tender, deliciously perfect, he conquered her will and her heart and her soul.

He lifted his head, arching it up and back so that the line of his jaw and the black of he eyepatch towered above her. His arms straightened the muscles hard, his bronzed skin wet with sweat and his back curved like a bow.

And he began to move. Riding her. Lifting her. Taking her with him into the sky, they surged through the storm and over the clouds and up to the stars, black and silver and bright with moonlight, clear and cold and chillingly beautiful. Higher and faster and stronger and faster and aching and faster and tighter and faster they rose until she couldn't breathe, couldn't think or be or know or want or hurt because they'd reached the heavens, flying so high that they were among the stars, the stars she loved, and they came, together, their bodies grasping and releasing and crying aloud their passion and pleasure.

Then, alone, and yet with each other, they began to fall, to drift back to themselves, to the arms that were holding them, the room that protected them, the bed that cradled them in comfort and love.

He was rocking her, his face touching hers, his lips caressing her forehead and eyelids, his heart beating against her breast.

"Don't let me go," she said and felt his smile.

"Never."

They were silent then, their hands exploring and caressing, their lips occasionally meeting, their bodies wrapped in the afterglow of loving.

Kayley held him against her and felt beneath her fingers the hard ridge of his scar.

"I want to know about this," she said. "I want to know everything about it, and about you."

"No, you don't."

"You mean, you don't want to tell me."

"If I did, you would hate me."

"Never," she said, and he wrapped his arms around her so tightly that she couldn't remember what she'd wanted to know.

Chapter Twenty-Five

Silence. A muffled quiet. The peaceful calm of hearing only the sound of two hearts beating as one. The rest of the world pushed away by the snow pressing against the window, against the door and the walls, the roof and chimney. Not falling. Just pressing.

Just quiet.

Just two.

Just now.

Jack lay on his back, one arm stretched out beside him, the other folded behind his head. On his outstretched arm lay Kayley, her face turned toward him, her gentle breathing pushing tiny puffs of warm air against his side. Hair as red as midnight firelight and as golden as morning sunshine was tumbled around her face and shoulders, her arm, tangled over and around her breasts and curling through Jack's fingers.

She frowned and moved slightly, worried and

263

searching, reaching out a hand to him in her sleep. He moved his arm from beneath his head and wrapped her fingertips in a calming hand. She sighed, almost smiled, and slept again.

Jack hadn't meant for it to happen like this. He hadn't planned on her smiles and her laughter or the way light sparkled in her eyes. He hadn't planned on dreaming about her and thinking about her and worrying about her. He hadn't planned on wanting her or needing her or watching her fall asleep in his arms or waking up with her in his heart.

For five years, he'd suffered and plotted and planned and waited. When the miracle of his release had happened, he'd thought himself ready.

She snuggled in closer to him, her lips so close to his chest that he could almost feel her kisses, so vividly remembered from last night. In the silence of the cabin, he heard again the ecstasy of her cries, the pleasure in her silken voice, the wonder in her laughter when he'd tickled her lashes with kisses.

She snuggled still closer, covering his leg with hers, resting her hand on his stomach and lifting her face onto his shoulder so that he could see the perfection of her face and the soft appeal of her sleeping frown.

He hadn't been ready for any of this.

I will destroy Sullivan, Jack promised himself. *This,* he kissed her forehead, *this won't stop me.*

Her lashes, so long and lovely, closed tighter, then opened.

"Good morning," he said, and his breath caught in his throat as she smiled at him.

"It's cold."

He pulled a blanket over her suddenly shivering body. "The fire died hours ago."

She hid a yawn against his arm. "Why didn't you save it?"

"I didn't want to wake you." He touched a finger to the tip of her chin. "Are you too cold for a kiss?"

"I don't think so. Would you like to try?"

"I'd love to," he said and, moving his finger to her smiling lips, traced the curve of the lower one, then replaced his caress with a kiss.

Soft, sweet, innocent.

He'd spent the night with a woman who made love like a sinning angel. Could she really be the same child who was kissing him now?

When he released her lips, she moved on top of him, warming him with her body, curtaining his face with her hair.

"I want more," she said, and his angel was back.

She tasted his lips with her tongue, sliding it slowly into his waiting mouth. Jack's body began to melt, his mind forgetting to hate, his heart forgetting not to love.

"How can you sleep in this?" she asked and, before he could stop her, slipped the knot on the rawhide laces of his eyepatch. He released his caressing hold on her to grasp the piece of leather before she could pull it away.

"I want to see," she said.

"It's not a pretty sight, Kayley."

She sat up, straddling him with her legs, her sleep-mussed hair falling about her in beautiful disarray.

265

"I want to see."

The set of her chin and the pout of her lips were impossible for Jack to argue with, especially when she began to lift herself off him and move away.

And it is tomorrow, he reminded himself, time to remember she was here as part of his plan, not as part of his life.

He lifted the leather away from his eye. He couldn't bring himself to look at her face and stared instead at the base of her throat where her pulse shimmered beneath her ivory skin.

"How did it happen, Clay?"

"I was stabbed."

He felt her stiffen.

"In the eye?" she asked, her voice choked with what sounded like sorrow, but which he knew was disgust.

He moved quickly to cover the unseeing stare of his left eye with the patch. She stopped him, closing her hands around his and pushing them away. Then she leaned over him and kissed the ruined eye, her lips soft on the shrunken flesh, her kiss gentle on his horror.

"Did the same man who stabbed you in the back do this?"

"Yes." He put the patch back on and jerked the laces into a knot.

"Did you kill him?"

He looked directly at her, dominating her gaze with his anger. "Not yet," he said through lips turned hard with hate.

"I don't want you to," she said, and the tense fear that edged her voice surprised him. Her eyes were wide, her lower lip trembling. "If you kill him, they'll take you away; they'll take you back to prison. You can't do it, Clay. Tell me you won't do it."

"What's wrong, kid? Worried I won't save your herd first?"

Pain shivered across her face. It was replaced almost instantly by anger. "You haven't even said if you'll take the job." She ran her hands down his chest in a cold caress. "Was the advance I paid you last night wasted?"

Jack's hate came roaring back, filling his veins with anger as hot as melted iron, pushing aside the tenderness, and the love, he'd almost deluded himself into believing were real.

"I want half the herd."

Her eyes clouded, reminding Jack of the death of his own delusion; then it was gone, and her eyes turned as clear and cold as her caress.

"A quarter of the spring herd," she said.

"Half of the current herd."

She stood, pulling with her a blanket which she wrapped around her. She stepped off the bed and crossed the cabin to look at the dead ashes of last night's fire.

"I can't afford more than a third, and it has to be the spring herd, otherwise you won't have an incentive to stop the rustling." She turned to look at him. "Please, Clay. I'm begging you to take a third."

"Half," he said, his voice like flint. Then it softened. "Of the spring herd."

She was silent for a long time. "Agreed," she finally said, her gaze falling from his.

267

A hard knot of desire rose within Jack, yet not because of how beautiful she looked in the reflected light from the snow-white window. It was because of how proud she'd looked even when saying please. It was the way her men respected her, and the way she respected them. It was how frightened she'd been for Jefferson Pollet's life and how, even though drowning in her own fear, she'd tried to ease Peters McDonnell's. It was because of so many things that Jack felt smothered by them.

But most of all, it was the pain he'd seen on her face moments ago when she'd realized he wasn't going to soothe her misgivings with sweet words and promises.

I wanted her to love me.

"You'll have to work alone," she said.

"Where's Sam going to be?"

"Since you want half my herd, he'll have to spend the winter trying to scare up unbranded cattle from the mountains west of the Rio Grande."

Jack got out of bed. He liked the way she refused to look at his naked body while he stretched. It made him feel powerful and aggressive, and as he crossed the room to her, he remembered with pleasure how it had felt to hear her say, *please* and *I'm begging you.*

"That means we'll be alone," he said and caught her arm before she could escape. "Just like we're alone now."

"We've already agreed on your wage, and this wasn't part of it."

"But last night was?" he asked and crushed her against him, pressing her to his hard, burning penis, forcing her to feel the proof of his lust for her.

She tried to meet his gaze with a disdainful stare. The attempt failed when her chin began to quiver. Her gaze fell. "No," she whispered, her voice hollow with pain.

"I'm sorry, kid," he said and lowered her head onto his chest, cradling her in his arms and bowing his head to kiss her hair.

"It was my fault; I called it an advance." She lifted her arms and slipped them around his neck while stretching on tiptoe to kiss his cheek. "I'm sorry."

"I want more," he said with a grin.

She shivered in his arms. "Build a fire first, and I'm all yours, Clay."

The name shocked him, reminding him that this morning it wasn't Jack Corbett making love to her. It was Clay. And like it was Clay's name she'd just said, it would be Clay's name that she whispered and cried and moaned when he was between her thighs. And it was Clay who grasped hold of her protecting blanket, stripping it from her with a quick, violent jerk as he said, "We don't need a fire, Miss Ryan."

Kayley shuddered beneath the sudden force of his mouth on hers. Plunging, devouring thrusts of his tongue. Angry sounds within his throat. Harsh caresses on her back, her waist and breasts.

His hands were like fire on her flesh. She tried to escape and was caught between him and the cold fireplace.

She cried out. Not in pain or fear. In need. Sudden

need. Powerful, strong, possessing need that flooded through her, from her, burning her thighs with her wet passion, causing her to grasp at his shoulders and dig her fingers into his flesh.

He pulled her up to him, raking her skin across the stones until his lips were on one of her aching, hard nipples. With one hand, he held her prisoner between the pain and pleasure of his sucking kisses and the cold stone as his other hand reached between her legs.

His caresses were hot and burning, rough and exciting. Fingers touching her, fingers inside her.

His mouth, biting, sucking, licking.

She bent her knee and pressed her foot into the back of his leg, arching her hips into the grasp of his fingers. She raked her hands across his shoulders, down his back, her nails scratching through the sweat of his effort, the sweat of their lust.

His arms were like timbers beneath her bruising touch, her force matching his, her caresses quick and firm and stroking, stinging and burning, rhythmic and fast.

His penis, hard and hot, throbbed against her leg. His teeth were on her nipple, his mouth sucking it in and his tongue licking it and his lips kissing it. His heart was beneath her hand, pounding, surging, beating so fast it frightened her.

"Clay," she cried, and pushed her hand down between them to grasp his swollen manhood.

He pulled her away from the stone edifice, carrying her down with him onto the rug stretched before the cold hearth. Before she could even catch a single breath, he was kissing her again, devouring her, biting her lips, her breasts, running his tongue across her stomach, and lower.

His lips were in her private hair, his tongue tasting her, forcing her to tear and clutch with desperate fingers at his shoulders while he parted her legs with his hands and held her motionless before him as he put his mouth close against her, kissing her, kissing her deep, deeper, wet kisses, passionate kisses, taking from her and giving to her and destroying her.

"Clay," she pleaded again.

Suddenly he was on top of her, crushing her, warming her. He raised himself up on one arm. With the other, he lifted her up against him, bringing her so close to his face she could feel the heat of his breath on her lips.

"Open your eyes," he commanded, and she cowered before his anger.

She couldn't obey, couldn't let him see her shame and her need. All she could do was hold on to him, her hands around his waist and pressing into the granite hardness of his muscled back.

"Open your eyes, Kayley," he ordered again, and touched the tip of his penis to the wet heat between her legs.

Her eyes opened, and she found herself a prisoner of his silver stare. A sob tore from her throat, and she began to tremble and quake.

A darkness, like black lightning, flashed through that pale gray lake of anger. The stiffness of his body melted.

"Say my name," he whispered, the pain in his

voice tearing at her heart. "Please, say *my* name."

"Clay."

He turned his face into her hair.

"Clay," she said again, her voice crying the word, her breath sobbing the name.

His arm, where it held her to him, stiffened around her. His shoulders became rigid, his back hard beneath her fingers, his hair, long and dark, falling across his forehead and onto her lips as he lowered her to the rug.

"Clay," she said a third time, and he entered her. Fast and deep and thrusting. Hard and raging. Strong and passionate.

"Wrap your legs around mine," he told her as he drove himself deeper into her, pushing her up and almost off the luxurious fur of the rug beneath her.

She obeyed him, putting her legs over his and holding herself steady with their embrace as he pulled out of her and entered again. Faster, harder, his sweat falling like rain on her fevered brow. His arms so rigid beneath her anchoring touch that it was like holding on to forged metal.

Pulse of pleasure, flashes of fire. Warming her, burning and freezing her. Throbbing arcs of energy poured like darkness through her, filling her legs and arms, her stomach and chest, drawing her down, dragging her inward, making her tighten around him. Quickening, flashing, like spasms of lightning, finding and grasping and centering.

Faster, harder.

His breathing expelled like explosions of gunfire while his body rode her, his gaze holding her

272

prisoner, his face like stone carved by a sculptor during a moment of anger and ecstasy.

Faster.

Her cries filled the space between them, his own gasping groans of agonized pleasure covering her, surrounding her.

Harder.

Climbing, higher, higher, darker, grasping, holding, clutching until—an explosion.

Inside of her. His. And hers. Together.

Like their hearts. Like their heartbeats.

Sinking into a muffled quiet.

Then, silence.

Chapter Twenty-Six

Clay rolled away from Kayley and stood with a fluid, catlike motion. He towered above her, tall and forbidding, a sudden stranger.

"The storm's over," he said. "I'll saddle the horses; you cook breakfast."

She sat up, pulling the discarded blanket to her and wrapping it over her nakedness.

He put on woolen underwear that reached from his neck to his wrists and ankles, then wool pants, a corduroy shirt as dark as his hair, and the belt that last night had pressed against her. He shrugged his wide shoulders into a greatcoat and, after putting on his hat and gloves, was gone, leaving her without a word or a glance.

She sat and shivered and stared at her toes where they pushed from beneath the itchy blanket.

He's only going to the shed. There wasn't a reason for him to say good-bye.

When he returned, she was dressed, and the cabin was filled with warmth and light from the fire she'd built. Coffee was boiling, bacon was sizzling, and a skillet of cornbread was propped up in front of the fire so its surface would turn crispy and brown.

"How are the animals?" she asked while turning the bacon, which didn't need turning.

"Cleo broke into a sack of grain and is bloated up like an elephant. The horses are fine." He rolled the sleeves of his shirt to his elbows and came to stand beside her. "Need any help?"

"No," she said, harsher than was necessary.

"That's right, you never need help."

She stared at the mantle. It was one great piece of stone, chipped and carved into shape and bearing the chiseled likeness of the McDonnell family coat of arms. She stiffened against the word family, refusing to let it break through her veneer of control.

"The first Christmas I spent in boarding school, when the other girls were getting ready to leave for the holiday, Alice Raleigh asked me to come stay with her. I can't remember any other moment during my years in school when I was that happy. Not just because I wouldn't be alone for Christmas, but because that's my birthday, too, and I couldn't bear the thought of spending both of them alone."

Kayley moved the bacon off the fire, set the coffee on the hearth so it wouldn't boil dry and lifted the skillet of bread, taking it across the room and setting it on the table beside the lacy plant. She traced a finger across the cornbread's crusty surface.

"When Alice told her mother about her invitation, Mrs. Raleigh looked at me as though I had the plague and hissed in Alice's ear, 'I understand you wanting to help the poor thing, but having her in our house is

275

out of the question. What made you do such a thing?' And Alice, poor, sweet, terrified Alice, said, 'She begged me, Mother.'"

Kayley turned the cornbread out of the skillet onto a plate. She tried to set the skillet down, but couldn't make herself release the handle. She just stood there, holding on to it with both hands.

"I survived that first holiday without Alice Raleigh's help, and I've survived without help ever since, spending every Christmas and birthday alone while I waited for my father to send for me. That's when my real life would begin, I told myself, when Poppa sent for me. Everything else was just make-believe."

"How long did you wait, Kayley?"

"I was nine years old that Christmas, and I was twenty when my father sent for me."

She wasn't aware of Clay moving, and yet suddenly he was there, taking the skillet away from her and putting his arms around her, enveloping her in warm corduroy and wool. Holding her up. Holding her together.

She knew it wasn't twelve years of being alone at Christmas that caused her to hurt so much inside. It was knowing that soon twelve would become thirteen, and, because she'd finally realized that her father would never be well, thirteen would become fourteen, then fifteen and sixteen, stretching out into eternity and forever and always.

The snow outside the cabin was so deep it came almost to Kayley's chin as she slogged along behind

Clay through the tunnellike path he'd forged earlier to the shed.

"Maybe we shouldn't go yet," she said. Her voice hit the walls of snow around her and came bouncing back like a flat echo.

"Another storm would seal us in for the winter." He stopped walking so suddenly that she bumped into him. "That's not such a bad idea," he said, turning to wrap her in a bear hug made clumsy by the layers of clothes they wore and their coats, which had grown stiff with the cold.

"The rustlers would appreciate your sacrifice," she said and laughed at his scowl.

"If I can't have the whole winter with you, can I have a kiss?"

"Our lips will freeze together!"

"I don't mind if you don't."

"Kiss me," she said, and he obeyed, igniting her passions anew.

"I don't mind about the rustlers so much anymore," she said when he moved his kiss to her eyes and forehead.

"I do."

He pulled her along after him into the animal-warmed shed. The air smelled rich and raw. Kayley drew a deep breath of it into her frozen lungs before looking around.

It was big for a shed. One end was filled with stacks of hay and sacks of grain and the tin bathtub. The other end had been divided into two stalls. Tavira and Louisiana were crowded in one, Cleo and Boxer in the other, none of them looking very pleased by the arrangement.

While Clay went to get the horses, Kayley looked at a stacking of shelves that displayed a varied assortment of cans, jars, tools, and a candy box filled with marbles. Beside that chest of glassy treasure, was a tin of arsenic.

"What's wrong, kid?"

He was right behind her.

"A rat," she said.

"Not again. Where?"

She pointed at the shelf with the tin of arsenic.

"That's supposed to kill them, not attract them."

She didn't say anything. She just stared at the arsenic, seeing dead cattle, birds, rabbits, deer and Sip and Silly, and Snow's tears.

Clay turned her to face him. "You think I poisoned Antelope Springs."

She stared at the front of his coat. "You had no reason to," she said, trying to convince herself that it was true.

But it's true, she told herself. *He didn't have a reason.*

"I had the opportunity. I was there the day before I came for Toro."

"You didn't do it. I don't believe you did it."

"Say it again, Kayley, only this time, look at me when you say it so I can see if you mean it."

It took her a long time to lift her eyes to his face. She was almost blinded by the intensity of his silver gaze.

"I don't believe you did it."

"Good girl." He patted the side of her face with a gloved hand. "Now, let's get going and find out who did."

Chapter Twenty-Seven

The foothills of the Manzanos had received only a few inches of snow, the valley even less. The day turned warm as they rode, and when they reached the R Cross in the early afternoon, the only snow to be seen was on the white-capped mountains towering above them.

Standing on the veranda, with one shiny boot on the end of a bench where Elda was sitting and with one tailored shoulder leaning against the front wall of the house, was Vance. One glance at him was enough to make Kayley feel horribly gruesome, bundled as she was into so many layers of Clay's clothes, which he'd insisted she wear.

"Otherwise you'll freeze" had been his argument. And so they'd begun to tuck and fold and tie and pin the cuffs and waists and shirttails and collars that now made Kayley feel like she was wallowing in wool.

Elda went into the house, but Vance remained on the veranda, his foot still propped on the bench while Kayley tumbled off Louisiana.

"Is Sam back?" she asked Snow, who'd limped out of the barn. "I thought your foot was feeling better."

"Elda hit it with a poker, and I don't want to hear a word from you about it now or ever. As for Sam, yes. He's been back, was gone again, and now he's back again."

"What's Vance doing here?"

"Came for breakfast, stayed for lunch and probably decided to wait for supper to see if you came back so he'd have somebody else to brag to about his fall herd."

Bede jumped out of the adobe corral almost on top of them. Kayley hadn't even known he was in it. "Four hundred and fifty head," he announced. "That's what the Lucky Ace sold."

"That's a lot of cattle," Kayley said, unable to prevent herself from thinking that the number almost matched the drop in the R Cross herd.

"Especially considering he doesn't have any ranch hands working for him," Clay said. He'd unstrapped Cleo's pack saddle and was lifting it off her. She brayed enthusiastically as he turned her loose in the corral.

"He has men working for him," Kayley said.

"He had four hired guns working for him."

"Here we go again," she said and rolled her eyes in exaggerated despair.

"The boy ain't talkin' just to hear his gums flap," Snow said. "That bunch at the Lucky Ace packs enough hardware to give them kidney sores. Bede, fetch a handful of empty sacks out of the barn and start rubbin' these horses down. I'll get feed bags for them."

When they'd left, Clay said, "If you keep defending Moore like that, Kayley, I'm going to be forced to shoot him."

"Is that an admission of jealousy?"

He assumed a look of terror. "Those are frightening words to a single man, girl. Tell you what, I promise not to shoot him unless you tell me to, or unless he's trying to shoot me."

"I'll hold you to that," she said and felt herself blush in response to his sudden grin.

"Is that a promise?" he asked, leaning close to whisper in her ear.

"Sam!" she cried and ran across the yard to where Sam had just appeared on the bunkhouse porch. "How's Poppa?" she whispered before Clay could join them.

"He's the same. I told the men he was not to be discussed with Clay." Sam's voice regained its normal tone as Clay stepped onto the porch. "I was just setting out to look for you, Miss Ryan. The storm on the mountain had me worried."

"Louie and I got a little cold; but he remembered the way to the cabin, and Clay thawed us out."

"She was stiffer than old man Peters' underwear," Clay said. "Seems we're going to be working together for a spell, Butler. Kayley's offered me a third of the spring herd to end the troubles you've been having."

She looked up at him in surprise.

"Too bad you didn't start sooner," Sam said. "Maybe you could've stopped them from dynamiting Gallinas Spring."

Kayley was staggered. "When did it happen?"

"We heard it last night. Snow said it sounded like a

cannon instead of thunder, and we went to check it out. The spring's completely blocked. The boys are down there now starting to clear it out. We also lost close to a dozen cattle that were there to drink."

Bede came staggering onto the porch, his arms filled with Clay's belongings. "I'll show you where to bunk, sir."

"I don't like sleeping in crowds," Clay said. "I'll bunk here on the porch, but you can take my gear inside, son."

"It'll be too cold to sleep out here," Kayley protested.

"Don't worry, kid, I'll keep my boots on." He glanced at the sun. "It doesn't look like we're in for any more storms, so I'd better change before we head for Gallinas." He tugged on Kayley's braid. "You should peel a few layers off before you overheat, too."

"I have to talk to Vance first."

"Don't wait too long. You don't want him to think you're fainting because of him."

Kayley dragged her feet as she crossed the yard to the house. Vance always knew more about her than she did herself. Would he be able to look at her and know what had happened on the mountain?

"Congratulations on your herd," she said as she climbed onto the veranda. "You must be a born rancher."

He didn't take his foot off the bench or his shoulder off the wall. He just stood there, looking at her with disapproval in his eyes. "Where have you been?"

"Hiring Clay."

"All night?"

Her face flushed hot. "There was a storm."

He struck the veranda floor a sharp blow as he lowered his boot off the bench. "Two inches of snow was enough to keep you barricaded on the mountain with him?"

"That question doesn't deserve an answer." She turned to go inside, and he blocked the door with his arm.

"I want to know what happened on that mountain, Kayley. Your reputation is at stake."

"My father's men have kept Poppa's illness a secret; they'll do the same with my personal life."

"Men won't work for a whore."

Kayley fell back from him.

"And I won't marry one."

The world seemed to be tilting beneath her.

"You want to marry me?"

"Try not to act quite so shocked. After all, I did tell you that I loved you. I'd planned to wait until you'd outgrown your schoolgirl infatuation with that man. Now I see it's getting worse, not better." He pulled her into his arms. "Let me take care of you, Kayley. And don't say you don't need me. I know you do. Bede told me the herd count was low at roundup."

She pushed away from him. "He shouldn't have."

"Say you'll marry me, and say it now while there's still time for me to save the R Cross."

"It's not my fault our cattle are being stolen."

"I wasn't accusing you, my dear." He surrounded her again with his arms, subduing her effort to escape with his superior strength. "I'm not letting you go until you admit that you need help."

"I already have; that's why I hired Clay. He's going

283

to stop what's happening."

"You think so?" Vance asked, and his tone was as bruising as his embrace. "He's not stopping this."

His mouth came down on hers, crushing and hurting her, cutting her lips with his teeth as he raped her mouth with a kiss she couldn't avoid or escape.

That morning, beside the cold fireplace, Clay had kissed her in anger. Instead of violating her with it, though, he'd excited her with it, allowing the violence of their emotions to explode into passion, not punishment.

Vance was trying to make her suffer, to hurt her and humiliate her. She was repulsed by his kiss, and by him. When he finally released her, he stepped back from her and gave her a victorious smile.

"Are you finished?" she asked.

"For now."

She wiped her mouth with the back of her sleeve. "Then, I'm going inside to see my father."

She had to pass Vance to reach the door. Although ready to recoil from any attempt he made to renew his embrace, he didn't touch her, and she gave a relieved sigh as she stepped into the house.

"It's just a matter of time before you say yes to me, my dear," he called after her, his mocking voice trailing her like a wolf stalking its victim. "Just a matter of time."

Kayley took off her excess clothing and heaped the rumpled items on her bed before going to see her father. It was dark inside his bedroom except for ribbons of hazy light that filtered through the closed shutters, falling onto the bed, encasing Sullivan Ryan in a aura of faded light. And with him, Elda.

She was seated on the edge of the bed with her back to the door, completely unaware of anyone's presence except the man beside her as she pushed his hair back from the scar that purpled Sullivan's forehead. Her touch was soothing, gentle.

Loving, Kayley thought.

Her fingers tightened on the brass doorknob. "You love him," she said, and took a cruel delight in the start of surprise that brought Elda's hand jerking away from Sullivan's brow.

"How long?" Kayley asked.

Elda stood with regal dignity. "Do you hate your father so much that you want no one to love him?"

"I don't hate him." She crossed the room to kiss him. His eyes were closed, and she felt guilty for being spared the agony of looking into his dark stare.

"Then, why does it anger you that I care for him?" Elda asked.

"You love him."

Elda looked down at Sullivan. "Since the first time I saw him. He made me feel special."

Kayley remembered her father's one visit to the boarding school. His dancing eyes had caused Mrs. Potter, the widow of perpetual mourning, to actually smile and laugh. After he left, she'd treated Kayley like a daughter. When Sullivan failed to make another visit to the school, Mrs. Potter's fawning attention had turned to bitterness, as though the child were to blame for the father's lack of interest.

He must have affected other women the same way.

I shouldn't be upset just because Elda Moraillon fell prey to his charm.

"Did he ever talk about me?"

Kayley heard herself ask the question before she even realized she was thinking it. She wanted to take it back, to snatch it out of the air before it reached Elda. She didn't want anyone to know how desperate she was to know the answer, not even herself.

"Once," Elda said, and Kayley's heart seized up inside her from happiness, and disappointment. "He said that if you were as much like your mother as he expected you to be, you'd be perfect."

"When?" Kayley asked, her voice almost a whisper. "When did he say it?"

"The day he sent for you. I have work to do," Elda said and left.

Kayley sank to her knees beside the bed. "Were you disappointed, Poppa? Is that why you didn't have supper with Vance and me that night, because you wanted perfection and all you got was me?"

Chapter Twenty-Eight

Kayley balanced on the edge of a keg of molasses and tried to see into the depths of the second-highest shelf in the provisions storeroom. The room smelled the way she'd imagined Peters McDonnell's cabin would smell. She wondered if she could persuade Clay to install a window in here.

She couldn't see anything, even with the aid of a lantern, so she brushed her arm across the shelf, hoping to come into contact with the trunk for which she was searching. The only thing she found was dust. It billowed into the air, resettling in sneeze-provoking layers on her face and hands and hair and clothes.

The keg teetered beneath her as she reached for a higher shelf. She would have traded the keg for a bigger one, except it was the only one there. The storeroom was empty except for the molasses, a sack of sugar, a box of candles, and several stacks of evil-smelling soap.

The door, which had refused to stay open during

her search, opened now. "Are you checking supplies?" Gunning asked as he entered with a draft of chill afternoon air and sunlight. "If you are, it shouldn't take long. What happened to the supplies Snow brought back from Santa Fe?"

Kayley jumped down. "That's what I asked Elda. She said we've already used them. If I didn't have to pay for another load, I'd be glad. An empty room is much easier to search."

"Are you still looking for that trunk?"

She nodded and pushed the box of candles to the left, peered behind it, then sighed and collapsed onto the sack of sugar, whose fullness had been depleted by frequent use.

"How big was this trunk?" he asked, looking from the candles to her.

Kayley divided the dust-moted air with her hands, visually describing a trunk the size of a freight box.

"About that big, best as I can remember." She kicked her toe into a scattering of dried beans. "I'm sure I saw it beneath Poppa's desk the day I arrived. If that's where he kept the old ranch records, maybe I'll find receipts for the loan payments Claude Asken claimed Poppa didn't make."

"Perhaps my sister knows where it is."

"I asked. She doesn't remember ever seeing it but said she'd look for it this morning while I read to Poppa. She didn't find it, though."

"Yes, she did."

Kayley looked up and saw Bede Moraillon standing in the open door of the storeroom. He didn't have his usual whipped pup expression, and she realized that he never looked that way except around

288

his mother.

"Sorry I interrupted, Miss Ryan. I came to get Sam a bar of soap and heard you and Uncle Gunning talking."

"Sam and Clay are back?" Her spirits lifted so quickly that she jumped to her feet to keep from getting dizzy.

"Just rode in." Bede reached a skinny arm in front of Gunning to the stacks of soap.

"Take one for yourself, too," Gunning said and handed Bede a second bar.

"I've been mucking out stalls. About that trunk, it's a small one, right?"

Kayley nodded.

"Ma's got it in her room."

"Why would she put it in there?"

"It was already there. She had me pull it out from under her bed; that's how I knew she'd found it."

"Where's your mother?" Gunning asked.

"Ma had Snow drive her to Tajique so she could argue with that woman that comes here to do the washing. You want me to take the trunk over to the main house for you, Miss Ryan?"

"If it is the one I'm looking for, Elda would've said something before she left."

"She opened it, and there's a lot of stuff in it, like receipts we get when Sam trades cattle or buys supplies."

"It sounds like what I want," Kayley said. "Why would it have been under Elda's bed?"

Bede shrugged. "If you wanna look to be sure, it's right inside Ma's room. I'll unlock the door."

He was gone, out of the storeroom and leading the

way to his mother's room behind the kitchen before Kayley could protest. He was lighting a lantern when she and Gunning reached it. At first Kayley wondered why, then she saw the thick curtains that prevented even the smallest ray of sunlight from coming into the room.

"Ma likes privacy," Bede explained. "I think it looks like a dungeon."

The dismal impression was heightened by the boxes and crates that were stacked and packed and stuffed everywhere in the room.

"What is all this?" Gunning asked.

"Ma's things from back east. When we came out here, she thought she'd have more room, and she brought everything we owned."

"I wrote her describing exactly how much space she'd have," Gunning said.

A photograph displayed on the mantle caught Kayley's attention. "That looks like Vance," she said, pointing at one of the unsmiling, light-haired men standing stiffly inside the frame. Between them was a boy almost Bede's age with equally light hair and eyes bright with impatience. The man resembling Vance was holding on to the boy, forcing him to stand still for the photographer.

"That's Uncle Ivo. The other man's my father."

Gunning stepped closer to see the photograph. "I never met Alba. He's a fine-looking man. Is this you?" he asked Bede, indicating the boy.

"I don't know who it is. Uncle Ivo died when I was a baby."

"We'd better check the trunk," Kayley said.

It took her only a moment to recognize the small

trunk Bede showed her as the one she'd seen beneath her father's desk. She knelt and opened the lid. The receipts Bede had mentioned were there, along with account books and letters and a lot of paper that looked like garbage.

"This is it," she said and closed the lid. "I think we should leave it here until Elda returns. I don't want her to think I'm spying on her."

"I shall speak to her about this," Gunning said. He was looking at the photograph as he spoke. "She should've told you that she found the trunk before she left."

Bede closed the door to his mother's room and locked it. "Sam's gonna have my hide for not getting him his soap sooner."

"We'll protect you, won't we, Gunning?" Kayley said, and they fell into step beside him.

Clay was nowhere in sight, but Sam was in the juniper corral brushing burrs from Old Joe's tail. It was a task that usually required the mare being tied head and foot and thrown to the ground.

Kayley was wondering at Old Joe's surprising tolerance when, at fifty feet away, she caught the first whiff of why Sam had asked for soap in the middle of the week. The stench suddenly surrounded her as a pair of familiar arms encircled her from behind, pulling her into an embrace rank with the smell of skunk.

"Let me go, Clay! I can't breath."

Gunning pinched his nostrils closed and backed away from them. Bede just stood there grinning and looking embarrassed.

"Give me a kiss first," Clay said and turned her to

face him. "What have you been doing, kid? You look like we smell."

"Then, I must look pretty terrible."

"It's just terrible how pretty you look."

She laughed as she pushed free from the odorous confinement. "What happened?"

"Sam and I made a new friend last night."

She edged away from him to catch her breath. "I hope you didn't bring him back with you."

"Old Joe wanted to," Sam said. "She's been as sweet as peppermint ever since we started stinking."

"Maybe she doesn't like clean people," Bede said. He moved up to the roan's head. Old Joe snapped her yellow teeth at him, and Bede jumped away. "Guess I'm wrong," he said with a sheepish grin.

"How's the spring?" Kayley asked Clay.

He leaned back against the corral fence and hooked his right boot heel on the lowest rail. "Ruined. It'll take weeks to clear the rock away, and that's no guarantee the flow hasn't been diverted by the blast."

"Were there any wild horse tracks around it? I've spotted the white stallion in that area several times."

"The only horses that have been near Gallinas were wearing shoes. Sam and I were getting ready to follow them when our new friend wandered into camp and spooked Boxer, who spooked the skunk, who sprayed us."

"Here's your soap," Bede said and tossed Sam one of the two bars. He slipped the other in his back pocket. "For after I finish the stalls," he said to his uncle.

Clay reached out to tug on the collar of Kayley's gingham dress. "Maybe you should join us, kid. You can scrub my back, and I'll scrub yours, again," he said, breathing the last word into her hair as he leaned close to her ear.

"Miss Ryan doesn't discuss bathing with the hired help," Gunning said, accentuating the last two words so heavily, and in such a pompous tone, that Kayley turned to look at him. His eyebrows were arched, and he was glaring at Clay.

"Yes, sir!" Clay barked, snapping to sudden attention and grinning at Gunning. "Who gets the horse trough first, Butler?"

"You smell worse, but I've got the soap."

"Not anymore," Clay said and snapped out his left hand so fast it was a blur. He grabbed the soap away from Sam and tossed it in the air, catching it and then placing his fingers around it precisely in a strange manner. "Ever hear of a game called baseball, Butler?"

Sam nodded.

"Good. I'll pitch, you catch. Gunning's the batter." Clay moved out into the yard, turned and began to wind his arm around and around like a windmill. "Here she comes!" he shouted and acted as though he were going to throw the soap at Sam. Instead, he heaved it straight up in the air.

"Infield fly!" he shouted as Sam went diving after the soap, hitting the ground with his face several feet short of the falling bar.

"You're safe, old man." Clay slapped Gunning on the back before turning to Kayley and chucking her under the chin. "See you later, kid." He and Sam, who'd retrieved the soap, disappeared behind the bunkhouse.

"I'd better get back to work," Bede said and chased after them.

"Kid," Kayley murmured. She looked down at the tucked pleats on the bodice of her dress. "Do you think I look like a kid, Gunning?"

"I wouldn't know, miss," he said in a very embarrassed tone.

Kayley laughed at him. "I'm asking my best friend an important question, so stop blushing. I want to know if my dresses are too young for me?"

"You always look charming, only, maybe, just a little young."

"What you're trying not to say is that I dress like a schoolgirl. But that's all I've ever known except for school teachers, and they always dress like someone just died." She looked down at her dress again. "Tomorrow, Gunning, I'm going to Belen, and I want my best friend to go with me. If you will."

"I'd be honored, miss."

Jack came out of the bunkhouse. He and Sam had spent all afternoon scrubbing and scraping and soaking and scrubbing again. Even though Bede had assured him that the smell of skunk was no longer on them, Jack could still smell its stench.

In Lansing, the prisoners had frequently been forced to go weeks without bathing. The rancid smell of their sweat, combined with the black filth of the coal they'd been forced to dig for the state, had disgusted Jack.

The stench of the skunk reminded him of those years in hell, and his hate was burning fresh and hot when he noticed Kayley standing alone in front of the veranda.

He stepped from the darkness into the light that seemed to surround her. "I thought you'd be knitting or doing whatever it is women do after supper."

The fringe of her shawl shivered in the breeze like dancing white icicles. "I was just looking at the sky before I turn in for the night. The stars are so bright tonight."

"Take a walk with me."

She lowered her gaze from the heavens to him. "I'd love to."

They walked along the edge of the arroyo under the naked branches of the cottonwoods that reached up in stark relief toward the Milky Way's river of brilliance. Jack pointed at a small cluster of stars giving off a quivering, misty light.

"The Pleiades. They're my favorites. They look more like diamonds than all the rest."

"Or dewdrops in morning light." She was looking up at them, her face lovely in the pale light and her hair like dark fire.

Hate, Jack reminded himself as he looked at her. *I'm here because of hate, to destroy what belongs to Sullivan and to claim what is mine.*

But the lines between the two were becoming blurred, and in the middle was this shining girl.

He pulled her to him, the warm, soft feel of her causing an ache of need deep within him.

"You smell like soap," she said.

"You smell like clover." He brushed his hand across the side of her face and stroked it down the length of her unbound hair. "Sam and I'll be gone several nights. Tell me how much you're going to miss me."

Her arms slipped around his waist, and he felt the touch of her hands on his back beneath his vest.

"I'm going to be very busy and probably won't think of you at all. When you get back, I'll look surprised and say, 'Were you gone? I didn't even notice.'"

"Liar."

She smiled up at him, her cheek dimpling and her eyes filled with stars. "I'm not very good at it, am I? I'll miss you terribly, even though I will be very busy."

"Knitting?"

"I'm not very good at that," she said with a guilty grimace. "Mrs. Potter was always horrified at the things I created with my knitting needles. 'A waste of yarn,' she'd say and then start ripping it apart. So while you're out chasing rustlers, I'll be going through a trunk where my father keeps his old account books and receipts."

Jack's heart raced. "Sounds exciting," he said with a yawn.

"Stop that," she said and playfully poked him in the ribs. "You devil, now I'm doing it," and her laughter dissolved into a yawn.

Sam was leading Old Joe and Tavira out of the corral.

"I have to go," Jack said.

"Why did you tell Sam we agreed on a third of the herd instead of half?"

"Because I'm a kind-hearted person." She started to laugh again, and he squeezed her until she stopped. "I'm doing it because when I find whoever's causing the trouble you're having, I want Sam and his men here to back me up, not on the other side of the territory chasing cows. If you keep smiling at me like that, kid, I'm never going to get any work done, so stop looking adorable and kiss me good-bye."

She stretched up onto her tiptoes. It wasn't enough, though, and he had to lean over to let her reach him. Her lips were soft against his, and he drank deeply of their sweetness. It took an effort to let her go.

But as he rode away, it wasn't Kayley he was thinking of; it was Sullivan Ryan's trunk.

Chapter Twenty-Nine

Kayley held the paper-wrapped package in front of her and pressed close to her, a shield against the fear that the dress wasn't right, that it was too suggestive, too mature, too everything except perfect. And yet it was perfect. Soft and shimmering and perfect.

There'd been an entire rack of ready-made ladies' dresses in Hunting and Company's General Merchandise Store in Belen. Becker's had contained a similar rack, and so had Hirschberg's and Scholle's. Kayley had been overwhelmed by the selection available, but not Gunning. He'd rejected them all, each for a different reason. The pink was too pale, the blue had the wrong lace, the yellow suffered from too many ruffles, the green didn't have enough ruffles, the black was too matronly and the red not matronly enough.

Kayley had given up ever finding anything to please him, when in the dimly lit back room of Felipe Chaves' store, Charity Calhoun, who was working for Señor Chaves, had shown them a dress made of magic and moonbeams. The moment Kayley saw it, she thought of Clay and how she'd feel wearing it for him.

"Perfect," Gunning had announced.

"Señorita Calhoun's mother, she made it," Señor Chaves said as he turned the dressmaker's dummy, to which the creation clung, around so that Kayley could see the dress from all angles. "It will make you look very much the lovely lady, Señorita Ryan."

Kayley had immediately bought the dress, not because of his flattery, but because of the anticipated light of surprise and pleasure in Clay's eye when he saw her in it. And now, even though she doubted herself and the dress, she didn't doubt Clay's reaction to it.

Señor Chaves finished writing the receipt for her purchases, which included enough supplies to restock the ranch storeroom.

"Anything else, señorita?"

"What are those?" She pointed at three blue-labeled cans behind the counter.

"Smoked oysters. A luxury not many can afford. I used to sell many. Now not even one."

The day Kayley had arrived at the R Cross, while she'd babbled about her trip from Boston and how wonderful the ranch house was and how very incredibly happy she was to be there with her father, Sullivan Ryan had sat at his desk eating, with unconcealed pleasure, tidbits from a blue-labeled can that she realized now had contained smoked oysters.

"I'll take them," she said. "Do you have any more?"

"No, señorita. Would you like to order more?"

"I'd like that very much."

"This brand"—he rubbed a thumb across the label on one of the cans—"it comes from Boston and takes much time to arrive."

"I understand. Just let me know when you have them in stock again." She smiled. "My father likes them."

Charity Calhoun, who was young and blond and very pretty, smiled at Kayley. "I'll order them for you today."

While Señor Chaves added the cost of the oysters to the receipt, Kayley crossed to the front window of the store. In the street outside, Francisco, the oldest Chaves son, was helping Gunning load the R Cross wagon.

Gunning's confrontation with Elda over the need for these supplies had been unpleasant. She'd argued that Sullivan had given her the responsibility to order supplies and that Gunning had no right to take the job away from her or imply that she'd mishandled the task.

"I've looked over her household expenses," Gunning had explained to Kayley. "And beginning last fall, the size of the orders have been increasing. Since spring, they've doubled. She's negligent and wasteful, and that's not something that can be tolerated."

"Your signature, señorita," Señor Chaves said as he handed Kayley the receipt.

She winced at the fifteen-dollar cost of her dress, and the additional five dollars for a pattern and the yards of material Gunning had insisted she buy.

"A lady must have more than one dress," he said when she protested the extravagance, "no matter

300

how beautiful that one dress."

Kayley scribbled her name. *"Gracias,"* she said to Señor Chaves. "And thank you," she said to Charity before picking up the package of oysters and fleeing the store.

In the sun-drenched street outside, Kayley accepted Gunning's offered hand of assistance into the wagon. Only it wasn't his hand, she realized when she looked at the elegant fingers squeezing hers.

"Vance!" She stood with one foot poised in the spoke wheel as she stared up at him in surprise. He was dressed all in black, except for his shirt, which was creamy white with a diamond stickpin. His hat was placed so carefully among the molded waves of his hair, his head looked like a sculpture.

"My dear," he said with a smile. "I thought you'd be toiling with your men at Gallinas."

"I had an errand." She scrambled the rest of the way into the wagon. "What are you doing in town?"

"I prefer cards to cattle, so I left my men to do their jobs and came looking for a poker game. It was luck that brought me to Belen today instead of Socorro. Tell me, my dear, do you think the labors of Sam Butler and his flock will be able to restore your little spring to usefulness?"

"They're trying."

"I suppose with that man Clay's help." Vance's dark hazel eyes turned black. "I'm telling you this for your own good, my dear. That man is trouble. It would surprise me if he wasn't the cause of your trouble."

She pulled her hand away from him. "I like trouble. Good luck with your game, Vance. I'm ready to go, Gunning."

He cracked the reins across the backs of Gypsy One and Gypsy Two. The mules twitched their ears backward, and when greeted by Gunning's, "Ho, gittup," they sauntered forward.

When they reached the end of Belen's main street and rolled onto the flat green land that bordered the Rio Grande, she couldn't stand her guilt any longer.

"I shouldn't have been so rude to Vance. It's just that he makes me feel so inadequate that I get mad at him and can't hold my tongue."

"I've never cared for him."

"Was he Poppa's friend very long?"

Gunning urged the Gypsies to increase their speed from a shuffle to a walk. "They met in Santa Fe last December, and he came back to the ranch with Mr. Ryan."

"So they could play cards?" Kayley asked.

"That was their main source of entertainment," Gunning said, "until your father lost half the ranch in March."

"And Vance was staying at the ranch all that time? Now I know where all our supplies went."

Gunning turned to look at her.

"He was living at the ranch, and this summer he ate most of his meals there," she explained. "You've seen how Elda loads his plate, just like she does Bede's."

He faced the mules again. "It's something to consider." There was a scowl on his face.

"I was joking."

His expression didn't change. "I know, miss."

"Maybe whoever's stealing Poppa's cows is stealing our supplies."

"The lookout would see him."

Kayley thought of her midnight walks to Quarai that always went unchallenged.

"Only strangers are challenged," Gunning said, surprising her by reading her mind. "And the lookout is only posted at night."

"You'd see anyone who came in during the day."

"If Mr. Ryan is restless at night, I sit with him and then sleep during the day."

"Elda would notice someone driving off with a wagon of supplies. She can see the storeroom from the kitchen, and even if she wasn't in the kitchen, she can hear a harness jingle within two miles of the house and would investigate."

Gunning turned to look at Kayley again. "Yes, she would, wouldn't she?"

"Then, it's settled," Kayley decided, unwilling to believe rustlers and dynamiters were lurking so close to the house where her father lay helpless. "Vance is responsible for all those missing beans."

"I believe you're right, Miss Ryan. But I suggest a lookout be posted constantly, just in case we're wrong."

"You worry too much." She thought again of the price of the supplies they'd just purchased. "Worriers have good ideas, though. I'll tell Sam when he and Clay return," she said and unconsciously hugged the dress to her. "I hope it's soon."

Jack knelt in the gravel to get a better look at the tracks he'd found. "They're recent. Not more than two days old."

He walked to the top of the gully and looked west, the direction the tracks were headed. Fogged by distance and the fading afternoon light, the limestone ruins of Gran Quivira topped a rise southwest of the gully which had washed down from the slopes of Los Jumanos Mesa. He'd chased Satan's Angel in this direction the day he'd first met Kayley. Had the impressive disappearing act simply been a jump into this deep trough?

"It matches the tracks at Gallinas and those I found at the branding fires," Willie Pete announced after looking at the prints. He unfolded his long legs and walked a short distance west, where he knelt again. "This one's from a different horse, and the rider's right-handed."

Jack nodded. He'd already noticed the tendency of the horse to drift right, as opposed to the Gallinas' tracks that drifted left.

"Most of the men in New Mexico are right-handed," Sam said. He handed Tavira's reins to Jack. "You're the only exception around here."

"One of Moore's men straps his gun on the left."

"So does Slowhand. But he draws with his right."

"Cavalry man," Jack said.

Willie had walked a few more yards away from them. "Wild horses," he said and pointed at the ground.

Jack went to look. An unshod print with edges so sharp they could have been carved with a knife was imprinted in the soft dirt. "The white stallion," he said. There were other prints with Satan's Angel's. Most of them were indistinct, except for one wearing iron shoes with a bulge on one side.

"That's Sophia," Willie said.

"She's got splayed feet," Sam explained to Jack. "Takes a shoe like that to cover her foot. It's hard to believe she's able to keep up with the stallion. Miss Ryan'll never stop trying to catch him now, even if it's just to get Sophia back."

"She thought a lot of that little paint, didn't she?" Jack asked.

"Mr. Ryan should've put a hole in that nag's head instead of making it a present to her," Willie said.

"Why didn't he?"

Sam slapped his reins against his knee. "Willie, see if you can find any more tracks."

"Sure thing." Willie mounted his bay and rode along the widening path of the gully.

"Why is it," Jack asked when he and Sam were alone, "that whenever Sullivan's name comes up, you close down the conversation?"

"We're here to work, not gossip about the boss."

"I don't want to gossip; I want to know what's so important that he can't come back here and deal with these problems himself instead of leaving his girl to face the trouble."

"We're wasting daylight."

"And I'm wasting my breath asking you about Ryan."

"You're a fast learner."

Willie came riding back. "Nothing."

"They didn't just fly away," Jack said. "Since our backs are to Los Jumanos, we'll ignore the east. Willie, you take the north. Sam, you've got the south; I'll go west."

305

"Two shots for success," Sam said.

"If we don't find anything, we'll meet back at Gallinas tomorrow," Jack said, and Willie rode away.

"What's the sentence for these men when we catch them, Butler?"

"A tall tree and a short rope," Sam said, "unless Miss Ryan's with us. Then they go to the sheriff." He spun his mare, and her feet sent out a shower of gravel as he spurred her south.

Jack mounted Tavira and rode west. When he'd ridden far enough to be out of sight of both Sam and Willie, he turned Tavira north and put the big Arabian into a ground-eating gallop, straight for the R Cross ranch house.

Chapter Thirty

It was late when Kayley and Gunning reached the ranch. Darkness had long since dimmed the colors of the Manzanos, and the Salinas Valley lay like a giant carpet of shadows beneath a sliver of moon.

"This don't look like no little bit of shoppin' to me," Snow said as he and Bede jingled their way off the bunkhouse porch. "We was missin' that much stuff?"

"The storeroom was empty," Gunning said.

"Except for a lot of dust," Kayley added as Snow helped her down.

He indicated the package she held. "That must be the little bit."

"It's a dress."

"A purty one?"

"Very pretty." She slid a finger beneath the package's binding string. "At least, I think so."

"Then, he will, too, girl."

"Who?" she asked, staring at him in what she hoped looked like wide-eyed bewilderment.

"Stop flappin' them lashes at me. You know who I mean, and I know who you bought that gettup to impress. Now, you and Gunnin' get inside and let me and the boy here deal with this wagon. Come on, Bede, stop standin' there draggin' your bottom lip and get that harness unharnessed and them knots unknotted and that rope unroped."

"I saw Charity Calhoun," Kayley said to Bede. "She didn't have any of her mother's fudge for sale, but she told me to tell you hello." Bede's mouth worked like a fish out of water. "Snow, would you put this in the storeroom for me?" She handed the trail cook the sack of canned oysters. "It's a Christmas present for my father."

"I'll put it right next to the candles so you can find it easy. What are you doin', boy?" he barked at Bede, who had managed to twist the reins around his feet and was causing Gypsy One to bawl a protest, which brought an answer from an unseen, but audibly recognizable, Cleo. "Not again," Snow moaned and covered his ears with his hands. "I'd shoot that critter; but her hide's too tough for bullets to get through, and she's too dumb to die anyways."

After Kayley put her new dress in her room, she checked on her father. He was asleep. She pushed the hair from his forehead and kissed his sunken cheek before going to the living room and starting to work.

She dumped the contents of Sullivan's trunk, which Bede had put beside the desk, into the center of the floor. There were six leather-bound cashbooks like the one on her father's desk which he'd filled with addresses and notes. These had been used for accounting, although like the other book, no dates were legible inside the branded front covers.

The cashbooks that covered the last five years of the R Cross history were less fancy. Kayley put them in a separate stack and began the momentous task of sorting the receipts and letters and heaps of ticket stubs from theaters and opera houses as far away as Boston and San Francisco, and as close as Santa Fe.

She'd been sitting cross-legged on the floor for more than an hour when Gunning entered the room. "It's late, Miss Ryan. You should do that tomorrow."

"I want to ride to Gallinas tomorrow and see how the men are doing. Is my father still asleep?"

"Yes, miss. I just left him."

"I'll check on him before I go to bed." She smiled up at Gunning. "Thank you for helping me today."

"There's no need to thank a friend, miss."

"And there's no need to call a friend miss."

A ghost of a smile flickered among the muscles in his stoic face. "It's a habit."

"I wish you'd break it."

"I'll work on it. Good night, mis—my friend."

"Not perfect," she said with a laugh, "but it's a start. Good night, Gunning."

Soon after he retired, she began to feel the effects of the long day and decided to call it a night. But once wrapped in the warm comfort of her nightgown, she couldn't make herself slip into bed. The contents of her father's trunk, which she'd left heaped in the living room, called her back to their cluttered midst.

She scooped the stack of letters from the floor and sank into one of the overstuffed chairs in front of the banked fire. With her feet tucked beneath her and her hair flowing across her shoulders and over the arms of the chair, she began to learn about the father she never knew.

Her candle was a mere stub when she finished the last letter. She watched the flame struggle to survive while she struggled to come to terms with what she'd learned.

Gunning's friend, Jack Corbett, had been not only the ranch's original owner; he had also been her father's partner. When Corbett had mysteriously disappeared, Sullivan Ryan had taken over sole ownership of the ranch, changing its name from the Crescent C, which she'd realized was the brand on the white cashbooks, to the R Cross.

Her father had then tried to sell the ranch, but the lack of adequate fresh water to support the massive herds that cattle companies wanted to graze on the rich valley grasses had defeated his efforts.

It was the letter from Elda Moraillon that had defeated Kayley. It was dated May of last year. It thanked Sullivan for inviting Elda and Bede to the R Cross during his April visit to Boston, and for the money he'd sent to pay for their train tickets.

That had been the last letter Kayley read, and now it refused to fall from her numb fingers. It clung to her with such determination, she wondered if she'd ever be able to let it go.

She pressed her face against the arm of the chair. "I wish Clay were here," she whispered, and the candle flame died, plunging the room into darkness and her wish into silence.

Slowhand Smith was standing lookout on the roof

of the ranch house. He lifted a hand of greeting to Jack, who returned the salute before riding Tavira into the wood corral. He left the stallion there and crossed the barren ground to the veranda.

It was almost two in the morning. As he'd expected, no lights gleamed from inside the house. He tried the front door. It was latched. He ran his hand up along the left side of the doorframe, his fingertips searching for an unnatural indentation in the oak. When he found it, he pressed on it. Inside the doorframe, a flurry of unseen activity resulted in the dull sound of the inside latch springing open.

"Thanks, Gramps, for the woodworking lessons," he said as he pushed the door open. Once inside, he offered a silent thanks to whoever kept the hinges so well oiled.

The house was quiet, just the ticking of the mantle clock disturbing the stillness. A red glow of light radiated out from the banked fire. Papers had been scattered across the blue rug and around the clawed feet on his grandmother's chairs. Jack ignored them in favor of searching the desk. He crossed the room with silent steps. There was no trunk under it or beside it, and the desk itself was locked.

Before risking discovery by searching Kayley's room for the trunk and the desk key, he decided to check the papers. His boot struck a solid object with a thud. He stood motionless until no answering sounds were heard in the house, stepped sideways to avoid whatever he'd kicked, and walked into a trap of crunching papers.

Instead of trying to find his way through the maze, he backtracked to the desk and moved along the wall

311

to the closest window. The hinges on the shutters weren't well oiled, and they squeaked as he opened them.

A sound, like the mumble of disturbed sleep, echoed the sound of the hinges. Jack turned to look at the moonlit room and saw, snuggled into one of the chairs, Kayley Ryan.

As he watched, her lower lip became fuller, making it look like she was about to cry while her right hand made motions as though trying to release the paper she held.

The way she sighed and frowned and reached out reminded Jack of being in his cabin with her in bed beside him, naked and asleep and the glory of her hair tangled from love-making.

He knelt beside the old chair and caught a silken curl between his fingers, bringing its fire to his lips and letting its scent carry him deeper into that delicious memory of their night of passion.

His gentle caress of her hair melted the frown of worry on her face, and her lower lip stilled its tremble.

"Sweet child," Jack whispered, and her lashes, golden even in the moonlight, lifted slightly, revealing two sleeping pools of perfect blue.

Blue, like Sullivan's eyes.

Jack dropped the red curl and bent to his task with the bitter taste of his hate staining his mouth and heart.

The subject of three of the letters were his and Sullivan's original contract discussions. Jack folded them into his pocket. The rest were useless. He left

312

them on the floor. The only thing he hadn't read was the letter in Kayley's hand. He touched a finger to the inside of her wrist and began to stroke the pulse beneath her soft skin. She clutched the paper tighter. He kept stroking. A soft moan escaped her lips, and her fingers relaxed.

He caught the letter as it floated to the floor. The script was so faint he had to take it to the window and hold it up to the moonlight before he could read it. It had been written by the housekeeper, Elda Moraillon, and was addressed to Sullivan. She called him "my love" and promised she'd be with him before the month was out.

"Threatened is more like it." Jack said as he remembered her unenthusiastic reception to his joining the R Cross crew.

Kayley stirred at the sound of his voice. She sat upright, blinking in confusion at her awakening. He knelt beside her, dropping the letter and catching her face between his hands to kiss away any sound of fear she might make at seeing someone in the room with her.

"I missed you," he said after she stopped resisting him and began to return his kiss.

"I'm glad." She slipped her arms around his neck and smiled. "I dreamed you were kissing my wrist."

He turned his head and pressed his lips to the place he'd been stroking. "What's all this mess?"

"Lots of lies," she said and waved her hand in the direction of the trap Jack had walked into earlier. There was the trunk she'd mentioned to him, along with piles of receipts and stacks of cashbooks.

313

His heart quickened in recognition of the books chronicling the early success of the Crescent C Ranch, its downfall due to a few bad winters, then its brush with bankruptcy after the 1873 cattle market catastrophe, and its quick recovery after an injection of cash from a Boston investor, Sullivan Ryan.

Those books were Jack's vindication, his salvation, his dream come true. And they were stacked not two feet away from him. If he'd seen them earlier, instead of a cascade of golden-red curls, he'd be on his way to Santa Fe right this minute.

"What it it?" Kayley asked. She turned his face toward her. "I've never seen you like this, like there was a fire burning inside of you."

"There is," he said and claimed her mouth with a savage kiss. Everything he'd dreamed about in prison was within his reach. The proof he needed to reclaim the land Sullivan had stolen from him, and the price Jack wanted in retribution for that treachery.

Kayley was that price, the cost Sullivan would have to pay for his sins. Her innocence, her heart and happiness, and most especially, her love. Jack would settle for nothing less. Once he'd flung that in Sullivan's greedy face, then tossed it away like a spent shell, that's when Jack would finally be completely free.

He slanted his kiss across Kayley's willing mouth while pulling open her robe and gown. When he closed his hand around the fullness of a breast, she sighed into his kiss and arched herself into his grasp.

It was an offer Jack didn't refuse. He tore his lips from hers and grasped her legs, forcing them out in

314

front of her as he knelt between them in front of the chair. Then he imprisoned her lips again with his kisses.

He jerked the hem of her gown to her knees, then higher, following its rise with cruel caresses that made her try to writhe away from him. He held her tighter, treating with vicious delight the beauty he'd known in both tenderness and anger, and with ultimate pleasure and unmatchable passion.

This time he didn't want pleasure; he wanted satisfaction. He jerked her closer to him and pressed his full weight onto her, forcing himself against her yielding gentleness with such savagery that she began to buck and twist beneath him and gasp for breath around the brutal hardness of his tongue.

"Stop it, Clay, you're hurting me," she pleaded when he released her lips and mouth to draw his own desperately needed breath.

Jack pulled her out of the chair and onto the paper-strewn rug, where he yanked her gown to her waist. The gown moved higher beneath the urgent lifting of his hands to her breasts which were firm and full and shaking with her gasps of fear. He crushed her quaking body beneath him as he filled his mouth with the flushed red flesh of her right nipple, then her left.

He slid down her quivering body until his lips were poised above the cold fire of her passion. It was then, just as he was about to spread her legs, that he realized she was crying and trying to cover herself with ineffective hands.

"You bloody bastard, you bloody cold-hearted

bastard," she said, her eyes closed tightly and her body rigid beneath him. "You one-eyed bottle of panther piss, you fly-ridden pile of cattle droppings, you tick-bitten chunk of rotten meat, you worthless pail of spit."

Jack's rage had faded at the first sight of her tears, but it was the painfully perfect enunciation of the curses that affected him most. Her voice was the only thing over which she still had control, and to hear her trying to hold on to her courage through it was more devastating to him than any tear could ever be.

He sat up and covered her nakedness with her gown and robe. Except for her hands, which she clenched into fists and held rigid against her sides, she didn't move. She just lay there, eyes closed while she spat out curse after curse.

"You ignorant farmer of land that should be grass, you overgrown piece of grizzly gut, you bandy-legged, flat-seated excuse for a man."

"That's it." He grasped her hands and pulled her into a sitting position. "Why don't you stop stumbling around it and just say what you mean, kid?"

Her eyes snapped open, and she glared at him. "I didn't want it like this. I wanted what we had before. I wanted it because I wanted you and because I wanted to punish Poppa by doing something he'd disapprove of happening in his own house." She stopped and took a shaky breath. "I'm stumbling again. What I wanted, was for you to make love to me, Clay. Not rape me."

It was what Jack had been doing. So why did it hurt him so much to hear those trembling lips accuse

316

him of his crime?

"What did I do that made you want to hurt me?"

"It wasn't anything you did, sweetheart."

He touched the side of her face hesitantly, fearing she'd turn away.

"There's so much you don't know about me, Kayley."

"There's a lot about me that I don't know. But I do know that I don't want you to hurt me." Her eyes opened. "And I know that even after what just happened, I still want you to make love to me."

She almost couldn't finish. But she did. And when she'd made it all the way through her declaration, Jack swept her into his arms and claimed her lips with a kiss as deep and penetrating as the ones he'd forced on her, only this one wasn't forced. It wasn't punishing or cruel or hurting or angry. Because this time he wasn't taking; he was giving.

She received his gift with a smile and a sigh. He demanded more response by biting and nipping at her lips, by licking them and sucking them and tasting every perfect inch of her face until her sighs became moans that filled his mouth and chest and soul with so much desire he could hardly stand.

He carried her past the trunk, pausing to glance at the stack of white cashbooks and reassure himself they were real. Then across the living room he carried her, a treasure of immeasurable value that belonged only to him. Now, tomorrow, and forever, Kayley Ryan would always belong to him.

"Which room is yours?"

"Facing east."

317

"That bed's too small." He stopped outside the carved oak doors of the room that had been his bedroom. "How about in here?" She slipped her tongue into his ear. "It's also closer," he added.

"No," she said as she withdrew her tongue. Before he could ask why not, she began to batter at his chest with her fists. "Put me down, put me down this minute!"

The desperate note in her voice caused him to obey, standing her on her feet and releasing her from his clinging embrace.

"I heard him call me," she said and threw open the double doors with a sweeping push of her hands. She ran on bare feet into the room and across the moonlit floor to fall on her knees beside the huge bed. She clasped at something there, something so frail and wasted it couldn't really be a hand.

But it was a hand, and she pressed it to her cheek in loving gentleness while looking into the face of the specter who lay beneath the blankets without hardly disturbing their folded perfection.

"I heard you; I heard you call me." She raised up from her knees to look into open, staring eyes that were the color of death.

"Kay . . ." the creature's ghastly voice wept, and Jack's heart froze in recognition.

"Say it again, Poppa, please, say it again!"

"That's not your father," Jack said.

She turned to look at him, tears making silver streaks across her pale face. "He was hurt and he had a stroke. I'd stopped believing he'd ever get well, but I was wrong." She turned back to the skeleton face on

318

the pillow. "You are getting well, Poppa; you have to so you can tell me why you sent for her and not me."

"Stop it, Kayley. Stop it right now!"

Jack advanced with angry steps into the room, intending to drag the pitiful imposter from the bed and force a confession from the sagging lips. But he couldn't make himself move any closer than the foot of the bed. He just stood there, his fists clenched around the bedpost and his hate pounding inside him like a heartbeat.

"That's not Sullivan," he said, desperate to make himself believe.

The dark, staring eyes narrowed, shifting their empty stare from the ceiling to Jack. He felt their touch on his face like the scalding heat of a branding iron on bare flesh.

"Cor . . ." Sullivan said, spitting the sound out like it tasted dirty.

The emaciated body began to rise from the bed, the thin fingers of one hand clutching at Kayley, the other hand clawing the air in deadly promise as they reached for Jack, who didn't know whether to be sickened by his discovery or to laugh at it.

"He's never been like this before," Kayley said.

She was trying to push him down, to stop his grasping and clawing and to pull her hand free from his frantic hold on her. The scrawny fingers caught in her hair and dragged her face so close to the drooling lips that Jack saw her recoil.

"Kay . . ."

"Let me have him, Miss Ryan," Gunning said as he entered the room. "Please, sir, step outside. Your presence is upsetting him."

"What happened to him?" Jack demanded.

Gunning emptied the contents of a small bottle labeled opium into Sullivan's mouth as he clawed at the air again, trying to reach Jack. The darkness disappeared from his eye, and the unearthly blue blazed like a blast of cannon fire.

"Kill him!" Sullivan cried, surprising all of them. "Kill him, Kayley! Kill him!"

She fell back from the bed. "He spoke, Gunning, he actually spoke."

"It's just a response to his panic." Gunning said. "His fear has caused him to overcome the paralysis. It won't last."

"Kill himm." The drug had begun to take effect. Sullivan's raging words were slurring, and his hands fell onto the bed beside him. "Kill himm ann marreee moorr . . . se . . . lll . . . ran. . . ."

The paralysis took possession of his face again. The blazing hate in his eyes faded into numbed darkness.

"Marr . . ." His body went limp and his chin fell onto his chest. "Moor . . ."

"He'll sleep now," Gunning said. He laid Sullivan in the depression in the bed that looked like a shallow grave. "I'll stay with him the rest of the night, Miss Ryan."

Jack was aware of Kayley leaving. "How long?" he asked, his gaze grabbing hold of Gunning's and forcing him to answer.

"Almost seven months now."

"Is there any hope?"

320

A shake of Gunning's gray head was the only answer.

"This won't stop me from taking what's mine," Jack said.

"If I thought it would, sir, I'd have brought you to this room the day you arrived."

"How did it happen?"

Gunning pushed the straggling hair from Sullivan's forehead. There, gross in its purple color and chiseled with perfect sharpness in the skin and the bone of Sullivan's skull, was the familiar hoof print of the white stallion.

Chapter Thirty-One

Cold air swept down the canyon and past the ruins of Quarai, pooling and pressing in around Kayley where she stood at the edge of the arroyo. Below her, between the walls of red earth, trickled a stream of water that reflected the moonlight like a ribbon of silver beneath the starlit wash of the sky.

Clay came to her, standing so close she could no longer feel the settling wind. She expected him to hold her. He didn't touch her, though, and she wondered at his reaction to the scene he'd just witnessed. She looked up at the sky, then quickly back down at the ribbon of water.

"Tonight was the first time I've ever heard my father say my name. He said 'Kayley,' and then he told me to kill you." She looked up at Clay. "Why would he say that?"

"That's why you want the white stallion, isn't it?"

She shivered and wrapped her arms around herself. "I hate him. Not so much because he tried to kill Poppa, but because he came back to do it. He was free, and he came back to destroy my father."

The sliver of moon sailing the sky above them was bright enough to paint Clay's dark hair with light and to accent the rugged lines of his face with harsh beauty.

"At school, I dreamed of the day I'd be with my father. Then this happened, and I began to dream of the day he'd say my name." She closed her eyes. "I'm not going to dream anymore."

Clay touched the side of her face, tracing a finger along the path of her tears. "These prove that you haven't stopped dreaming. Only someone who dares to hope and wish and want can cry." He put his arms around her. "Only someone who dares to dream, Kayley."

She leaned her forehead against his chest and looked down at her hands where they held so tightly to the buckle of his belt. The silver shone as brightly in the moonlight as the handle of his pistol.

"You should have this engraved, too." She tugged on his belt. "C for Clay."

She lifted her face to smile up at him. The moon was directly above them. It was a C, also, just like the engraving on his gun.

"C for crescent," she said, and her voice sounded like it belonged to someone else, someone too afraid to cry. Someone who was being destroyed.

"C for Corbett," she said and backed out of his embrace.

Jack couldn't believe how much the hurt in her eyes hurt him.

"I've been so blind," she said and took another step away from him. "It was there right in front of me every time I opened my father's desk. I guess you were right; I am just a kid, too stupid to realize that the man she thought was making love to her was actually stabbing her father in the back."

She spun away from him. He blocked her escape, grabbing her arms and forcing her to stop. "At first, yes," he said and shrank from the hate in her eyes. "But not on the mountain, Kayley, not in my bed."

It was the only truth he had to give her. Why it was so important that she believe it, he didn't know. Maybe it was those carefully spoken curses or that her father had never said her name, or maybe it was just how empty his arms felt without her. Whatever the reason, it had suddenly become more important than revenge or justice, even more important than hate.

"The tears frozen on your face during the storm, Kayley, those were my tears. I'd thought I'd lost you, and I knew it was my own fault because I wanted you to run after me."

"Then, you should be happy. Not only did I run after you, I even begged you to take part of my father's herd in payment for stopping what you were doing to it. And tonight I wanted you to make love to me to spite my father. No wonder you were in such a hurry you wanted to go into the first room we passed."

"Kayley—" he began, but she stopped him by jerking away from his grasp so suddenly she almost fell.

"Don't say it!" She covered her ears. "I won't listen to you say again that it was just you and me. It was never you and me. It was you and my father. I'm just the road you traveled to get to him." She turned and ran, lifting her robe and gown in clutching fingers, running away from him and up the steps to the veranda.

He stopped her by blocking the doorway. He wanted her to look at him; he needed to see in her eyes if there was any chance, any hope, no matter how slight.

But she kept her face turned away from him. At first he thought she was just avoiding looking at him. Then he realized that she wasn't staring at the moon-shadowed darkness on the veranda; she was looking into it, and at the bench beside the door.

When she moved toward it, he tried to stop her. He was too slow. She reached the bench before him and picked up the cashbooks he'd put there before going to her beside the arroyo.

"So this is what you wanted." She looked at him with eyes of ice. "What's in them that's so important you risked having to take me to bed again just to find them?"

He couldn't stop staring at her fingers clutching the soft leather. "Proof that I didn't embezzle partnership funds."

"I thought you were in jail for murder."

He looked up at her in surprise. Where had she heard that?

"Attempted," he corrected. "Except that I was the one who was almost murdered."

"And yet you were the one the court convicted. There must've been evidence."

"There was," he said with a harsh laugh. He walked a few steps away and dug the heel of his boot into the wood floor of the veranda. "Twenty thousand dollars worth of evidence. Ten thousand to lock me up, ten thousand to take my ranch away."

"You accused Claude Asken of taking a ten thousand dollar bribe from a convicted confidence man," she said, and her voice sounded like glass that was being shattered. "That wasn't my father. He isn't a criminal."

"You don't know that, Kayley." Jack turned to face her again. "The only thing you know about Sullivan Ryan is that he wants me dead and he doesn't want you at all."

He wanted to take the words back. But all he could do was watch her shoulder the truth of them. She looked so very alone and young standing there before him, and so pale he feared she might faint. For a moment, he thought she was going to turn and run again. Instead, she lifted her arms and pushed the cashbooks at him.

"Take them," she said. Her voice was as forcibly controlled now as it had been earlier. "You earned them."

"You don't know what these can do to you, Kayley."

She crossed her arms in front of her. "If I keep them, it means I believe you and not my father. Trust is the only connection I've ever had with him. I'm not going to let you or these books or the contents of that trunk in there take that away from me." She walked to the edge of the veranda. "Slowhand?"

"I'm here." The voice floated down from the top of the house.

"Clay is leaving. If he comes back, kill him. That's

326

my father's order." She met Jack's hard stare. "And it's mine."

"Yes, Miss Ryan."

"Good-bye, Clay." Her chin lifted slightly. "Or does it give you more pleasure to hear me say, Good-bye, Jack?"

He couldn't let it end like this. He couldn't just walk away knowing how much he'd hurt her. He caught her arm, crushing it with his fingers and dragging her so close he could smell the night wind in her hair.

"Please," he said.

"Please what? You have your proof, you've heard me beg, and you've seen Sullivan Ryan drooling like a half-wit while he babbles inanities and worthless threats. What else could you possible want? Pity?"

His heart turned to stone, and his hand fell away from her. "You're right, there isn't anything else here I want," and he walked away.

Kayley stood in the center of the living room. Around her lay the refuse of her father's life, evidence to disprove the lie she'd spent her entire life believing. Clay had almost changed that.

Clay.

She sank into the chair where he'd kissed her and heard again her voice as she asked him—no, begged him—to make love to her.

Gunning entered the room, the lantern he carried spilling dirty light onto Kayley's face. She turned away from it.

"Why didn't you tell me who he was?" she said.

"Because I owe him a great debt, and because he'd changed. When he came here that first day, I realized he wasn't the same man who bought hand-tailored shirts and had bigger gold nuggets embedded in his boots while he was looking for an investor to save his ranch. This Jack Corbett was wearing plain boots and store-bought shirts."

"And so, because of this debt, and his change of wardrobe, you didn't tell me that he was here to destroy my father."

"I didn't tell you because I knew he wouldn't go through with it."

"Why would you think that?"

"I saw how he looked at you, and I knew that he'd never be able to hurt you. You see, my friend, Jack was looking at you the way I looked at Melissa."

Kayley stared at the fire for a long time. Then she slowly stood. "You were wrong," she said and bent to gather the contents of the trunk, filling it again with its secrets and sealing away her father's past.

Chapter Thirty-Two

The Lucky Ace Ranch wasn't what Kayley expected. It wasn't anything except a split-rail corral draped with drying hides. Two horses were confined in the corral, and they were spending their time biting and kicking each other. Near the corral was a leanto built of logs and canvas which housed saddles and other gear. And set away from the corral was a shack so ramshackle and small and filthy it made Kayley think with fond memory of her first sight of Peters McDonnell's cabin.

She wouldn't have even known she was at the Lucky Ace if Vance's brand hadn't been burned on the front of the shack. Even though she easily recognized the playing card with the single diamond, until she saw it here, she hadn't realized how infrequently she'd seen it on cattle in the valley.

From behind the shack, came the sound of rapid firing. Six shots, then another six, then a short silence for reloading and the routine was repeated. She'd been hearing that same staccato of noise ever since reaching Los Jumanos Mesa.

She stayed astride Louisiana and called, "Hello!" during one of the short silences.

Two men sauntered from behind the shack, their pistols drawn. "Look who's here," one of them said. Kayley recognized him as Clive Savely. The other man was Bill Terkell, who in comparison with Clive, almost looked respectable as he dropped his gun into his holster with his left hand.

But then, who wouldn't, she thought and shuddered in disgust at the sight of the mean-faced Clive.

They were still walking toward her. She tightened up on Louisiana's reins, and he backed away from the advancing pair, taking her closer to the corral.

"These hides have the R Cross brand," she said. She rode along the fence to check all the hides. "Why have you been killing my father's cattle?"

"We got hungry and couldn't find one of our cows," Clive said.

"So you ate six of my father's? Where's Vance?"

"He ain't here. Just us." Clive grinned, revealing teeth the color of dead moss. "And you."

Kayley's skin crawled. "Tell him I came by," she said and whirled Louisiana away from Clive's grasping hand.

Terkell made a grab for her foot. Louisiana spun into him, knocking him down.

"You're gonna regret that," Terkell said, and Kayley put Louisiana into a run.

Within a few feet, though, she whirled around and rode back to the corral. Leaning over from the saddle, she hooked her fingers in the rope catch that kept the gate closed. With a quick jerk, she lifted the catch and

330

swung the gate open. The quarreling horses bolted for freedom while Kayley again turned Louisiana west to escape.

"Damn that bitch!" she heard from behind her, followed by a shot.

She rode into the thick stands of junipers for protection. When they were safely several miles away from Clive and Terkell, Kayley worked her way back to the trail.

Her insides had already been twisted into knots by the contents of her father's trunk and by the painful revelation of Clay's real identity. Now that the danger of the confrontation on the mesa was over, her stomach began to cramp with spasms of horror and revulsion.

She doubled over in the saddle. "Please, God, I can't stand any more," she gasped against the side of Louisiana's neck.

"Kayley!"

The shout came from down the trail. She sat upright to see who it was, her hands and arms still doubled across her stomach.

Ahead of her on the trail was Vance. He was riding his black mare toward her, looking exactly as he had the first time she'd seen him standing beside her father in front of the R Cross ranch house. Everything about him was so unlike Jack Corbett that when Vance swung down from his mare and reached for her, his arms outstretched and welcoming, she fell into his embrace without hesitation.

"Vance," she said and pressed her face against the smooth satin of his quilted vest.

"What's wrong?"

"Your men, I was looking for you and went up to your headquarters, and your men tried to—"

She couldn't finish. Her fingers clutched at him, trying to draw him closer so she could lose her fear and hurt in the comfort of his embrace. Only he wasn't embracing her. He was peeling her away from him like a leech from a repulsed victim.

"You were asking for trouble when you went there, my dear, so you shouldn't be surprised you found it."

She realized then that he wasn't alone. His two other men were sitting on their horses with knowing grins on their faces that reminded her of Clive and Terkell.

"Do you really live in that place?" she asked while trying to restore some of her self-control. She moved way from Vance and reached for the stirrup on her saddle for support.

"I have a room in Socorro so I can be close to the gaming tables. The cabin is just for my men." He straightened the rumpled sleeves of his coat and smoothed his vest. "What's this all about?"

"You were right about the ranch." She sighed, and the sound of her defeat deepened her already bottomless depression. "I can't run it. I want you to take it over."

"What brought about this long-expected surrender, my dear?"

She stared at her right foot as she scuffed it across the ground. "Nothing in particular."

"It's my guess that one-eyed trail bum has something to do with this."

"I don't want to talk about him," she said and met Vance's gaze. "I just want to hand over control of the

332

R Cross to you and go back to my father."

"What's my saying yes worth to you?"

She hadn't thought he wanted anything except her to admit she'd been wrong. "What do you want?"

"You sound surprised, my dear. Surely you didn't expect me to take on such a Herculean task in exchange for nothing more than your gratitude."

"Of course not. I just don't know what you want."

He ran a hand across his mare's neck as he came toward Kayley, not stopping until she was pressed between him and Louisiana.

"I want to know what happened between you and Clay on that mountain."

'I hired him." She couldn't see Vance's eyes through the shadow cast by his hat. But she could feel them on her, watching and waiting for an opportunity to see the truth, or the lie, in her words. "And last night I fired him. My infatuation, as you called it, is over. You won, Vance. You were right; I was wrong."

"I don't care about that," he said and bent to kiss her.

She thought first of his men watching, then forgot them as his tongue touched hers and her pulse quickened. But that was all. A moment of heightened anticipation, of wanting and waiting to be lifted up and into shared pleasure and passion. Then nothing. Just a kiss. Demanding on his part, obedient on hers.

His swollen response to their kiss pushed against her thigh, and she suddenly had the same horrible feeling of being violated that she'd suffered last night when Jack Corbett's hate had turned his desire into near rape.

She turned her face away from him. His fingers tightened on her shoulders, sending shock waves of pain down her arms and up her neck.

"Let me go, Vance."

He dropped his hands onto her waist. "Not until you tell me if that bastard Clay got inside these tight pants. I have a right to know if I'm getting another man's leavings."

She could feel his fingers reaching inside her denim pants. That touch, that intrusive, unwelcomed touch, helped her meet his accusing gaze without flinching.

"In marriage, Vance, or here on the trail with your men watching?"

His smile was as unfeeling as his kiss. "If Clay beat me to the prize, there's no need to wait for a preacher. If not, then you can consider yourself safe until the wedding night. I wouldn't want to do anything to jeopardize the legality of our union. Either way, though, we will be getting married, my dear, because that's my price for stopping the little problems besetting your precious R Cross."

She should be happy. He wanted to marry her, even though she could no longer offer him what every man wanted in a bride. All she had to do was say yes, and he would take over the ranch.

She frowned. "You don't even like cattle, Vance, and yet ever since Dr. Easterday said my father's condition was hopeless, you've been trying to take over the R Cross. Why is having control over it so important you're willing to marry a whore?"

"Is that an admission, my dear?"

"It's not me or the ranch, is it? What terrible wrong

did *you* suffer at my father's hands that you think this will undo?" She forced his fingers out of her pants and pushed him away from her.

"You catch on quickly," he said and turned to rub a hand down his mare's neck. "My interest is in the big money cattle companies are paying for ranches all over the southwest. My problem is that they're not interested in my small piece of landscape."

"Joining it to my father's piece isn't going to help unless you can turn salt water into fresh."

"That is a problem, but apparently one that can be overcome."

"My father spent five years trying to overcome it."

"And I think he made it."

Nothing Kayley had found in Sullivan's trunk supported Vance's statement, yet he seemed so sure of himself.

"What do you know that I don't?" she asked.

"I know why he sent for you."

The wind rushing down the slope of the mesa roared in her ears. "Why?" she asked, and though she thought she had shouted the question it sounded no louder than a whisper.

"Not long after I'd won that fateful game with Sullivan, I was in Socorro with a little redhead sitting on my knee. Your father came staggering up to me, smelling of whiskey and failure, and asked me if I liked women with hair that color. I confessed that I did have a weakness for them. A few weeks later, Sam was driving you up to the veranda."

"That was a coincidence," Kayley said.

"Was it? You said yourself that your father has failed in his attempt to sell the R Cross. Losing the worst half of it to me should've made him ecstatic. Instead, he tried to buy it back. That sparked my interest, so I refused. Then that incident occurred in Socorro, and a few weeks later, what do you know but Sullivan is being reunited with his long lost, and coincidentally, redhaired daughter.''

A cold chill swept over her.

"You still don't get it?" Vance asked. "Sullivan finally found a buyer for the R Cross; only they want all of it, not half, and he brought you here to help him get my half back."

"That's a lie.''

"Ask him; he'll tell you.''

"He can't talk.''

"You told me yourself that he said the first part of your name. What else has he been saying to you that you've been dismissing as grunts?''

Marr moor.

That had been the first thing her father said after his injury. He'd repeated it constantly, mumbling it over and over until sometimes Kayley had wanted to scream from having to listen to it.

Marr moor. Marry Moore.

She folded her hands across her stomach again. "How did you know?''

"Elda tells me everything that happens on the R Cross, including the interesting fact that Sullivan received a letter from the Prairie Cattle Company the same day he tried to buy the Lucky Ace back from me.''

"I went through all of Poppa's papers last night. There wasn't a single letter from that company. And even if there was one, what makes you think they'd still be interested? They haven't tried to contact Poppa since I've been here. But let's say they do still want it. We get married and you stop the trouble the ranch is having and then we sell it. What happens next?"

He shrugged. "We'll be rich, of course."

"Gamblers are never rich. No matter how much money they have it's always just enough for a stake in the next game."

"You've been listening to range gossip again, my dear."

"What happens after you sell the ranch?" she asked, her voice rising. "What happens to me, your wife, your partner for life? Will you sell me, too, or just give me to your men as a Christmas bonus?"

"Stop this, Kayley."

"What you accused my father of, Vance, it's a lie. I'm not a bribe. I'm his daughter. He sent for me because he wanted me. That's what I'm going to believe ño matter what you say or Elda says or what anyone else says."

She swung into the saddle. Her legs were too weak to support her, and she gripped the saddle horn with white-knuckled hands.

Vance moved toward her. "You're talking like a fool."

"I'm not a fool," she said. "Not anymore." She reined Louisiana away from him. "And the next time your men get hungry, tell them to make sure it isn't an R Cross steer they point their rifle at, or I'll be pointing mine at them."

Chapter Thirty-Three

Kayley turned Louisiana into the adobe corral and tossed her steaming saddle on the floor of the tack room. She was headed for the house when Sam Butler surprised her by stepping out of the barn and asking, "Got a minute?"

"Always."

He dropped the sack of cornmeal he was carrying beside the corral and propped his elbows on the top rail. "I just got back from Gallinas. The boys said you were there looking for me this morning."

She leaned against one of the corral posts and told him what had happened with Vance that morning and who Clay really was.

"That explains the order Slowhand said you gave him last night."

The way Sam was avoiding looking at Kayley, she knew he'd been told about more than just her order. He pulled his arms off the rail and walked a short distance away. He kicked at the ground, then squatted and began scratching in the dirt with a small stick.

"When you were outside—" He made a few more stabs with his stick, stopped and looked up at Kayley, then back at the ground. "I feel responsible for you, Miss Ryan, and if you tell me this is none of my business, there's nothing I can do except keep quiet; but I'll not be happy about it."

Kayley knelt in the dirt with the chicken scratches between them. "Ask me what you want to know, Sam."

He dropped the stick, but kept his gaze fixed on the ground. "You were—Slowhand said that you were with Clay and you were—in your night clothes."

Sam's face was so red beneath the brim of his hat that Kayley would have laughed if it hadn't been for how much she loved him at that moment.

"Nothing happened, Sam."

"He didn't insult you?"

Jack Corbett had manipulated Kayley, he'd taken advantage of her, he'd used and betrayed her, and yet, he'd taken nothing that she hadn't offered him.

She picked up the stick and began adding her own scratches to the dirt. "No, he didn't insult me."

"Are you turning him in to the sheriff?"

"We don't have any evidence against him, other than an empty tin of arsenic in his shed. I could as easily accuse Elda of the same crime." She laughed, the sound of it hurting her throat. "He even has an alibi for the night the spring was dynamited." She dropped the stick. "We need to check with that Kansas prison to see when he was released. If it was prior to the first drop in the herd count, we'll have something against him. And if he did escape, like Mr.

339

Parker said, we won't need evidence."

"I'll send the telegram today," Sam said. He picked up the stick and poked at one of the scraggly lines in the dirt between them. "About this morning, do you believe what Moore said about your father sending for you?"

"Yesterday I'd have answered no to that. Today I can't answer it at all. Why, Sam?"

"Last year, there was a man here representing the Edinboro firm that finally formed the Prairie Cattle Company. Mr. Ryan took him around the ranch; then they left for Santa Fe together. If something did come out of that and Vance has suspected it all along, why did he wait until today to tell you about it? After all the trouble we've been having, what happened to make him decide this morning that it was time to lay his cards faceup on the table?"

"He insisted on knowing what had happened between me and Clay. Not my firing him, but personally. Maybe Vance really is in love with me, and he's afraid I'm falling—"

She stood abruptly and turned to look out across the valley.

After a long minute of silence, she heard Sam's spurs jingle as he stood.

"I'd better get this cornmeal into the storeroom. I found it mixed in with the grain." He went to the corral, and Kayley watched him lift the discarded sack with an ease that belied its hundred-pound weight.

"Are you going to be okay?" he asked, his face hidden by the bulging sack.

"I'll be fine, Sam."

"Anything I can get you in town?"

"How about five hundred head of cattle?"

He switched the sack to his other shoulder and eyed Kayley. "You sound just like my wife, always wanting more than a man can possibly provide for her."

"I didn't know you were married."

"Neither did Abigail. She thought her daddy bought me for her. Must've given her quite a shock when I decided to emancipate myself one Saturday afternoon. One minute she was calling to me from the kitchen to do something; the next minute I was headed west."

"You mean that she doesn't know where you are?"

"If she did, she'd be here on the next train, telling me to clean my boots and stop rattling my spurs and wanting me to hang curtains and clean the bunkhouse windows and telling me to get a second job so she could buy a new bonnet and a bigger bustle and a house someplace where a man can't see a horizon farther off than the end of her apron strings."

"Married life was really that bad?" Kayley asked through her laughter.

"It wasn't anything to be volunteering for again." His shoulders slumped beneath the weight of the sack. "Maybe I'll wait for tomorrow to ride to Belen. I'm feeling mighty tired all of a sudden."

"Must've been that second job."

"Nope, it was those curtains. Fooling with those things always did wear me out faster than hauling steers out of mud. After I get rid of this sack, I'm taking a nap." He moved off to the storeroom.

"Sam," Kayley called after him. "Thank you."

He stopped and turned around. "For what?"

"For making me forget to cry."

"Thinking about Abigail always has that effect on me, too."

"It sounded more like she made you want to cry."

"Not as long as she's east of the Mississippi and I'm west of it."

"Put the sack away, Sam."

"Yes, ma'am."

Chapter Thirty-Four

The weather had turned so unseasonably warm that Jack didn't need a fire, but he kept it burning anyway. It gave him something to stare at other than the corner of the table. That's where the Crescent C cashbooks were stacked in a neat pile, their leather bindings clean and white and waiting.

All he had to do was take them to Santa Fe. Lew Wallace would look them over and write an order that would go to the territorial Supreme Court justices, who would write an order that would go to the land office, who would write an order that would go to the president of the Second National Bank, who would write an order to fire Claude Asken and dispossess Sullivan Ryan.

All Jack had to do was glance at that stack of books, and he could see himself collecting his pot of gold from the end of that order-writing rainbow. Only he didn't care about the gold anymore, not the gold, not the ranch, not even Sullivan Ryan.

All Jack cared about was staring into the fire and

watching the flames dance and flow and sway. They reminded him of an avenging angel's crimson hair, of a dimpled cheek and a siren's song of laughter, and of eyes so blue that Jack knew he'd never be free from their sparkling spell.

With that sentence he could live. What he couldn't live with, and what kept the cashbooks sitting unused on the table, wasn't the hurt that had overflowed those beautiful eyes the last time he'd seen them. It was the love.

"The second pot of gold," Jack said and kicked at the embered remains of a pine log that left a burned scar on the plain leather of his boot.

Chapter Thirty-Five

"What's wrong with him?" Kayley asked. Her arms were around Louisiana's neck, and they ached from her effort to keep the gelding from falling either into the corral wall or onto her as she led him up and down in front of Snow.

He'd already stared into the gelding's sunken eyes and beneath the sagging tail, and he'd run his hands all along the gelding's back and sides where the dull chestnut hairs appeared to all be turned the wrong way.

Now Snow was watching Louisiana's wobbly legs and his strange manner of walking, which looked like he was picking his way through a tumble of logs, not across the bare ground.

"Locoweed," Snow diagnosed. "We'll need hot lard or melted bacon fat. The other three horses and the Gypsies ain't showin' no sign of bein' poisoned, but we'll dose them anyways just in case. We're gonna need help, too. This ain't gonna be easy."

Kayley left the staggering Louisiana in Snow's

care while she ran to the kitchen to tell Elda what they needed. Then she went to find Gunning and Bede.

"Must've been put in his hay," Snow said as they carried out the first buckets of melted lard. "You're tallest here," he said to Gunning. "You pour that grease down Louisiana's gullet while Miss Ryan and me hold his mouth open. Bede, you help your uncle."

Gunning's aim with the melted lard was good, but it wasn't perfect. By the time the animals had been dosed with the poison remedy, Gunning, Bede, Kayley, and Snow were all coated with grease.

The warm weather brought a swarm of flies to aid in their discomfort, along with a flock of crows. The smell of the lard had also attracted a turkey buzzard, which hung in the air high above them, waiting and watching for an opportunity to see if the smell was an invitation to a tasty meal.

While Louisiana was being led backward out of the corral and backward into the barn and backward into his stall, the lard began to work by producing a massive, poison-ridding bowel movement. The flies were inspired to a new level of excitement, the crows to a fresh serenade of raucous cawing, and the buzzard brought his soaring loops closer to the ground.

"Why backward?" Kayley asked.

Snow handed her a shovel. "Locoweed makes them spooked of gates. You start cleanin' up this mess while Bede brings in the other horses and I get the mules."

"I must see to Mr. Ryan," Gunning said when

346

Kayley passed the shovel to him. He stepped so high over a pile of greasy droppings that he looked like he'd been eating locoweed.

"Why didn't we just leave them outside where we wouldn't have to worry about shoveling this?" Kayley asked Snow.

"Locoed horses have a problem with fallin' over when they drink. If we couldn't get them back up, they'd die. Anyways, we'd still have to clean up the corral, too, to keep the coyotes and wolves from comin' in tonight. Might even get a mountain lion down here sniffin' around, and with the other men down at Gallinas haulin' rock, we ain't got no chance of guardin' the stock unless they're inside."

"In other words," Kayley muttered as she staggered to the wheelbarrow with a load of steaming dung, "shut up and shovel."

It was dark before Kayley and Bede dumped the last load of manure in the arroyo east of the house. And it was midnight before she was able to scrape the last dollop of grease off her. She braided her freshly washed hair, dressed in clean clothes and wet boots and went to the barn.

Fresh dung scented the air, and a few flies hovered over the droppings. The other horses were eating the grain Snow had fed them. Only Louisiana wasn't eating. His eyes were still unfocused, his legs still wobbly, and he looked as though he'd lost a lot of weight in the last twenty-four hours.

Kayley went to him, standing close to the stall door so she could stroke his nose. He pulled away from her.

"It's okay, boy. I know it's just the locoweed

347

working on you, but you'll be better soon."

She pulled a crate filled with Sam's blacksmith tools across the floor and propped it against Louisiana's stall door. The next morning, when the first ray of light forced its way through the knotholes in the pine siding on the barn, it found Kayley still sitting on the crate, waiting and watching for a sign that Louisiana was better.

Her vigil had been in vain. The chestnut gelding still didn't know her.

Snow looked over the other horses and pronounced them fit to ride. Kayley immediately hoisted her saddle onto the back of the white-faced sorrel Jack had ridden the day of the Antelope Springs fire.

"Give me your pistol," she said to Snow after she'd mounted. "I'm going bastard hunting."

He handed her the long-barreled Colt, handle first. "Them birds are buzzards, girl, not bastards."

"Who said anything about birds?" she asked and headed north.

Chapter Thirty-Six

Jack closed the door of his cabin with his shoulder and crossed the room to drop the supplies he'd just purchased in Belen onto the table. His plans hadn't included spending the winter on the mountain, but now he was ready to withstand a siege if it didn't last more than a month.

The distinctive sound of a pistol being cocked outside the cabin caused him to jerk his left hand onto the handle of his holstered gun as the cabin door was thrown open. Out of the resulting flood of sunlight, came a flash of fire and the explosion of a shot.

He pulled his gun as he hit the floor, hearing as he fell the thud of a bullet striking wood. Splinters showered onto his face. He looked up at the ceiling and saw an indentation where the bullet had hit.

His surprise at his assailant's poor aim was doubled as he heard a very irritated and very feminine voice say, "Damn it, I missed."

He backed off the pressure of his Colt's hammer.

"Kayley?"

The only answer was the sound of the gun being cocked again.

"Hold still," she said, and he threw himself under the table as her second shot was loosed. Another thud of bullet into wood was heard, and the floor vibrated. He began to laugh.

"Kayley, put that gun down before you hurt yourself."

A third shot cut short his laughter. The bullet whizzed so close to his cheek that he felt its hot breath. Before it hit the wall behind him, he'd catapulted himself out from under the table toward the pile of firewood. He grabbed the nearest log just as Kayley stepped into the cabin and out of the glaring light. She had the gun pointed at the floor and was biting her lower lip in concentration while trying to pull back the big Colt's hammer.

As Jack lay there, staring up at her, the world shifted beneath him. Everything around him and within him suddenly changed, and time itself stopped, allowing him to hold on to the moment he first realized that he was in love.

With a woman who's trying to kill me, his common sense reminded him, and he heaved the heavy log at her just as she brought up her arm to fire.

The exploding crash of a shot filled the cabin. Jack was on his feet and lunging at her before he realized that the cringing reaction of her face wasn't from surprise at the unexpected blow from the log, but from pain.

The pistol fell from her hands, which were only inches from her face. Her eyes closed in a faint, and he caught her in his arms as she fell.

"I meant to knock the gun away from her. I swear, God, that's what I intended. Don't let her die," he prayed as he carried her to the bed.

He laid her on the quilt she'd been wrapped in the night they'd made love. Her head fell over onto the pillow, revealing to him an ugly stain of blood on her right temple.

Jack wiped the blood away with numb fingers, revealing a tiny cut marring the perfection of her skin. There was also a splinter. He glanced up at the ceiling and saw two indentations. Then he closed his eyes and offered a silent prayer of thanks.

Steam hissed into Jack's face as he poured boiling water into a bowl and carried it to Kayley's side. He dipped a clean piece of what had been his best shirt into the bowl and used it to wash the dried blood from her face and hair.

The skin around the tiny cut was swollen and beginning to bruise. He cleaned it as gently as he could, but even the slightest touch caused her to frown and turn away from his ministrations.

"Hold still, Kayley."

She stopped moving. With the point of his knife, he pressed down on the tender flesh and pulled the splinter from her torn skin.

The golden lashes fluttered, then opened. She looked around with an expression of uncertainty.

"What happened?"

"You tried to kill me. It's a good thing I shaved this morning or you would've had me with that third shot."

"I would've had you with the second one if you'd

held still like I told you." She lifted a hand to her temple, and her eyes became suddenly enormous. "You shot me!"

"No, I didn't. I hit you with a log."

"You bastard!"

He laughed at her anger. "Sweetheart, you were trying to kill me."

"And I'm going to try again," she said and leapt from the bed to the floor.

Jack had the advantage of knowing where her gun had dropped. He reached it a split second before she did and planted his foot firmly on it. She threw her entire weight against his leg in an attempt to dislodge him. It didn't work.

"I wish whoever burned your boot had set fire to you instead," she grunted, her face almost as red as her hair as she tried again to push him away from the pistol.

Jack grasped her shoulders and dragged her to her feet. "That's enough," he said and pinned her arms to her sides to stop her violent struggles. "You're not big enough to take me on, kid, so calm down and tell me what this is all about."

"You know what it's about, you yellow-livered buzzard!"

"Humor me, Kayley."

"You poisoned Louisiana. He almost died; he still might." She broke then, her voice and her anger and her resistance crumbling at the same time.

Jack's hold on her turned from restraining to supporting. He lead her back to the bed and wrapped the quilt around her. Even though the heat in the cabin was stifling, she was shaking as though freezing to death. He sat on the bed beside her and rubbed her back.

"What makes you think your gelding was poisoned?"

"Snow said somebody put locoweed in Louie's hay." A new wave of chills caused her teeth to chatter.

He lifted her, quilt and all, and carried her across to the fire he'd built while she was unconscious. With his foot, he dragged his chair close to the hearth and deposited her in it.

"Why am I so cold?"

"You're in shock."

"Killing you would've shocked me; missing was just a disappointment."

"Then, I'm glad you're just disappointed." He searched through the packages on the table for the tea he'd purchased.

"Why haven't you used them yet?" she asked.

He followed her gaze to the cashbooks on the corner of the table. He went back to the fire and sprinkled the tea into the kettle of hot water.

"I'm not going to use them," he said.

"What does that mean?"

"It means I don't want revenge anymore. It means I'm not going to contest Sullivan's ownership of the ranch. It means"—he knelt in front of her and took her hands in his—"it means, Kayley, that I lo—"

"I don't believe you," she said, her voice overpowering his. She jerked her hands away from him. "And I'm not drinking any of that tea. I don't want to be poisoned, too."

"I didn't poison your horse."

"It had to be you. No one else hates me."

"I don't hate you, Kayley."

Her eyes filled with tears that shattered the light from the fire into a thousand rainbows. "You hate my father."

"He tried to kill me."

"So did I."

"It must run in the family," he said, and the tears spilled over her lashes.

"Don't say that," she begged. "We're not a family; we never have been."

She didn't resist when he pulled her to him. She buried her face against his shoulder, and he tried to still her sobs with his embrace.

"Vance said Poppa only sent for me because he wanted me to marry Vance because Poppa wanted to get back the property he lost to Vance because Poppa finally found someone to buy the ranch but he needed all of it not just half."

Jack stifled his laughter. "Do you think Moore's right?"

She sat up, sniffed, and wiped the tears from her face with the back of her hands. "I don't know why Poppa thought Vance would want to marry me."

"Any man who took one look at you would want that, kid. Or something similar."

Her eyes shied away from his teasing smile. "But Poppa didn't know what I looked like. He hadn't seen me in twelve years." She pulled the blanket closer around her. "Jack," she said and was stopped by a sudden quivering of her lips. "The night you—we—made, I mean, did something similar, was it—" She stopped and took a steadying breath. "Did you

354

mean it when you said what we did wasn't because of my father?"

He pulled her to her feet. The quilt fell to the floor, and he wrapped the fragileness of her in a protecting embrace.

"It was because of you," he said. "And what we did, Kayley, was make love."

She looked up at him, but her eyes didn't quite meet his. Instead her gaze went past him. She stiffened, and even though he was still holding her, she felt suddenly far away from him, withdrawn and cold.

He turned with her in his arms to see what she was looking at. He was so surprised that he didn't try to resist when she broke away from him. She went to the supply shelves, took down a can of kerosene with one hand and a new tin of arsenic with the other.

"You don't have a lantern, Jack. What do you use kerosene for, to burn the bodies of all the rats you kill?"

"Those aren't mine, Kayley. Someone put them here while I was in Belen."

"And you just happened not to notice them when you returned."

"You started shooting at me before I had the chance."

"The locoweed, you cut that in the meadow around the beaver pond, didn't you? I remember smelling their flowers the day I came to buy Mr. McDonnell's land." She took a shuddering breath. "Why did you have to use it, Jack? You already had your precious books. Why didn't you just take them to the governor and let him set to rights all the wrongs my father supposedly had done you and leave Louisiana alone?"

"I didn't do it, Kayley, and I won't do it, because I love you."

She looked as though he'd struck her. "Don't say that."

"It's true," he said, begging her to believe with his voice and his touch as he drew her to him. Instead of fighting him, she laughed, and his hands fell away from her.

"It's so funny you saying that to me. Of everything you could've said, that's what I least expected." Her smile faded. "What's even funnier is that I'm so desperate for someone to love me that for a moment, I believed you."

"I *do* love you."

She looked away from him. "It didn't work that time."

Jack's gaze fell on the cashbooks. He picked them up, his fingers spreading like a caress across the white leather. Then he threw them in the fire.

Disbelief turned the clear blue of her eyes to violet as the flames began to burn the white leather, turning the mark of the Crescent C to cinders and ash.

"That doesn't prove anything," she said in a hoarse whisper.

"It does to me."

She took a step back from him. "I wish I'd shot you."

He handed her the gun. When she didn't take it from him, he forced it into her hand, uncurling her fingers from inside her palm and closing them around the Colt's handle.

"I used all the bullets."

"Only four."

"You took the rest out."

"You're making excuses."

Her hand began to shake. She laid the pistol on the table and folded her fingers back into her palms. "This doesn't prove anything either, except that I'm a coward." She went to the door and threw it open to the sunlight and fresh air.

"What will prove something, Kayley?"

She turned to look at him. "Give me back my faith in my father."

He crossed his arms in front of him. "I don't believe in the worship of false gods."

She glanced at the burning books. "And I don't believe in miracles."

Jack looked again at the small bruise on her temple. "But I do," he said after the door closed between them. He turned to look at the horsehair rope hanging from the wall beside him. "And I know how to make you believe, too, kid."

Chapter Thirty-Seven

Several times on her way back to the ranch house, Kayley thought she was being followed. Her attempts to catch her pursuer were in vain. When she finally reached the ranch, the combination of her surprise, the pain from her bruised temple, and her inability to hate Jack Corbett had given her such a terrible headache that it took her several minutes to realize the significance of the wagon pulled close to the provision storeroom.

The wagon was stacked high with supplies, and when Kayley finally realized that, she reached into her belt for Snow's pistol. Her fingers closed on leather instead of wood and steel.

"I left it in the cabin," she groaned.

But they don't know that.

She rode the white-faced sorrel up to the wagon and shouted, "You in the storeroom, come out with your hands up!"

Snow's weathered face peered around the edge of the door. Kayley almost collapsed in relief.

"You've been readin' too many dime novels, girl.

What happened to my gun?"

"The buzzard got the drop on me," she said and touched her temple. "I thought someone was stealing our supplies. What's this wagon doing here?"

"Sam sent it," Snow said.

Kayley dismounted and tied the sorrel's reins to the back wheel of the wagon. "Why did Sam send us a load of supplies?"

Francisco Chaves came out of the storeroom. "Señorita Ryan," he said and nodded his broad-brimmed felt hat to her.

Kayley dug through the few phrases of Spanish she knew to ask, *"Qué es esto,* Señor Chaves?"

"Señor Butler ordered *esto* from *mi padre.*"

"Why?" Kayley asked. "I mean, *por qúe?* Or is it *por qué no?*"

"Por qúe," Snow said. "And the answer's because we needed supplies."

"But Gunning and I brought back a load not two weeks ago."

"I remember unloadin' it, but they ain't here now. See for yourself."

Kayley went into the storeroom. It was as empty as it had been the day she looked for her father's trunk. The only difference was now the box of candles was missing and the sack of cornmeal which Sam had been carrying when he told her about his wife was slouched in the corner.

"My oysters are gone," she said and ran her hand across the shelf where Snow had put them. "And it's my fault. I forgot to tell Sam about Gunning's suggestion we post a lookout all the time."

Francisco had followed her into the room and was digging in the pocket of his shirt. "Señor Butler say to bring the supplies when this arrive for you." He handed her an envelope.

"*Gracias*." She went outside while she ripped the envelope open, almost tearing the telegram inside in her haste.

Jack Corbett had received a governor's pardon for the conviction of attempted murder, the pardon based on the failure by the prosecution during the trial to produce either a victim or the accused, and the state's current inability to locate the ruling judge. An early release had been granted for the charge of embezzlement based on exemplary behavior by the prisoner during his interment.

Jack had left Lansing four weeks prior to Kayley's meeting him near Corbett Springs, which was five months after the first confirmed drop in the herd count.

The telegram added to her confusion, and her headache soared to new heights of pain.

"*Mi padre* sends this." Francisco handed Kayley a bill for the supplies along with another piece of paper. "And Señor Butler, he sends the note."

Miss Ryan,
There's a little business I need to attend to, the boys are going with me. We'll be back by Christmas. Snow can take care of things until then. Tell him we won't miss his cooking on the trail.

Sam

"What is it?" Snow asked.

Kayley handed him the note. "Francisco," she said, "tell your father that after Christmas, Sam will bring in enough cattle to settle our account."

"*Mi padre,* he says if your *vaqueros* keep eating so *mucho grande,* he will be able to retire soon."

"How wonderful for him," Kayley said.

"Givin' this to me ain't gonna do no good." Snow thrust Sam's note back at her.

"I forgot," she said and read it to him.

Snow crinkled his face into a menacing scowl. "I'll have to buy a new gun just so I can shoot that Butler when he gets back."

"I might take a shot at him, too," Kayley said, "even though he didn't know about Louisiana being poisoned before he left. When you finish unloading these supplies, install a lock on this door."

"Don't have a lock."

"Buy one when you buy that gun."

Kayley found Elda in the kitchen scrubbing the table with a brush so stiff it would've raised blood blisters on the toughest longhorn in the territory.

"I owe you an apology," Kayley said. She leaned against the counter and crossed her arms in front of her.

"What for?" Elda looked up, her eyes narrow with suspicion.

"I thought our missing supply problem was your fault, but it isn't. We're being robbed."

Elda resumed her vigorous scrubbing. "Do you

know how?''

"No," Kayley said. She rubbed her tired eyes with tired hands. "I just know that whoever's doing it took the smoked oysters I bought Poppa for Christmas."

Elda's arm stopped in midstroke. "I didn't know we had oysters."

"They were in a sack beside the candles. The last three cans in Belen."

"Sullivan loves oysters." She dropped her brush onto the wet table. "Where's Bede?"

"I haven't seen him. Maybe he's keeping watch on Louisiana."

Kayley rubbed her eyes again, this time because the caustic-looking bubbles on the table were beginning to dissolve into deadly vapors. "I'm beginning to feel a little sick myself. What is that?"

"Lye. It's the best thing to use to clean after these men."

"You won't have to worry about most of them for a while. Except for Snow and Bede, the rest have gone off somewhere and won't be back until Christmas." It was only three weeks away, but it seemed like a lifetime. "What am I going to do without them?"

"When I was young," Elda said, "there were troubles I couldn't handle. I married Alba, and he didn't expect me to handle them. It was his responsibility."

"Sam told me that his troubles started when he got married."

"A man doesn't need a wife, but a woman needs a husband. You shouldn't have turned down that Vance Moore when he asked you."

362

"He didn't ask me anything; he told me."

"It must be a wonderful thing to have a man who wants you so much."

Kayley thought of Jack Corbett throwing the cash-books in the fire. "It would be," she said, "if I could believe it was really me that he wanted."

Chapter Thirty-Eight

Afternoon on Christmas Eve. Kayley was sitting on the crate outside Louisiana's stall. The gelding's skin was quivering, his eyes were fogged, and his breathing was as silent as her father's. It was the fourth time he'd come down with the same sickness, and the fourth time she'd heard Snow diagnose the problem as locoweed.

"But where's he getting it?" Kayley asked. "He eats the same hay as the other horses, and they're fine."

"If I knew the answer to that, girl, he wouldn't be sufferin' now."

"Maybe it's not locoweed," she said. "Maybe it's just this weather making him feel so bad."

It was making her feel bad, too. It was too warm to be almost Christmas. It felt like summer.

Christmas should be cold, the way it had been in Boston with freezing winds whipping in from the ocean and whistling through the masts in Boston harbor and rushing into the window of the dormitory in Mrs. Potter's Boarding School for Young Ladies.

There was no last-minute bustle from Mrs. Potter as she left to visit her sister or frowning anger because there was nothing to do with Kayley except leave her alone with a warning that if the judge who controlled her trust ever learned of this lapse, the least of Kayley's troubles would be that she had to spend the holiday alone.

Christmas in Boston hadn't been perfect, but it had been familiar. Here there was nothing even remotely familiar: no cold wind, no snow or ice, no holiday tree in the common room and no sounds of carols drifting on the night wind from the nearby churches and faraway carolers.

"Miss Ryan." It was Gunning, his voice coming from outside. He stepped into the ribbons of sunlight that filled the barn with dust-moted brightness. "There's someone here to see you."

Kayley's hopes jumped, and she ran to him, holding on to his arm as they went out of the barn together. She expected to see four mustached smiles. Instead, she saw Jack Corbett.

"I got orders to shoot you," Snow said.

"You'll need this," Jack said and tossed the long-barreled Colt to the old trail cook.

"You must be crazy, boy," Snow said. He looked the gun over. "Did a good job cleanin' it, even oiled the wood handle. Loaded it, too. Trustin' fella, ain't you?"

"Give me a minute with him alone," Kayley said, her emotions once more in a turmoil of confusion.

"You sure, girl?"

She nodded and heard Snow's spurs retreating back into the barn. Gunning slipped away from her, too, and went toward the house.

"I brought you a present, Kayley," Jack said and glanced beside him, trying to take her gaze with him.

She didn't want to stop looking at him, though. She wanted to hold on to this moment, to memorize everything about it, every breath, every beat of her heart. What the present was didn't matter to her. That he'd brought one was everything.

When finally she did look, she didn't believe what she saw at the end of the horsehair rope he was holding. Sophia. Ugly little Sophia, her splayed feet polished and freshly shod, her splotchy brown and white coat curried and combed and shining in the sunlight, her ratty mane and stubby tail combed and braided and tied with trailing ribbons of blue and gold and crimson and silver.

"You can come closer, kid. I promise not to bite."

"I'll hold you to that," she said and ran to throw her arms around Sophia's neck. "You made her look beautiful."

"She's with foal," Jack said.

Kayley laughed up at him. "Can you imagine what it will look like? Not even the white stallion's bloodline will be able to overcome poor Sophia's lack of class."

"She's not so bad."

"Yes, she is," Kayley said, her voice muffled by Sophia's beribboned mane. "It must've taken you forever to find her and longer to make her look like this. Why did you do it?"

"Because the stallion didn't need her. You did." His hand touched her hair so softly it was like a stirring of breeze. "Merry Christmas, sweetheart," he said, the wish a whisper on the wind.

Kayley turned to him, wanting to thank him, wanting to say so many things, but he was gone, disappearing as quickly and as completely as the stallion, leaving her feeling that maybe, just maybe, miracles were real.

Chapter Thirty-Nine

Kayley couldn't sleep. Her mind was too completely filled with thoughts of Jack Corbett, of his smile and his gentle touch on her hair, and of his gift.

Could it really be true that he cared for her? Had he really given up his hate for her father? She wanted to believe that he had; she wanted to believe it so much that she ached inside.

She slipped out of bed and paced the short length of her tiny bedroom. But even that activity was fraught with dangers, for with each pass across the room, she had to pass through the starlight her bedroom curtains could not contain.

The night sky had always been her friend and ally. Now it was an enemy, reminding her of the night she'd stood inside the circle of Clay's arms and discovered his deceit.

And yet tonight, when she wanted to remember how much he'd hurt her, all she could think of was him throwing the cashbooks into the fire and the touch of his hand on her hair.

Merry Christmas, sweetheart.

The words were calling to her, beckoning her out into the night. She stopped fighting them, and herself, and let her nightgown fall from her.

Over her bare flesh, she pulled the dress made of moonlight, the folds of silk clinging to her, holding and caressing her. Her hair streamed across her shoulders and down her back like crimson waves as she ran out of her room and down the hall, stopping outside her father's room and slipping into its silence.

His eyes were closed, his breathing peaceful. His hands, where they rested on the cotton quilt, weren't shaking so much tonight, and the purple scar on his forehead looked pale in the spill of moonlight.

From deep within the silence of the house, she heard the ticking of the mantle clock. A chime, muted and far away, marked the hour.

"Merry Christmas, Poppa," Kayley whispered.

She left his room, moving on slippered feet through the living room where the only light was a single candle above the mantle. Gunning was sitting in one of the chairs pulled close to the hearth. She couldn't see his face, just his hands hanging limply over the arms of the chair.

Kayley walked quietly past him, opening the front door, silent on its hinges, and she stepped out into the night.

The air was warm, the winds gentle. The Manzanos stood tall and dark behind the sandstone ruins of Quarai, sentinel guardians looking down in silence on Jack as he waited for midnight, and for Kayley.

Midnight.

He didn't need a clock to tell him when it came, just the night, softening around him, cloaking itself in magic and promise. Christmas. A day of rejoicing, a day of love and sharing.

Seconds passed.

He knew she'd come.

Seconds became a minute.

She would need the stars tonight; she would need the sky and the ruins. He knew she'd need them, just like he'd known she needed Sophia.

One minute became two.

Two became three.

"Please come," Jack whispered, and then suddenly, appearing from out of his need and his prayers, there she was. Standing before him, not as a child, but as a woman. Wearing a silken gown the color of moonlight. Wrapped in silver light shining down from a sky so bright with stars it had to be unreal, just a wish, just a dream.

"Thank you for Sophia." Her voice was as soft as the night.

"I have another gift for you," he said and handed her a flower of living lace. "It bloomed this morning. It was the first thing I saw when I awoke."

Her fingertips touched his as she took the flower from him. She let the touch linger, then pulled away and lifted the flower to her lips. "Did you really grow this, or are you just saying you did so I'll be impressed?"

"Are you?"

She lowered the flower. "I telegraphed Lansing Prison."

He leaned back against the wall. "And now you think I bribed the telegraph operator to lie."

"There's no one else to blame."

"Then, why are you here?"

Her eyes closed. "I don't know."

He started to reach for her, then stopped, realizing that this time, it was her chasm to cross.

"It's not me, Kayley."

"I wish I could believe you."

The walls of the old church caught her first two words and repeated them, once, twice. She turned and walked a few steps away from him. When the last echo faded into silence, she looked up at the sky.

"Show me the Pleiades."

He went to her, standing so close he could smell her hair and see the stars reflected in her eyes. "There," he said and lifted his arm to point. But she wasn't looking at the sky now. She was looking at him. He lowered his arm around her.

"Kayley," he whispered as he bent to kiss her.

She touched her fingertips to his lips. "No names. No yesterdays or tomorrows. Just tonight."

"It's too late for that, Kayley."

She tried to pull away. He stopped her by taking her face between her hands and turning it up to him.

"Sweetheart, I need to know that there's something more than just make-believe between us."

"Don't ask me this. Please, Jack."

"Just say yes or no."

Her lips trembled, and her eyes became bright with

unshed tears. "I can't."

"I'm not asking for promises or commitments, I'm asking—"

"You're asking me if I love you."

He was silent for a long moment before asking, "Do you?"

"Yes," she said, breathing the word softly, desperately. "I love you, Jack Corbett." She stopped trembling. "But, I don't believe that you love me."

"All I ask for is one miracle at a time," he said and drew her to him, wrapping her in his arms and touching his lips to the silk of her hair. "I want to make love to you, Kayley. Yes or no?"

"Please," she whispered, "yes," and he tasted her tears in her kiss.

Kayley turned her face into his shoulder as he lifted her and carried her across the flagstone floor to where the sky was their only roof, where corbels carved centuries ago supported the darkness of the night and the brilliance of the stars.

"Not here," she said. "Not in the church."

"Where better than a place built to celebrate love?" he asked.

Celebrate love. Not fear it or beg for it. Celebrate it. Believe in it.

Maybe these ancient walls knew the secret to believing; maybe within them she could find a way to take her trust beyond the night and into the day. Maybe here she could learn to believe in miracles.

Jack stood her before him, and she lifted her hands

372

to his face, touching his skin, touching his lips.

"Here," she whispered.

And then she felt the magic—in his smile, in his kiss, in his hands and his arms as he touched her, embracing her.

Silken moonbeams fell to the floor, illuminating a silver crescent, unstrapped and set aside. Boots and slippers were pushed off and away amid denim discarded in starlight.

Wind and darkness, warming and concealing, moss like satin on her skin.

Whispered sighs against her lips professed the reverence of his kiss.

His hands molded her, inspiring and creating her.

Touching his tongue to hers, he touched her heart with kisses and her love with wonder.

His body rose above her, his legs pushing between hers, his need reaching for her, his strength entering her. Filling her.

Light and heat and fire and sky surrounded them, their love like notes of music, slow and even, rising and falling, rhythmic and straining.

Whispers on the wind. Songs of night rose up and over them. Surrounding them. Candlelight, shadowed by centuries, came to life around them. Chanted hymns. Sacred dreams.

Past and future, merging, blending. Infinite beauty. Stars and moonbeams. Dust of planets, clouds of creation.

Joy. Shared, equal. Complete and absolute.

He gave to her a whispered pledge, a promise of tomorrows not spent alone, of tomorrows spent together, forever and always.

"All you have to do, my love, is just believe."

The night was cooler now, the warm winds hushed, the mountain breezes pooling around them as they lay naked together among the scattering of their clothes and the silence of the ruins.

"I'm cold," she said, and he kissed her hair.

"I'll warm you."

And he did, touching his lips to hers and kissing her. Putting his hands on her flesh and caressing her. Covering her with his body and entering her.

Swift and fast, he climbed onto her and into her, sweeping her, sudden and quick, into passion. The stroke of his thighs against hers. The taste of his kisses in the darkness. The feel of his heartbeat in the night.

As he thrust faster, rhythms of ecstasy threaded through her body. Desire and darkness made her cry out and clutch him, fingers against his flesh, hands upon his shoulders. Touching his hair, his face, his lips, she heard him moan and felt him sigh, and knew he was hers, even if just for one night.

Passion—hot and fluid, like melted iron—ran through his veins, filling his mind and arching his spine and thrusting his hips faster and harder and deeper and stronger.

He felt her stroking his legs with fingers of fire, then touching his back, molding his arms, finding his shoulders, grasping his hair.

Darkness and passion and pain and desire. Heavy and deep, deeper and harder, sweetness and light. His, just his, only his, she was his.

Stronger. Pulsing. Echoes of yesterday raced through his head. Promises and lies. Five years in hell and one night in heaven.

Had he really stopped hating? Was he really in love?

Yes.

Somewhere, far off in the night, they heard the sound of an eagle, screaming and high. It hunted its prey as the first light of dawn streamed over the valley, into the canyon, over the walls of the ruins and into the church where they lay entwined, arms and legs and hearts, tangled and together.

"It's morning," Jack said and rose above her. "They'll come looking for you soon."

Pulling her up, he caught her to him, holding her against him for a moment, feeling her heart beating against his chest, watching her lips and eyes smile up at him.

"It's my birthday."

"That's why I brought you the flower."

"To impress me?"

"To please you."

They dressed in silence. Kayley was afraid to speak, afraid to even think. She put her hand in Jack's and let him lead her into the *sacristy*, through the passageway, across the *porteria* and into the open-air patio of the *convento*. There she broke away from him, running a few steps ahead to better see the crimson dawn.

"Watch out!" he cried and caught her arm, dragging her back from the edge of what appeared to be an opening in the ground.

"What is it?"

"A kiva. An Indian ceremonial chamber. There's another one outside the *convento* walls."

Kayley leaned over to peer into the black depths of the kiva. "I've never seen either of them."

"Pueblo ruins always have kivas."

"Like caves to hide in."

"Or to fall in. The white stallion fell in the other one."

Kayley straightened up and looked at him. "The mark on his side, it's your brand, isn't it? What happened? How did he get loose?"

"I bought him from Madison Blackwell, who lived near my grandparent's farm. Blackwell named him Satan's Angel because he said the stallion couldn't be broken.

"I was determined to ride him, though. On the trip to New Mexico, whenever I came near him with a saddle, he went for me, teeth snapping and hooves flying, trying to break me before I got a chance to break him.

"When we got here, I had to throw him and tie him before I could brand him. When that iron touched him, he screamed, a terrible scream, unlike anything I'd ever heard at the time. Then he stopped and he lay perfectly still. When I cut him loose, he bolted straight through the corral gate and headed for the terrain that was most familiar to him, the mountains.

Jack took her hand and lead her to the second kiva.

"He fell in here. The men went to get ropes, and I went to get my gun, thinking we'd have to kill him or he'd kill us. When we got back here, he'd vanished."

"Like at Gran Quivira."

"Not exactly. Here, he jumped out of the kiva to escape. At Quivira, I think he jumped into one, or into a ditch or pit. There's a lot of those around that area. There's also a good-sized gully washing out of the mesa north of the ruins that he could've used to escape, just like he used the arroyo to get close to the ranch house."

Her heart was beating so fast that her head hurt. She felt faint and dizzy and so excited that she couldn't think.

"That's it! Every time the chase gets too hot for him, he runs for Gran Quivira, then he disappears." She frowned. "No, not every time. Sam said he chased the stallion into the salt flats once, and he disappeared there."

"Mining pits," Jack said. "Laguna del Perro is full of pits and shafts."

"Satan's Angel," she said, her excitement rising again. "It's a good name. I'll be sure to call him that just before I kill him."

"What if he kills you instead?"

"I promised my father I'd destroy the stallion."

Jack put his arms around her. "And I promised myself that I'd destroy your father. Let the past go, Kayley. Don't let yesterday's hate destroy today."

In the shadowed depths of the kiva, she saw the reflection of her father's face, not the way he looked now, but the way he'd looked the day he left Mrs. Potter's without Kayley.

"How can you stop hating?" she asked.

"By beginning to love."

She closed her eyes and let him hold her. But the night was over, and the magic of the walls no longer embraced them.

"I have to go," she said and stepped out of his arms.

"I'm worried about the ranch, Kayley. Let me help you save it."

"You're who I'm trying to save it from!"

"Then, let me help you catch the stallion. That way you can keep an eye on me to be sure I don't cause any trouble."

"You blew up Gallinas while I was with you."

"Long fuse," he said, and she couldn't help laughing at his grin.

"I'll let you ride Tavira," he said, and her laughter stopped.

"You always know just what to say to get your own way, don't you?"

"I'm learning, kid," he said and slipped his arms around her again.

If only she could believe.

"Why are you doing this?" she asked.

"Whoever's waging war against the R Cross brought the battle pretty close to you when they poisoned your gelding. I want to make certain you're not in the way of their next attempt."

She leaned her forehead against his chest and closed her eyes. If it was a mistake to love him, why did it feel so right?

He kissed the top of her head, and she squeezed her eyes tighter.

"I have to go to my cabin to get Boxer and Cleo. I'll be back tonight."

"Do you promise?"

"I thought you didn't believe in asking for promises, kid."

"So did I," she said and broke out of his arms. She made it halfway across the meadow before she began to run, her flight from him suddenly as blind as her love for him.

Chapter Forty

The sound of thunder was the first thing Kayley noticed as she approached the ranch house. Vance Moore was the second. While his men lounged on the bunkhouse porch, he was waiting for her on the veranda. Elda was with him, her expression and manner so intense that Kayley wondered if the housekeeper was giving him one of her lectures on proper deportment or untidy cowhands.

When he caught sight of Kayley coming across the yard, he turned away from Elda to glare at Kayley. "Where have you been?"

She climbed the steps onto the veranda. "Picking a flower to celebrate my birthday," she said and held up the floral lace for him to see. "I'm twenty-one today, Vance, which makes me too old to be glared at like a naughty child."

His expression quickened into a smile. "That's wonderful, my dear. Now you can marry me without needing consent."

380

Gunning walked out of the house. "Or she could marry me."

"Or me," Sam Butler said as he appeared from around the corner of the house.

He'd barely made it onto the veranda before Kayley was throwing her arms around him. "I knew you'd make it back."

"Gosh, Miss Ryan." He didn't know what to do with his hands, so he straightened his hat.

"If you ever go off like that ever again, you'll get two hugs when you get back."

"If Abigail had threatened me like that, I'd be on the train headed for St. Louis right now."

"You *do* miss her," Kayley accused him.

"I never said that," Sam hedged.

"Who's Abigail?" Vance asked.

"His wife."

"What's goin' on down there?" Snow asked, peering down from the roof of the house.

"I'm hugging Sam."

"What's he gettin' all that sugar for when I ain't gettin' none?"

"Because he's not on the roof."

"I'll be right down." Snow disappeared back over the edge. The clomping of his boots and spurs was drowned out by the thunder as it grew louder and closer. Then the ground began to shake and shudder.

"Earthquake," Elda said and grasped Vance's arm.

"Is that the sound of success?" Gunning asked.

"Sure is," Sam said. "To the head."

"Success at what?" Kayley asked while trying to see whatever it was they were looking at south of the ranch house. All she could see was a cloud of dust billowing and rolling along the ground close to the Manzanos.

"Cows!" Bede shouted, jumping onto the veranda. "There's cows coming yonder." He pointed at the cloud. "A whole bunch of them."

"Why are they coming this way?" Kayley asked.

"And why are they raising so much dust?" Vance asked.

"Because that's what cattle do," Sam said. "And they're coming this way, Miss Ryan, because they're your Christmas present, from Gunning and the boys and me."

"I don't understand."

"Neither do I," Elda said as she glared at her brother.

Gunning ignored her. "You told me, Miss Ryan, that you'd like to see 477 cattle come running into the yard looking for roundup." He paused as the dust cloud suddenly split open and longhorn cattle began rushing out of it and into the yard. "There they are," he said.

"All yearlings," Sam said. "Straight up from John Chisum's ranch."

It felt like Kayley's heart was swelling inside of her. "I can't believe this," she said and slipped her arms around Gunning to hug him. "They're beautiful and you're beautiful and I think I'm going to cry." She cut off Sam's attempt to escape and gave him another hug that turned his face crimson and caused the brim of his hat to be fatally crushed in his determination to hold on to it.

"My turn," Snow said as he appeared out of the dust. Kayley turned Sam loose and hugged Snow, who returned the favor so enthusiastically she thought she was going to be crushed.

Slowhand Smith and Joe Duke rode up beside the veranda, dusty and sweaty and grinning from ear to ear. "Merry Christmas, Miss Ryan!"

Joe's black face turned a shade paler, and Slowhand's smile changed direction. "You look different in that dress," he said.

"Both of you get down off those horses and let me hug you." She went out to pull at their trouser legs.

"You first," Slowhand said to Joe.

"No, you first," Joe said.

"Me first," Willie said, striding up to Kayley. "I never had a redhead hug me."

She lifted her arms to try, but he was too tall and had to almost bend double to let her reach him.

"You have new feathers in your hat," she said.

"From these two turkeys," he said and lifted the birds off his saddle horn. "Shot them this morning for Christmas supper, along with a bunch of quail."

Slowhand and Joe Duke were still on their horses. "You can't stay up there forever," Kayley said to them.

"We can try," Joe Duke said and rode his horse into the milling cattle.

"You ain't leavin' me alone with her," Slowhand said and spurred his mare after Joe.

"Do you think you'll be too tired tomorrow to help me catch the white stallion?" Kayley asked Sam. "The mystery of his disappearing act has been unraveled.''

"Kivas," Sam said.

Her eyes widened. "How did you know?"

"It was my idea," Gunning said, "and I asked Mr. Butler to check those southern ruins."

"There's plenty of places the stallion could jump into around there," Sam said.

"And we're going to check them all," Kayley said.

"Tomorrow," Sam said. "Today, all I want to do is rest my saddle sores."

"And eat these here birds," Snow said. He held Willie Pete's limp game aloft before shuffling off to the kitchen.

"I hope Mrs. Moraillon's going to cook those and not you," Sam called after him. "I don't want to eat shoe leather for Christmas. You hear me, Snow?" He ran off after the old trail cook.

As quickly as everyone had arrived, they all disappeared, leaving Kayley and Gunning alone.

"Where's Elda?" she asked. "And what happened to Vance?"

"They went inside after the cattle appeared."

Willie, Joe Duke and Slowhand were herding the longhorns out of the yard, with Bede's help. He'd mounted his mare and was shouting and flailing his hat at the cattle, which seemed determined to ignore him. Whichever way he tried to turn them, they went the opposite.

"Is Mr. Corbett joining us for breakfast?" Gunning asked.

Kayley looked at him in surprise. "How did you know Jack was here last night?"

384

"You forget, my friend, I was in love once, too."

Kayley opened the door on her father's room and stepped into the silence. He was awake and staring at the ceiling with empty eyes. As she kissed his cheek, his forehead bunched into a frown.

"What is it, Poppa?" she asked, then gasped as Vance swept her into his arms.

"Marry me today," he said. "I'll send my men for a preacher or priest or judge or whatever you want."

She pushed away from him. "It's not what I want that matters to you; it's what you want, and that's the title to the R Cross."

"If you think those cattle out there will make a difference in what's been happening to this ranch, Kayley, you're wrong. Come spring roundup, they'll be missing, along with the rest of your herd. You'll default on your mortgage, lose the ranch to the bank and that'll be the end of the fairy tale."

"And marrying you won't end it?"

Even though his lips curled into a smile, his eyes had gone completely blank, as though something inside of him had just died.

"Whatever happened to that sweet child Sullivan introduced me to?"

"She grew up, Vance."

"I spent Christmas last year with your father, and I wanted to spend it this year with you; but it's become painfully obvious that I'm no longer welcome in this house. Good-bye, my dear."

She stopped him from leaving. Jack had been right

the day of the fire when he'd said Vance was pompous, condescending, and reproachful. But he'd also been her father's friend and, for several months, his house guest. Even though she didn't feel she owed anything to Vance, she did to her father.

"Have supper with us," she said, "you and your men. And tomorrow, when we ride out to find the stallion, go with us." She hesitated, then said, "I could use your help, Vance."

"You really want me to stay?"

"Yes," she said, and thought it ironic that she'd never lied to anyone in her life before he convinced her to keep her father's illness a secret, and now she was lying to him.

"Then, of course I won't go, my dear," he said, and she had the feeling she'd been outmaneuvered. "I'd better go and make certain Elda's using sage stuffing in those turkeys instead of apple and sausage."

"I like apple stuffing."

"I don't." He started to leave, then stopped. "I almost forgot; I brought your mail from Belen." He pulled a handful of letters from an inside pocket of his jacket.

"If you keep this up, Vance, my father's men will forget where the post office is. I can't remember the last time anyone else picked up our mail."

He smoothed the front of his jacket where the letters had been concealed. "I won't need to pick it up anymore, my dear. The job is all theirs from now on."

*   *   *

386

It was the kind of night Kayley loved, bright with stars and moonlight, silent and warm. She rubbed her hands across the velvet softness of her dress. She'd just finished making it yesterday. The velvet was blue, and it matched her eyes so perfectly she felt like a piece of the sky itself.

Ever since the first shadow of evening had flowed down the slopes of the Manzanos, she'd been waiting for midnight. Jack hadn't said that's when he'd return or that he'd even be at the ruins waiting for her. But Kayley knew he was.

She left the shadowed darkness of her room, going down the hall past her father's silent room, past the closed door of Gunning's bedroom, and the closed door of the spare room that Vance had appropriated for his own use.

The living room was dark and smelled sweet from the lopsided pine tree Joe Duke and Slowhand Smith had given her in exchange for a promise not to hug them.

"It's a bribe!" she accused them when they tried to strike the deal with her.

"It sure is," Joe Duke had said.

"Will it work?" had been Slowhand's concern.

It had, but only because they'd caught her in the outhouse and refused to release her until she agreed. Elda had been appalled by the impropriety of the escapade, Bede had laughed so hard he fell off his horse, and Snow had accused them of being so stupid they couldn't see through a ladder.

It had been a perfect Christmas. But now, as the clock in the living room chimed, it was over, and

Kayley was ready to make the day after Christmas just as perfect. She eased the front door open, stepped onto the veranda without a single board squeaking, and eased the door closed behind her.

"Good evening, my dear."

"Vance," she said, sounding like an out of tune piano. "I thought you were asleep."

He was sitting with his boots propped up on the front wall of the house. She wanted to slap his feet down and tell him to go to bed, but restrained herself. As Mrs. Potter had so often said, "You can catch more flies with honey than you can with vinegar."

Kayley had spent an entire month assisting in the kitchen for asking what anyone would want with a bunch of flies. After that, she'd accepted Mrs. Potter's pearls of wisdom without questioning them because, as Mrs. Potter herself had so often said, "A pearl is just an oyster's way of vomiting." It wasn't much of a creed to live by, but it had kept Kayley out of the kitchen.

"I thought it was much too nice a night for sleeping," Vance said. "What's your excuse, my dear?"

"My room was stuffy."

"You should try opening the window."

"I don't like sleeping with an open window."

"It was just a suggestion, my dear. No need to sound offended. Sit down and we'll talk."

"I really don't have much to say, Vance."

"Then, I'll talk. Are you anxious about something?"

She stopped wringing her hands. "What makes you say that?"

"You look anxious, you sound anxious, and you're acting anxious."

"Very perceptive of you," she said and wished his chair, in which he was tipping back, would fall.

"Did I ever tell you about the first time I met your father? He was behaving much the same as you are right now. It was in Santa Fe at the City Beer Hall last December."

"The only place of amusement in the city," Kayley said as she sank onto the bench beside the front door.

"Everyone else had dropped out of the game except your father and me," Vance said, "and Sullivan was raising my bets like he was made out of money."

"A wonderful story!" She jumped to her feet. "I'm so glad you told me. I think I'll take a walk."

"It's not over."

"Oh," she said and slumped back onto the bench.

"Anyone else would've thought your father perfectly calm. But to a professional like myself, it was obvious he was sweating bullets."

"That sounds uncomfortable," she said and wiped her brow.

"Good evening," Jack said, stepping out of the shadows beside the house and into the bright spill of moonlight in front of the veranda.

Kayley leapt to her feet, then immediately sat back down on the bench. "You startled me."

"I'm not surprised," Vance said, "considering that you fired him."

"He's here for the same reason you're here," Kayley said.

"Because it's a nice night?"

She had to sit on her hands to keep from knocking his boots off the wall.

"It is a beautiful night," Jack said. "I was just up at the ruins enjoying it."

Kayley almost jumped to her feet again. "What a coincidence," she said instead. "It's such a warm night that I couldn't sleep so I came outside intending to go up there but Vance was here because it's such a nice night that he couldn't sleep and he stopped me to tell me a story about meeting my father."

Jack struck a match on his thumb and touched the flame to one of his cigars. His hat was pulled low across his face. The light from the match blazed across his features, accenting the hard line of his jaw and the darkness of his eyepatch. He shook out the match, plunging his face back into shadows as he stepped onto the veranda and leaned a shoulder against one of the roof posts.

"Sounds like an interesting way to spend a few minutes. Go on with your story, Moore."

"Why don't you catch him up to where I left off, my dear?"

Kayley worried her bottom lip. "You were in a saloon, and Poppa was eating bullets. No, that doesn't sound right."

"Sweating bullets," Jack supplied.

"Yes, that's it, and because Vance is a professional, he noticed the sweat right away. Go on, Vance."

"Well," he said, giving Kayley a look of undisguised suspicion. "Sullivan kept raising me, although I knew from how nervous he was that he didn't have anything in his hand. I had an inside straight," he said in an aside to Jack, who smiled benignly and took his cigar out of his mouth to study the ash hanging on the end. "Anyway," Vance went on, "I finally called Sullivan. He didn't even have a pair of anything, just a handful of garbage."

"And he invited you to the R Cross," Kayley said. "End of story."

"You're behaving most peculiar," Vance said. "I'm worried about you, my dear."

"Me, too," she said and began fanning her face with her hands. She suddenly stopped fanning and frowned at Vance. "If you knew Poppa was bluffing in Santa Fe, why didn't you know he was deceiving you when he bet the water rights of Laguna del Perro?"

Vance pushed his chair back a little farther. "He showed me a map and told me to take my pick of which waterhole I wanted. He was so drunk he could barely unfold the map. I didn't think anyone that drunk could cheat me, so I took the biggest."

"But it says salt flats on Poppa's map."

"Not the one he showed me."

"Try sleeping with your window open," Jack said.

Kayley looked up at him in confusion.

"The reason you came out tonight," he prompted. "Just open your window and that will solve the problem."

Her eyes widened. "Oh, yes. That's a good idea."

Vance sat his chair abruptly upright. "You told me you don't like sleeping with an open window."

"That was before I knew you tried to take

advantage of my father while he was drunk.''

She was impressed with her own poise as she stood, opened the front door and entered the house. The moment she was inside, she lifted her skirts and ran to her room, fearing that Vance would appear behind her at any moment. She shut her bedroom door, locked it, threw the window open, then stood shivering in the corner for what seemed like hours before a pair of hands pushed a bottle of wine and two glasses through the curtains to her. She took them and stood back for Jack to slip into the room.

"I can't believe I made such a fool out of myself,'' she said while he lit the candle on her dressing table. "I just fell apart when I came out and saw him sitting there. And did you see his boots? Right up on the wall like he owned the place! And saying my father was drunk, then admitting he tried to cheat him. The nerve of some people!''

Jack had opened the wine and was pouring it. With a glass in each hand, he advanced on her, looking terribly tall and very much like a pirate in the half light of the room.

"You talk too much,'' he said when he had her backed up against the wall, then covered her mouth with his, silencing her nervous need to babble with a kiss that took her breath away and left her hanging limply against him when he finally released her lips.

"I love you,'' he said and handed her one of the glasses.

"Even though I talk too much?'' she asked as he drank from his own glass.

"I know how to stop that,'' he said and kissed her

again, his lips tasting like wine. His free hand explored the velvet front of her dress. "You don't dress like a little girl anymore. I like this better." He slipped his hand into the low-cut bodice. "Much better," he said and claimed her lips in a kiss that sent her head spinning and her wine spilling.

"I think so, too," she said and pushed him onto her bed, pinning him there with her body while she lowered her lips to his to force her own kiss on him.

It didn't take much force.

Chapter Forty-One

Fog blanketed the camp of the stallion hunters at Corbett Springs. It was the second morning after Christmas; it was dark and cold, and dawn was still several hours away when Kayley finished her second cup of coffee, which reminded her of Elda's lye soap.

No smells of breakfast cut through the damp air, just the juniper wood sweetness of the fire. Snow bent close to the flames to stir the coals beneath the dented tin pot.

"There's cold biscuits in one of the packs," he rasped in an attempt to talk in the hushed tone Sam had ordered everyone use. "I'll dig them out for you."

"I'm too nervous to eat, Snow."

Vance and his men appeared out of the fog. "Good morning," he announced, and Kayley silenced him with a glare. "Sorry, my dear. I forgot the rules."

"Where's breakfast?" Clive Savely asked.

"Ain't none," Snow said.

Kayley tossed out the dregs in her cup. "The

394

stallion might scent it," she explained.

"And he can't smell the fire?"

"Snow wouldn't let me go out without something hot to drink first."

"How about the rest of us?" Vance asked.

"There's enough for everybody," Snow said and pointed at the tin cups beside the fire. "Pour your own."

Jack and Sam came into view leading saddled horses. "He's all yours," Jack said as he handed Tavira's reins to Kayley.

She ran a hand down the big gray's neck. "Except for that one time at the ranch house, I've ridden Louisiana every time I've gone after the stallion."

Sam squatted beside the fire. "I don't think you'll be riding him anymore, Miss Ryan."

"He'll have to be put down, won't he?" Kayley asked and felt the warm reassurance of Jack's hand on her shoulder.

"If he's no better when we get back," Sam said. "Joe Duke's keeping an eye on him to see if he can catch someone slipping something into the gelding's feed. It's almost as though someone had a personal grudge against him since the other horses aren't getting sick." He grimaced as he swallowed a mouthful of coffee. "This stuff's strong enough to haul a wagon."

Willie Pete rode into camp. "The stallion's in a canyon about a mile south of us. It's that box canyon where you and me roped that bear a few years ago, Sam. Must be forty horses running with him, including that buckskin mare of mine. He's pacing in front of the opening, nervous but not sure why."

"Let's get moving before he figures it out." Sam dumped out the rest of his coffee. "Listen up," he said, and the other men appeared out of the thinning fog to gather around him. "Slowhand, you have more experience chasing mustangs than the rest of us, and Clay knows this stallion the best. Either of you want to add to or change what I lay out here, go ahead."

"What do you mean, Clay knows him best?" Vance asked.

"Nine years ago, I put my brand on him," Jack said.

Vance's eyes narrowed.

"We're wasting time," Kayley said. "Go on, Sam."

He picked up a stick to use in scratching his plan in the dirt. First he drew the box canyon, then detailed the three approaches to its entrance.

"Snow will be bringing fresh horses to the ruins after the chase is over, so that leaves ten of us to split between these routes. The one running to the east is the hardest to hold, which makes it the most likely route the stallion will take out of the canyon. It's also the most direct path to Gran Quivira. I want Miss Ryan there with me and Slowhand."

He glanced over at the four Lucky Ace hands. "Sethy, you told me you'd had some experience with horses in Texas. You, Moore and Terkell take this southern approach. Clive, you and Piebald Anderson get the western route. It has the least chance of being used since it's almost straight up the side of a mesa. The stallion would lose the advantage of his speed there, but there's no telling what he'll do once he's spooked, so be ready."

Sam pushed his stick into his drawing at the eastern edge of the box canyon's opening. "Willie, you'll be up here on the rim. Fire two shots if the stallion takes a direction I haven't mapped here and start laying down a trail we can follow. That leaves Clay." Sam stood up and dusted off his hands on the back of his pants. "Where do you think you'll do the most good?"

"Halfway between Kayley and the ruins. The Arabian she'll be riding can easily keep up with the stallion, but the rest of you will be pushing your mounts before they reach the ruins. I'll be waiting with a fresh horse to help her finish the chase and to make certain he doesn't turn on her like he did Sullivan."

"Good idea. Let's do it, then," Sam said, and the men broke away to get their horses.

"I'm a little afraid," Kayley said when she was alone with Jack and Sam.

"Get over it," Jack said. "Otherwise, you'll be making mistakes and taking chances that you can't afford to take. Once Satan's Angel realizes you're onto his disappearing act, you'll never get another chance."

Kayley lifted her chin. "I won't need one."

"That's the spirit, sweetheart," he said, and his smile made her feel that maybe she really was as brave as she was pretending to be.

Willie rode up beside them. "I made this for you, Miss Ryan." He handed her a rope so thin and stiff it felt like wire. "Braided yucca fibers," he explained. "I've been working on it all summer. Use it after you've caught him. He won't be able to break it like

397

he broke your father's rope."

Slowhand reined in alongside them and untied his own rope from his saddle. "Tie this to the back of her saddle skirt, Clay. That way if she loses hers, she'll have a spare."

Snow pushed in beside her. "Put these in your shirt pocket, girl." He handed her two biscuits the consistency of horseshoes. "If you get hungry, eat them. If that devil goes after you, hit him with them."

"I'll remember that." She slipped the biscuits into her pocket. "How about you, Sam? Any last words of wisdom?"

He smiled and put a hand on her shoulder. "Give him hell, boss."

She turned her face away from him and the other men. It took a moment for her eyes to clear. When they did, she accepted Jack's offer of a leg up into Tavira's saddle.

Vance had been talking to his men. Now he rode up on his black mare. "What's this, a prayer meeting? The cards are already shuffled, folks, let's start dealing so we can get this game finished." He rode away, followed closely by Bill Terkell, who'd slipped a rifle into his saddle holster, and Clive Savely, who was eating something out of a blue-labeled can. Behind them were Piebald Anderson and Sethy.

"Nothing left to say after that," Sam said and swung into Old Joe's saddle. "Move it out, men." They rode off ahead of him, leaving Kayley alone with Jack.

His hand was resting on her left boot, and as he looked up at her, his eye flashed like silver. "I'll be looking for you," she said.

"I'll be there," he promised and squeezed her toes. "Good luck, kid."

After he turned away from her to mount Boxer, Kayley reached down to touch the forty feet of braided horsehair tied to Tavira's saddle beside her right knee. It was the same rope Jack had used to snatch Sophia away from the white stallion.

A good-luck wish and a good-luck omen.

I need a miracle, Gunning, not luck.

It seemed like a lifetime since she'd said that.

The crimson colors of dawn had faded to gold, and the gold was turning to blue when Kayley heard the first shouts that signalled the stallion had broken out of the box canyon.

She was waiting astride a nervous Tavira at the mouth of the eastern gulch. When the last shout faded into silence, her heart leapt into her mouth, and she took firm hold of Tavira's reins as he spun in an eager circle, ready to join the chase.

She heard the ring of horseshoe on stone. Tavira steadied. Her own breathing calmed, and then Sam and Old Joe broke out of the gulch ahead of her.

"Where is he?" she shouted.

"He cut back from us and headed for Moore and his men. Slowhand's on his heels."

Kayley turned Tavira south to the opening of Vance's approach. She had the gray in full stride when the stallion appeared ahead of her. Vance's mare was right behind him, along with Sethy's skinny sorrel. Kayley kept tight control of Tavira, not letting him give too much too soon. As she drew even with Sethy and Vance, Slowhand appeared out of the canyon.

The stallion was so far ahead she could barely see him. She let out a little rein, and Tavira surged forward. Vance and Sethy fell behind. It was between her, Jack and Satan's Angel now.

The land beneath her began to rise. It turned hard, and the ringing sound of Tavira's shoes made Kayley remember being here the first day she met Jack.

"The arroyo," she said, and the wind threw the word back into her face.

She reined Tavira to the left, away from the leap that would land him in soft dirt. Eastward they ran until just before the great boulder, then down, down into the arroyo, leaping and flying and falling and landing—on firm ground.

Through the narrow opening and around the boulder they ran. Ahead of her was the collapsed side of the arroyo. She loosed her grip on Tavira's reins, leaned forward over the pommel of her saddle, and as the gray stallion gained his full stride, Kayley reached for her rope.

Up, up the side of the arroyo they raced, and out onto the grassy plain. In the distance, Gran Quivira's weathered limestone glistened in the sunlight. Between Kayley and the magnificent beauty of the ruins, was the white stallion.

At the base of the hill crowned by the ruins, he turned, swerving, changing directions and speed, curving around the hill and streaking out across the valley floor, heading north and east toward the gully Jack had told her about.

"Jack," Kayley said as she reined Tavira after the

stallion. When the gray had steadied into the new direction, she looked around. Nothing, just grass and sky and the sound of her breathing, harsh and angry.

She felt empty, her arms and legs wooden, her heart slowing and almost stopping.

He promised.

The white stallion had disappeared while she looked for Jack. Her heart in her throat, she kept Tavira running toward the last place she'd seen the stallion. She saw the gully. Tavira dove into it, and there, standing, not running, just standing, was the white stallion.

He threw up his head in surprise, turned and ran. Tavira was so close behind him Kayley could taste the bitterness of the white's sweat on the wind. She slung out the horsehair rope, releasing its coiled tension, caught the edge of the loop and lifted it, holding it, leaning into it, swinging up with it, out with it, and letting it go.

It hissed through the air, uncurling its forked tongue, sliding and hissing and spitting its threat at her victim. And failing.

She grabbed the rope back to her, snatching and clawing at it, and when she saw the loop had closed, threw it from her and grabbed for Slowhand's rope.

The gully had reached Los Jumanos Mesa. The stallion soared up and out, flying into the sky, landing and running again without a break in stride. Tavira followed, game and eager and with every bit as much heart as Louisiana.

Back to the west, the white stallion ran. Straight for Gran Quivira. No hesitation. No tossing his head to taunt her. No snorting or snapping his teeth. Just running. Head down and nostrils flared, feet flying and desperation creeping into the dark hate in his eyes.

Kayley shook out Slowhand's rope and slid her fingers along its supple curves, reaching for the loop.

The white stallion surged up the side of the hill to the ruins. Through the ancient mounds he ran, twisting and turning in dizzying cuts. Past crumbling heaps and piles of earth and around a wall.

Tavira turned so close around that same wall that Kayley's knee brushed the time-darkened stones. On the other side of it, she pulled him to a rearing stop. When his front hooves crashed back to the earth, she spun him once, twice.

The white stallion was gone.

Amid the ruins of a once prosperous and populous people, in a place where Salinas pueblo dwellers lived and loved and died, in a land where droughts and Spaniards and Apaches had affected the destruction of a civilization, the stallion had vanished.

It was still and peaceful on the hill. The sky was blue and the limestone bright in the warming sunlight. The air had that shimmering quality that made this valley so special, so uniquely pure and beautiful. The wind was gentle, and clouds, like a bouquet of white flowers, were spreading themselves across the northern horizon.

Kayley's arm fell to her side. The limp rope dangled around her foot and stirrup, reaching almost to the black earth beneath Tavira's feet. The gray stallion shifted his weight, took a step away from that towering wall, and his ears pricked forward. His body tensed; his spine arched.

On the breath of the wind, came the scent of sweat. The sound of breathing, a rasping, raw sound. In the distance and to the west, Kayley saw her men riding toward her. She recognized Sam and Willie, saw Slowhand and Vance and Sethy's thin sorrel.

But Tavira wasn't looking west. He was looking south.

Kayley dropped the reins and let him move forward. One step, another, a third and fourth until Kayley saw in the shadow of the mighty wall of the ancient Church of San Isidro an opening in the ground.

Tavira walked on silent feet close to that hole. Kayley's arm lifted, her muscles tensed, the sun moved higher, the shadow disappeared—and there, below her, within feet and inches and trapped in an Indian ceremonial chamber, was the white stallion.

The loop shook free; the rope lifted and fell. And the stallion was hers.

When Sam and Old Joe made it to the top of the hill, Kayley was sitting on a tumbled pile of stones, her hat off and her face turned up to the sun.

"Where's Jack?" she asked.

"Where's the stallion?"

"This way," she said and led him to where Tavira was standing outside the walls of the old church, two ropes stretching from him into the kiva below.

"You did it, Miss Ryan, you roped the devil himself. No offense, but I never thought he'd get caught."

"Now tell me where Jack is."

"I haven't seen him since he cut away from us and

headed this way."

Kayley laid her hand on Tavira's neck. "He promised, Sam," she said and turned to greet the arriving men.

Kayley was standing beside the kiva, looking down upon the stallion. His mouth was flecked with the foam of his hate, his muscles bulging and rigid. His feet had dug at the floor of the kiva until the hardened earth had been rent and lay crumbled around him.

He'd tested and retested the strength of the rope that bound him. The horsehair was strained but holding; the yucca fiber was tight with strength.

Beside the towering wall where Kayley had thought she'd lost him, the men were quenching their dusty thirst and talking about the chase. Vance left them and crossed the uneven ground to stand beside Kayley.

"Well, my dear, it appears your friend had more than just the name of Clay; his feet were made of clay, also."

"And you knew this would happen, so you sent Savely and Terkell to keep an eye on him."

Vance kicked a stone into the kiva. Tavira was keeping the stallion pulled so close to the side of the kiva, all the big white could do was paw anew at the broken earth and roll his eyes upward in hate. "There was just something about him that I never liked," Vance said as he smiled down at his helpless foe.

"Something that reminded you of a bluff."

"Yes, just like that."

"Aren't we lucky he didn't fool you by showing you a map?" Kayley asked and turned away from him. "Let's get him out of here, Sam. I'll ride Tavira."

Sam, Slowhand, Willie and Sethy mounted fresh horses. "Let him rip," Sam said, and Kayley swung into the saddle.

She left the double ropes tied around her saddle horn, but eased off one, then two twists of the ropes, letting them fall slack. Satan's Angel was watching her, his eyes rimmed with white and the black of his pupils huge. When he had enough room to shift his hind legs away from the vertical wall of the kiva, he gathered himself and leapt straight up and out, landing and spinning in Kayley's direction.

Before he completed his turn, four more ropes dropped around his neck, were snapped tight and tied to saddle horns.

"We got him," Slowhand said.

The white tried to cut to the left, then the right. Then he stood still, lungs heaving, eyes blazing, and front left hoof repeatedly striking the ground.

"Make sure that twine's tied tight, boys," Sam said. "The first one to lose his hold on the stallion will be eating my right boot with my foot still in it. You sure you don't want a fresh horse, Miss Ryan?"

"Tavira's fine," she said, and the gray stallion pawed the ground in eagerness. Kayley envied his excitement. All she felt was betrayed.

Chapter Forty-Two

By midafternoon, the white clouds to the north had spread and turned black, the darkness and the storm engulfing the entire northern sky. Not a single flash of lightning relieved that menacing front. The only movement was its fast spread to the south, reaching out threatening fingers of rain toward the ranch, then boiling over itself and swallowing its threat, then reaching out again.

The wind had stopped; the light from the descending sun was chill and bright as it poured in beneath the lowering clouds. Everything in the landscape stood out in startling relief, every blade of grass, every twisted limb of juniper, every cresting rise that lay before the tired stallion hunters.

Satan's Angel fought them every step of the twenty-five miles to the R Cross. By the time they drew within the last mile, his body was so dark with sweat that he looked as gray as Tavira. The white's muscles were quivering with exhaustion, and his breathing sounded forced and painful. But he didn't stop fighting, testing the men's strength, testing Kayley's will, testing his own courage.

As they topped the last rise south of the ranch house, the first flash of lightning ripped across the sky: west to east, bright and blinding and sudden and terrible. And the thunder, so loud it was deafening, so strong it shook the ground beneath them, sent the horses into stunned motionlessness. Even the white stallion stopped his fight for freedom and stood still.

Kayley took advantage of his momentary lapse to look below her. She expected to see flickering lights of greeting. What she saw, was fire.

"Sam," she said and felt the stallion's struggles begin anew. "The ranch," she said, still not believing.

"Cut the stallion free," Sam said, and she whirled Tavira around, dragging both Arabians almost off their feet in the sudden tangle of ropes and confusion.

"No!" she ordered. "Bring him in. Even if I lose everything else, I'm not losing him!" She flipped the double ropes off her saddle horn and thrust them into Sam's hands. "Bring him in," she said again, turned Tavira and put him into a run.

Down the rise and toward the mountains she raced, into the first lashing breath of the storm, through the flashes of silver fire and the billowing thunder, on she raced, Tavira giving her the last of his strength in a valiant show of heart.

Into the yard they galloped where fire and smoke towered around them. The barn was completely engulfed, the bunkhouse was on fire and the veranda was sparking with fresh flames.

A terrifying scream of pain and fear rent the air, then died away into silence as she fell from the back of the exhausted stallion, grabbing at the ground and forcing herself to her feet. She ran across the yard and onto the veranda where fire and cinders rained down around her like the storms of hell.

The front door flew open beneath her bruising push. The living room wasn't on fire, but it was thick with smoke and a smell that wrenched Kayley's stomach. Down the hallway she ran, past her terror and to her father's room. From the far end of the hall to his door, the floor was on fire.

Again she was almost overcome by the smell, dear God, the horrid stench of burning flesh, human flesh, so near she could see the outline of a person laying in the fire before her, so far away she knew she could never reach it.

She started in fear at the feel of someone grabbing her and spun to see the body still laying motionless within the flames. But someone was holding on to her, pulling at her, dragging her back from the fire. Blindly she fought the hands, struggling to reach the door and throwing it open to the roaring fury within.

Within that fiery hell, from among the licking, devouring flames, someone appeared carrying a blanket-wrapped body. The hands grabbing at Kayley dragged her back from the inferno. She could no longer resist them. Her lungs were aching for fresh air; her face and body were scorched by the heat and the horror. She staggered through the living room and across the burning veranda and down into the yard. Gasping and choking and crying with fear, she fell in the dirt and looked up at Jack Corbett.

"It's Gunning," he said and laid the blanketed body before her. "He's unconscious."

"My father," she said and reached for him.

"Hold her here, son," Jack ordered and pushed her back into the clutching hands.

"Please don't fight me, Miss Ryan," Bede said, and Kayley turned to stare at him, realizing it had been he who pulled her from the house. "I can't hold you; and if you go in, I'll have to go after you again, and I'm too scared."

"My father's in there," she said and stopped struggling as she saw trailings of smoke rising from the blanket in which Gunning was wrapped. "Help me," she said and threw off Bede's hands. Together they tore the smoldering blanket from the unconscious Gunning. Bede ran to douse it in the water trough.

Gunning was breathing, his chest rising and falling, his eyes dilated as though he'd been drugged. Bede came running back and covered his uncle with the wet blanket. When he was finished, he fell to his knees beside Kayley and stared wide-eyed at Gunning.

"He's alive," she said. "How did this start, Bede? What happened?"

"Clay's what happened," a man said, and Kayley looked to see Vance Moore standing over them.

"What makes you think he did this?"

"Clive saw him."

Kayley realized he wasn't alone. Clive Savely was with him.

"What did you see?"

"He took out the black cowboy, and while I was lookin' for Terkell, I think he got him, too; the barn

409

was fired."

"I tried to get Louisiana out," Bede said, "but I couldn't get to him, Miss Ryan. I'm sorry."

"Louie," Kayley said and looked past the boy to the barn. The scream she'd heard, that horrible scream.

Sam appeared out of the darkness of the storm and the light of the fire. "Jack," Kayley said to him. "He went back inside and hasn't come out."

Sam ran for the house. She tried to follow him. Vance stopped her. Seconds later, Sam staggered out of the house, alone and beating at smoking burns on his shirt and pants.

Kayley went limp and sank to the ground at Vance's feet.

Faces floated above her. Voices swarmed around her. Elda, "How did it get inside the house?" Sam, "Form a line and get those buckets moving." Vance, "It was an accident." Bede, "I don't care what you say; this wasn't right." And through it all, the calm profile of Clive Savely as he looked around him with a smile of satisfaction.

Kayley became aware of a strange feeling seeping through her numbing shock and heartache. She stood and turned and saw Jack walking toward her through the haze of smoke from behind the house. His clothes were burned, his hair scorched, and his arms were filled with a body hanging limp from his sagging embrace.

She ran to him, but stopped when she reached him, held at bay by his complete lack of expression.

"How'd he get out of the storeroom?" Vance asked.

"Must've kicked his way out," Clive said. "I'll tie

him up this time."

"He's dead, Kayley." It was Jack talking. "I didn't get to him in time."

"How'd you get out of the house?" Sam asked. He took the bundle from Jack.

"Bedroom windows." His arms were empty now, but Kayley couldn't make herself step into them.

"That's my father, isn't it?"

"I'm sorry, Kayley."

Clive pulled Jack's arms behind him and wrapped rope around his hands. His face was pale beneath the stain of smoke and ash. He sank slowly to his knees while holding Kayley in the black center of his eye. Then it rolled back into his head, closed, and his body went limp before her.

She wanted to reach out to him. She wanted to feel something, anything. Instead, she just stood there and watched while Clive dragged Jack away, his boots leaving deep tracks in the ground.

The storeroom, the kitchen and Elda's rooms were the only places not touched by the fire. Except for the living room, which the men had saved with their bucket brigade, the house was destroyed.

The storm had unleashed its drenching fury to extinguish the last flame. Now, while the rain continued, Kayley stood at the kitchen window and looked out at the charred heap that held the body of Louisiana. And she looked at the storeroom. In it was Jack Corbett, the man who'd sworn to destroy Sullivan Ryan and who'd risked his life to carry Sullivan's dead body from a flaming hell that, according to Clive Savely, Jack had started.

"I didn't see anything," Joe Duke said. He'd been shot in the back, the bullet going all the way through his shoulder. "I was on the roof and heard a shot. The next thing I knew somebody was dumpin' water in my face."

"That was me," Slowhand said. "Your shirt was on fire."

"Tell me what you saw again, Clive," Sam said.

"Just what I done told you twice. Clay shootin' and then runnin' to the barn."

"Why was Terkell's body found in the house if Clay went to the barn?" Sam asked.

"He probably took Bill out," Vance said, "after he escaped from the storeroom. I don't know why you keep going over this."

Elda came into the kitchen from her room, where Gunning had been taken. Kayley turned away from the window. The kitchen was crowded, the men having nowhere else to go to get out of the rain.

"How is he?" Kayley asked Elda.

"Awake now."

"I'll go see him," she said, but Elda shook her head.

"He needs rest."

"We all need rest," Kayley said and pushed her way through the men to the door. Bede was standing beside it, his hair matted from the rain and his face set into rigid lines of anger. "Thank you for trying to save Louisiana," she said to him. "I'm glad you weren't hurt." His eyes lifted to hers. She tried to smile, but couldn't, and left the room.

A lantern pooled yellow light in the main room of

412

Elda's quarters. Kayley carried the lantern through to the bedroom where Gunning lay among sheets so white it almost hurt to look at them.

"How are you feeling?" she asked and set the lantern on the dresser before crossing the room to sit on the bed beside him.

"Terrible. How's Mr. Ryan? Elda wouldn't tell me anything."

"My father's dead," Kayley said and wondered at how easy it was to say those words. It was as though she'd suffered the pain of his dying years ago, not hours.

"Someone drugged me."

"Clive Savely swears it was Jack who started the fire, so he must've drugged you, too."

"Before I drank my tea, I smelled kerosene."

"That's what he used to start the fire. They found the empty cans behind the bunkhouse. We lost it, the barn, most of the house, and almost, you. And Poppa."

"You don't understand; Jack would never use kerosene because of what happened to Melissa."

"You told me she was taken by Apaches."

Gunning struggled to sit up in the soft bed. "She was, and Jack brought her back. Alive."

"But the grave, I thought—"

"She didn't want him to bring her here because in the house was where they raped her the first time. Right on the hearth."

Kayley drew back from the remembered image of Gunning sitting beside the hearth on Christmas Eve.

"Jack took Melissa to the Stormer ranch and came for me. When we reached the Flying S, I didn't wait for Mrs. Stormer to bring Melissa out to me in their front room. I went directly to the room where she was. When I burst through the door, she fell to her hands and knees and scurried across the floor away from me. Her face was so twisted with fear that I almost didn't recognize her.

"I went to her, wanting to touch her, wanting to hold her and prove to myself that she was really there. She was making little whimpering sounds and clawing at herself and the wall behind her.

"Jack was dragging me out of the room when suddenly Melissa calmed down, and I saw in her eyes that she'd finally recognized me. Then she looked down at herself, at the scratches on her arms from her own fingernails and the blood on her hands from trying to dig through the wall to escape. She stood up and said, 'I must go outside.'

"We let her go alone, thinking she wanted to regain her poise while she washed off the blood. I promised Jack I'd let her come to me when she was ready. Not a minute later, through the front window, we saw something burst into flames. Jack broke the door down getting out. When he tried to get near the fire, it ran from him."

"It was Melissa," Kayley whispered, horror making her voice sound hollow and far away.

"She'd used kerosene, Miss Ryan. I could smell it then, just like I smelled it today. There wasn't any way to stop her from running from us, and no way to save her if she'd stopped. Then the screaming started. There was a shot, and I saw Jack putting his gun away. After that, there was just the sound of the flames."

414

Kayley couldn't believe how calm Gunning sounded, as though he were relating a story he'd heard or read, not one that he'd witnessed and that had so dramatically changed his life.

"Don't you see? He knew that she'd used kerosene, too. It wasn't Jack that did this; it couldn't have been."

"Then who?" Kayley asked.

"I know," a voice behind her said, and she turned and looked into Bede's dark hazel eyes.

Chapter Forty-Three

It was dark inside the storeroom. Kayley turned up the flame on the lantern. A hole in the side wall let in rain and a damp cold that made her shiver. Laying on the floor before her, heaped against the shelves as though thrown there like a sack of grain, was Jack. She hung the lantern from a hook in the wall while Sam entered behind her and knelt beside Jack.

"Look at the back of his head, Miss Ryan."

The swollen lump of matted hair and flesh on the back of Jack's head made her shiver again.

"Cut him loose," she said, and Sam sliced through Jack's bonds. "Willie, help Sam get him out of here."

They half lifted, half dragged Jack out of the storeroom and into the rain. When they reached Elda's room, Bede held the door open, closing it after they were all inside. A fire was blazing in the fireplace, and the boxes and crates had been pushed aside to make more room.

Jack was placed on the sofa and smothered in warm blankets. Kayley held him against her while

Sam cleaned the wound on the back of Jack's head; then he was laid back on a mound of pillows.

Gunning, who was still groggy from the drug he'd been given and ill from the smoke he'd inhaled before Jack saved him, had been moved to a chair in front of the fire. "Give him some whiskey," he said.

When Sam returned a few minutes later with a bottle, Joe Duke, Slowhand and Snow were with him.

Joe was propped up in the other chair in the room, and after everyone had taken a drink of the whiskey, he looked at Kayley, whose eyes were running and insides burning as a result of her own drink from the bottle.

"I heard a shotgun, Miss Ryan. Not a pistol."

"And Corbett didn't have a shotgun," Sam said.

"Corbett?" Snow asked.

"I'll explain later," Kayley gasped. Even her teeth felt like they were being melted from the inside out by the whiskey, which she'd been surprised to discover wasn't anything at all like wine. "Right now," she wheezed, "I want Bede to repeat what he told Gunning and me."

It was the feel of her hands on Jack's face that pulled him out of the darkness that clouded his mind. It took a long time for him to see the first flickering of light through the haze of his pain. When he finally did, he saw her looking down at him with so much love on her face that he didn't think it could possibly be real.

"Kayley." His voice sounded harsh as it tore out of

his smoke-burned throat.

"I'm here." Her hands stroked the sides of his face again.

"How's Gunning?"

"I'm fine, sir."

The familiar voice came from somewhere in the room beyond Kayley. Jack didn't look for his old friend because he didn't want to look away from the love in those beautiful blue eyes smiling down at him.

"Did you get the stallion?" he asked, and tears spilled over her golden lashes.

"She got him," Sam Butler said. "Trapped him in a kiva."

Jack covered Kayley's hands with his own and turned his head to kiss first one of her palms, then the other. "Good girl."

"When did Savely and Terkell hit you over the head?" Sam asked. "Before they brought you to the ranch or after?"

"Both." Jack probed at the lump on the back of his head. "They said Kayley had been hurt. I put my gun away and was mounting Boxer when the lights went out. I woke up as they were putting me in the store-room, so Clive put me back out. The next time I came to, I smelled the fire and kicked my way out of there."

"And saved me," Gunning said.

"Then you went back for my father," Kayley said, and he felt the tremble in her fingers as they closed around his. "Jack, is there a place in the house where Poppa might've kept documents that Gunning doesn't know about?"

"My grandfather's desk." He ignored the sick throbbing in his head to sit up beside her. "The second drawer down has a false bottom. And behind the largest cubbyhole in the back of the desk, there's a locked box that can be pulled out."

"That's what she's been looking for," Gunning said.

"Poppa even told me about the drawer once, but I didn't understand."

"What's going on?" Jack asked.

"We'll tell you later," Kayley said. "Right now, Sam and I have a plot to hatch."

Jack pulled her into his arms. "I want to know what's going on now, kid."

"I'm trying to save your smoky hide from the lynch mob Vance is trying to work into a frenzy."

"Does that mean you don't think I'm responsible for the fire?"

"Or for anything else that's happened on the R Cross, except me falling in love with you. I hold you completely responsible for that."

He lifted a hand to her face, wanting to make certain her smile was real. "That's one crime I'll gladly plead guilty to, sweetheart. What happened while I was unconscious to make you believe me about the rest?"

"I always believed you. That's what I didn't believe." With a soft kiss on his cheek, she was gone, leaving him alone with a bandaged Joe Duke, and a pale and propped up Gunning.

"Tell me what's going on, old man, or I'll come over there and beat it out of you," Jack said.

"Hardly likely with a knot on the back of your head as big as your ego, but I'll tell you anyway."

Kayley carried the box from the desk cubbyhole, and Sam had the desk drawer, which he'd removed under her careful scrutiny. "I don't want it scratched," she'd repeated so often that she thought Sam was going to shoot her. Despite the advice she'd given him, he'd managed to wrest the drawer from the cherry-wood desk without hurting it, or her.

Now they were entering the kitchen from the courtyard. Vance and Snow, Bede and Elda were the only ones in the kitchen, Slowhand and Willie Pete having taken the three Lucky Ace men outside for a drink of whiskey, and a few twists of rope around their feet and wrists.

"Are you any good at picking locks, Snow?" Kayley asked and put the box in the center of the table. Sam placed the desk drawer beside the box and lifted out the drawer's false bottom, revealing a flat metal box built into it.

"Where was the small box?" Elda asked.

"In the back of one of the cubbyholes," Kayley said. "The key to the desk doesn't fit them, and I need them opened."

In truth, Kayley hadn't tried the desk key. The cigar box where she'd kept it had been destroyed, along with its other precious contents.

"You don't need one," Bede said. "Ma can open them, just like she used to open Papa's money box back home. Can't you, Ma?"

420

Elda didn't respond to Bede's question, but Vance did.

"Shut up, boy."

Bede sidled away from him. "You remember, don't you, Ma? When Mr. Ryan used to visit us in Boston. You told me you were cashing checks for Mr. Ryan and Papa didn't need to know, just like nobody on the R Cross needed to know that I was taking messages to Mr. Moore. Show Miss Ryan how you did it, Ma. Open them up for her."

Snow reached for his gun as Elda lifted her hands above the table. When they proved empty, he relaxed his caution. But only a little.

"I'll need that thin knife," she said, acting almost as though she were in a trance as she stared at the box and the drawer. She reached for the drawer first. She slid the point of the blade into the brass lock, and with a maneuvered turn, the lock came open. She started to lift the lid, but Sam stopped her, taking the drawer and putting it on the table in front of Kayley, who forgot about the other box as she began looking through the contents of the drawer's secret compartment:

Her father's will, folded and sealed with red wax.

A map of the R Cross showing Laguna del Perro as Laguna del Grande, and with no mention of salt flats or salt water.

Papers for the two thousand dollar loan taken out last September from Claude Asken.

Dated the day after the loan, a copy of a report signed by a property acquisition agent acting for the American Mortgage Company in Edinboro before it formed the Prairie Cattle Company. The report certified that Laguna del Grande was fresh, not salt water, as shown on the Colton territorial map.

A letter dated March of this year from the Prairie Cattle Company expressing their interest in buying the R Cross Ranch. Penciled on the bottom of that letter, in Sullivan's handwriting, a list of ways to recover the Lucky Ace property from Vance Moore. The last item, was Kayley.

Vance had been right. She was a bribe.

"Now do you believe me?"

She looked up at him. He was reading the list over her shoulder.

"I don't have a choice," she said.

"Finding it now is like hearing a dying wish from your father," he said. "Make that wish come true, Kayley. Marry me."

"What makes you think that they"—she smoothed a hand across the letter—"are still interested in the R Cross? This offer was made in April."

"This," he said and pulled from the inside pocket of his jacket another letter. "They want an answer before the end of the year or the offer's forfeited. That's only four days away, Kayley."

"So you had your men set fire to the barn to frighten me into trusting you, after Clay was arrested for their crime. And what about you, Elda? What was your part in this?"

The cubbyhole box had been opened. Elda was holding a packet of letters it had apparently contained.

"Let me guess," Kayley said. "Those are from you to my father."

"He promised me that if Alba died, he'd marry me," Elda said. In her voice was the same emptiness Kayley had felt when Jack hadn't been waiting for her at Gran Quivira.

"But he didn't," Kayley said, and the letters slipped out of Elda's hands. "So you decided to make him pay for that, first with his supplies, then his cattle, and finally his ranch."

"How did Moore get mixed up in this?" Snow asked.

"Gunning figured that out," Kayley said. "He's Ivo Moraillon's son and Elda's nephew."

Bede's eyes grew wide. "The boy in the photograph in Ma's room."

"Moore," Sam said. "Moraillon."

"Exactly," Vance said. "How very clever of dear Gunning to figure it out."

"My father messed up your plans, though, didn't he, Elda?" Kayley asked. "He lost only half the ranch to Vance, the worst half, and then was struck down by the white stallion before you could get the rest of it from him."

Elda's hands were back under the table. "It would've been a simple problem to overcome if Sullivan hadn't brought you here."

"Sorry to spoil your plans."

"They wouldn't have been spoiled if Vance had listened to me," Elda said. "Only he had to do things his way."

Kayley lifted her eyes to Vance. "By waiting for me to grow up?"

"He's just as weak as the rest of the Moraillon men," Elda said. "Always so noble, always thinking a miracle will happen to further their cause without them lifting a finger to do it themselves."

Bede had picked up the letters Elda had dropped and was looking through them. "This says you gave Mr. Ryan a lot of money to invest in a ranch, Ma." He looked up at her. "I remember when I was nine or ten, a deposit Papa was supposed to make for his boss got lost. Mr. Arram thought Papa stole it, and he fired him." Bede's face fell. "Only he didn't steal it, did he, Ma? You did."

"Give me those," Vance said and snatched the letters away from Bede.

"So it wasn't just Poppa not marrying you," Kayley said. "You wanted the same return on your investment that he got from his with Jack Corbett."

"It's gone beyond that now," Sam said. "Now it's murder."

"Sullivan was dying anyway," Vance said. "I just had Clive and Terkell hurry nature along a little because I knew that while Sullivan was alive, Kayley would never marry me, no matter what we pinned on Clay."

"You said it was an accident," Elda said as her face went suddenly pale. "Just a spark that got into the house somehow."

"It would've taken a lot more than a spark to start the floor burning," Kayley said.

"That's why I had my boys pour kerosene on it," Vance said.

The kitchen door burst open, and Jack entered. "That's what I've been waiting to hear, Moore."

Vance twisted Kayley's right arm behind her back. She cried out in pain, then surprise as she felt the jab of Vance's gun in her ribs.

"Let her go, Moore, or you'll be as dead as Terkell."

"Did you use one of those fancy shots of yours on Bill?" Vance asked.

"No, city boy." Jack stalked farther into the room. "I broke his neck."

A chill shuddered down Kayley's arms. When Vance felt it, he laughed. "Better be careful, you're frightening our girl here. She might decide she likes me better after all, Clay, my friend."

"Try Corbett," Jack said.

Kayley felt Vance tense. "So that's what you're doing here."

"I'm here because of what you're pointing that pistol at, Moore. Let her go."

Somewhere during the last exchange, a shifting of positions had taken place. Elda was still at the table, but Sam had moved over behind her, putting himself between Vance and Bede. Snow had disappeared entirely.

And Jack, who had been keeping his gaze fixed on Kayley, reassuring and comforting and calming her, was now looking directly at Vance. The muscles in Jack's face had hardened, and his eye was the color of iron.

Kayley took firm hold on her courage. "Vance," she said softly. When he glanced down at her, she shifted her weight into him, knocking him off balance. Elda's hands appeared out from under the table again. She gave a bitter cry as she threw a folded piece of paper at Vance.

Kayley flinched as it hit him, and as her left arm

was grasped by unseen hands.

"Get her out of there!" Jack shouted, and she was jerked away from Vance just as an explosion shattered the room, thundering and roaring and flashing fire so close to her that she felt the air shudder.

She was thrown to the floor as Jack's gun blazed.

Sam shoved Elda out of the chair and onto the floor.

Another shot by Jack.

A second shot close to Kayley, only this time she didn't feel anything except Snow falling on top of her.

A third shot by Jack.

Someone in the room groaned.

Silence. A thud as something hit the floor near her.

From beneath her trail cook covering, she saw the folded paper Elda had thrown in Vance's face. Kayley reached for it, catching it with the tips of her fingers and pulling it back to her.

It was her father's will.

"It's over," Sam said. "You can let her up, Snow."

There was a grunt like a drum being kicked by a mule as Snow lifted himself off her. "You hurt, girl?"

"No. Where's Jack?" She raised her head and looked directly into his silver gaze.

"It's over, sweetheart." He swept her up and into his arms.

"What happened?" she asked.

He was holding her as though he'd never let her go. "Vance was hit, but no one else."

"He's not dead," Snow said. He was kneeling beside Vance, who was lying on the floor with his feet toward Kayley.

"I want to see him," she said.

"You sure?" Jack asked.

She nodded, and he carried her to Vance. Three patches of red were spreading across his shirtfront. She fell to her knees beside him while Jack knelt behind her.

"Vance," she said.

The dark hazel eyes turned to her. She slipped her hand into his grasp.

"Was there ever a time you would've said yes to me?" His voice wet and thick.

"There was a time," she said, and he squeezed her fingers.

"I really did fall in love with you that first night," he said, and his embrace of her fingers failed.

Jack lifted her away from him while Snow closed the pale lids over the dark and staring eyes.

"Is he dead?" Elda asked.

"Deader than a can of corned beef," Snow said.

"Please, Snow," Kayley said. "Where's Bede?"

"I'm here," he said, and she saw him in the far corner of the room.

"Are you hurt?"

"No. It's just so strange all that's happened."

"Why don't you go out to your Uncle Gunning? He'll be worried about you."

Bede started to leave, then stopped and looked back at his mother. She was standing in front of the stove, her arms crossed in front of her as she watched Snow and Sam lift Vance and carry him out into the rain.

"I'm sorry, Ma, I just couldn't let it go on no longer."

"This could've all been yours," Elda said. "Now we don't have anything."

"I don't want anything that came from what you stole from Papa. I don't just mean that bank deposit, but every time you opened his money box. It made him cry, Ma. Did you know that? It made him cry."

"He's just a boy," Elda said when Bede had left. "When he's grown and knows what it's like to always work for someone else and have nothing to show for it, he'll think different. Then he'll think I did right to want so much for him."

Kayley held up the will. "This is what you've been looking for, isn't it?" She tossed it to Elda. "Go ahead. See if it was worth it."

As Elda broke the red wax seal, Kayley turned into Jack's embrace. "I don't want to know what it says," she said into the warmth of his shirt.

"I leave all my possessions to my daughter, Kayley Marie Ryan," Elda read aloud. She sounded like she was strangling in anger. "I gave him everything I had, and he left it all to you."

Sam came into the kitchen. "I have the wagon ready to drive Mrs. Moraillon into Belen."

"Why?" Elda asked. She threw the will onto the table. "Isn't that enough? Do you have to press charges against me, too?"

"It's Bede who wants you taken in," Sam said. "He says he wants to clear his father's name."

"My—my son wants this?"

"He's Alba's son, too," Jack said.

Elda stiffened her shoulders. "Yes, I know that. Every time I look at him, I remember." She shook off Sam's guiding hand and left the kitchen without

428

another word.

"I'm sorry about Sullivan, kid," Jack said as he rubbed Kayley's back and shoulders. "I know he wasn't a great father, but like Elda said, he left it all to you in the end."

"It would be easier for me to appreciate that if he'd remembered my name right. It's Kayley *Ann*."

He leaned against the edge of the table and pulled her between his legs. His hands caught at the ends of her hair as he hugged her close. "Did you ever wonder how I knew your name that first day?"

"At the time. Later I was too busy trying not to love you to wonder about anything."

He grinned and kissed her.

"The night Sullivan decided to end our partnership, he told me about you."

Kayley leaned her forehead against Jack's chest. "He must've not had much to say."

"He said you looked beautiful with the sea breeze in your hair."

Her heart grew still within her. One time, one single solitary time in her twelve years at the school, the students and staff had gone on a field trip. It had been when Mrs. Potter's sister left for a trip to England. Kayley had stood on the very end of the pier and lifted her face into the wind, letting it tear her hair from its binding braid and fly free around her.

That had been last year in April, when Sullivan Ryan was visiting Elda Moraillon in Boston.

"And he said that you sang like an angel."

When Kayley was fifteen, she'd performed a solo during a church Easter service. Because her voice had been anything other than angelic that day, she'd never been asked to sing again.

"And he said that you rolled a hoop better than any other girl in your school."

"You're making this up," Kayley said and lifted her head to look up at Jack. "He couldn't have known about those things."

"Then, how did I know about them?"

"Poppa was watching me?"

"Not every day, but enough to know you were exactly what he needed to win over Vance Moore."

"Hold me," she said and buried herself in Jack's embrace. "Why didn't you tell me this before?"

"You didn't need to know before."

He smoothed the hair back from her face.

"So what do you want to do now, kid? I'll understand if you want to sell the ranch and start over elsewhere. There's still a few days left until that deadline I overheard Moore talking about."

"There's only one thing I want," Kayley said. She went to the door and looked out at the rain sheeting from the silent sky. "Starting first light, I want to make the white stallion pay for what he did to my father."

Chapter Forty-Four

It took two days for the ground to dry enough to begin the process of breaking the white stallion. It wasn't too wet for burials, though, and there were three of them in the little cemetery. Sullivan Ryan was placed beneath the spreading branches of an ancient apple tree. Vance Moore and Bill Terkell were buried beside the unnamed dead.

When the morning finally came for Slowhand to begin his work, Kayley told him about the warning Madison Blackwell had given Jack about Satan's Angel.

"Just leave it to me, Miss Ryan," Slowhand said. "I learned my business from the Mexicans, and they learned theirs from the Spaniards." He mounted his dun mare and walked her around the perimeter of the high-fenced branding corral while his rawhide rope swung above him in a wide, curling sweep.

The stallion paced in a circle, keeping the width of the corral between him and the rope. His hide steamed in the cool air. His eyes were bright with caution. His nostrils were flared and his tail was carried high.

The rawhide rope hissed as it cut through the air toward him. He whirled, but the rope had its way and settled around his neck. It tightened with a jerk. The dun mare stopped in the middle of her stride and fell back, bracing her forelegs to wait.

It took only seconds for the stallion's plunging to bring the rope up tight. The mare dug her hooves in, and the stallion found himself on his back. His eyes bulged nearly out of his head in surprise and pain. There were no sounds of breathing, no attempt to regain his stance.

Kayley curled her shaking hands around the top rail of the corral. Seconds ticked by with Slowhand waiting and the stallion choking.

"That's it," Slowhand finally said.

Sam and Jack entered the corral and moved in so close to those razor-sharp hooves that Kayley saw Sam flinch. They loosened the rope just as the stallion's tongue began to show. Freed from certain death, he exploded onto his feet while the men leapt to the top of the corral fence, a six-foot jump that they both made without missing.

The stallion went mad. He plunged and kicked and crashed his hooves onto the ground in straight-legged fury. But the rope didn't shake off. The mare worked to hold a constant pressure on the rope, keeping the stallion both furious and captive.

When he'd circled the corral completely, he turned toward the gate. The boards and pinewood braces looked exactly like the gate he'd crashed through twice before, once when escaping Jack Corbett, once when freeing his imprisoned mares.

Only this time it didn't break. The logs the men had braced the gate with groaned, but held against the stallion's madness.

The tremble in Kayley's hands stopped. This time it was going to happen. This time he wasn't running away from his past. This time, satisfaction would be hers.

It took an hour for the stallion to give up his attempt to break the rope and crash through the door. At the end of the hour, he stood ready for the next step in Slowhand's training.

A hackamore was forced over the stallion's head. The special halter was attached to a stake rope, and the dun mare left the corral for a well-deserved rest while the stallion learned his next bitter lesson.

Too much pulling against the cruelly designed hackamore would result in his breathing being cut off. The stallion, not realizing his danger, ran at a gallop to the end of the stake rope. His hind legs were thrown into the air and his head bent double beneath him as the hackamore crushed his nose. Three times he came close to breaking his neck before he stopped trying.

Kayley shivered as she watched him learn defeat. Jack climbed onto the top of the corral fence to sit beside her. Without taking her gaze off the sweating stallion, she leaned her head against his arm. She loved how no matter where she touched him, he felt so strong, so protecting and safe.

"Give it up, kid."

"No, Jack."

He stroked his hand down the long rope of her

braided hair. "When the prison doors swung open, Kayley, I thought I was free. But I wasn't. Not until I stopped letting the past control my life was I really free. Not until I stopped looking back, and started looking forward."

"I'm going to see him broken," she said.

"There'll come a day when you won't remember the reason you did this. You'll just remember the cruelty. Then it'll be you who breaks."

"What I'll remember, is that my father never had a chance to know me as anything other than a bribe."

"He had twenty years' worth of chances, Kayley."

She closed her eyes. "I'm not letting the stallion go," she said, and didn't open her eyes again until she felt the corral fence give beneath her, and she knew he was gone.

Slowhand was in the corral again. He was walking this time, holding a blanket and lugging a saddle. He dropped the saddle out of the stallion's reach and began to whip the blanket back and forth over the steaming white back.

The stallion cringed and jerked away. Slowhand rested his hand on the stake rope. The hackamore tightened, and the stallion held still. Slowhand moved his hand up the rope until he was touching the stallion's nose. The nostrils flared, the black eyes widened until they were rimmed with white, but the stallion didn't move.

"Blindfold him," Slowhand said. Jack pulled a red bandanna from his pocket and put it over the stallion's eyes, knotting it to the sides of the hackamore.

Kayley's throat went dry as every muscle in Satan's

Angel's body began to tremble like a frightened foal.

The blanket began to whip across him again. He withstood his fear and agony bravely, his only reaction the continued trembling of his body and the occasional turning of his head to try to look past his blinder.

Slowhand lifted the saddle and tossed it across the quivering back. The stallion bolted away from it, came up short on the stake rope and began to pitch, hind hooves flying, front digging, teeth snapping in a desperate attempt to free himself of all the horrors to which he was being subjected.

Jack and Slowhand moved to the outer fringe of the corral and waited for the stallion to calm. A dozen times the routine was repeated: the feel of the saddle, the maddened fight for freedom, the hackamore bringing him under its cruel control. Finally, when the saddle was tossed on him, he stood still, his determination to rid himself of it conquered by pain.

Slowhand bravely reached beneath the stallion's trembling body and grasped the girth, dragging it up and into the iron ring before him. He pulled it to the end of the cinch. The big buckle of the special breaking saddle caught quickly in the holes of the girth, and with a sudden jerk, the saddle was secure.

The stallion discarded his resolve to withstand the indignity and began to pitch again. Jack grasped the sides of the hackamore. Using his full weight, he forced the stallion's head down and sideways while Slowhand tightened the cinch again and again until the stallion was forced to stay his fight to draw whatever breath the hackamore and the crushing girth allowed.

The bandanna was ripped away, and there he stood, angry and ashamed of his submission, eyes bloodshot and body dark with the stinking lather of his sweat.

Slowhand grasped hold of the flank girth. Kayley couldn't breathe as she watched the hairy thing being drawn tight across the stallion's stomach, sinking deep into the softest part of his body.

Instead of fighting again, as she expected, he stood firm, fighting now only with his courage, his strength to endure, his hate.

Jack held the stallion's head in an iron-tight grasp while Slowhand untied the stake rope and looped it around his fist. His left foot lifted to the stirrup. The stallion tensed, and Slowhand sprang into the saddle.

Jack turned the stallion's head loose and ran for the fence. The R Cross hands let loose a yell that filled the canyon behind them and came bouncing back as an echo just as the stallion began to pitch with all the hate and terror, all the rage and fear, all the savage wildness and all the towering courage that he possessed.

Nose between knees, legs straight and back arched, he ran from one end of the corral to the other, plunging and furious and desperate. Up and down. Back and forth. He dropped first one shoulder almost to the ground, then the other, jumping into the air, twisting around and coming down facing the other direction until Slowhand's face went as pale as Kayley's felt.

It went on for minutes. Hours. A lifetime.

Then the stallion stopped.

There was blood streaming from his nose where

436

the hackamore had sliced into his tender flesh. There was foam dripping from his mouth. His body was scarred by the cutting rowels of Slowhand's spurs.

And the stallion's eyes, the eyes of the devil, the eyes of hell, were staring through the rails of the corral fence at the sweeping expanse of the Salinas Valley the way he might look through a tiny window at a sky bright with stars and dark with dreams and chill with unreachable promises.

"Let him go," Kayley said.

The voices of the men fell silent.

"Let him go," she said again. "But don't let him know what you're doing. Let him think he's breaking free."

Slowhand turned the stallion and spurred him toward the staking post. Satan's Angel quivered as he walked the short distance, his freedom and pride curbed into obedient slavery.

Slowhand dismounted and lashed the rope to the post again. "Give me a knife," he said and caught Jack's knife by its deer antler handle.

Slowhand slipped the sharp blade beneath the flank girth. The stallion recoiled from it, even though it didn't cut him. The blade split the hairy girth almost all the way through; then Slowhand did the same thing to the front girth.

He tossed the knife back to Jack and began running his hands slowly up the stallion's neck. The white skin shuddered beneath his touch, but Satan's Angel didn't pull away, even when the hated touch moved over his ears and onto his muzzle.

Slowhand talked to him, murmuring and soothing and telling him worthless words while he slowly loosened the binding straps of the cruel hackamore.

Kayley tensed at the same moment as the stallion. The bloodshot white of his eyes disappeared beneath lowered eyelids. The trembling muzzle became suddenly motionless. The flicking ears stayed their movement. He looked beaten and resigned, except for those half-closed and watching eyes.

The heavy logs were being lifted quietly down from the gate. When the last one had been laid aside, the men climbed back onto the corral fence to reassure the stallion that nothing had changed. He was still a captive, and they were the captors.

He wasn't watching them, though. He was watching Slowhand edge around to the other side of the staking post. His hands were still hooked inside the hackamore, keeping it pulled tight and secure, assuring that for another few seconds, there would be no attack.

Jack and Sam leaned down over the top rail of the fence, reaching their arms out to Slowhand. He judged the distance from the staking post to them, turned back to the stallion, and released the hackamore.

The stallion bared his teeth, threw up his head, and screamed. The sound spurred Slowhand into action, sending him racing on bowed legs across the corral toward Jack and Sam.

Satan's Angel streaked across the corral after him. The stake rope snapped tight when he reached its end. The hackamore ripped off his head. The stallion lunged for Slowhand, but the bronc buster had reached the outstretched hands. Jack and Sam lifted him out of danger and dropped him outside the corral in a plummeting thump of dust and grunts.

The stallion planted his forefeet on the ground and began to pitch. His back feet flew almost over his head as he fought the saddle in a frenzy of pitching. The flank girth gave first, then the front girth, and the heavy breaking saddle fell to the ground and was pummelled by the flying hooves of the raging beast.

"When he breaks out, jump in the corral!" Jack called out to Kayley.

The stallion reacted to Jack's voice by running straight for the gate. Faster, faster, furious and determined, throwing his heart and body into the rush. And breaking free. A splintering of wood and bending of metal and cracking of bolts, and he was free.

Kayley dove into the corral, landing on her side and knocking the wind out of herself. From beneath the bottom rung of the fence, she watched the stallion turn back to the corral.

His gaze, black and bitter and grand in his victory, met the silver stare of the man who'd once before tried to break him, of the man who'd scarred the perfection of his skin with a brand and who'd burned into the stallion's heart the searing taste of hate. He reared and screamed his triumph, then began to run.

Kayley got to her feet. Covered with dust and smiling with satisfaction, she watched the white stallion race away from her, running toward his dreams. Running free.

The last she saw of him, his head was held high and his tail and mane were streaming behind him like the banner of a unconquered warrior.

The men had gathered around Kayley. At first no

439

one said anything; then Snow took off his hat and held it crushed against his chest as he smiled at her.

"When you said let him go, girl, I was more surprised than a slut dog with her first porcupine."

"I was a little surprised myself. Not quite that much, but a bit."

"You're all right, Miss Ryan," Willie Pete said.

"She'll do," Sam said.

"Maybe she's not such a bad choice for a wife, after all," Jack said, and wrapped Kayley in the magic of his embrace.

"Are you proposing to me?"

"No, I'm staking a claim on you, kid."

"Close enough. I accept."

"Of course you do," Jack said with a grin. "What half-smart female would turn me down?"

"After we're married, I want to talk to you about this ego of yours," she said, and he kissed her smile.

Chapter Forty-Five

It was one of those days when the sky was so blue it hurt to look at it, the air so clean it hurt to breath it, the light so pure it shimmered and danced like fairy dust in the breeze sweeping down from Quarai.

The smell of the fire had faded beneath the relentless pressure of time. The new floor being put in the ranch house was of flagstone, and the new bunkhouse was made of adobe. The barn hadn't been replaced yet. The adobe bricks for the stable area were still in the form of mud and straw, waiting to be molded together.

The ground in the little cemetery was damp with last night's dew. Kayley lifted the hem of her skirts as she left her father's grave and crossed to where Gunning was standing beside the grave of his wife.

"The marker's beautiful," he said and looked down at the cross-shaped marble between them. On it was carved, *Melissa Pauley Brison, Beloved Wife of Gunning, Killed by Apaches*.

"A gift for a friend," Kayley said.

"After Melissa died, Jack told me that if I stayed here, I'd never have anything except painful memories. I couldn't leave, though, because while I was in the same house where we'd lived, I could hear her laughing at his boots, or see her pretending to pout about some silly nonsense so I'd hug her, or listen to her singing a song she'd forgotten the words to, so she'd made up her own, only she'd also forgotten the melody, so she'd made that up, too. But when I left the house, for even a second, I saw her burning."

Kayley went to him and put her arm around him.

"The first time I saw you sitting beside your father, waiting for him to get well, even though you knew it was hopeless, I realized that what I'd been doing was waiting for Melissa to come back and be the way I remembered her. Since then, when I look out the windows of the house or step out onto the veranda or come up here, I don't see Melissa burning anymore.

"That was the gift you gave me, dear friend." Gunning ran his hand across the last engraved line. "This was for her."

They walked arm in arm to the edge of the cemetery. Below them, spread out across the dirt yard, were the men of the R Cross Ranch. Willie Pete was on first, Sam on second, and Snow was behind third base, bribing Cleopatra with a peppermint stick to prevent the mule from joining the game, again. Joe Duke, his shoulder newly healed, was the catcher, and he squatted in the dirt waiting for the batter to take the plate.

Because all the men were wearing their spurs, chaps, hats and riding gloves, they looked as though they were waiting to wrestle steers instead of play their first game of ball.

Willie Pete was even wearing war paint. "My grandfather told me never to face anyone holding a club unless I was prepared for battle," he'd explained to Kayley.

Jack was showing Bede how to hold the baseball bat, correcting his awkward stance, giving him some last-minute advice before Jack threw the boy his first pitch.

"I told Bede that we were giving him a partial interest in the ranch," Kayley said, "since it was his mother who actually invested in it, not my father."

"He told me," Gunning said. "He wants to know if he can have the money, instead, so he can pay back the man his father was accused of stealing it from."

"I'm sure Jack will agree to that."

"Strike two," Joe Duke announced, and Bede kicked dirt over the rock plate at his feet.

"Have you heard from Elda?" Kayley asked.

Gunning shook his head. "She was always a tough one, even when we were children. I never did understand her."

"Strike three!"

Bede started to toss the bat away in disgust. Jack stopped him and put his arm around Bede's shoulders. Although Kayley couldn't hear what Jack was saying, she knew he was rebuilding the boy's confidence, telling him that the next time, he'd do better.

"Jack's a good man," Gunning said.

Kayley smiled up at him. "You told me that once before."

"We'd better join them before he thinks I'm trying

to steal you away."

"Would you do that?"

"Who knows what I'd do if I were a few years younger and he wasn't so good with that pistol."

"Kayley!" It was Jack shouting to her while he pointed at the rise south of the ranch where a wagon had just appeared. "Reverend Mathieson from Socorro's almost here, kid! Get down here so we can get married!"

Kayley lifted her silken skirts and ran down the path from the cemetery, leaving Gunning to close the gate while she was met by the loving embrace of the man to whom she was about to pledge her love and her life.

"Who's that in the wagon with him?" Sam asked. He shaded his eyes against the sun. "It's a woman, and she's waving something."

"Looks like a curtain," Bede said.

Sam's face went completely white, and he grabbed Bede's shoulders. "Saddle Old Joe for me. Move it, boy!"

As Bede ran to the corral, Sam turned on Kayley, who was trying to hide behind Jack.

"Miss Ryan," Sam said, making a tremendous effort to control his voice. "You sent for Abigail, didn't you?"

"I needed a bridesmaid."

"I knew it," Sam said and bolted for the corral.

"Where are you going?" Jack called after him. "I need a best man."

Sam came to a reluctant stop. "What about Gunning?"

"I'm giving my best friend away."

"Willie Pete?"

"I believe in saloons, not marriage. Besides, I don't want to mess around with the spirits in that church at Quarai. Ghosts don't like me."

"Snow?"

"I'm gonna sing."

Kayley laughed at Jack's groan.

"Slowhand or Joe Duke?"

"We're not gettin' that close to Miss Ryan," Slowhand said.

"She might hug us," Joe Duke added.

"Looks like you're stuck, Sam," Jack said.

The wagon rolled into the yard, and a female voice cried, "Sammy, darling!" before the wheels came to a stop.

Sam's shoulders drooped. "I'll get you for this, Miss Ryan, if it's the last thing I ever do."

As he trudged over to greet the long lost, and very pretty, Abigail Butler, Kayley saw the light of love that sparkled in his eyes, and she knew her impulsive telegram to St. Louis hadn't been a mistake.

"Poor fella," Jack said, and she jabbed him in the ribs. "Another of those, sweetheart, and I won't give you the present I have for you."

Kayley crossed her fingers behind her back. "I promise to be good."

He went to the garden. "Look," he said when he came back, and opened his hands to show her a rose, its petals soft and red and perfect. "I've never seen them bloom this early in the year."

This man with the patch over his eye was every bit as dangerous, overwhelming, stubborn, arrogant, and intimidating as he'd been the first time they met.

445

And yet, as he stood there so tall and broad-shouldered, and with his heart in his hands, Kayley realized he was also very different from the man she'd been so frightened of, and intrigued by, that day.

That difference filled her with so much love that it was like a physical pain deep inside her, a pain more welcome and wonderful than any pleasure could ever be.

"It's a miracle," she said.

"Yes, sweetheart, it is."

Jack wrapped her in his arms, holding her close and safe against him. And Kayley knew that she'd finally come home.

FIERY ROMANCE

CALIFORNIA CARESS   (2771, $3.75)
by Rebecca Sinclair

Hope Bennett was determined to save her brother's life. And if that meant paying notorious gunslinger Drake Frazier to take his place in a fight, she'd barter her last gold nugget. But Hope soon discovered she'd have to give the handsome rattlesnake more than riches if she wanted his help. His improper demands infuriated her; even as she luxuriated in the tantalizing heat of his embrace, she refused to yield to her desires.

ARIZONA CAPTIVE   (2718, $3.75)
by Laree Bryant

Logan Powers had always taken his role as a lady-killer very seriously and no woman was going to change that. Not even the breathtakingly beautiful Callie Nolan with her luxuriant black hair and startling blue eyes. Logan might have considered a lusty romp with her but it was apparent she was a lady, through and through. Hard as he tried, Logan couldn't resist wanting to take her warm slender body in his arms and hold her close to his heart forever.

DECEPTION'S EMBRACE   (2720, $3.75)
by Jeanne Hansen

Terrified heiress Katrina Montgomery fled Memphis with what little she could carry and headed west, hiding in a freight car. By the time she reached Kansas City, she was feeling almost safe . . . until the handsomest man she'd ever seen entered the car and swept her into his embrace. She didn't know who he was or why he refused to let her go, but when she gazed into his eyes, she somehow knew she could trust him with her life . . . and her heart.

HISTORICAL ROMANCES BY VICTORIA THOMPSON

BOLD TEXAS EMBRACE (2835, $4.50)

Art teacher Catherine Eaton could hardly believe how stubborn Sam Connors was! Even though the rancher's young stepbrother was an exceptionally talented painter, Sam forbade Catherine to instruct him, fearing that art would make a sissy out of him. Spunky and determined, the blond schoolmarm confronted the muleheaded cowboy . . . only to find that he was as handsome as he was hard-headed and as desirable as he was dictatorial. Before long she had nearly forgotten what she'd come for, as Sam's brash, breathless embrace drove from her mind all thought of anything save wanting him . . .

TEXAS BLONDE (2183, $3.95)

When dashing Josh Logan resuced her from death by exposure, petite Felicity Morrow realized she'd never survive rugged frontier life without a man by her side. And when she gazed at the Texas rancher's lean hard frame and strong rippling muscles, the determined beauty decided he was the one for her. To reach her goal, feisty Felicity pretended to be meek and mild: the only kind of gal Josh proclaimed he'd wed. But after she'd won his hand, the blue-eyed temptress swore she'd quit playing his game—and still win his heart!

ANGEL HEART (2426, $3.95)

Ever since Angelica's father died, Harlan Snyder had been angling to get his hands on her ranch, the Diamond R. And now, just when she had an important government contract to fulfill, she couldn't find a single cowhand to hire on—all because of Snyder's threats. It was only a matter of time before she lost the ranch. . . . That is, until the legendary gunfighter Kid Collins turned up on her doorstep, badly wounded. Angelica assessed his firmly muscled physique and stared into his startling blue eyes. Beneath all that blood and dirt he was the handsomest man she had ever seen, and the one person who could help her beat Snyder at his own game—if the price were not too high. . . .

Available wherever paperbacks are sold, or order direct from the Publisher. Send cover price plus 50¢ per copy for mailing and handling to Zebra Books, Dept. 3233, 475 Park Avenue South, New York, N.Y. 10016. Residents of New York, New Jersey and Pennsylvania must include sales tax. DO NOT SEND CASH.